Praise for

CHUCK WENDIG and
ZERØES

"ZERØES is a very powerful development of the idea of science as magic, with a cast of unwitting sorcerors' apprentices. It asks a lot of real-world questions, both moral and practical, and it builds a lot of documentary information into the story, as good sci-fi should. It might make you nostalgic for Mr. Gibson's "Neuromancer": Life was so much simpler back in the '80s."

Wall Street Journal

"[A] high-octane blend of nervy characters, dark humor and bristling dialogue . . . smart, timely, electrifying."

NPR

"ZERØES is a taut, complex techno-thriller with something much darker and deeper at its core than mere espionage."

Richard Kadrey, *New York Times* bestselling author
of the Sandman Slim series

"A Matrix-y bit of old-school cyberpunk updated to meet the frightening technology of the modern age . . . An ambitious, bleeding-edge piece of speculative fiction that combines hacker lore, wet-wired horror, and contemporary paranoia in a propulsive adventure that's bound to keep readers on their toes."

Kirkus Reviews

Also by Chuck Wendig

ZERØES

A NOVEL

CHUCK WENDIG

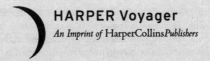

HARPER Voyager
An Imprint of HarperCollins Publishers

This book is a work of fiction, and while it sometimes strives to get details right about hacker culture and the actual act, be advised that it also takes liberties with the subject in order to tell a story.

HARPER Voyager
An Imprint of HarperCollinsPublishers
195 Broadway
New York, New York 10007

Copyright © 2015 by Chuck Wendig
Cover image © by Mohamad Itani/Arcangel Images
ISBN 978-0-06-241317-8
www.harpervoyagerbooks.com

First Harper Voyager mass market printing: June 2016
First Harper Voyager hardcover printing: August 2015

Harper Voyager and ⟩ is a trademark of HCP LLC.

Printed in the U.S.A.

10 9 8 7 6 5 4 3 2 1

This book is for all the zeroes out there

The Trans-Mongolian Railway

The train clacks on the tracks, rocking side to side. A hundred smells come together—garlic in an iron wok, wet goat, a tin pail of piss—and nausea forms a rolling boil in Chance's belly. He's not sure the last time he had something to eat. But he has a water bottle within reach, the clear plastic red with steppe dust.

He takes a sip. His throat hurts like a scraped knee.

The three men across the table watch him drink. The water tastes sharply of minerals. He's not sure where it came from—they probably filled it up from some spigot on the train. He hopes where the tourists sit. Not where everyone else sits. Or worse, where he saw that yak.

Chance tries to sniff, but his left nostril is blocked with dried blood.

"Do you need anything?" the translator asks. His mouth shows the faintest curl of a smile. His coal-black hair is shot through with veins of silver.

"Oh, *now* you're being nice to me," Chance says. His words come out a stuttering croak—the sound of a door creaking and juddering against its frame. The three Chinese men—the old cinder block with the caterpillar eyebrows, his attaché with the razor-sharp line of a mouth, and the translator—stare at him as if he's got a third eye.

"We have questions," the translator says. He's not translating anything yet—the other two haven't spoken aloud, not today. They chattered plenty when they pulled him out of Moscow, though the translator didn't do much translating then, either. Mostly he explained what was about to happen. *We are going on a journey. We are putting you on a train. You will not struggle or you will meet an unfortunate end. And so will your friends.* Then he said the horrible magic words: *We have Aleena Kattan.*

So now here Chance sits. Feeling sick. And dizzy. And jumpy. Like a spark dancing at the end of a fraying wire.

The old man nods to the attaché, who whispers a string of Chinese to the translator. To Chance's North Carolina ears, it doesn't sound like much at all except a series of hissing murmurs.

The translator nods. "My friends want to tell you that you are not highly skilled and so they find it strange to be talking to you about this."

"That's not much of a question."

"Please comment upon it."

Panic is a nest of snakes inside his heart. He knows they want something from him, but he doesn't know what. Two days ago they tried asking him questions and he didn't understand and so they blackened both of his eyes and took a telescoping baton to his left knee and worked the rest of his torso over with fists before abandoning him here, in this room. Now they're back and he still doesn't know what they want.

"I don't understand," he says, drawing a deep breath past cracked lips. "I get beat up a lot, and my brain's pretty rattled, so help me understand the question—"

The old man's mouth tightens into a scowl.

The attaché backhands Chance.

His head rocks to the side. He tastes blood from his teeth biting the inside of his cheek. *Spit or swallow?* He opts to swallow, which only makes his queasiness surge.

The translator says with great enunciation, as if Chance is both American *and* stupid, "Your *technical* skills are not worthy."

It occurs to Chance that the translator doesn't translate any of his words to the other two men. They understand English. They just can't—or won't—speak it to him. "That's probably true."

"So why are we talking to you?"

Chance thinks he understands now. "You're saying I'm a pretty subpar hacker. That's probably right. So how am I here?" He winces and swallows more blood, tries to smile. "I was selected."

"By your government."

"If you say so."

"By Typhon, then."

His smile broadens. It is mirthless and red toothed. "If you say so."

"How did you stop Typhon?"

Now Chance laughs. A ragged, raspy sound. "Who says we *stopped* it?"

PART ØNE

THE SELECTØR

CHAPTER 1

Chance Dalton

Chance is underneath his lemon-chiffon Plymouth Duster, trying—and failing—to fix an oil pan leak, when he hears the crunch of gravel under boots. He starts to slide out from under the car when someone says, "So it was you."

Hands grab his heels, drag him the rest of the way out from under the car.

He looks up, sees three guys standing over him. Two are football players: Ryan Bogardian and Anferny Derkins. Quarterback and linebacker of the Yellowjackets, respectively. Ryan is built like a great white shark—long, lean, fast as thrown lightning. Derkins looks like the love child of a freight train and a bank safe.

The third guy's older than the other two by a good stretch. Got a lot of gray in that bristly, unkempt mustache. Got a lot of rust on that socket wrench in his hand, too.

Well, shit. Chance wipes his hands on his shirt and starts to get up, but Ryan puts a boot on his chest and presses him down.

It's the older man who speaks first. "You don't *look* like a computer nerd."

"I'm not," Chance says. It's not a lie. Not really.

Bam. A hard kick to his ribs from Anferny Derkins. Chance feels something give. The pain is like a rock through a window. He cries out, rolls over—

Hands hoist him to his feet. Slam him up against his Plymouth.

"I don't know what y'all think I did—" Chance says, trying not to wheeze.

The old man pistons a fist into his midsection. Pain blooms. The guy comes up on him like stink on a skunk, presses the length of the socket wrench against Chance's throat. Chance struggles, tries to catch his breath, feels blood gathering above his neck and in his cheeks like water in a balloon, and suddenly his brain is like a too-big fish in a too-little fish tank where kids keep slapping the glass. *Boooom, booooom, boooooom. Don't tap the glass, kids.*

Derkins is laughing. Bogardian is just leering, chin out, tongue resting on his lower lip like a slug. His eyes are flinty, catching light but reflecting back only darkness. Darkness and spite and maybe a little hate, too.

Maybe a *lot* of hate.

Black dots like blobs of ink dip and swirl in the margins of Chance's vision. His heartbeat is like a kick drum in his neck, his cheeks, behind his eyes.

The guy finally pulls the wrench away.

Chance gasps a painful intake of air.

"This your car?" the old man says. He begins to pace the length of the Plymouth as Derkins and Bogardian pull Chance away.

"Naw," Chance says, and he hears the smart-ass comment about to come tumbling out of his fool head and he tries to catch it, but it slips its leash and bolts through the door. "That's my little pony. Actually, she's a unicorn. Her name is Princess Glitternuts, so be real nice to her—"

Pop! A fist crosses open air, slams into his eye like a Mack truck.

Now Bogardian's smiling. The ex-quarterback reels back the fist, holds it next to his head like a trophy, gives it a sweet little kiss like he's kissing a puppet.

"That was a good hit, boy," the old man says, running his hands along the Plymouth, along paint the color of a dark forest. "You still got it, Ry."

"Thanks, Dad," Bogardian says.

Chance blinks, coughs, says, "Can I ask you something?"

Bogardian shares a look with his father.

"Who told you?" Chance asks.

"Who told us what?" Bogardian says, gaze gone slim.

"That I did what you think I did."

The elder Bogardian pipes in with a laugh. "One of your fellow hacker buddies sent around an e-mail. Showed us who was the one sticking the broom handle up our ass."

"I'm not a hacker," Chance says. He's not. He knows people. He knows how to figure them out, break them down, but he's bush league. "I don't *have* any hacker buddies."

"No," the father says, grinning wide. "I guess you *don't.*"

The quarterback hits him again. Right in the breadbasket. *Oof.* Chance can't help it. He doubles down.

"Lemme ask you another question." He breaks into a coughing fit. "How'd it feel?"

"How'd *what* feel?"

"How'd it feel when you lost your scholarship, you rapist assho—"

His head rocks back with the force of another hit. His lip splits against his own teeth. Blood flows as Derkins flings him to the ground. Suddenly Bogardian is on top of him, fist rising and falling like a hammer slamming a post into dry earth. Chance cries out.

Not because of the pain. That's bad. Hell, that's *awful.*

He cries out because he sees what's about to happen next.

Bogardian's father raises the socket wrench.

And begins busting the windows of Chance's one true love: his Plymouth Duster.

Ø Ø Ø

The double-wide trailer sits at the south end of the family's old farm—a farm that's gone to hell because Chance doesn't know how to keep it up, the property overgrown with tall grass and poison ivy. There's an old apple tree that's so burdened by kudzu it's taken the shape of an arthritic T. rex.

Chance shuffles past the old barn with a drunken lean and heads into the trailer, each lift of his foot up the cinderblock steps a certain agony. His ribs feel like someone stuck a knife between them. Once inside, he makes a beeline for the sink. He pushes aside some dirty dishes. Spits a line of blood against the white porcelain. Wiggles a back tooth with his tongue. Then licks his split lip.

Chance winces, stoops, washes up. The terrible thought runs laps through his head: *If they know, who else knows?* And just who the hell is out there telling people he did this? How does anybody even *know*?

If someone knows, then that means the authorities might know, too. That means the media might find out. And if he gets drawn into that, then what? He'll get run out of town. And not before having his ass beat up and down the highway, too. Worst of all, Faceless will come after him. He did what he did using their name. *Their* cred. If his getting caught means unmasking the masked—well, they call themselves Faceless for a reason. They can do a lot more than beat him up. They can hack his life to little bits.

He just wants to keep to himself. The thing with the football team and their "rape posse," well—he had to get involved. *Had to.* It was the right thing to do. (And a small voice reminds him, *And you had a debt to repay, didn't you?*)

Now he's got another, different kind of debt to repay.

Revenge for the Duster.

Chance heads over to the laptop. Loads up Facebook. Ignores all the memes and cat GIFs and people outraged about this, that, or the other thing and instead heads to the search window. He pulls up Ryan Bogardian's account. Lots of folks standing by the football player. He sees one comment: *I know you didn't rape those girls, RB, but somebody ought to.*

That gets Chance mad. But that's not why he's here. He looks to Ryan's list of friends and family. Ryan's old man isn't on the list. He didn't look like a Facebook user, though it surprises Chance just how many folks *are* on Facebook these days.

But Ryan's *mother* is on it, though. Marylou Bogardian. That'll do.

Chance looks at her account. Sees the e-mail address she's got associated with it. Then he uses that to log in as her. If he had enough time he might be able to figure out her password—older folks don't use nearly the amount of protection they should. Half the time it's *password123* or a cat's name or something you could figure out by poking around their photo streams for ten minutes.

He doesn't feel like wasting the time. He checks the box that tells Facebook that he—Marylou—has forgotten the password. It says she'll get a new password via e-mail, but he clicks the box that says she doesn't have access to that e-mail address anymore. Then Facebook asks for a new address, and he puts in a dummy one he's been using.

Here the site asks him a security question. *What is your mother's maiden name?*

New browser window. He goes back and starts poking through Marylou's profile. It's pretty spare. Mostly passing around political stories that could be disproved by a cursory Snopes search. So Chance heads off to one of those ancestry sites.

There she is. She's got an account. Got her family tree all pretty and public. Mother's maiden name: Kiplinger.

Back to the Facebook window. He types it in. His phone

dings. Chance snatches it off the desk and resets Marylou's password to *mysonisarapist*. Then he uses the password to log in as her. His blood's pumping, racing through his veins like a bullet ricocheting down a metal pipe, and he starts writing a new status for Marylou Bogardian. A status about her precious son, Ryan.

I would like to apologize for my son, Ryan. I know now that Ryan did those things to those poor girls and he is a rapist monster. I blame myself and I blame my husband, who was abusive to us and who cared only about beer and football and those magazines about having sex with horses. My son is a rapist. My husband is a wife-beater. May God have mercy on all our souls.

"I hope this shit goes viral like a case of monkey flu," Chance says. He moves to click the Post button.

His monitor goes dark. All that's left is a bright white pinprick.

"What the—"

The monitor clicks a few times. *Click. Click-click. Click-clickclick.* Then it comes back on.

The Facebook screen is gone. In the center of the screen sits a little pop-up window. Like from an old Windows 95 machine—bad resolution, blown-out pixels. It warps a little, the colors go funky.

The pop-up window reads: KNOCK-KNOCK.

Chance thinks, *I've been hacked.*

Then the monitor goes dark, and just as it does, the door to his trailer flies open—splintering at the already wobbly hinges, coming off as it swings wide.

Two men enter. Cops. SWAT. Feds, CIA, NSA, Chance doesn't know who—but they've got helmets and shiny visors and black armor.

Chance doesn't have time to figure out who they are or what they want. He's up on his feet, his body complaining against the sudden movement. A gun goes off. The laptop spirals and shatters in a rain of black plastic.

His ears ringing, Chance runs.

He doesn't make it far. Someone is already in his bedroom. The butt of a shotgun cracks hard across the side of his head and he goes down against a rickety end table he picked up at a yard sale. His clock radio catapults across the room. He paws at the bed, trying to stand up—

A man steps into view. An older black dude with close-cropped hair and big muttonchop sideburns. He's a tall bundle of sticks stuffed into a rumpled government suit.

The man pops gum in his mouth. Pops it as he chews. "They beat your ass pretty good, huh," he says.

"You hit me," Chance says, but the words sound mushy. His face aches.

"And I'll do it again if you try to run."

Chance coughs. "I don't know you, but way I figure it, you're trespassing."

That gets a chuckle. "I'm allowed to trespass," the man says. No Southern twang, none of that easy, muddy North Cackalacky slide. His words are short. Clipped like with a little pair of scissors. "I'm Mr. Government."

Then Mr. Government sticks a stun gun to Chance's neck and the world goes bright and alive.

CHAPTER 2

DeAndre Mitchell

SAUSALITO, CALIFORNIA

DeAndre presses the earbuds into his ears with two pokes of his long fingers, swings his legs out of a Honda Accord that's not his, and walks over to the gas pump. He tells his jailbroken iPhone to play some music. Chiddy Bang queues up. He thumps drums on his chest with one hand as he pumps gas.

Then he holds his phone over the card reader for five seconds.

He feels the phone vibrate as it finds the Bluetooth signal. It starts the download. Credit card numbers—hundreds of them, digits and mag stripe data from all the people who used this pump over the past week—zip into his phone. It vibrates again when it's done.

DeAndre pockets the phone. Bobs his head to the music. Slaps an open-palm drumbeat against his thighs. Then he stops pumping gas—just six bucks worth, not even two gallons—and gets back in the car and drives away.

He'll sell 90 percent of these credit card numbers. The carder markets online always have scammers looking for fresh dumps of digits. At ten bucks a pop, that makes today a three-thousand-dollar day. And this ain't the only place he's running skimmers. He's got devices at the Valero off 82, at the Sev on Shoreline, at the Safeway on Marina. After a couple of weeks he'll move 'em to new locations. Cycle 'em around.

He'll turn the other numbers into plastic. He's got a top-shelf card printer, spits them out fast. He gets a refresh of cards, can use them quick, then toss them.

All that will come later. Right now, it's time to go see his moms.

This is going to be a good day, he thinks.

And it will be. Until it's not.

MARIN CITY, CALIFORNIA

The houses on Nogales Street aren't much to look at. Like a bunch of shoeboxes sitting next to one another in an ugly line. The hedges between them are dead or overgrown.

DeAndre parks the car, gives the side-eye to the housing project across the street—the Olima Apartments, where a bunch of reedy, weedy gangbangers mill around mismatched lawn furniture in the middle of the apartment courtyard. A few whoop and yell as he gets out—they don't know him and he doesn't know them, but that's how they are.

DeAndre could have been one of them. Thinking he's a little Tupac in the making—so proud they all come from the same town as the long-dead rapper—slinging drugs and packing a nine. But his moms kept him straight. She made DeAndre do his time at the library. At the comic book store. At the two-dollar movie theater. Most important of all, in the computer lab at the library. He did anything to get out of that house. Anything to get away from those bangers and slangers across the street.

Miss Livinia pokes around the front lawn of the little lemon-yellow house next door to the one he grew up in. She's all hunched over, a little pile of raisin-wrinkled lady squinting from behind praying-mantis eyeglasses. She's picking pieces of mailbox out of the overgrown grass, setting them on a flattened cardboard box to collect them.

That's when DeAndre sees—it's not just the mailbox. The house is all shot up. Windows broken. Bullet holes in moldy siding. A gutter hangs loose. He hurries over, calling, "Miss Livinia, hey."

The old woman lifts her head—a small act that seems to take a lot of effort. Her pinched eyes search him up and down. Finally she adjusts her glasses and laughs. "That you, Stringbean?"

"Yeah. It's DeAndre, Miss Livinia."

"All right, all right, I'm sure I got some candy in the house for you. Got some M&Ms, the kind with the peanuts in 'em—but they're getting harder to find, you believe that? Those chocolates are a *classic* and nobody seems to want 'em anymore. But that's the way with old, good things—"

He laughs and stops her from going inside the house. "No, Miss Livinia, I don't need any candy. I'm good."

She looks him up and down behind the lenses of her bug-out spectacles. "You need to eat something, boy. You skinnier than a cat's tail. I'll make you some chicken and rice."

"I gotta get to my moms," he says. "But yo, what happened to your house?"

"Those dopeheads came by and shot it up. They musta thought Demetrius was back in town, but he ain't even out of jail yet, those donkeys."

"Damn! You okay?" Demetrius, her grandson. Always used to push DeAndre around, beat him up after school, steal his shit.

She waves him on. "I'm fine, Stringbean. I'm fine. God ain't seen fit to take me yet and no dopeheads spraying my gutters with bullets are gonna be the ones who do it." She sighs and *hmm*s. "Guess I do need a new mailbox, though."

He grabs Livinia's hand. It's dry and papery, like the pages of a Bible. DeAndre makes sure to turn his back to the slingers across the street. He presses a handful of money into her palm: just shy of five hundred bucks. She peers down at it like she's trying to read the fine print on a newspaper ad—then her eyes go big enough to match those glasses of hers. "This what I think it is?"

"Take it, Miss Livinia. Buy what you need."

"Boy, whatchoo been up to lately?"

"I got a job."

"It a good job?"

"It's a real good job."

Ø Ø Ø

His moms answers the door. She looks him up and down with an eyebrow cocked so high he thinks it might float up above her head and take off like a spaceship. Then she laughs and gives him a big hug and tells him to come inside, get something to eat, he's too skinny. She turns and sways those big hips, sashaying to the kitchen.

But DeAndre doesn't go inside. Instead he calls after her.

"Moms," he says. "Let's take a ride. I got something to show you."

"What are *you* gonna show *me*?" she says with a wry smile.

He winks and waves her on.

MILL VALLEY, CALIFORNIA

"Whose house is this?" his moms asks, again with the arched eyebrow. "This is a richie-rich house. You got business here?"

The house is—what did the real estate agent call it? Mission style. Three bed, two bath. Couple of palm trees out front. Privacy fence with pretty flowers climbing all over it. Little fountain burbling and gurgling. Pool in the back. Golf course across the street.

"This ain't business, Moms," DeAndre says, laughing. Then he fishes into his pocket, past his phone, and fetches a set of keys. He dangles them in front of her.

"What the hell is this?"

"They're keys."

"You're a smart-ass, you know that?"

It's a familiar refrain, and DeAndre has a familiar response: "Smart-ass is better than a dumb-ass."

"Yeah, yeah. You still didn't answer the question. Why you dangling a set of keys in front of my eyes like I'm a little kitty cat? I don't care much for shiny things."

"You oughta start."

She sits there, quiet for a second. Finally, she says, "You're telling me this is your house. That what you're telling me?"

"I'm telling you this is *your* house."

Blink, blink. "What'd you just say?"

He drops the keys in her lap and claps his hands, thrilled by having taken her by surprise. The woman's a rock. She isn't surprised by *anything*. All his life she's been five steps ahead of him. But not this time.

He hops out of the car and yells for her to follow after.

Ø Ø Ø

Inside the house. Big foyer. Spanish tile. Steps made of some kind of redwood going up to the second floor. He takes her right to her favorite place: the kitchen. This one has granite countertops, stainless steel appliances. DeAndre doesn't know much about that, but the real estate agent said that's what everybody wants. He understands why. It looks nice. Feels nice, too—the counters are cool to the touch, clean and smooth. Like he could lay his head on one after a hot day.

Moms walks through real slow, real cautious, like she's afraid if she moves too fast the whole thing will come down around her ears like it's made of playing cards. "This is an expensive house," she says.

"You don't know that."

"I *do* know that. I know who lives in Mill Valley. Rich white people."

"Middle-class white people, Moms."

"They're rich to me. And I thought rich to you, too."

"I got money now, Moms." He figured this conversation would come. He swallows a hard knot and steadies himself. "I got a good job now."

"What kinda job?" Now she's studying him real good. Way a cat studies a mouse. That's how he feels, too—like a mouse pinned by a heavy paw.

"I work with computers."

Now her hands are on her hips. "What kinda computers?"

"The kind with a keyboard and a monitor." Before she can say it, "I know, I know, smart-ass. I'm doing some programming, okay? It's good money. Shoot, good money doesn't even cover it." He sees her suspicious look, pulls it back a little. "I got a good deal on the house. Foreclosure-type deal. A . . . a . . . whadda they call it? Short sale. Low interest and all that."

DeAndre neglects to mention that he's got the kind of money you could spread out on a bed and roll around in the way a dog rolls around in its own mess. Enough money that if he ever lost any of it, he could be like, *Yo, whatever, I'll just go buy more.*

She's still got that look. Like she doesn't believe him. Like she's picking him apart with a fork and tongs the way you shred meat.

But then her expression softens and a big goofy smile spreads across her face and she crashes into him with a big hug. "I always knew you'd make something of yourself," she says.

He kisses her brow. "Come on, Moms. Let's go upstairs, check out the bedrooms."

Ø Ø Ø

The master bedroom's damn near as big as the whole downstairs of the house on Nogales Street. His moms does a slow orbit of the room, whistling low and slow like she's seeing something she just can't believe. Each whistle followed up by a little *mm-mm-mmm*.

DeAndre laughs.

But his laugh gets cut short.

Out the window, he sees something that doesn't make sense. Past the pool, past the patio furniture and the built-in Weber grill, he sees a black round something. Like a bowling ball covered in fabric. Hiding in the shrubs and vines next to the pretty purple flowers.

A radio squelches outside.

DeAndre's palms glisten with cold sweat. It's five-oh. The cops. *It's the cops.* That's no bowling ball. It's someone's *head*. A helmeted head. A cop in SWAT armor.

"Hey, Moms," he says, trying to stop his voice from cracking, trying to stop the panic from leaching out. "You, uh, you hang here for a minute. I gotta run out, meet the real estate agent for, ah, a quick thing at the corner diner."

He ducks into the bathroom. Travertine tile. Shower big enough to have a party inside. A shower with a *window*. A window that looks out over the neighbor's house.

∅ ∅ ∅

DeAndre thinks, *I can do this.* He can jump. Like they do in the video games. Free running. Parkour. Whatever they call it.

He climbs up, crouches in the bathroom window like a gargoyle. He's tall but lean, and can close himself up like a folding chair if need be. He looks down at the stone wall separating his moms's new house from the neighbor's place. The wall is as wide as DeAndre's foot is long, and just ten feet away. Beyond it is the neighbor's house, with a sloped roof. If he can make it to the wall, he's free.

The trick is, he's got to run—but they've got to *follow his ass,* too. He runs and they go kicking down the door to this house, what will Moms think? If she doesn't have a heart attack, she'll know his job is a lie, the house is a lie.

She'll know *he's* a lie.

He swallows hard. Catches movement down below, up past the little shed along the side of the house, near the birdbath.

He jumps. His feet plant hard on the flat top of the wall—the shock goes up through his knees, into his hips, a javelin of straight pain, and he knows he should have crouched more as he hit to absorb the shock, but no time to worry about that now.

Now he's landing on the neighbor's roof, cracking a terracotta tile and sending it spinning to the ground. He hears another radio squelch and mumbled police chatter. Just to make sure, he calls out, "Up here, homies."

Someone calls out in alarm from below. The cops. Good. He scrambles to stand, spits blood, jumps to another roof. He slams his shoulder hard against a window—it's just a screen, and it pops out as he tumbles inside, pitching forward against what is mercifully plush carpet. He hears a high-pitched shriek and realizes it's his own.

He hurries through the house. Carpet on his feet, air in his teeth, no time to think. He runs through the hall, sees a woman in frumpy pink panties throwing clothes into an over-under laundry machine. DeAndre gives her a panicked look—*sorry, lady*—and a little wave. She screams. He runs into a master bedroom the color of Caribbean waters. He flings open the window and—

Long jump. Ignoring the pain now. Adoring the freedom. His hands catch the ledge of another house's roof—and here he has it all played out in his head. He'll plant his feet. Kick off like a swimmer. Wrap his arms around a palm tree like a stripper at her pole and then he'll be up on another roof with some kickin' Assassin's Creed moves—

The gutter he's holding onto shifts downward. It makes a *gonk* sound, then rips out of its moorings and breaks away from the roof.

DeAndre lands hard on his ass bone and feels firecrackers of pain popping up his spine, into his neck, to the base of his skull.

He hears the crackle of shrubs and hedge. *Incoming.*

He wants to lie down and whimper, but that ain't an option. So he's up. Running toward the sounds of traffic, past a little swing set, past a hibachi grill, to a breach between two tall bougainvillea hedges. That breach means freedom. He sees the road beyond it. Cars and trucks whipping past. Once he hits the street, that's it. He can go anywhere—lose himself in the park, disappear into traffic, grab a golf cart.

He charges hard for the breach in the hedge.

Someone steps in his path.

He cries out, "No, no, no, no!"

A shotgun goes up, then off.

DeAndre drops. Gasping. He can't breathe. He can barely see. Everything is a strobing white light of pain, up and down, left and right, wheeze, cough, whine. He feels around his midsection for the hole. Looking for the blood. But nothing. His shirt's not even torn.

A man steps into view. Tall, like he is, but not so lanky. Broad shoulders, bit of a gut straining against the white shirt and black jacket. African American, like him. Darker skinned. Midnight skin.

The man lets the nickel-plated pump-action hang by his side. "Hey, DeAndre," he says. "My name's Hollis. You busy right now?"

CHAPTER 3

Aleena Kattan

Reminder," Melanie the vampire says, standing at the front of the room by the whiteboard. "Next Thursday is the Fourth of July, and the Wednesday before we're doing Cruiseapalooza, where every floor is a different"—she makes bunny-ear quotes in midair—"'cruise destination,' and here on the accounts floor we're going to be Hawaii, so, aloha, mahalo, dress Hawaiian."

Aleena sits at the back of the room, listening to Melanie—whose skin is the alabaster hue of a river-logged corpse—drone on and on. Mel's the wrong person to lead the department and these monthly staff meetings. Everyone hates her. She's got a voice like a mosquito humming in your ear. But that's middle management for you: smart enough to get promoted, stupid enough to have to stay.

Aleena thinks a lot of these people are stupid.

She feels bad about that. It's very judgmental. But she also feels these people are due a bit of judgment. This batch of half-done cookies is an ignorant, corn-fed lot happy to watch sitcoms on their too-big TVs while the rest of the world struggles and cries and burns. They have their own problems, but Aleena knows they're not real problems. Like the hashtag says: #firstworldproblems.

Her phone vibrates in her pocket. A text. She pulls out the phone, gives it a quick look. Her heart lodges in her throat.

The text reads, in Arabic: *We are advancing—the timetable has moved up*

The message is from Qasim.

She texts back: *I'm not ready. Nobody told me!*

Khalid has been shot—sniper fire

Her pulse goes from stopped to stampeding horses. *No, no, no.* She tries to think. It's 10 A.M. here, which means in Damascus it's 5 P.M. Where are they? What are they doing right now? Not the protest.

The station. They're attacking one of the state's TV stations. Trying to take it over in the name of Suriya al-shaab, the people's station, to broadcast truth in the name of those who oppose the regime. That's today. That's *now*.

Her phone buzzes: *Get to a computer*

Not now. She can't. *She can't.* She needs this job if she's going to do her . . . other work. Firesign is one of the country's biggest ISPs. She has nearly infinite bandwidth here, and as smart as they think they are about network security, she can dip in and out with ease.

Leaving a meeting, she'll draw attention. She looks up, makes sure nobody sees her texting. Sends the message: *Can't right now find someone else.* It has to be someone else. They have others like her. She knows they do, even if she doesn't know who they are.

Qasim texts back: *Nobody else—only you—get to a computer!*

Then a second text: *Please Aleena*

Before she knows what she's doing, she's standing. The chair stutters and groans against the floor as she pushes it back. Everybody in the room—and the entire department is here—turns to look at her. Melanie stops speaking. She has a look on her face like she smells something dead.

"Is there something wrong, Aleena?"

"No," Aleena blurts. "Yes. I . . . have to use the bathroom." Stupid, stupid, stupid. What is she, in fourth grade?

Melanie echoes the sentiment. "We're not in kindergarten, Aleena. You're supposed to go before you get here. Uh, hello."

A quiet murmur of uncomfortable laughs from those gathered.

"I don't feel well." Aleena holds her hand over her stomach. Her brother Nas always said, *You want to get out of a day's work, just tell them you have diarrhea. Nobody will ask you to come in if you've got the shits.*

"Go," Melanie says, her look of disgust deepening.

Aleena hurries toward the door, ignoring all the looks that follow her out.

Ø Ø Ø

She texts as she walks, all of it in Arabic.

What do you need from me?

Qasim returns: *We can't get into the station without Khalid you need to shut down their broadcast*

She texts back: *How am I supposed to do that?*

Qasim sends four texts in rapid succession.

You're the one with the bag of tricks Aleena

They're broadcasting lies and we can stop them we can show the truth

Please Aleena

Others have been shot—we are pinned down

Aleena responds: *I'm working on it*

She jogs down the hallway.

Ø Ø Ø

This would have been her plan all along. To hack the broadcast. That's the power of what she does. Nobody needs to die. Nobody needs to step in the way of a sniper's bullet. But some of her people over there, they want to make a show of it. Qasim and Khalid said they needed the people to see them doing it—masks and homemade flash-bangs and AKs chattering. So that when they took over the state media, *other* media around the world would show images of them storming the stations.

They don't understand what she does. Not really. Not yet. But her fingerprints and those of her fellow "hacktivists" were all over the Arab Spring. Helping protesters kick through firewalls, setting up wireless hot spots or dial-up access, running direct denial-of-service attacks on government websites, hacking the sites to deface them, spreading restricted images and videos across social media, leaking secret documents.

She threads her way through the cubicle farm. There's been some talk about moving to an open floor plan, which would be terrible for what she does. These fuzzy gray cubicle walls give her all the privacy she needs.

She navigates the grid, turns right at the copier, left at the paper cutter—

Someone is sitting in her cubicle. Right in front of her computer.

He's government. She can see that by the way he sits, the dark suit, the earpiece nesting in his ear. Though she wonders about those muttonchops: an unusual style. He's opening her drawers. Rifling through files. Humming.

She has to go. She's busted. Aleena knows the stakes—if they catch her, she'll end up in a dark hole in some desert. Her and every Muslim goatherd suspected of terrorism, lorded over by soldiers with high-powered weapons.

But she also knows the stakes in what's happening right now. She needs to help Qasim. She can't keep anyone from dying today. But maybe by ending the government broadcast, she can get the rebels—*her* rebels—international attention. She can save people going forward.

The truth can save people.

And that means she has to work.

Aleena pivots before the government man can see her. She hates leaving her computer behind, but everything there was done through a proxy—she has no evidence on that system. And while she has items in the desk she would otherwise want to keep (lip balm, snacks, an appointment book), none of it is meaningful, nor does it point to her *activities* in any actionable way.

She stops in the break room. Kay Weldon is there—one of the executive secretaries. Red hair like a helmet, shellacked with so much hair spray it reminds Aleena of her brother's Lego figurines, like you could pop the hair on and off with ease.

"Aren't you in Melanie's meeting right now?" Kay asks. Kay knows everyone's schedule. Kay called Aleena "Lana" for two months straight, then "Leena" for two more.

"Over early," Aleena says. She tries to make it chirpy but knows it comes out bitchy. Fine. Whatever.

"Where is everyone, then? The cubes are still empty."

Aleena looks at the snack machine. She needs Kay out of here. Now. "They're still talking about Cruiseapalooza."

"Shouldn't you be talking about it, too, Aleena?"

Aleena tenses up, hears the words come out of her mouth before she can yank them back in. "Shouldn't you be keeping your piggy nose out of everyone's ass, Kay?" The acid in her words is regrettable, but it does the trick. Kay's face puckers like a stress ball squeezed in a heavy hand.

"Well, then." She bustles past Aleena and out of the break room.

Time to hurry. Aleena goes to the snack machine. Reaches under it. Finds the cell phone taped there along with the USB key containing her suite of hacker tools: port scanners, portalware, worms, Trojans, keyloggers. She's no script kiddie. She designed these all herself. They have her signature.

She heads to the elevators. Outside, in the cubicle farm, are two men in suits. One woman, too. Just as the woman looks in Aleena's direction, Aleena drops down behind the fax machine table.

When the woman looks away, Aleena hurries to the elevator.

Ø Ø Ø

White floors. White ceilings. Bold humming fluorescents.

And beneath them, row after row of black boxes and blue lights winking. It's quiet down here. Calm. Just the vibrations in the floor, the hum of the cooling fans, the little chirp and whir of hard drives running.

One of Firesign's many server farms. For hosting. For directing traffic. For the company intranet. Aleena's not supposed to be down here. But a hacked key card made it easy.

She grabs the cell she plucked from under the snack machine, unspools a cable, plugs the USB right into a random server—doesn't matter which one, she just needs the connection to the Firesign pipe. Down here it's *pure bandwidth*—useful for the encrypted video she's about to send and receive, but not strictly necessary. No, why it's important to be in this building is because most connections in America are loaded with speed bumps meant to slow the connection down. It's all monitored, as if every line has a little virtual bug clamped to it. But here, at the source, it's all open. A screaming, streaming river of unburdened data.

She fires up the phone. Opens a telnet port. Some privileged hackers think cracking computers in the Arab world is easy, like Arabs are all a bunch of dirt merchants with wireless signals coming in through a Pringles can to shitty old ten-pound laptops with security as sophisticated as a password that's someone's birthday. It was that way once, and still is in some places, but that world caught up fast. With the combination of DIY, get-it-done attitude, and a sudden flood of high-tech gear coming in from the UAR or Qatar, everything has changed. That's true across the whole Middle East—maybe more so in Iran.

Translation: they've gotten good at protecting themselves.

But she's better.

She opens up her port scanner, uses her own breach-map software to find the vulnerabilities. It doesn't take long before she's digitally kicked open a backdoor into the Syrian state television station. This is bare-bones stuff: a command prompt. She starts sniffing for the ports of the consoles filming, mixing, and broadcasting the feeds.

There—

And then her phone's screen goes dark.

What the— Aleena looks up. The server to which she's attached is dark, too. No blue lights. No hum. Still as an alien obelisk.

She unplugs, starts to plug into the next one.

The phone rings. Which is odd, because it has no cell service. Doesn't even have a SIM card. It's rigged. Jailbroken to be used only for data.

The name on the call is "PROTECTED."

Don't answer it.

But she's a curious girl. Always has been. Aleena curses under her breath and answers.

"Aleena," says the voice. A gruff voice. Short. Sharp. Gravel rattling in a cup.

"Wrong number," she says.

"This is Hollis Copper, Aleena. I'd like to speak with you."

"Gotta go," she says, and hangs up.

The entire server bank goes dark. One at a time, like a series of lights going out down a long hallway. It seems so simple a thing, but she knows what it means. You turn off a bank of boxes like this, the ISP grinds to a halt. Firesign would never consent to that. Someone's got a finger on a very big switch. She's compromised.

She races back to the elevator. She stabs the button. It lights up, but doesn't ding. Then the button goes dark. She hits it again. It lights up. Goes dark.

They've cut off access to the server room.

The phone rings. She pops the back of the case, pulls the battery, flings it away from her like it's a scorpion found inside a boot.

All the lights on the floor go out. For a moment, all is dark, and Aleena is left with her own breathing, her own rushing blood in her ears. But then the backup lighting flicks on, and everything is cast in a red emergency glow.

She thinks fast. On the ground floor, they'll be waiting. Garage floor, too. So—where? She could hide. Duck into a janitorial closet.

Wait. The old skybridge. Runs across to the ISP's second building—which they sold last year to a developer who diced it up into smaller offices. They closed the skybridge, but it's still *there*. Sixth floor? Seventh? She doesn't remember. She'll figure it out. She throws open the stairwell door—

And there stands the man with the muttonchops. In one hand, he's got a Taser. In the other, a foil-bubble pack of gum. He pinches the pack, pops what looks like a Chiclet into his mouth. He grinds it between his back teeth and smiles. "Hey there," he says.

Aleena just stares. Feral. A cornered animal.

"Aleena, I take it. Nice to finally meet you."

"I didn't do anything wrong. People are getting hurt. I have work to do."

"I got work to do, too," he says. "So let's get right to it. Are you going to make me Taser you, or will you join me of your own accord?"

She thinks about it. "You're going to have to Taser me," she says. "And you'll have to carry me up several flights of stairs by yourself. You're older. In your fifties. It won't be pleasant. My sincerest hope is that it takes a few weeks off your life."

He sighs. "At least I'm told you don't have a heart condition," he says. "So let's hope your medical records are right."

Then he fires the Taser into her stomach.

CHAPTER 4

Reagan Stolper

Courtney Gurwich is in love.

She never expected it. Not like this. Not . . . *online*. But dating's hard. She doesn't have a lot of time in her life these days, and the last thing she wants to do is go to a bar because she already manages an awful chain restaurant called McGlinchey's. It *has* a bar, one that comes stocked full of slacker staff and rude customers. Whenever she's there she hears all the cheap, crappy, toxic come-on lines the guys at those places say to try to get in a girl's pants. It's all very *pathetic*.

Courtney's not like that. She hasn't had many boyfriends. She's almost thirty, and it's not like she's a virgin or anything, but—most guys, they just want to get right into it. All that pawing and panting and fumbling to get the bra off and then it's another ride on the Amateur Hour Express, where they hitch and grunt and she lies there staring at the ceiling fan and then it's all over but for the shower swiftly after.

Then she met Dave. She decided to try online dating, and it wasn't even a week after putting up her profile that she met him. He e-mailed her and was sweet and polite. Handsome, but not too handsome. Clean-shaven. A little heavy but not so much that it bothered her. In fact, she likes a man who has some heft to him. He was Christian, too—that was a good sign. It's not like she's a Bible-thumper or anything, but she goes to church once a month and wants someone who believes in something bigger than himself.

One problem: Dave lives in Portland. Oregon, not Maine. Still. He made her laugh. They started e-mailing. He asked her lots of questions, responding with compassion and kindness and, above all else, wit. He even wrote to her, "Lot of girls say they want a sense of humor but never seem to mean it, but I'm glad you do."

She did like it. She liked *him*. She started dreaming of Portland.

Now it's been three months. They've e-mailed on and off. They've spoken on the phone a few times. Skype, too, though only through headphones—his camera's busted.

Today's the day. He's flying in. She's going to meet him down at Frick Park. Then they're going to go to dinner—and she thinks she'll bring him back here. He said he'd stay at a motel but she told him he could stay here. He was playful about it but not rude. "Why would I come to your house?" he asked.

She danced around it but eventually typed: "So we can have some fun together."

> **HIM:** Whatever do you mean? ☺
> **HER:** ;)
> **HIM:** You're naughty.
> **HER:** For you, maybe.
> **HIM:** How about a preview?

She didn't know what he meant but he said *her* camera was working so maybe she could do a little routine for him. Like a striptease or something. She'd never done that, and she balked a little. But then she admitted she'd imagined what it would be like and so she decided to oblige him, thinking it *would* make a nice preview for what was to come.

Courtney turned on the camera. Did a dance as sexy as she could. She maybe rushed it a little bit—took off her clothes too fast—and it was hard to know how much he could see and how much he couldn't. She tried to push her breasts together to make them look bigger. She kissed the air. Bent over, waggled her beehive. Hiked her panties down as she did it—slow and seductive, or so she hoped.

Then she lost it and started laughing and he laughed too and told her he had to go get packed. Because he'd see her tomorrow.

Now it's tomorrow.

Ø Ø Ø

Dave does not exist.

Courtney Gurwich gave Dave explicit instructions where to meet her in Frick Park. She told him there's a bench that faces an overlook of trees, and nobody ever seems to sit on it. The bench has a little plaque attached that says DONATION: JAMES AND ANN TROXEL and she always says a little thank-you to those two even though she doesn't know who they are. Because she loves that bench.

Courtney shows up right on time. She is not the type of person to be late.

But Dave is not sitting on the bench. What sits there is a laptop. And playing—*looping*—on that laptop screen is Courtney's striptease. Her awkward, unsexy, graceless striptease. Someone has edited the sound so that whenever she moves, the laptop speakers belch out bold, realistic fart noises.

Courtney tries very hard not to cry. She sees a Post-it note stuck just below the laptop's keyboard. With a hesitant hand she snatches it up. Then she sees it's not one Post-it, but several layered on top of one another. She reads them one by one, each message like an arrow fired into her quaking, clammy flesh.

Courtney
You crabby stuck up beeyotch
suck a thousand dongs in Hell
I sent this video to all the McGlinchey employees
also uploaded it to your FB page and sent a link to all the
contacts in your e-mail using your e-mail address so they
think it came from you
FUCK YOU you fucking twat
Love, Dave Who Doesn't Exist You Dummy
P.S. you should've never fired Carlos you racist ho
And that's when Courtney loses it. She screams. And
sobs. And takes the laptop and wings it off the overlook.

Then she collapses in a heap and cries, pulling at her hair
until clumps of it come out in her hands.

Ø Ø Ø

Dave is a construct of Reagan Stolper.

He is one of her many constructs. She created him months
ago for the sole purpose of fucking with Courtney Gurwich.
Courtney the McGlinchey's Dictator. Courtney the White-
bread Half-Christian Assbitch. Courtney, who once referred
to Carlos the line cook as a "wetback." Courtney, who once
told Reagan she was fat.

Reagan decided that Courtney's firing Carlos—because
she said he was "leering" at her—was the last straw, and so
she started spying on Courtney, even hacking her Master-
Card account. (*So* not hard, what with the password being
her dog's name.) She saw a line item for an online dating site
and that's when the idea hit her, like a magical meteor cast
from the heavens.

Now Reagan sits a quarter mile away, in Frick Park, at
a picnic table not far from the Reynolds Street Gatehouse.
She does a few quick finger-swiping video edits on her An-
droid phone. Like tying a child's shoelaces, it's that easy.
She takes the brand-new video—the laptop's webcam was
on and so it recorded a reaction video of Courtney seeing

herself galumphing about nude—and uploads *that* online. She's not sure which one is her favorite, really. The awkward Courtney slut-dance, or the one where she cries a lot and flips shit before flinging the laptop into the woods.

That was a pretty good laptop, but Reagan's glad to lose it. Sometimes *sacrifices must be made* in the search for *sweet lulz*.

She wonders if maybe she should call Courtney. Put on her Dave voice one last time—for kicks. She has a naturally deep voice and it's easy to do.

But then her phone dings and the upload is finished. Time to go home.

Reagan heads back to her car.

Ø Ø Ø

She doesn't see the man in the backseat at first. Reagan hops in, fishes around the glove compartment for her pack of smokes, and then someone in the backseat says, "Looking for these? You shouldn't smoke."

Reagan reacts fast. She reaches deeper into the glove compartment, wraps her hands around the pepper spray, whips around and hoses the backseat with the stuff. The man thrashes around like a cat covered in bees.

Reagan throws open the car door to get the hell out of there.

Ø Ø Ø

Reagan hoofs it to the bus stop. Then takes the bus to her apartment.

She thinks about calling the cops, but given who she is and what she just did to Courtney Gurwich, maybe that's not such a hot idea. Instead, Reagan decides she'll go back to the car the next day, when creepy backseat black dude will be long gone. She seems to remember him wearing a suit. Odd for a tweaker. Or for a homeless guy. Though sometimes they buy third-hand suits from the thrift shops.

Tired, she staggers into her dirty butthole of an apartment, throws her phone and bag on what little counter space she has—

"Pepper spray, huh?" says the man in the suit, rounding the corner by the coat closet and stepping into the kitchen. Reagan utters an incomprehensible curse—some panicked pastiche of *fuck* and *shit*—and grabs a knife out of the block next to the oven. She slices through the air with the serrated blade. "I'll stab the crap out of you," she says.

The man blinks a pair of raw, red-rimmed eyes. He sighs. "I'm an agent of the government," he says, and flips his identification toward her. "Spraying me with that toxic shit already gives me complete and total license to stick a bullet in you. Stabbing, slashing, or slicing me open will get you a lot worse than that."

It's now Reagan notices he has a gun in his hand. A black, boxy pistol. The knife wavers. "How'd you get here so fast?" she asks.

"You left your car with the keys in the ignition. I took it."

"That's stealing."

He laughs. "I call it 'licensing public goods *for* the public good.' "

"That's clever. You think you're really clever."

"Maybe. You think you're clever, too. And maybe you are, because that's why, right now, I got a team of folks on the way. I'd like to have a conversation with you somewhere other than . . . here."

She thinks for a minute. "I like conversations." She sets the knife down on the counter. "Let's go."

"No fight?"

"No fight. I'm curious."

His eyes narrow. "They say curiosity killed the cat."

"Well, I'm no pussy, dude. So let's do this."

CHAPTER 5

Wade Earthman

Wade wakes out of a dream of burning jungle and screaming women, of helicopter rotors and machine gun fire. He hears something he first thinks is part of the dream but soon realizes is not: the sound of a helicopter's blades chopping the air.

Wade drops down off his bed—a bed handmade by a local boy down the road, a real autistic type who doesn't do well with people but can make a set of fresh-cut logs sing beneath saw and sandpaper. He groans and winces. He's old now, and feels the movements of the morning especially keenly; often he feels like a beater car that takes a while to start up. But this, *this* has him starting up—regardless of the arthritis squeezing his knees and the popcorn crackle of his back.

The sound of the chopper thuds up through his feet and down from the rafters of his attic bedroom, so he rushes to the window, peers out.

He can't see it. But he can hear it passing overhead. *Black helicopter,* he thinks.

That's when his alarms go off. Klaxons and red sirens.

Loud enough and bright enough to wake a dead man out of his dreamless sleep. That means someone's breached the perimeter. Coming over the cattle gate. Probably cut the electric fence.

It's over. They're here.

Ø Ø Ø

It's just past midnight and Wade's got the man on this side of the cattle gate pinched neatly at the center of the rifle's night-vision crosshairs—the rifle, a .30-30 lever-action, is his coyote gun. Coyotes are always trying to get in here, take his chickens. Any time he sees one of those tricksters traipsing down his driveway or through his irrigation ditches, he drops it. If he sees coyotes on the butte behind his house, he leaves them alone—he figures they're not bothering him, he won't bother them with lead to the lungs.

Out here, coyotes are like rats. Now he's got a whole new rat to worry about: the fella who just climbed over his cattle gate. Black fella, he thinks, though it's hard to tell through the infrared scope. No matter the color of the man's skin, this damn sure counts as trespassing, which means he could peel this son of a bitch's scalp like an orange with a squeeze of the trigger. The bullet would cross the four hundred yards between them, give this fella one hell of a surprise.

Still. He hesitates. He's never killed anybody before. Also, not many black fellas up in these parts. Killing one would be problematic. They'd say he was a racist, but Wade's sure that he's not—he wouldn't be shooting this person because of his skin color but because he's planting his feet on Wade's land. That's Wade's *property*. He's got signs up all over down there: NO TRESPASSING. DON'T TREAD ON ME. FUCK THE DOG, BEWARE OF OWNER. All of them hand-painted.

Wade looks closer. The black fella ain't alone. Two others are coming up along the sides. Two more come in from the east. All jacked up in military gear.

It's time to get his bug-out bag.

Ø Ø Ø

The BOB, the bug-out bag, is a duffel filled with water, beef jerky, dried fruits, some cookies (shut up, cookies are delicious), a first-aid kit, a rain poncho, a cammie suit meant to match the scrub desert of western Colorado, a change of socks and underwear, a radio, a flashlight, a netbook, a hunting knife, a .380 Smith & Wesson pistol.

It's not meant to get him far. It's meant to get him to his bunker, out there in the BLM—the Bureau of Land Management territory that he technically doesn't own, but hey, the government doesn't seem to want to do much with it either.

He slings the bag over his shoulder. He passes by his computer room—a series of old and new desktops and laptops piled floor to ceiling. PCs. Macs. Unix boxes. Servers running his BBS software. Disconnected from the Internet. Hooked up only to phone lines. These are his babies. He's been sysop of these bulletin board systems since he was a much younger man. Since before the Internet even mattered. Liberty Bell BBS. The Shadowlands BBS. The Patriot's Amendment BBS. Havens away from the clamor and the overconnectedness of the Internet. Receptacles for information. *Dangerous* information—or, at least, information dangerous to the government. WikiLeaks ain't got shit on the cables and memos he's got in these boxes. Classified information loyal dial-up customers have been giving him and his other users for a decade now—men and women in the service, across various agencies, in police departments across the country. Patriots, every last one of them.

Wade brushes a gray ringlet out of his eye. Thinks for a moment that he might want to shed a tear or two over all this—his life's work. But he has neither the time nor the inclination toward sentimentality. So he flips the switch on the wall. A series of electromagnets beneath the floorboards hum like yellow-jacket wings in a wasps' nest. The noise rises to a crescendo and then it's gone.

Wade opens a small desk drawer, and from behind it pulls

a little remote control—the kind that starts fireplaces, like the one he has downstairs under the big-ass elk head hanging there. He's not sure if this is going to work.

He presses the button. At first nothing happens. But suddenly, behind the vents and inside the cases of the computers, he sees a faint orange glow—and then a small shower of blue sparks followed by a sound that conjures the memory of Fourth of July sparklers. *Kkkkkshhhpop.*

In each system, a little fire burning. The hard drives melting down to worthless slag.

Those fires may go out. They may not, might burn the house down. That last part is regrettable, of course. He owns this place. This is his home. He beat the system and the home ownership scam and bought this place outright in cash, not feeding the greedy banks their pound of flesh month after month.

Still. The cost of doing business.

He heads downstairs to the four-wheeler parked out front.

∅ ∅ ∅

The night air is cold here. Whistling through his shaggy hair, keening through his teeth. The quad bounds away from his house, away from the agents, away from captivity—he knows what they do to people like him. Like Bradley (or is it Chelsea now?) Manning or that snooty WikiLeaks fuck or that NSA fella, Snowden, or hell, any of the good patriots who break the poisonous chains of command to give their true bosses—the American *people*—a hard dose of high-test truth for once in their lives. They catch him, they'll put a bag over his head and throw him in some black-site prison in eastern Europe where they'll experiment on his brain or torture him for information like something out of that movie *Marathon Man.*

Or worse, they'll just shoot him in the head and dump him in a hole.

Probably that one, actually.

But they won't catch him today. He knows this area. They don't.

The quad rocks and shudders, and he hears a sound like gunfire. Four *pops,* maybe not loud enough to be guns going off, which means—

The quad's momentum, dead. The four-wheeler suddenly handles like he's driving through mud despite everything out here being flat and dry as a skipping stone. The tires are blown. All four of them. *God damn it!*

Wade hops off the quad. He kills the engine. He pulls the .380 out of the BOB and tears the lining of the bag to get at another small remote control.

He looks back. Behind him, twenty feet back, sits a strip of spikes rolled out on black rubber. The strip is half covered in scrub and dirt. They didn't just lay this out. This has been here for a while. That bakes his noodle a little. How'd they know? Then he realizes: tire tracks. He makes this run once every two weeks. For practice. That means they've been watching him. More than that, *studying* him. They knew where he'd go. They knew to place the tire strip right here.

That means his bunker is compromised.

He has backup plans. Up at the reservoir he has an old dirt bike stashed. If that fails, he could hoof it all night to 70, thumb a ride somewhere—if he makes it that far. And given that he hears the shuffle of clothing and armor and the loose rattle of weapons in hands, he knows now that he will not.

Two soldiers come over a scrubby berm of dirt and stone. They've been waiting for him. Of course they have. One has a shotgun. The other, a small submachine gun tucked against his shoulder. Moonlight gleams in their helmet goggles. He sees a band of winking green behind the goggles—night vision. He forgot to pack his own night-vision goggles, didn't he? Shit. Guess it doesn't matter now.

He drops the pistol, but keeps the remote.

They hold him there for a while, their guns up. A cold wind sweeps over the area, kicks up a red cloud in the darkness. Nobody says a damn thing. The remote is small, but feels heavy in Wade's hands.

A few moments later, the black fella shows up. Panting a little, with four other soldiers jogging alongside. "Wade Earthman," the fella says.

"'Sright."

"Hollis Copper."

"That's a helluva name."

"Says the man with the name Earthman."

Wade frowns. "It's not Earth*man,* like you're saying it. It's *Earth*man. It's from the German. Erdmann, I think."

"Okay." Hollis dusts off his pants. "What you got there, Wade?"

"Mr. Earthman, if you please."

"Question remains the same no matter how I address you."

Wade tilts the little remote. "This old thing? It's a remote control."

"Okay. You going to tell me what it does?"

"You predicted me coming out here on the quad, but looks like you didn't predict what I might do when you caught me."

"Our models aren't perfect."

Wade grunts. "I press this button"—his thumb hovers just over it—"and we all blow to king hell and back."

"Oh yeah?"

"Oh yeah. I got fifty-five-gallon drums buried all over the place out here. Hard digging in this ground; had to use an excavator I rented from Grand Junction. And even still, lot of stone. Just the same, I managed to bury these barrels—a dozen of them—and wire 'em all together and set them to a trigger box and antenna that—drumroll, please—connects up to this little doohickey right here. Did I mention that each one of them barrels is loaded to the tippy-top with . . . well, let's just say I hit this trigger, it's going to get real hot and real noisy around here. Two of those twelve barrels are here with us right now, like ghosts waiting to be called up out of their graves. One over there under that hill.

And one *right* under the ground where you're standing, Mr. Copper."

That last part's a lie. Two barrels are buried nearby. If Wade blows those barrels they might die from the debris, but it won't be the explosions that take them out. But the government man has bought the lie, because he stiffens. Hands flexing in and out of fists.

"You're willing to just blow yourself up," Hollis says.

"'Sright. I'm old."

"I wouldn't call sixty-three old."

"It feels old."

"Sorry to hear that, Wade. I have a third option I'd like to discuss. Can I get something from my pocket without you turning this place into the end of a *Die Hard* movie?"

"I said, call me Mr. Earthm—"

Copper holds out a photograph. It's wallet size blown up to eight and a half by eleven. Printed out from a color laser. It flutters and flaps in the wind. Hollis nods, and one of the soldiers points a gun at the photo, clicks on a flashlight at the end of the barrel.

That's when Wade sees whose face is in the photo. "Shit," he says. Everything inside him goes slack, like a fishing line after the fish has bitten off the bait and gone to the current.

"You going to come with us, Wade?"

"Come on, man. You can't do this to me."

"I'll ask one more time. You going to put that remote down and come with us?"

The photo. The girl's face. Wade sets the remote down on the seat of the quad. He lets the duffel slide off his shoulders and thud into the dust. Then he holds up his hands and puts them behind his head, and closes his eyes as they swoop in to claim him.

CHAPTER 6

The Hook

They each end up in a room, alone, after a long flight on a C-130 military plane. Seated at a table. Walls of cinder block. Black ceiling, black floor. Glass of water. Little sleeves of cookies—Fig Newtons, Oreos, Chips Ahoy—laid out in front of them.

They each hear a similar pitch. Though each pitch is tailored differently, because Hollis Copper knows that everyone has a story and if you want to speak to someone, you better find a way to speak to his or her story.

Ø Ø Ø

Hollis: "How are the cookies?"

Chance: "Little stale."

"Our pastry chef is on vacation."

"I bet."

"You know why I'm here."

Chance shrugs, trying to play it cool. "I know, man. I know. Overdue library books. I'm a slow reader, what can I say?"

"You're a funny guy."

"I was hoping for 'handsome gentleman,' but I figure that's reaching."

"Shut up."

Chance shuts up. Hollis can see, despite all the lip, the kid is scared pissless. "Two of those football players you messed with are facing a year, maybe five if the judge is a hard-ass who doesn't give much of a shit about football. But my guess is, around where you live, *everybody* gives a shit about football."

"Shoot, I played baseball."

"Yes, you did. Pitcher. Good arm on you, I heard. You *also* ran the computer lab all four years in college, which leads me to my next point. Way the laws are set up, what you did and what those boys did is not equal in the blind eyes of Lady Justice. They'll do a couple years. But *you'll* do ten."

Chance stiffens. "Ten for what? You haven't said what."

"You *know* what." From behind him, Hollis pulls a white mask attached to a black hood. Looks like the one from the serial killer in that movie *Scream*. He gestures with the mask as he speaks. "Nice mask. A Faceless mask. Bunch of iconoclast punks throwing stones at giants. We've been looking to get one of them on the hook for a while and—well, look at that—now we got *you*. Chance Dalton, aka Shad0wman91. That's a zero instead of the *o,* and a 91 for the year of your birth, right? So. You hacked a couple websites. Broke into some e-mail. You went on the Internet and exposed a little cabal calling itself the Yellowjacket Rape Posse. Shit that would have stayed hidden because everybody wanted it hidden. But you can't turn a blind eye when this shit gets to Myspace, isn't that right?"

The kid looks freaked. "I don't know what you're talking about." He crosses his arms over his chest, tucks the flats of his palms under his armpits. "And nobody uses Myspace anymore."

Hollis ignores that. Computers aren't his thing. "I'm not

judging you. Those boys will get far less than they deserve. You ask me, they deserve to have the same thing done to them that they did to all those girls. But then again, I'm a real Old Testament, eye-for-an-eye, karmic-debt type."

"I don't think karma's in the Old Testament."

"I'm not a big reader."

"So." Chance gnaws his fingernail. "Who told them? Bogardian and his pops. How'd they know it was me?"

"Another hacker sold you out."

"I'm not a real hacker. I got no grudges against anyone. No one's got any grudges against me." But Hollis can see the kid trying to figure it out.

"It was a troll type. Just messing with shit to mess with shit."

"Oh."

"You think you were doing the right thing. And by my standards, maybe you were—even if the reason for what you did was a little *complex*."

There. Now Chance looks really panicked. He's wondering: *How does Hollis know?* But Hollis knows. He's got a pretty good idea why Chance did what he did. Everybody's got a dark secret, and this one is all Chance's.

"Like I said," says Hollis, "those boys deserve more than they're going to get and they're going to get more than most folks around your town think they deserve. But it's not my standards that matter. I'm just one bee in the whole damn hive. What matters is the law. The laws of this country. And by doing your little computer thing—which honestly I don't understand and don't much care to—you broke the law. And I'm here to collect."

"This isn't how it works. You haven't . . . you haven't shown me a badge or . . . or . . . produced a warrant. I want a lawyer."

Hollis needs to seal this deal. He doesn't know why they want this kid—Chance Dalton seems like a bit player with middling skills—but they do. So he steps up from across the table, throws the *Scream* mask down, knits his hands in front of him. "Hey, don't misunderstand. I'm not here to arrest you. I'm here to offer you a choice."

"Choice? What kinda choice?"

"One year or ten years."

"I don't understand."

"You do ten years behind bars or you do one year with me. Working for the government. Doing some . . . odd jobs. You still get to do your computer thing, don't worry."

Chance clutches his ribs. "I want a lawyer."

"You lawyer up, this deal turns to smoke. Grab it before it's gone." When Chance hesitates, Hollis shrugs. "Not like you got much else going on, *Shadowman*. You go back home, those football players will eat you like a cookie." Hollis pops an Oreo in his mouth, crunches down hard.

Chance closes his eyes. Draws a deep breath. "All right," he says. ". . . All right."

Ø Ø Ø

Aleena: "I want a lawyer."

Hollis: "You lawyer up, this deal turns to—"

"Where are we?"

"You can worry about that later."

"Hour-and-a-half flight, fifteen-minute drive. I'm guessing D.C. area. Virginia?"

"Okay, so you get the *clever* badge."

She wrinkles her brow. Looks down at the cookies. "Muslims don't eat cookies. We're not allowed to have processed sugar. Islamic dietary laws."

He laughs. She's quick, not like that last joker. "That's no dietary restriction I've ever heard about. Besides, we both know you're not actually Muslim."

"So you know quite a lot about me. Do you also know I'm an American? I know my rights."

"Whatever. As I was going to say, your kind doesn't get a lawyer."

"My kind. You mean Arabs."

"I mean *terrorists*."

She freezes. "I'm not. I'm not a terrorist."

"No, I know that. But that's how it'll play. And the laws work easier for us if we just slap that scarlet letter across your chest now instead of later. You're Syrian. You got family there. Muslims. Doesn't matter that you're not religious. Which, I have to say, begs the question why you're involved at all in the Arab Spring."

She blinks. "Those are people who can benefit from my help. As you noted: I have family there. They like freedom. I like freedom. The reasons are not complex." She stiffens, like she's got a little more steel back in her backbone. "By the way, *begging the question* is not that. It's a logical fallacy. Where a statement attempts to prove itself by including the conclusion within the statement: *This girl is a terrorist because the law says so, and I am the law.*"

"Enough with the pedantic nonsense. Let's cut to the chase, Aleena. I can help you. All you gotta do is come work for us."

"Us." She says that word like a curse.

"The United States government."

"I neither like nor approve of this government."

"But as you note, you *are* American. Which means this is your government as much as it is mine."

"This government hasn't been mine in a long time."

One of those *types*. "You and I are going to have to differ on that point. I say you live here, it's your government. All the bells and whistles. All the warts and wrinkles. You want the job?"

She gives a stiff shake of her head. "I want a lawyer."

"Answer's still no."

"Please—"

"I thought you were smarter than this. Top of your class at Emerson. Folder full of recommendations. I guess you're still a little dumb, too."

"Excuse me?"

"You're not looking at the long game, Aleena. We got you, so let's say we file you under T for Terrorist. What happens to your family, you think? You have a big family, Aleena. Mother. Aunt. Little brother. They might pass the smell test. Maybe they won't. Doesn't matter. They're going to be in for it. The accusations. The *threats*. If you're a terrorist, then far as the rest of the world is concerned, so are they."

She pinches her eyes shut, like she's trying not to cry. But then she opens her eyes and her stare bores a hole right through his chest and into his heart. Hollis thinks, *She wants to leap across this table right now, wrap her hands around my throat, and kill me.* He doesn't blame her. This is dirty pool and he knows it.

Aleena: "You're a bully. Your whole country, a bully."

"We have work that needs doing, and I'll say whatever I have to in order to see that work done, Aleena. Last chance. You in?"

She stares off at an unfixed point. "What choice do I have?" she asks.

Ø Ø Ø

DeAndre: "Man, fuck you." He pushes the cookies away.

Hollis: "That's not very friendly, DeAndre."

"Government bitch. You don't know me."

"Oh, but I *do*, DeAndre Deleon Mitchell. How do I know thee? *Let me count the ways.* Online handles: Cardshark. Scarface. Darth Dizzy. Mister Freeze. All sound like cartoon names to me. You're a carder. A spammer. A scammer. A movie pirate. You're like the Swiss Army knife of hackers. You've got card skimmers and backdoors and botnets— and I don't even know what those things are, that's just what they tell me."

"So who are you?" DeAndre asks.

"I'm a friend. Here to offer you a deal."

"A deal."

"Uh-huh. The United States government knows what naughty business you've been up to. And they would very much like to bring the hammer down and pound you flat like a crooked nail. Unless you decide to play nice. Come work for the government for one year."

"Sounds like prison."

"It'll be much nicer than prison, I promise. It's a lodge." DeAndre's face twists up in confusion, probably imagining he'll be skiing and drinking hot chocolate by the fire or whatever. Hollis laughs. "That's what we call it, anyway. It's in the mountains. Real pretty."

DeAndre sniffs. "You want me to turn traitor. Be a white hat all of a sudden."

"I'm sorry—white hat?" Hollis suddenly feels old.

DeAndre laughs, but it's not a happy sound. "Man, you really don't know this stuff, do you? White hats: good-guy hackers, hacktivists, SJW social-justice types. Black hats: thieves and pirates and all that scum and villainy shit. No? You're here to offer me a deal but you don't know dick about this stuff?"

"Think of me as a *collector*."

"What I see is a brother who's really a white dude done up in Grade A, high-quality blackface. A traitor to the skin."

Hollis scowls. "Don't try that solidarity shit with me, son. Won't fly."

"You didn't grow up poor?"

"My father was a dentist. I went to Princeton. You and me, we aren't alike."

"Okay, okay." DeAndre swallows hard. "You're telling me you don't have a moms you want to take care of?"

"Not one who'd like me paying her in stolen money. If I tried that, my mother would whip my ass till it turned baboon blue."

DeAndre sighs. "Yeah. You and me got *that* in common, at least."

"The deal is, you work for us, and your 'moms' gets to keep that house. Don't worry, she doesn't know anything. Yet. I met her at the house, told her you're working with us on special contract. She can go on believing that her son is a productive member of society, that she raised you right.

And you can avoid prison. Or, well . . . You probably got the money to afford a sweet lawyer, but no matter what happens, your mother will know who you are. She'll see through your bullshit to the con artist you are."

"Fuck you, man."

"Take the deal, DeAndre."

"Fuck you, man!"

They sit there in silence for a while. DeAndre looks edgy. Itchy. Like he knows what he's got to do but doesn't want to be the one to do it. So Hollis does the work for him. "I'm going to assume by your silence, you're in," he says. "If that's a true statement, then all you got to do is sit there, stay silent, keep staring at me like you want me dead."

DeAndre says nothing.

Hollis nods. "Welcome to the team."

Ø Ø Ø

Hollis: "So what happened to you, Wade? You're sixty-three. Been working with computers since they were, what, the size of this room and ran on programs made out of paper punch cards. Promising programmer. Could've been a Steve Jobs, Bill Gates type. Now look at you. You look rough, Wade. Like a field gone fallow."

Wade: "I think I'm pretty."

"Come work for us," Hollis says.

"I'll pass."

"You won't. We know what you've been up to. We know about the Doorstop worm. We know about the Globe hack. We know about the Shadowlands, the Liberty Bell, all that. We know about every soldier and spy and government file clerk who comes to you with a classified unredacted memo in hand, and we can plug every leak and burn every one of those traitors. But that's not what matters. Not to you. They get sacrificed as part of the cause, you're okay with that because you've done it before. But you *do* care about *her.* You care about Rebecca."

And here he slides that photo across the table.

Wade flinches.

Good, Hollis thinks. Wade probably thought he had severed all the threads and tethers to Rebecca. Wade's *daughter.* But nothing stays secret, no matter how deep you bury it. Thanks to Typhon.

Wade tries to lie—"I don't know anybody named Rebecca"—but Hollis hears the shake in his voice, hears how Wade's throat tightens with emotion.

"Rebecca doesn't know who her father is, Wade. But we'll tell her. Hell, we'll *show* her. Daddy with his crazy online bulletin board systems and his cache of guns and ammo— that's right, we know how much ammo you've been buying up. Daddy with his explosive barrels buried in the desert. Daddy the traitor. The crazy man. She'll think she's the daughter of a real Waco wacko, some Tim McVeigh type."

"That's cold."

"Life's hard, Wade. You know that. You were in 'Nam, right? You've worked for us before. So come on back. I'm offering you a year's worth of good clean government work putting your skills to use. And I know you're going to say yes, because the second you tell me no, I'm going to get on the phone and tell Rebecca just who her daddy really is. It'll break her heart. She seems nice. Be a real shame."

Wade doesn't have to say anything. All he has to do is nod, and that's it.

Ø Ø Ø

Hollis: "I'm a little behind on the times, I admit, but everything in your file says you're a Class A Internet troll, responsible for no end of hacking and surveillance and online bullying and an all-around attitude of mucking about in people's lives—"

Reagan: "I'm in."

"What?"

"I said I'm in."

Hollis blinks. "If I may be honest, I don't understand."

"You're here to offer me a deal. And it's some weird under-the-table, off-the-books thing because you put a hood over my head and flew me here and I haven't seen a lawyer and your identification doesn't have any agency listed—which suggests NSA, or some ghost agency nobody's ever heard of—and so since you haven't killed me (and, honestly, why would you?), I can say with some certainty you're going to offer me a deal. Probably a job."

She must see the look on his face, because she says, "Oh, what? Think I don't know you guys like to scoop up black-hat hackers and crackers and scammers and trolls and make them turn tricks for John Q. Law? You're offering me a job and I'm taking it."

He eyes her warily. "I don't have to convince you?"

She shrugs, grabs a Fig Newton. "I quit my job a few weeks ago. I hate my apartment. I hate my town. I have a cat somewhere, and I hate that cat. He's weird. He reminds me of Gollum. Piss on my old life. I'm in."

Well, that's five out of five. Though Reagan is one he needs to watch. She's *too* eager. She's a snake you invite into your house, then wonder why it bit you.

Golathan—that prick—will be happy.

CHAPTER 7

Hollis Copper

NSA HEADQUARTERS, FORT MEADE, MARYLAND

Locked and loaded," Hollis says, throwing down five folders on the desk. Ken Golathan looks up with a cheek bulging with half-eaten PowerBar. He pauses midchew, fans the folders out like he's about to do a card trick, then keeps chewing.

"Good, great, yes," Golathan says, his interest already flagging. That's how he is. Always sounds like he's only partly present, only temporarily invested in the conversation at hand. "So we're solid, then. Another five guests at the Hunting Lodge."

"Where'd you find these people, anyway?" Hollis asks. "They're not exactly high value. I gotta admit, Ken, I'm feeling like my talents were a little bit wasted here. You don't bring out big guns to shoot pigeons off your mailbox."

"You a big gun now? The ego on you." Golathan sniffs, squints. "Trust me, this was curated at the highest level."

"Typhon selected these people. That's what you're telling me."

Golathan gets a mean look. Vulpine. Vicious. Like he's

about to tear a chicken into wet gobbets and red feathers. "We don't talk about that, Copper. We don't just throw that name around. But yes. That's how it came about. Like I said, this has been curated. They've been selected. You're not important enough to worry about what's going on here, you feel me?"

"You're an asshole," Hollis says.

"That I am." Ken shows off his big white teeth in a celebrity smile.

"Whatever. Consider our time together done. It's been fun."

"Mmm. Fun ain't over, Copper."

"I'm sorry?"

"You're still on the hook."

"Listen, I did what you told me to do. I've got work back at the Bureau. I've got a partner. I don't work for you."

"Oh, but you do." The NSA administrator stands up, plants both hands on the desk, and leans forward like he's leering down a teen girl's shirt. "I got you on loan."

"You have your own people for this."

"Eh. We're not real *out-amongst-the-people* types. Plus, with a Fed on my payroll, even temporarily, everything looks neat and clean and interagency."

"I'm part of the CYA." *Cover your ass.*

Golathan picks a bit of granola from a molar. "Mm-hmm."

"Last ass I want to cover is yours. I want out."

"Door's thataway, then. Except, let's remember, I know things about you. So until I say so, you're on my hook, little Copperfish."

Inside, Hollis is picturing a dartboard with Golathan's face on it. He bites back any further comment and asks, "What other geniuses you want me to wrangle up?"

"Same five geniuses. You're going to be their babysitter."

Anger spikes like a hot pin through Hollis's heart. "What?"

"That's right. You're going to the Lodge. You're going to watch these little turds and make sure they all roll in that same direction. You brought them into this world, and you're going to stay with them all the way to the end."

"Why are you doing me like this, Ken? This about Fellhurst?"

Golathan sneers, doesn't answer the question. "I got a job to do, chief. I see a hammer nearby and I need a hammer, I'm going to pick it up. I'm going to use it until I'm done with it or until it breaks. So stop asking me stupid fucking questions and get back on the plane and usher our new 'hires' out of their hidey-holes and to the Lodge where they belong."

Hollis stiffens. He feels the pressure of Golathan's boot on his neck. This is about Fellhurst. Has to be. And Golathan will punish him for it. Again and again. Hollis knows he has to find a way to turn the tables. Get one over on Golathan.

But for now, he does all he can do: he grits his teeth and says, "Done."

CHAPTER 8

The Compiler

The house feels empty.

Gordon Berry paces, and each footstep echoes through the halls of his home, like the *clop-clop-clop* of a nervous horse. He pops his knuckles, and the pops echo, too.

He has the sense of being sucked downward—like a misstepping adventurer in an old serial, caught in a pit of quicksand. He remembers his parents, who grew up in Pennsylvania's "coal cracker" region—the band of coal-mining towns upstate—telling stories about coal silt. Like quicksand, but black as the devil's heart. Sometimes, they said, it would pull you down like a child popping a gum bubble and sucking it back into his mouth—so fast you'd blink and the person would be gone. Other times it was slow and crushing, like wet concrete. You'd breathe in, then out, and the slurry would tighten like a constricting snake—no way to get another breath. You'd suffocate long before the mire filled your mouth and throat.

That's how he feels. Like he's being pulled down. Slowly.

Surely. Everything constricting—with every breath out it gets harder to breathe.

He's losing it all. His home. His wife, Janine. His daughter, Sue—graduating this year from Georgetown. His *practice*. The lawyers have made sure of that. His wife has made sure of the rest.

He knows that if she's been vile to him, he made her that way. His indiscretions with patients whetted her into a serrated blade. Bright and flashing and angry. And now she's sawing his life apart.

He doesn't blame her. He hates her, a little. But he doesn't blame her.

It's this pacemaker. That's what he blames. He's got an arrhythmia. An uneven heartbeat. For a long time the meds worked well enough—enough to control the fainting spells and shortness of breath. But then he had the heart attack. Tachycardia. Again, that feeling of being crushed in a vise, by a snake, under a hard and heavy boot. He thought he was dead. He *was* dead—clinically, for twenty-three seconds. And those twenty-three seconds—meaningless in any other context—changed everything. They changed his world. His outlook.

He was alive again. A second chance.

Some folks become newly religious. Gordon became something of a hedonist. New foods. New exercise equipment. New trips abroad. The indiscretions. Nine of them.

Now he's living through lawsuits and divorce and—

A light flutter in his chest stops him in his tracks. It's a tickle. No—an itch. Deep, beneath the breastbone. The kind of itch he can't scratch, though he's certainly going to try. He has this moment, this revelatory, Saul-becoming-Paul-on-the-road-to-Damascus moment, *this sudden epiphany* when he thinks he should call Sue, should call Janine, should call all his patients and tell them he's sorry.

But that doesn't last long. Because suddenly his limbs seize. Pain goes through his chest as if a locomotive is punching a hole through the mountain that is his body. He feels like a Christmas tree lit up from tip to stump, every branch and needle alive with pain and electric with fire.

One moment he's standing. The next he's on the ground. Trying to speak. Trying to say something. *My heart,* he thinks. No. *The pacemaker.* Damn thing. He always said it was too weird, sticking something like that in his chest. His computer gives him a blue screen full of illegal operations twice weekly. Last week his toaster shorted out, almost caught fire. And he's supposed to believe a pacemaker won't go south? Now it has.

He tries to get up, but he's weak. The world wobbles. He hears sounds. Like his own pacing footsteps still echoing, even though here he is, flat on his back.

A shadow falls over him.

Those aren't imagined footsteps. They're real.

A ghoul stands tall over him. A man, or something that was one once. Greasy dark hair barely managing to cover up the unevenness of his skull—like someone bashed him in the side of the head with a bat, collapsing the bone without ever letting it heal. His eyes are cold and dark, like chips of flint. A scar runs from the base of his left eye all the way down to his thin, froglike lips—lips that, on that side, tug upward in an uncomfortable facsimile of a half smile. Tattoos like ants crawl up arms that are long and lean as braided ropes—inked all the way from his wrists to the sleeves of his black T-shirt. Little symbols. Words that don't make sense. Numbers, too. Like a code, a cipher.

Gordon tries to say something. *Help. Get away. Who are you?* But all that comes out is mush-mouthed burble, his lips stuck together with strings of spit, his tongue like a roll of bloody gauze in his mouth.

He reaches out. Paws at the monster man's steel-toe boot.

The boot rises, lands on his hand. The bones pop and break. Gordon cries out.

"Don't need your hand," the man says. His voice is devoid of inflection, empty of emotion. "Just need this." He grabs Gordon by the back of the head. With his free hand, he sticks a syringe in the side of Gordon's neck.

Everything starts to slew sideways, like a car on black ice. Gordon hears snippets of a conversation, one-sided. Then a handful of words, clear as a bell ringing in the darkness:

"It's done," the man says. "We have number thirteen."

PART TWØ

THE LØDGE

CHAPTER 9

Hackaway House

The SUV carves its way through dark pine forests. Morning sun passes through the pleached trees, dappling the windows of the vehicle. Chance can tell they're heading up. *Ascending*. Into the mountains, he guesses, though what mountains, he's not sure. His head still feels gummy from whatever drug cocktail they gave him last night.

He woke up in this car about an hour ago. The driver—an implacable dude, stone faced and staring forward—never once acknowledged Chance's presence. Chance tried talking to him. Making faces. Yelling. Kicking the chair. *Are we there yet? Are we there yet? Are we there yet?* Nothing. Big-jawed guy stayed silent as a brick wall.

The doors on the SUV won't open. No handles. Like what you get in a cop car. Chance was in a cop car once. In high school he got drunk with Jay-Jay Burgos on Yukon Jack and the two of them hung out on the shoulder of a defunct overpass, spitting on the cars below—until Jay-Jay thought it would be funnier instead to *piss* on the cars below. And damn if it wasn't—at least, until he whizzed right on a cop cruiser. (Hell, it was funny even then.)

The car takes a hard bounce as it cuts off the narrow road on which they've been driving and turns onto a red gravel drive. Chance's teeth vibrate together. That plus his empty stomach and the drugs from the night before have him feeling suddenly queasy.

And hungry.

Hungweasy.

Ugh.

This stretch of bumpy gravel is long—not a driveway as much as it is a road. They go for five minutes, maybe ten, and then tires skid on loose stone. Out front, Chance sees a chain-link fence and a gate. The fence is tall—thrice his height, easy. Ringed with loops of razor wire, in which are caught leaves and branches. The gate is mechanized: nobody around but them to watch it click, hum, and drift open.

The car passes through. The gate whirs, then closes behind them. The chain link rattles as it shuts. Stone-Face moves the car forward again.

Another ten minutes go by. Forest all around. Rocks, too—boulders painted with green moss. They pass by a little waterfall not far off the "road," white water frothing and gushing like a stab wound.

Then, ahead, Chance sees it.

Hollis Copper called it the Hunting Lodge, but this isn't one building; it's a whole damn complex—a series of cabins and pods connected by decking walkway, lots of redwood and dark wood. The cabins are modern—boxy and clean, like something out of an Ikea catalog, plunked down in the middle of this tract of mountain forest. All of it stands surrounded by another—shorter, just above head height—fence. Another drunken loop of razor wire decorating the top.

Another mechanized gate. Stone-Face eases the car through and they park in a line of identical SUVs underneath a broad metal awning.

"Are we there yet?" Chance asks, as snarkily as he can muster.

Stone-Face gets out of the SUV, stone faced, and opens Chance's door: "Yeah. Get out."

Stone-Face pulls a long duffel bag out of the back of the car and shoves it into Chance's arms. *Oof.* "The hell's in this?" Chance asks.

"Your clothes."

"I didn't pack anything."

Stone-Face shrugs. "We packed for you."

"I hope you remembered to pack underwear. I don't wanna have to go commando in this place. It's damp up here, man, I don't wanna get some kinda crotch fungus—"

Stone-Face suddenly grabs him by the ear and slams his head into the back of the SUV. Chance cries out, pulling away. Ear ringing like a bell.

"Shut your mouth," Stone-Face says. "You keep babbling that brook and we'll dam it up for you. You're here to serve a purpose, you little skidmark. That purpose is not to irritate me. Thinking you're a fucking comedian." Chance gives him a sneer, but that just sets the man off further. Asshole reaches out, grabs for Chance again, cups a meaty hand around the back of Chance's neck. "You wanna have a go at me? I'll throw you in the Dep so fast your dick will shrivel. You know what happens—"

"Roach," comes a voice. "That's enough."

Stone-Face—or, apparently, Roach—gives Chance's neck one last *squeeze,* then fakes a laugh. "Sorry, Agent Copper. Just giving our newbie a short, sharp shock."

Chance pulls away. "Whatever, dickhead."

Roach's jaw tightens.

Hollis Copper comes up, steps between them, gives Chance a look. "You don't know when to shut up, do you?"

Chance shrugs. "I figure it says as much in my file."

"It does. Let's go. Bring the bag. You have some people to meet."

Roach gives him one last look as they head up a set of aluminum stairs.

Chance gives him the finger. It's a dumb move, but nobody ever said he was smart.

Ø Ø Ø

Hollis strides along, long limbs swinging like branches. Chance loops the duffel around his back and grunts as he bears its weight, hurrying to catch up. As they walk up over the gravel lot, Chance can see that the tops of the parking canopies are lined with solar panels—photovoltaic octagons. There's a big building in the center of the complex; standing near it is a tall white post with a trio of triangle-shaped pieces framing it, each like a rack for billiard balls. Chance knows what it is, because they'd put one in not far from his house: a cell tower.

"Hey, ain't you gonna give me the nickel tour?" Chance asks.

Hollis, without stopping, points. "That's the main building. That's where you eat. There's a rec room in there, too. On the other side, basketball court and lap pool. Over there"—he points to gray composite pods with black windows, windows through which Chance can see the smeary glow of monitors—"is where you'll work. Some of the pods are individual. Some of them are team pods. You get assigned 'em as they come up. Past that—"

Coming up on them is a young Indian or Pakistani kid staring out from behind a set of too-big glasses, like the kind a shop teacher might wear. Walking with him is a wispy sylph in a long tie-dyed dress, her skin so pale that she might as well be one of those see-through anatomy dolls in science class. She's older by a good bit—not old enough to be Chance's mother, but definitely, like, older sister age. She turns her gaze away as they pass, looking frightened.

The boy gives a nervous nod and an anxious laugh (*heh-heh*).

Hollis gives them a nod. "Dipesh. Miranda. Past that," he continues, "are the cabins."

"And the Dep? Where is that?"

"You don't wanna know about the Dep. Where it is doesn't matter."

"What the hell is it?"

"Like I said, Mr. Dalton, you don't want to know."

Chance grunts. "All right, fine. Those two that just passed. They hackers, too? Everybody here a hacker?"

Hollis stops. Turns toward Chance. "Two types of people here, Mr. Dalton. Prisoners and guards. Are the prisoners all hackers? To the number, yes. Are the guards all capable servants of the government who know how to extract results? Yes. All that being said, on a good day, this place is pretty cushy. Not everybody gets along, but everyone plays well together, and on those good days, our relationship is more like *babysitters* and *children*. On days when folks don't get along, that's when it becomes clear that no matter how nice the view, no matter how *fresh* the mountain air, you're still trapped in here until your time is done. And you do what we say."

"That's, uhh, real good to know." Chance offers a stiff smile.

"So everyone here is a hacker. Question is, Dalton—are you?"

I'm not, he thinks. *I'm a poser.* But he nods. "Yep, yeah, sure."

"Then let's go meet your bunkmates."

Ø Ø Ø

Chance steps into the cabin. The doors must be pretty well sealed against sound inside and out, because soon as he opens the door, the noise of the argument is like a slap to the face.

"—I said I'm an *atheist,* okay? You don't need to use language like that around me. I find it offensive," a young woman says as she plucks shirts out of a carry-on bag. Chance is struck by the intensity of her eyes—dark yet bright at the same time, like chips of shiny coal catching light. She pulls out each article of clothing and folds it with stiff hands and bloodless knuckles, like at any point she might let a shirt drop and haul back and pop the older fella with the gray mop of hair right in his gin blossom nose.

The old fella says, "Quit it with the politically correct word-police horseshit. I didn't mean *jihad* like jihad-jihad, I just meant you were really doing a jihad on those clothes—I mean, hell, look at you. You're folding them like it's a religious war."

The woman spins around, eyes narrow, lips curled in a scowl. "Oh really? You would've used that same word if you were speaking to her?" She gestures first toward another young woman, in a loft space above—a big girl splayed out on a bed, using a duffel as a pillow, a wide grin that could only be described as *shit-eating* smeared across her face. "Or him?" Now she points to a lanky black dude—maybe Chance's age, early twenties or so.

That dude says, "Naw, no way, uh-uh, don't drag me into whatever this is."

Hesitantly, Chance steps in through the door with Copper just behind him. The cabin's an A-frame—narrow at the top, like some kind of ski chalet. Not much in there except three beds down below and two on the loft. Couple of bookshelves: all fiction from a quick glance, nothing nonfiction. A couch at the far wall. No kitchen. A small door that Chance guesses might be a bathroom and shower?

But most important: No TV. No computers. No phones. No connection to the outside world.

"Kids today," the older man says. "I swear, you are about as tough as a rain-soaked Kleenex. Everybody's so easily *offended*. As if that's the worst thing that's ever gonna happen to you, somebody saying something that puts a little grit in your panties? I was born in 1950, which means I saw some time in 'Nam, and let me tell you—"

Up on the loft, the big girl guffaws. "Man, really? We're shut up in this place with a crotchety old vet?" She laughs so hard she almost cries. "I wouldn't have pegged you for the type, gramps. You look like Ben & Jerry, not John Rambo."

The old vet waves her off. "Well, you look like you *eat* a lot of Ben & Jerry's."

That just makes her laugh harder. "Fuck, man, we haven't known each for a whole hour and"—here she wipes laugh-tears from her eyes—"already with the fat jokes? Suck it, old man. You know I'm a prime piece of real estate up here. My homie down there knows what I mean."

"Goddamn," the black guy says, "can't y'all just shut up for five minutes?"

Their voices all start to rise together again.

Hollis has obviously had enough, because he pushes his way in. *"Shut. The. Fuck. Up."*

Everyone shuts up. They don't quite scatter like cockroaches in the light, but they do freeze in place like spooked mice.

Hollis clears his throat, then nods. "Good. Here's the last of you. Chance Dalton, meet your pod. In order left to right: DeAndre Mitchell, Wade Earthman, Aleena Kattan, and up there in the loft, Reagan Stolper."

"'Sup," DeAndre says.

Wade gives a clumsy salute. "Dalton."

Aleena looks away.

Reagan gives him an obnoxious waggle of her fingers. "Ahoy, script kiddie. Welcome to the Good Ship Dipshit."

CHAPTER 10

The Babysat

DeAndre thinks as he walks:
Keep your head low.
Do your time.
These people gonna dangle bait in front of you—don't take it. Just do the bare minimum of what they say and run for the hills soon as they let you out.

His "pod"—man, how he hates that term, sounds like something out of some science fiction film, something out of Cronenberg—follows their new babysitter, Hollis Copper, back toward the main building. A building Hollis refers to as the Ziggurat, "because it is your temple."

The little know-it-all, Aleena, corrects him: "Ziggurats weren't necessarily temples. They were towers, on which a temple usually featured."

"Thank you for the history lesson, Miss Kattan," Hollis grumps.

The white boy, Chance, speaks up: "Shoot, I thought it looked like something out of an Ikea catalog. The funky angles and that blue frosted glass."

"The Billy Bookcase Building," Reagan snarks. "The Triple-B, bitch."

"Everybody pipe down," Hollis says. "Before we hit breakfast, you gotta know some rules." Here he stops walking and pivots like a revolving door. "The Lodge has, as I understand it, one helluva lot of bandwidth. This bandwidth is for use by the United States government and in service to our government's many needs, actions, and ideals. It is not for personal use."

He rattles on: No cell phones. No smartphones. No iPads or iPods. No pagers. (Reagan mutters: "Who the hell uses pagers?" DeAndre: "Time-traveling drug dealers from 2004.") No connection to the outside world—when he says this, that's when people lose their shit. Aleena starts talking about her family. Wade goes on about "I got a whole network of friends and family who you don't want trying to hunt me down." Reagan shrugs, says: "I got a sister and she's kind of a twat, but she'll worry." DeAndre's about to speak up, talk about his moms, but then he reminds himself again: *Head low, do your time, shut your mouth.* Repeats it inside his head like a mantra.

Chance looks at DeAndre, laughs a little like he's trying to cover up a deeper feeling, and then whispers to DeAndre: "I don't really have nobody to worry about me."

DeAndre mumbles back: "Then you're lucky, man."

Hollis talks over and past them: "No unsupervised media access."

And here, a new round of protests, Reagan loudest among them: "Hey, whoa, *hey.* I got a DVR schedule back at home that is a thing of beauty. It has risen to the level of art. I need my shows. I need my Netflix, too. Given our surroundings, I think we can all agree that a little *Orange Is the New Black* is a necessity—"

"I love that show," Wade says at half volume. "Some funny lesbos."

Everyone gives him the stink-eye.

"You want media access?" Hollis says. "Read a book. Books: the original TV shows."

More grumbles of dissent. Hollis goes on to add: No drinking, no smoking, no drugs. (A groan from Reagan.) No fighting. (Another Reagan groan.) No fucking. (Reagan mutters: "Then you might as well just kill me.")

"Tomorrow morning," Hollis says, "your service to this great country begins in earnest. You will be given tasks to complete both as individuals and as a team. Should you fail these tasks, you will be punished. Should you fail them repeatedly, you will be washed out and thrown back into the prison pipeline that you have—at present—avoided. Are we clear?"

A bunch of nods and eye rolls. DeAndre looks around: Chance looks nervous. Gone pale as a ghost, that one.

"Now, let's get you some breakfast," Hollis says.

Ø Ø Ø

"Breakfast is over," the woman says from behind the counter. She's got hair the color of a Weimaraner's coat shaped into something that resembles a wave about to crash down on a beach. The name on her white chef's coat: *Zebkavich*.

It takes them a while to find the cafeteria. Hollis obviously doesn't belong in this place—he takes them to a back door that's locked, then around the side where they have to wind their way through a hall of what looks like offices and supply closets, then back down a stairwell until finally, the cafeteria.

It's a big room. Lots of round white tables with people sitting around them. Lots of light, too, from tall windows—though the light is muted, filtered as it is through the forest. Couple of arcade machines sit tucked in a lounge. Plus an air hockey table.

DeAndre's looking around when he hears the woman say that—*breakfast is over*. He sucks air between his teeth. "Aw man, what? I'm hungry."

Hollis holds up a finger. "Deb—"

"Zeb," she corrects. "Short for Zebkavich."

"Got a first name?"

"Yes."

Awkward silence. Hollis sighs, then says: "Okay, ahh, Zeb—can you spare something for the pod here? They just got here."

"They *just got here* seven minutes too late, Agent Copper."

"You serious? You have absolutely nothing to spare?"

Her face scrunches up in a bulldog scowl. "Rules are rules, Agent. Surely you can respect that?" But then she sighs and says: "Here. Hold on one minute." She disappears into the back for a minute, then returns with a bag. "Bagels," she says. "Old bagels. From yesterday."

Aleena protests: "Hey, wait. I don't eat bread."

Hollis shrugs. "Then you don't eat." He thrusts the bag into DeAndre's hands. "Have a good breakfast. You got an hour, then you need to be back in your cabin."

Ø Ø Ø

Hollis leaves, and the rest of them all pick a table and take a seat. They pick at half-stale bagels like bored but hungry squirrels. Quiet, mostly— DeAndre thinks it's a welcome change from when they were all trying to tear each other new buttholes back in the cabin. He thumbs a hole in a puffy sesame bagel, peels apart the crust, and pops a piece in his mouth. Feels like he's chewing a bike tire.

All around them, the other—what? Hackers? Inmates? White hats? Whatever they are, they all sit around, finishing up their breakfasts. It's a pretty motley crew, DeAndre thinks. Mostly dudes. Some girls. The expected racial breakdown: not a lot of brothers, no sisters at all, couple of Latinos, and the rest a mix of Asians and whites. Different styles: a girl with a Mohawk the color of grape soda sits between a chunky Asian neckbeard in fly Reeboks and some gawky white kid who looks like he took his fashion cues from *D&D Dungeon Master Weekly*. Most everybody's young. Everyone looks tired, bored, angry, beaten down, beaten up. Hollow-eyed stares and the like.

As DeAndre stares at the hackers, they all stare back.

"I don't know many of these people," Reagan says, mush-mouthed around a wad of everything bagel. Specks of the "everything" dot her chin. "But I see we got at least one hacker superpower in the bunch." She nods toward the back of the room.

DeAndre turns. Huh. Well, damn. "Shane Graves," he says.

"Ivo Shandor?" Aleena asks.

Reagan winks and picks bagel from her teeth. "Bingo bango bongo."

Graves is tall, lean, broad shoulders—ropy without being skinny. He lopes between tables like a wolf or a coyote keeping the rest in line. He's never not smiling, but that smile ain't exactly happy. It's the smile of a shark. Or worse, a salesman.

"He's a high bar," Reagan says. "So I guess it's time to slap all our scrotums on the table. Show our *jewels,* as it were." When no one responds, she makes an impatient gesture—finger rolling like a barrel down from Donkey Kong's hand. "Your hacker cred, motherfuckers. Spit it out."

"Fine, since I guess we're all workin' together." DeAndre shrugs. "I'm nobody special, but I'm good at the game. Made a name for myself over the last couple years—been going by Darth Dizzy lately. Mostly switched everything over to the carder market. I know the guys who hacked Walmart."

Reagan whistles. "Oooh, you *know the guys.* Gosh, jeez, wow. Did you ever touch them? Can I smell you? What a hero!"

"Hey, man, shut up. You asked, I'm talking. I stick mostly to gas stations. Skimmers and shit. It's good money."

"If you don't mind people getting hurt," Aleena says. Her mouth tightens up like a greedy person's coin purse. "Stealing is stealing."

"Yo, whatever. What I do these days is a *victimless crime.* Money isn't money anymore. It's all just ones and zeroes."

"We're all just ones and zeroes," Wade says. "Trick is figuring out which of us are *ones* and which of us are *zeroes*."

Reagan interjects: "Sitting at this table, I'd say we're all *zeroes*." Then she holds up a bagel and makes a fart noise through the center hole. "Actually, that's a pretty good name. I've never been part of a group before but they always have names. Masters of Disaster. Lulzcult. Chaos Chess Cabal, or Triple-C. I say we're"—and here, said with some flare— "*the Zeroes*."

"Whatever, Reagan, you call us whatever you want. I'm just saying," DeAndre continues. "It's not like I'm reaching under somebody's mattress and stealing their hard-earned bills. Credit card fraud? All that's just data. And it's backed up and insured—it's damn near no different from, like, Bit-Torrent. I can copy the latest *Transformers* piece of crap and who cares? Same thing here, except I'm just copying dollar bills. I get one, you get one. Like Oprah and shit: *you get a dollar bill, you get a dollar bill, yoooou get a dollar bill!*"

"Whatever helps you sleep at night," Aleena says.

"I sleep just fine," he says. "And don't pretend that you don't do some illegal shit. You didn't get here by helping old ladies across busy roads."

"Lemme guess," Reagan says. "White hat. Arab Spring?"

Aleena says nothing. Wade grunts.

"More racist nonsense?" Aleena says.

"Hnnh?" the old man asks. "Nope. I'm all for the Arab Spring. Spread some democracy around that joint like butter on toast."

"It's not about democracy," Aleena. "Not like you mean it."

"And how do I mean it?"

"You mean America. You want to spread America."

"No, that's not it, either. Maybe some perfect world idea of America. But this country hasn't been a democracy in a long time. We ain't free like we think we're free. Politicians keep coming along, each stacking the deck just one more card deep in their favor and in the favor of the rich and powerful. Big companies. Big government. Big men." He's suddenly super serious. "It's all a rigged game, and you realize that soon as you start flipping through the rule book and none of this stuff even makes sense. Soon as you play a few rounds, you start seeing some common themes: the Bilgerbergs, the Trilateral Commission, MK-ULTRA—"

Reagan bleats an attention-getting laugh. "Yep. You're one of *those*. Conspiracy-nut alert. Lemme guess: you probably think one of them is run by the Jews."

"Well . . ." Wade furrows his brow. "I figure some Jews are in there somewhere."

"It *is* worth looking at Israel's influence over world politics," Aleena says.

Wade nods. "Sure is."

DeAndre shakes his head. Two minutes ago they were sniping at each other, now they're nodding at each other from across the table. Bridges burned, rebuilt, probably burned again before too long. *That's hackers for you,* he thinks. *They're a group of individuals every time. Don't work well together because to the number they're all freaks, mistakes, assholes, fringe-dwelling wack jobs who got a real bug up their asses about people telling them what to do.*

Reagan says to Wade while pointing to Aleena, "So we know her deal. What have you done, Earth Man?"

"*Earth*man. Emphasis on the first syllable. And I'm not telling you all what I do because it's none of your business. Just know that I'm old school. I remember punch-card computers, some of them big as a fancy mansion's walk-in closet."

"Fine, don't play our reindeer games." Reagan fauxpouts. "Now, let's talk about me. I am no hacker. I don't belong here." She feigns horror and exasperation. "Unlike all of you jerkoffs: I am innocent!"

"Bullshit," Wade says.

"I don't hack. I troll."

"Figures," Aleena says.

"It's true. I spend a great deal of my time trading in that most precious of currency: *lulz*. I fuck with people because it's funny. And because they deserve it. I expose people for who they are. All the hypocrisy and hyperbole. I'm frankly something of a champion."

DeAndre thinks she's serious. She doesn't have that flip tone anymore. This is a girl who has bought into the smell of her own stink.

It's now that Chance chimes in: "Man, you all are the worst. Trolls, I mean." He seems agitated—he takes a napkin and begins to tear it into ribbons like someone ripping apart a bedsheet in order to make an escape out a window. "I, ahh, knew this girl in high school. Didn't know her very well, but she got raped. And after the fact, she tried to tell people what had happened—though she didn't know who had done it to her since she was drugged at a party—and you know, it didn't go like I thought it would. I figured people would rally around her. They didn't."

"What happened?" DeAndre asks.

"They mostly treated her like she brought it on herself. You know, all that 'how was she dressed' and 'that's what happens at parties' garbage. But the real corker was that she started getting . . . messed with. By people that I think she didn't even know. These people, trolls, just finding her online and posting pictures of her and blog posts and Photoshopped . . . things. Just wearing her down. She eventually swallowed every drug she had in her family's medicine cabinet. They drove her to that. Shamed her to death."

Reagan arches an eyebrow so high it might as well float above her head. "Sucks for her, but maybe she really was asking for it."

Jaws drop around the table. DeAndre shakes his head. "What the actual fuck."

Aleena: "Yeah, seriously, are you joking?"

"Hey, you don't lock your car doors, it might get robbed. You drop chum in the water, you might get sharks. You go out to a party with a bunch of drunken asshole frat-tards and you wear skimpy-ass clothes with a whale-tail thong sticking out and a tramp stamp that's a Chinese character for 'do me up the butt long time,' then maybe, just maybe, you send an RSVP invite to all the rapists in the room."

"You're messed up," Aleena says. "Aren't you a feminist?"

"Ugh," Reagan says. "So uptight, those bitches."

"You know what your problem is?" Chance asks, suddenly angry. "No way to see yourself wearing other people's shoes. It's all about *me, me, me*. No care about anybody who ain't you." He thrusts out his jaw. "That's screwed up. *You're* screwed up."

"The word you're looking for, dear Chauncey, is *empathy*. And I'm not a fan."

"It's Chance. Not *Chauncey*."

"Sure, Chauncey. So, fine, let's talk about someone who isn't me. Let's talk about, ohhh, I dunno. You. We're all showing our balls here, so tell us what great feats of mighty hackery *you* have committed. Share with the rest of the class."

Chance leans forward for a moment, like all he wants to do is bury his head in his arms and take a long nap. Then he straightens up, stiffens, and thrusts his chin out. "I'm not much of anybody, but I was the one who exposed the Yellowjacket Rape Posse."

"Right, right," Reagan says. She snorts. "You and Faceless."

"You're one of Faceless?" Aleena asks, and she's about to say something else but then it hits DeAndre. His eyes go wide and he says:

"Whoa, shit. You were the one on the TV? Behind the mask with the . . . the . . . whaddya call it that modulates your voice—"

"Voice modulator?" Wade asks.

"Yeah. Voice modulator. Was that you?"

Chance nods.

And then a shadow darkens the table. A pair of hands falls on Chance's shoulders—long-fingered hands that suddenly grip the meat between Chance's neck and shoulders and squeeze. He winces, pulls away, and protests. "Hey, what the hell—?"

Behind him, Shane Graves is grinning like the fox that ate all the chickens. "Look at this table. Some real odds and ends here. You ever puke and then wonder where the hell all that stuff came from? That's what it's like looking at you guys. Who barfed all of you up?" He makes a gross face like he's catching a whiff of a dog fart.

"Ivo Shandor," Reagan says with no small amount of awe. *No,* DeAndre thinks, *that's not awe, that's* lust. She wants to climb him like she's King Kong and he's the Empire State Building. "Heyyyyy."

DeAndre's damn close to feeling the same way. Graves is a bona fide legend. Biggest, most public hacks? All him. Hacked the Google Car, drove it off a Bay Area cliff. Posted YouTube videos on how you hack an airplane, an insulin pump, a pacemaker. Has taken over Times Square billboards not once, not twice, but *five* times. He even caused a small stock market crash the day he hacked a bunch of news sites and put up a story about how China and all these other countries were devaluing the dollar and calling in a shitload of American debt. People lost *money* that day.

Then, about a year ago, the guy dropped off the map, like a ship sailing off the edge into the part labeled HERE BE DRAGONS. One day, the most public hacker everybody knows. The next: vaporware.

Now, at least, DeAndre knows where the guy's been.

"Now, this guy in particular," Shane says, reaching forward and mussing up Chance's hair. "He's the real superstar, isn't he? Big social justice champion on the YouTube and the boob tube. I hear those rapey football assholes are gonna go to jail. Nice job. Seriously. You made a real difference, buddy."

"Uh. Thanks?" Chance says.

"Thing is, though, you're not part of Faceless, are you? I know some of those guys. You were acting all by your lonesome."

Chance shakes his head. "C'mon, man, Faceless is just a . . . faceless organization; it's all anonymous; there's no, like, central council or leadership—"

"But you still gotta earn your way in. Still gotta do something to deserve the name and the mask. Did you earn your way?"

"My stunt says I did." DeAndre can tell Chance is trying to stay cool. But there's something going on underneath. Anger. Fear.

"Your stunt was a lucky hack on a dumb jock who didn't know how to cover his tracks. You're just a little script kiddie, couldn't hack your way out of a cardboard box even if I handed you a brand-new machete. You're gonna wash out. We don't have room here for amateurs. This isn't pool-hall karaoke, Dalton. This is Radio City Music Hall."

"This is *prison*," Chance says.

Again, Graves musses his hair. More aggro this time. He looks to the rest of the table: "Were I you, I'd jettison this extra weight ASAFP. Dump him over the side unless you wanna all go down with him."

"That a threat?" Wade asks.

"It is, Grateful Dead, it is."

Wade gives him the finger.

Graves just winks. "Enjoy your bagels, shitstains." He strides off back to his own pod—a couple of other white boys who look moneyed and privileged, plus some Latina with little shoulders and big hips and an Asian kid in all black, maybe thinks he's the Japanese Dracula or some shit. His crew all laugh as Graves returns to them.

Aleena buries her face in her hands. "So glad we're making friends."

Reagan just laughs.

Chance says: "Shit."

And DeAndre, well, he just reminds himself:

Keep your head low.

Do your time.

Don't take the bait.

CHAPTER 11

The Eye

The office they gave him must've once been a supply closet. It's still got the metal frames bolted to the wall where shelves must've sat, and the whole room still has that antiseptic stink, which calls to mind hospitals and high schools—two smells that haunt Hollis like a pair of vengeful ghosts.

He wonders if Golathan did that on purpose.

What the hell—*of course* Ken did this on purpose. That's who he is. Wouldn't surprise Hollis if the son of a bitch was pumping in those scents through the ductwork. Little injuries sent as a reminder of who is really in control.

As he sits at his desk, his monitor blinks on. It flashes a couple of times, then a green light winks above it. Golathan's face appears. He's stuffing his face with a forkful of salad. Dressing dripping.

"Agent Copper," Golathan says, crunching lettuce.

"Ken," Hollis says, trying not to show his surprise.

Golathan, even through the screen, detects it. "I startle you?"

"Nope."

"Uh-huh. And how's the pod's first day?"

"Just dandy."

"C'mon, don't shit me. I can smell a lie like a dead hamster in the walls. We had that a couple weeks ago, you know. Hamster in the walls, dead."

"At your office?"

"At my—? What? *No.* No, at home. Mandy brought home the class hamster—Scrubbers, I think his name was. Or shit, maybe he was a guinea pig? Whatever. Point is, the little fucker got out, got into the walls somehow. Died there. Stunk up the place. Had to convince the kids that he ran off to be with his own family somewhere and that the smell was just some septic fumes."

"That's a great story," Hollis says. "Really."

"Don't condescend. The story actually has a point, Agent Copper."

"Oh, and what's that?"

"Your job is to be the adult that lies to the children. You're in charge of your little group, so you're gonna have to make them dance for their dinner."

"They're gonna wash out," Hollis says. "They're not gonna hack it."

"Nice pun."

"Didn't mean for it to be one."

"If they can't—ahem, *hack* it, then fine, so be it. But we think they will."

"*We* think. You mean *you* think. Or Typhon thinks."

"There you go again, asking questions that are miles above your pay grade."

Fuck my pay grade, Hollis thinks. "What the hell *is* Typhon, Ken?"

"It's a program. Like I've said."

"And it picked these people."

Golathan takes one more bite of salad and shoves the plastic tray away from him as if suddenly he's offended by it. "It picked every one of those faces in that joint. Typhon even picked *you*. It crunches data. This is the result of that *crunching*."

"I don't like it."

"You don't have to like it. Just do your job." Golathan's finger appears suddenly large on the screen—blurry, pixilated, purple.

Then the call ends.

"Asshole," Hollis says, hoping Golathan can still hear him.

CHAPTER 12

The Stolper
Two-Step

They're walking back to the cabin. None of them are really talking to one another—they're walking together but they're not walking *together*. Chance hangs back even farther. He's been here, what, two hours? And he's already feeling like a rat with its tail caught in a trap, little claws scrabbling against the cellar floor.

God damn that Graves. He's right. Chance doesn't belong here. He's a rube, a newb, a poser. But it's here or it's prison. And it's one year here. Or maybe ten there.

He's gotta stay in the game.

His palms sweat. His heart hammers in the sides of his neck. He feels suddenly, overwhelmingly alone.

And that's when, of all people, Reagan Stolper hangs back. "'Sup, Chauncey," she says.

"Really wish you wouldn't call me that."

"Okay, jeez, fine. *Chance*. Hey, listen, don't sweat Graves."

He cocks his head. "Yeah?"

"Yeah. Fuck him."

"You looked awfully into him."

She shrugs, makes a face. "I really *would* fuck him. He's like a sweet-ass Popsicle I just wanna—" Reagan mimes sucking a Popsicle, then biting it. She smacks her lips. "Mmm. Yeah. And his résumé is *most impressive*. But I don't like people who think they're too big for their britches. I see egos like that, it stops mattering how frothy my panties get—my greatest urge is to knock that cocky parrot off his perch." She grins big, then musses his hair the same way Graves did. "Don't worry, Chauncey. I got your back."

Ø Ø Ø

Reagan whistles as she walks up to the basketball court. *Peter and the Wolf.* Doo-doo-dee-doo-dee-doo. There, on the court, stands Shane Graves. His babysitter, who she's pretty sure is named Rivera, stands there, too—practically nose to nose with him.

In Graves's back pocket is a phone. Black like volcanic glass. Thin profile.

Rivera's a slug. Might've been a lean cut of meat once— muscled of body, principled of mind. But now he looks like a mess. Sloppy. Tired. Everything *untucked*. Got all the hallmarks of being a drunk except for the smell of liquor coming off him.

They look, see Reagan sauntering over.

Graves takes the basketball he's holding, thrusts it into Rivera's middle. The hack makes an *oof* sound. He passes it back.

She hears Shane tell Rivera: "Take a hike."

Rivera probably doesn't want to seem like he can be pushed around, so he says, "Whatever, Graves, don't fuck up." But to Reagan's trained ear it sounds rehearsed: a bluff, some bullshit bluster. He passes her, gives her a look. "What?" he asks sharply.

She shrugs, keeps walking.

Now it's Shane's turn. Eyebrows raised. "What?"

"Hey, Graves. Or should I say Ivo Shandor."

"What's your name? Stapler?"

"You know my name. You know more about me than I do, probably. I know you got a phone. I know you probably have a laptop here. I figure you've got Rivera in your pocket, somehow. You were Hacker Supreme on the outside, so no reason to think differently here on the inside."

"So you're less of a zero than your cohorts." He spins the ball in his hands. Dribbles it a few times. "What do you want, Reagan?"

"It's more about what you want."

"And what do I want?"

"Besides a puppy? I'm guessing you have a hard-on for Chance Dalton." He cocks an eyebrow and she rolls her eyes. "No, not like that. I mean, you want to burn him down. Wash him out. Punish him. Am I right?"

"You are, at that."

A wicked grin cuts across her face. "Then I can help."

CHAPTER 13

The First Message

The Lodge shuts everything down at 9 P.M. A female voice over a loudspeaker tells them that everyone is to be back in their cabins by nine thirty, at which point the cabins lock.

Reagan is missing.

At first, fine, whatever. Everyone's nervous, it seems, but nobody really wants to acknowledge it. They keep peering out the door and the windows. All the other hackers—the prisoners, they have to remind themselves, since most of today it felt like they were just students on some kind of college campus hidden in the mountains—have gone to their pods, and only a few mill around. None of them seem to be Reagan.

"She's gonna get washed out, first day," DeAndre says.

"Good," Aleena says as she climbs the ladder to the loft. "Let her."

Chance says, "Couldn't that hurt all of us?"

"It does seem like our fates are intertwined," Wade says. "She messes up, we all gotta do the push-ups, you know?"

"Crap," Aleena says. "You think? *Crap*. She's going to screw us."

9:25 P.M. Still no Reagan. Everyone shuts up. Like speaking will somehow scare her away. The uncertainty in the room is killing them. What happens if she's not accounted for? Do they all wash out? Get packed back in SUVs and sent to prison?

DeAndre hurries around the room, whispers in everyone's ear—Chance assumes everyone gets reminded of the same thing: "They probably got mics or cameras in this room. You feel me?"

Nine thirty rolls around. The door seals with a vacuum *foomp*. There's a loud rattle as the lock engages. The lights in the cabin go out with a buzz and a click.

"Good night," Aleena says. And then she names them one by one until finally she says: "Good night, Reagan."

Time slows to a crawl. Like sap oozing from cold pine. Chance lies there in his cot. DeAndre and Wade nearby. Wade's asleep. When the old man snores, he sounds like someone throwing kitchen appliances into a wood chipper.

DeAndre's not making any noise, so Chance takes a, well, chance, and says: "You awake, DeAndre?"

"What? I am now."

"Sorry."

"Whatever, man, I wasn't actually asleep."

"I think I'm screwed."

"Huh?"

"I'm way out of my depth, man. I don't know what they're gonna have us do, but first day I'll be the guy who drowns in a puddle."

"You'll be all right."

I don't think so, Chance thinks. He's about to say something else, but from the loft, Aleena hisses:

"Shut up. I'm trying to sleep."

"We are, too," DeAndre says.

"Doesn't sound like it!"

DeAndre snorts a laugh. Chance does, too. But that's the last they speak.

Eventually, sleep reaches a tentative, hesitant hand and takes them all.

Ø Ø Ø

Hollis walks the nighttime perimeter of the Hunting Lodge. The forest is loud with chittering bugs. It's isolated up here. Way too isolated. Hollis doesn't do country mouse very well. He's a city mouse—born and raised in D.C. The Hunting Lodge feels too remote. So far off the grid you start to forget there's a grid in the first place.

Hunting Lodge, he thinks. Given the targets they go after, it's an apt name, if a little cocky. He wonders what his five hacker charges will think about that—they haven't seen what's coming down the pike. They don't know what they'll be asked to do. Up until now, everything's been theory. But tomorrow, it starts.

He doesn't have high hopes. Aleena is capable, but too principled. Reagan is a mystery—she claims she's just a troll, but his file on her is thick as three thumbs and it isn't just trolling. Earthman is old school, old tech, old man; wouldn't surprise Hollis to see him wash out. DeAndre's probably their best bet, here—capable, savvy, so far seems to know he should shut up and do the time. He puts on a good show, but Hollis thinks DeAndre is scared. That's good.

Chance, though—Chance is a worry. They should've just let him be. If the law brought charges against him for hacking into some e-mails, so be it. Let him tangle with the justice system, take his shot—the court of public opinion would be on his side (at least outside his own town, where they were ready to crucify him for screwing up their football season). But this kid doesn't really know what he's doing, and—

Somewhere not far away, a branch snaps.

Hollis stops. Listens. Peers out into the dark woods. Behind him, the lights of the Lodge shine bright—while it's lights-out inside the cabins, the pods, and the Ziggurat, out here the electric lights buzz and hum and shine. They cast fingers of light out into the trees, but that only goes so far, and—

Snap. Another branch cracks. There's a flutter of feathers—some night bird takes flight, is gone.

Hollis feels the weight of his Glock 21 hanging pendulous at his hip. The weight of consequence. He's taken his gun out too many times to count, even taken a few shots here and there, but he shot and killed someone only one time:

Fellhurst. Back when he and Golathan—

A rustle of leaves. *Just a deer,* he thinks. *Or a bear.* Are there bears here? Moose? Elk? Jesus, he doesn't know. He knows rats, pigeons, city raccoons, and skunks.

Still. Hollis pops the holster latch, draws the gun. Heads down the steps toward the first fence. He thumbs the soft switch on the tactical light hanging from the front of the .45, and a beam of garish white light punctures the darkness like a pin. Casting a chain-link shadow as it shines: a series of dark diamond outlines.

Hollis shines the beam side to side. Nothing. His thumb reaches to turn off the tactical light—

Movement. Off to the left. He pivots, points the pistol. A person is out there. On the other side of the fence. Running almost silently through the trees. Hollis catches a glimpse of a thick frame, hunched over, a muss of dark hair, and then the figure is gone.

Hollis yells. Curses under his breath. Who the hell could be out there? The Hunting Lodge has *two* fences. Nobody gets between them—though, is the five-mile outer fence really guarded well? Probably not.

Hollis grabs the radio and calls in for backup. Time to do what the Lodge's nickname demands.

Time to go hunting.

CHAPTER 14

Evals

The alarm—it's not a clock radio going off, clicking over to some nineties-era one-hit wonder (that insidious earworm about walking five hundred miles), and it's not the happy chime of an iPhone. It's a honking Klaxon, a sound like what someone hears when they're in a submarine and the XO is yelling *dive, dive, dive!* Aleena sits up in her bed, her heart like a rat in a cage that just suffered an electrical shock—it beats so fast she thinks it's going to break out of her chest and run for the door.

By the time she covers her ears, the Klaxons outside stop. Everyone is sitting up in their beds except Wade. And that includes Reagan.

Aleena looks across at the smug, self-satisfied face. Reagan smirks, eyes squinting. She yawns, rubs her face. "What's up, little Kardashian?"

"I'm not a—what? I'm not Armenian. They're Armenian."

"What are you, then?" Reagan picks at the edge of a nostril. Flicks something away, maybe a bit of skin, maybe a booger.

"I'm *American*."

"Fine, whatever, I meant what nationality—"

"Syrian."

"Syria and Armenia share a border, so I was close."

"They do not share a border. Turkey is in the middle—"

Reagan giggles. "Like a sandwich. A delicious, Arabic, Muslim sandwich."

"Armenians aren't Arabs—I think they're just Armenians. And they're not generally Muslim, either, it's a Christian country—wait. *Wait*. This is what you do, isn't it? My brother does this to my mother. He winds her up. You're just winding me up."

"It's kinda my jam."

Aleena makes a frustrated noise. Down in the cabin, Chance and DeAndre are both standing over Wade. Wade is still rolled over, snoring like a grizzly bear with a bad case of sleep apnea.

She turns back to Reagan. "Where were *you* last night?" she hisses quietly.

Reagan presses a finger to her lips. Then leans forward as if she's gonna share a secret: "Nunya. Fuggin'. Business." Suddenly she's standing up, stretching and yawning in a loud, obnoxious way (Aleena realizes that this is Reagan's default setting: loud and obnoxious). Then she claps her hands and says: "Today is eval day. As I understand it, that means a simple black box *pen test*. You know the deal: an hour to shower and then a day to shine. Let's move."

"What do you mean a black box pen test?" Aleena asks.

"C'mon, little girl, you know what that is. Right?"

"Yes, damn it, I know what it is. But how do *you* know that's what's happening today? Nobody told us that."

Reagan pops a finger in her mouth like she's slurping on a lollipop, then holds it up in the air and says: "I just know which way the wind is blowing, sweetie pie."

Ø Ø Ø

Chance and DeAndre stand over Wade's snore-roaring body.

"If he wasn't making that awful sound, I'd think he was dead," DeAndre says.

"He sounds like someone moving furniture across a broken floor."

"I know, man. I can feel it vibrating in my feet. In my *teeth*."

DeAndre nudges Wade in the middle of the back with a knee. Nothing.

"Hey," Chance says, voice low. "What the hell's a . . . black box pen test?"

"You're joking, right?" DeAndre asks. But the look in Chance's eyes tells him this ain't no joke. "Oh," DeAndre says. "Oh, you really *are* screwed. A pen test is a penetration test. Like, you hit a company to see how vulnerable it is to . . . well, people like us." *Like me,* he thinks, but doesn't say. "White box means you get all the info you need to do the job. Black box means they're not telling us shit about the test. Means we go in blind, you feel me?"

"I don't feel you. Because I don't know what the hell I'm doing." Chance shakes his head. "It's fine. I'll . . . I'll figure it out."

"Okay. Cool." DeAndre doesn't hear a lot of confidence in the dude's voice, but it is what it is. He can't be sticking his neck out for somebody. Especially somebody he doesn't know from Adam. "Hey. What's the deal with Troll Girl up there? How'd she get in last night?"

"Damn, man, I dunno. She seems to be playing her own game and I'm not sure if we're allies, competitors, or pawns on the board."

"I hear that. I'd say that describes our situation in this whole *place*."

Behind them, a llamalike bleat as Wade Earthman rolls over and stares up at them through a curtain of gray ringlets. "Would you ladies kindly shut up? I am doing my damnedest to get some beauty rest down here."

"You snore like two pigs fuckin' in a cement mixer," De-Andre says.

Wade yawns. "Good morning to you, too, sunshine."

Ø Ø Ø

Hollis comes for them not quite an hour later. He looks haggard, like he hasn't slept. Even his sideburns look rough.

Aleena is still drying her hair, and starts to complain about how they only have one shower and bathroom for five people—

Hollis says: "I had a long night. Say one more thing and I'll pack your ass in an SUV and dump you on Rikers Island without a whiff of ceremony. Let's. Move."

Ø Ø Ø

Breakfast. Hollis stands off to the side, eating a banana. He needs the potassium. He keeps getting leg cramps after last night's tromping through the woods. By the time he and the other two guards—that thug, Roach, and another dim bulb named Chen—got back from scouring the woods (and finding neither shit nor Shinola out there), he just wanted to sleep. But leg cramps woke him up every hour, on the hour.

Of course, not finding anything out there haunted him, too. He saw something. He saw some*one*. Hollis put in a call early this morning to have a couple of guys go along the fence's perimeter to see if they could find a breach—but he could hear that they were just giving him lip service. Like it was some kind of joke. And maybe it was. After an hour out in the woods not finding so much as a single footprint, Roach and Chen looked at him like he was some doddering old man.

I just turned fifty, he thinks. *I'm not old.* But his leg cramps maybe tell him otherwise. So does the arthritis in his wrists. And his hips. *Shit.*

He finishes his banana, looks up, sees the pod sitting

around, looking mostly mopey, tired, confused. Scared, too. Everyone but Reagan—and, frankly, Hollis is starting to think that one doesn't get scared. Maybe she's a sociopath. The rest of them, though—hell, he suddenly hopes they *all* wash out today. Send 'em home so he can go home, too.

Maybe I am getting too old for this, he thinks.

Ø Ø Ø

Each of the smaller pod buildings is modular. Rounded corners. Eight-by-eight space. Not much there: a desk, a chair, an all-in-one desktop—no touch screen—with Ubuntu Linux as the OS. Mouse, keyboard, not much else. Behind the monitor is one camera. Behind the chair is the other. Both the operator and the monitor are therefore on camera. The five "Zeroes" are informed that every system is mirrored and tracked, and every aspect logged: every key tapped, every nudge of the mouse, even the ways that the *eyes* twitch.

By each computer is a folder that contains written instructions for the day's task.

The five pods in this group are all within ten feet of one another. Hollis opens the doors to each, says that if they have an emergency, they just need to say something out loud—the microphone on the cameras will hear. Otherwise, he says, he'll see them at lunch.

They all step in. The doors lock behind them.

And so begins their first day.

Ø Ø Ø

Aleena opens the file folder. Inside is a single sheet of paper. On it, printed in bold Helvetica:

PENETRATION TEST: CMG (CENTINAL MEDICAL GROUP)

She reaches for the keyboard. Her fingers hover over the keys without touching them. Her skin feels cold, clammy, covered in pinpricks. This isn't her. Working for this government? A government that doesn't mind what it does to her people? To *any* people who don't register as white, male, and, increasingly, upper class?

She has an urge to just push it all away. Shove the computer onto the ground. Get up, walk out, tell Hollis what he can do with his pen test, then drop the metaphorical microphone and wait for them to pack her into an SUV.

But then what? Will she go home and await the law? Will they just throw her into jail? Will it be a jail that people can visit, or will it be some *Silence of the Lambs*–style hole in the middle of nowhere, not on any map? The United States doesn't have a very good reputation when it comes to dealing with those it considers *enemies*.

And what will happen to her family? Ummi and Abbi— her mother and father? And oh gods, what about Nas? Nasir thinks he's all tough—little pot-smoking thug in training, listening to Jay Z and Kanye, pretending like he doesn't also sometimes watch *My Little Pony* when he gets really high. Prison would eat him up.

This is no big deal, she tells herself. A penetration test on a—well, all she knows is what it says. *Medical group*.

Then it's fingers down on the keyboard, and she starts cutting through the dangling digital vines with the heft of her data-machete.

Ø Ø Ø

Wade yawns, scratches his beard, scratches his balls, licks his chapped lips, looks up at the camera, smirks like a pissy little kid forcing a smile for the family photo, then reaches across and picks up the folder.

PENETRATION TEST: PALISADE SYSTEMS & SERVICES

He snorts. Speaks aloud, as much as to Them as to himself: "Really? You've got me trying to crack the shell on a defense contractor? You know I'm rusty at this, right?"

This isn't what he does anymore. He'd developed a pretty cozy routine, honestly—he was like the spider in the center of the web. He didn't have to hunt; all the prey came to him. Servicemen, spies, embassy workers, techies inside the NSA or CIA or FBI—people sending him sensitive information that he could decrypt, re-encrypt, and post across a variety of sites across the world. WikiLeaks changed everything: it popularized what he already did, which made it easier, but also made it all so damn diffuse. Now the market for information is blown open—some folks want to torrent the latest Hollywood cock-buster of a movie, others want to torrent cables and wires leaking the corrupt practices of a variety of world governments.

Not much money in it, but Wade doesn't care much for money. What Wade cares about is keeping the government out of people's goddamn business. If the American people couldn't have privacy, then neither could the American government.

Now they're asking him to crawl out of his web— difference between a garden spider waiting for its prey and a jumping spider who has to hunt down its food. He's too old to go jumping around. Truth is, he's rusty in more ways than one.

He waggles his fingers. The knuckles hurt. His wrists ache. Arthritis.

"You make me dance too hard," he says, "I'm gonna up and break a hip." He holds up the file folder again. "By the way, this some kinda joke? I remember these a-holes. Palisade. High-tech weapons and systems, got caught greasing too many wheels overseas." They fell prey to the FCPA—the Foreign Corrupt Practices Act. A little bit of mostly smart legislation that keeps American companies from influencing other nations (largely through that time-honored tradition of bribery). The act allows for what they consider "grease" payments—money paid to officials and individuals under the auspices of getting things moving along. But once folks start getting Lamborghinis and fancy bottles of champagne that cost a thousand a pop and appear in whole cases, well, that goes beyond just *lubricating gears*.

Wade didn't even know Palisade was still around. "All right," he says, waving the folder. "I'll play. I'm curious."

Ø Ø Ø

On the piece of paper:

PENETRATION TEST: UNTERIRDISCH ELEKTRIZITÄTSSYSTEM GMBH

DeAndre leans back in his chair. "German, really? Aw hell." He shakes the folder at the camera. "I don't speak the Deutsch, okay?"

The camera stares, implacable.

"Whatever," he says. "The work is the work." It isn't the human language he needs, anyway.

Ø Ø Ø

PENETRATION TEST: ARCUS LAND DEVELOPMENT

Reagan makes a sound like she's dry-heaving. "Land development? What is that, real estate? Bo-ring. Fucking *God*. And what the shit, Big Government, where's my coffee? If you want me to wear a white hat in service to your nonsense, then I *at the very least* require coffee. You know what happens when I don't get coffee? Nothing, that's what. Nothing happens. I sit here, I stare at the wall, then I fall asleep. You're asking a car to drive a thousand miles but forgot to fill the tank, jerks. Jesus, God, *crap*."

She sighs.

Waits.

Stares.

No coffee magically manifests. No elves bring it on a dogsled.

She yawns. "Fine. *This time,* you win. No coffee. Next time: coffee, or I stab a bitch."

She gets to work. Arcus will be easy. The other job, though, the *real* job? That's going to be a bit harder.

Ø Ø Ø

Chance gnaws a thumbnail. Then some of the dry skin around the nail till it bleeds. Shit. His heart is beating same way it used to when he'd go into school knowing there was a quiz he forgot to study for or homework he didn't do. It's the kind of anxiety you get in a nightmare—one of those mundane nightmares where you show up late to something, or you end up naked, having to recite the Pledge of Allegiance in front of a girl you like, for some reason that makes sense only to the architects of the dream.

The file folder sits, splayed open.

PENETRATION TEST: HARRINGTON CON-GEN

The computer sits, waiting.

Look busy. Chance nudges the mouse, waking the system from sleep. He knows this OS a little.

He finds the web browser. Opens it up. On a lark, he types CNN.

Blocked.

Entertainment Weekly?

Blocked.

Gmail?

He can practically hear the portcullis slamming down.

In a search window he types in: "Harrington Con-Gen."

It's some biotech company. Nice website, clean, bright, big fonts, all green and blue. And it's ConGen, not Con-Gen, but whatever. Looks like it's a company that genetically engineers—er, "modifies," in their parlance—insects for "accelerated and adjusted function." A few clicks deeper, he sees self-destructing mosquitoes, moths that spin spider silk, corn-eating pests that instead eat each other, some new honeybee. ConGen also specializes in the software necessary to genetically engineer plants and animals.

Chance has no idea what any of this has to do with anything. All he knows is, he has nothing. He finds a couple of e-mail addresses, a few phone numbers. But there's no intranet logon, no way into the company's systems from here. If he were a real hacker he'd know, but he's not a real hacker. He's a fraud. A guy who knows how to do the bare-bones basics: a script kiddie who can crack some e-mails, scare up an FTP password now and again, maybe use keylogger software or download Wi-Fi WEP/WPA breakers. Hacking Ryan Bogardian's e-mail was one of the easiest things he'd ever done. He got it on his *third* try—for God's sake, the password was *yellowjackets*. The name of Ryan's team. Then it was nothing to scroll through the dumb-ass's e-mail until he found what he was looking for: a link to a cell-phone video taken by one of his teammates, a little scatback named Barry Lattner—aka "the Flash."

Even thinking about that video damn near makes Chance puke up what little breakfast he actually managed to eat.

He took the e-mail, the video, forwarded it to every damn news station he could think of. Plus, Gawker, Jezebel, whoever, whatever. He found other incriminating e-mails, sent those, too. This wasn't their first "posse." They knew this rodeo all too well.

Of course, he was still pissed—especially since all the local news refused to pick up the story. Protecting hometown football, probably. That's when he bought one of those discount *Scream* masks and pretended to be a member of Faceless. He knew Faceless pretty well—had haunted the dead-chan forums, watched them do their thing. They'd been around a long time—since he was in high school—but they'd only recently started getting attention in the media as a group who could get things done, who could put pressure and move the needle when it needed to be moved. They went from trolls to warriors, from bullies to picking on bullies, and he dug that.

Pretending to be part of Faceless worked. It got him on TV. Ranting behind a mask and a voice modulator.

Now, here he is. He used his one trick.

Above him, one of the cameras beeps once, then twice. The green light goes red. The other camera—this one over the computer—does the same thing.

"Hello?" Chance asks aloud, feeling stupid for even saying it.

His screen flashes. Then, out of nowhere—a series of installation progress bars. Software loading. Whoa. A chat window pops up. A user named "Dutch Jellyfart" appears with a *bing*.

DUTCH JELLYFART: HEY DICK-KNOCKER

The return cursor blinks.

DUTCH JELLYFART: HELLOOOOOOOOOO

A graphic image shows on the screen: a breaching whale with its fin out of the water. Underneath: WHALE HELLO THERE.

Chance pulls the keyboard close, types a response—

GUEST: Who is this?
DUTCH JELLYFART: Who the fuck do you think it is?
IT IS I, SIDNEY FELDMAN.
GUEST: What?
DUTCH JELLYFART: Grosse Pointe Blank, wang-
nozzle. Uh, only the best movie ever. John Cusack is
my master now. Though these days he's looking like
a melting candle. It sucks when hot sexxxy people
get old.

Then up pops an emoji of a cute little piece of poop. So it's Reagan, then.

GUEST: I need help here.
DUTCH JELLYFART: No shit, Cumberbatch. I'm going to take over your computer for a little bit. Pay
attention to what I'm doing. TAKE NOTES. We good?

Does he trust her? He winces. What choice does he have?

GUEST: Okay.
DUTCH JELLYFART: YALL READY FOR THIS

That's when Chance discovers that he is not, in fact, ready for this. And worse, he learns why he never should have trusted her in the first place.

∅ ∅ ∅

Aleena's already hard-charging through the CMG infrastructure. With a pen she found in the drawer, she's drawn up a loose network diagram. Found a few vulnerabilities in the code, too—sloppy work, leaving doors and windows open like that. A half hour in, she's found bolt-holes into the company intranet, and once you're in there, who knows what she might find? E-mails. Bank transactions. Employee information.

She starts with contact lists, purchase orders, inventory requests.

Already she's starting to see that, for some goofy reason, their biggest client of the past twelve months is . . . the Department of Transportation in D.C.? Huh. Why would the DOT need medical equipment?

Then she sees something else.

The code is a mess. And someone is using that mess to their advantage. He or she is rerouting information to a bunch of different IP addresses. She follows the trail back out, expecting the hacker to have used a proxy, but doesn't find one—whoever did this is cocky, either thinks he or she won't get caught or just doesn't care.

The IP addresses to which the info is being rerouted are Chinese and South Korean. Huh. She's about to dig deeper when she hears it—

Someone nearby. Pounding on the pod walls. Yelling in alarm. It's muffled—these things are pretty well insulated against sound. But it doesn't mask it entirely.

Oh no. Is that—

Is that Chance yelling?

Ø Ø Ø

Wade's gotta take a break. He's frustrated. Pissed off enough he's thinking of taking the keyboard and cracking it over his knee like a rotten stick. Palisade is still up and running. They're either ironclad or he's too soft to make a dent. If it's the former, hey, he's good. If it's the latter? He doesn't know what happens then. But he damn sure doesn't want to wash out of here.

He can't handle their telling Rebecca all about him. That girl's been through a hard enough life not having a father, let alone discovering that the one she never met is some kind of—well, he knows how they'll spin him. Doomsday-prepping libertarian half-a-hippie conspiracy nut. Might throw *domestic terrorist* in there somewhere. Traitor to the stars-and-stripes. Treasonous old windbag—like Snowden without the sex appeal.

So, he's gotta get this right. He's about to go back to the keyboard when—

Somewhere nearby: thumping, yelling, and then a crash.

Ø Ø Ø

DeAndre has this problem. He wants what he can't have. That's always been true, really—it started as a collector's mind-set. Like, when he was playing Magic: The Gathering or Pokémon, he'd covet those rare cards—with Pokémon, Shining Charizard, or even better, the first-edition Charizard. For Magic he finally got himself one of those Beta Black Lotuses, but *shit,* he wanted an Alpha Black Lotus *something fierce.* Of course they only made eleven hundred of those bad boys, and they went for ten grand or more. It was the same thing with rare toys—the original Optimus Prime, or the first Storm Shadow figure (v1: "Cobra Ninja"). Both those were expensive, too.

And that's how a collector mind-set turns into a thief mind-set. Thing was, he was too chickenshit to steal things off shelves—and, for the most part, all the rare, collectible stuff wasn't on a shelf anyway, it was on eBay or locked away in the back room of some comic book or game store.

So he started stealing *money* instead. Online. Hacking PayPal accounts or picking up credit card numbers here and there. The slope wasn't just slippery: it was damn near frictionless. And now, here he is, trapped in a room, working for Mr. Government because he couldn't keep his hand out of the cookie jar—not 'cause he likes cookies but because he can't stand *not having any.*

And here, once again, he's confronted by that old demon: that old collector spirit that sees something he can't have, which makes him want it all the more. This time it's a little part of the Unterirdisch Elektrizitätssystem network structure. Everything else is pretty open and, truthfully, poorly defended—this is some Swiss cheese coding, right here. No need to penetrate at all—just stick your finger in and waggle it around like a worm. But then, buried in a tangle of subfolders—

It's lockdown. A series of folders buttoned up tight. Encrypted with bulletproof algorithms.

The company is a geothermal energy company. That's it. Nothing fancy, nothing exciting. They help design systems that draw energy from below the ground. Total snooze-fest. Which makes this all the more tantalizing—it's like playing a role-playing game and finding some platinum chest locked tight in a farmer's bedroom. Makes you want to bust that lock, see what's inside.

He needs to up his game. Dive down into the Deep Web and—

His pod shudders. Muted yelling. A crash.

What the hell?

Ø Ø Ø

Soon as Chance tells Reagan to go, she goes. She goes right to CNN. Or tries, but can't, because it's blocked.

It's blocked, until it isn't. More windows pop up faster than Chance can study them to see what they are, and next thing he knows, CNN is coming up. He catches a quick glimpse of news: something about North Korean aggression, Iran nuclear programs, a cat that called 911—

Then it's gone and replaced with back-end software. Almost like blog software—like WordPress except fancier—and he realizes with cold horror it's CNN's back end. Reagan pops open a window and starts writing an article same way you'd pen a blog post—title: "Agent Hollis Copper Found Fornicating Cows"—then backspaces and adds a "with" between "fornicating" and "cows."

Chance, out loud, starts to protest: "No, no, no, oh, c'mon now, stop—" He grabs the mouse, but the cursor isn't his. The keyboard doesn't respond either. "Shit! Damn." A chill sweeps over him. She's hacking him so it looks like *he's* hacking CNN.

Already the article is a paragraph deep—he can barely read it, can't even focus on it, though he catches some precious keywords and phrases like *deep fucking* and *dick-butt,* and he hears his own voice growing louder and louder in cries of frustration and he's pounding on the walls and the door but nobody's coming, and Reagan types ninja fast and he can't do a single freaking thing about it, except, *except*—

He reaches for the computer. Just as he gets his hands around the desktop, the screen flashes white, then red. Text pulses across the screen:

> She withstood all the gods, hissing out terror with horrid jaws, while from her eyes cast forth a hideous glare. And the gods did turn to common beasts.
> AND THE GODS DID FLEE.

Something about that sends a bolt of terror running through Chance, sharp like a pin. He pauses. Thinks: *What is this? Why is Reagan doing any of this?*

He grabs the computer. Wrenches it from its wires. *Pop, pop, pop.* Then he flings the computer against the wall. It's heavy. He's imbalanced. His heel skids out, and suddenly he's going ass over teakettle (as his grandma used to say)— head snapping against the chair, chair banging against the edge of the desk, monitor slamming forward with a crack. Pain radiates up his butt bone to his midback.

At least, he thinks, *it's done.*

But it's not. Soon as he starts to sit up, he hears footsteps outside shaking the decking beneath him. Then the door is sliding open. The sun is right outside the door, and all he sees is a pair of shapes. He puts his hands up for good measure, hears a *pop* sound—and then something sticks in his side and every part of him lights up like the Fourth of July.

CHAPTER 15

Undertow

They dragged Chance out. He remembers that much. The Taser knocked him sideways, made every part of him feel like it was imploding on itself—teeth pushing together so hard they might turn to dust, like chalk against a hard sidewalk. The other pod doors open and he sees his own crew there, staring at him in horror—someone throws him forward and he points at Reagan, is about to accuse her loud as he can manage, but then the Taser hits him again and all he can do is stutter-scream.

Hands underneath him. They pull him toward the far western corner of the property, then down a set of steps and over a broken stone walkway—moss underneath, weeds growing up, the path hedged in by curls of blackberry briar and sharp grass. A couple of blue jays complain in the trees overhead, take flight.

Out there is a building. Like a springhouse. Old stone. Looks like it wants to fall apart, like it's giving the world one last shrug.

Someone—Roach, Chance sees it's Roach, that brick-jawed bastard—starts unlocking a handful of padlocks from a door that clearly isn't the original door: red, metal, with a porthole window bolted into the center. They fling him inside. He slides across a new concrete floor, hits an industrial-looking office chair, which rolls away, caster wheels squeaking.

The springhouse is divided in two. One side is just this: the chair, a table, a toolbox. The walls are still old stone. Mossy, cobwebby. Millipedes crawl and centipedes run. Above, in the shelter of fluorescent light fixtures, cellar spiders spin silk.

The other side is behind a big Plexiglas divider. In there is something that looks like one of those lean composite storage boxes that might sit atop a Subaru Outback—it's got the shape of a shoe or a spaceship escape pod.

Chance rolls over. Looks up and sees three Lodge guards standing there—Roach, in his dark suit, and two others: a doughy guy with a patchy beard (name tag: Chen) and a grim-faced scowl-beast of a woman (name tag: Metzger).

"First day," Roach says. "First day you pull this shit."

"Most prisoners wait a couple days," Metzger says. When she speaks, the lines in her face turn to deep crevices. "But you? Ballsy."

Chen just laughs.

"I didn't—" Chance starts to say, but talking feels like he's trying to push sound through a tunnel of fiberglass insulation. "It wasn't—"

"Get up," Roach says, then steps behind him, picks him up, and drops him into the chair. "What's that?" Roach tilts an ear. "I don't like threats."

Chance protests: "Whoa, what? I didn't say—"

Roach pistons a fist into his side.

"God *damn* it," Chance says. Adrenaline kicks up like a fast storm and Chance launches himself upward, swings a clumsy fist—but Roach is fast, turns his head, gets clipped in the ear, then brings a hard knee up into Chance's middle. He doesn't let Chance fall, though: he grabs for Chance's back, holds him there as he knees him a second time, then a third. Then Roach shoves him back into the chair.

Chance gasps, pain radiating out from his middle—all the way down to his balls and up to the drumming pulse beat in his neck. He holds up his hands. "Stop. Stop."

"Time to give him the spiel?" Metzger asks.

"Think so," Roach says. He turns to Chance, plants his hands on the arms of the chair. As he talks, he gently eases the chair back and forth—a small, sickening movement. "Here's the deal. This is hacks versus the hackers. We hate you. We're stuck in here, same as you. Every one of us is away from our families, our friends, our lives, while we hang out in the middle of nowhere to babysit a bunch of nerdy, disrespectful, antiauthoritarian criminals. So now and again we like to blow off a little steam, but we can't just *do* that. We gotta have a reason. Good news is, you mopes tend to give us plenty of reasons, and so we drag you in here and we work you over. Then we toss you in there." He gestures with his chin over Chance's shoulder. "Into the Dep. Short for sensory *dep*rivation chamber."

"Oh, it's horrible," Metzger says. "Each of us hacks has to spend a half hour in there when we sign on to see what it's like."

Chen doesn't say a word but makes a sound: "Yuggghh."

Roach nods. "You go in there, you start to lose sense of time. You hallucinate. Piss and shit yourself. We put you in there for six-hour stretches—and each subsequent time you get sent to the Dep, it's another six hours. You get four turns in the box, and that last trip is a doozy—twenty-four hours long. We hook up an IV so you don't need to eat or drink while you're in there. After that, you fuck up again, we ship you out. Prison."

"This sounds worse than prison," Chance says.

Chen belly-laughs.

"You think?" Roach says. "Real prison sucks. Chen there used to be a guard at Rikers. Forty percent of the population is fucking schizo. Half of them will rape you soon as look at you. Guards like to go on blanket parties—anybody who stares at them sideways gets a blanket tossed over their heads and beaten with batons and chair legs. This is a vacation, you little hick. Hell, it even has therapeutic value, they say."

"REST," Metzger says. "R-E-S-T. Restricted Environmental Stimulation Therapy. We get to pretend this is good for you instead of a total nightmare."

"So," Roach says, leaning in close. "You ready for your first six-hour stint?"

"No, you don't understand," Chance says, swallowing hard. "I didn't do anything—I was there in the pod—"

"Oh, so you didn't hack the cameras so they played back a loop of you just sitting there, twiddling your thumbs? You didn't turn off the keylogger? You didn't then, for some mysterious reason, decide to *pick up your computer* and smash it?"

"I . . . I did that last part, but the other stuff, that wasn't me—I got hacked."

"The hacker got hacked. Sure, sure, sure. That sounds legit." To the other guards: "Metzger, get his legs. Chen, look lively—go open the door to the Dep chamber."

Chen nods, hurries over, pops the door in the Plexiglas.

Chance screams as Roach gets under his arms. "Get off me, motherfucker!" He kicks his legs and thrashes about—his foot almost catches Metzger under her chin but she yanks her head back and chuckles. They move him toward the door.

"Put him down."

Chance never thought he'd feel relief at hearing Hollis Copper's voice. But turns out pigs do fly, because that's what happens.

Except, the guards don't put him down. "Look who it is," Roach says. "You see something else out in the woods, Agent Copper? Maybe the Blair Witch is out there. Or Bigfoot."

"Shut up, Roach. Put Dalton down."

"Golathan sanctions this. He knows the deal."

"I don't care what he sanctions. One thing he *has* sanctioned is that you have a Taser hanging at your hip. I have a Glock."

Roach breathes heavily. Like he's pissed and wants to say something more. But instead, Chance watches the man nod to Metzger. They set him down. He scrambles away from them, almost knocking over the table and chair.

Hollis nods toward the door. "Let's go, Dalton."

Ø Ø Ø

They sit in Hollis's non-office. A repurposed supply closet, far as Chance can tell. *They must not like this guy very much,* he thinks. "Hey," he says, "I just wanna thank you—"

Hollis sits forward in his chair. "No. Do not thank me. What you tried to pull today is serious business, Mr. Dalton."

"I *didn't* pull any shit, dude. Okay? I got hacked. Reagan Stolper hacked me."

"That's a bold accusation."

"It's true. I mean—at least, *someone* hacked me. It had to be her."

Hollis crosses his arms. His eyes are framed in dark circles. He seems to literally chew on all this, his jaw working slowly, diligently, like he's got a sunflower seed stuck in a back tooth somewhere. "I don't understand much of what goes on here, and honestly, I don't care. Next time you get the urge to smash a computer, don't. You think you're getting hacked? Say something instead of destroying government property. Because right now none of this looks good for you."

"You gotta help me—"

"I don't. I *don't* have to help you. I'm not your friend, Mr. Dalton. I'm not your ally, your bodyguard, I'm not even your damn babysitter. I'm just a guy sitting around waiting for you flunkies to flunk out so I can go the hell home."

Chance levels his gaze. "So why'd you help me today, then?"

"Because I don't like Roach. And because, much as I don't like you, I also can't have my conscience burdened by letting you get your ass beat to a grapefruit pulp."

"Like I said: thanks again—"

"Shut up. You can thank me by just shutting up."

Ø Ø Ø

It's hours later that Copper finally lets him go. He tells him to skedaddle—Copper's word, *skedaddle*—to the cafeteria lest he miss dinnertime.

Chance heads downstairs from the administrative offices of the Ziggurat. His hands are balled up into fists. It's too much. He's already bad at this. Why the hell did Reagan hack him? All she had to do was let him weave together his own rope, tie his own noose, slip it over his neck, and kick out the chair. He didn't need any help.

He shoulders open the door, sees his pod sitting there at their table all the way toward the edge of the room— fringe dwellers. Reagan's not with them. The others see him coming, and suddenly it's a flurry of questions: *What happened? What did you do?*

"Where's Reagan?" Chance asks, voice a ragged rasp. "Where's the troll?"

Nobody points. All he has to do is follow their eyes. She's sitting all the way across the room. With Shane Graves. Ivo Shandor. Of course. *Of course.*

Reagan sees him looking. Her big pink cheeks stretch into a big cheeky smile. She winks and waggles her fingers in another toodle-oo wave. Shane sees her looking, then turns toward Chance. He grins and gives Chance a sarcastic thumbs-up. Then their whole table laughs and laughs and laughs.

Chance growls, starts to storm over. But DeAndre is up fast, stepping in front of him. "Whoa, whoa, whoa, firecracker. This ain't your move. Just sit down. Cool your shit. Eat some pizza."

"*He* set this up," Chance says, pointing to Shane. "That son of a bitch did me in. And one of our own helped him." How fast he's come to thinking of the pod as *his own*. A group to which he belongs. "I wanna go break bad on his ass with a dinner tray. I can't hack a computer worth a damn, but I can sure hack his nuts with my foot."

Aleena is next to him now. "DeAndre is right." Her hand on his arm is warm and cool at the same time, and just that small touch feels unusually nice. Chance looks down at it and she pulls it away quickly. She clears her throat and stands up straight.

"I'm gonna go cool down," Chance says, and walks away from the table. He heads to the rec room side, checks out the arcade cabinets. On the way he feels eyes on him—Shane and Reagan staring holes through him like cigarettes burning through a bedsheet. He feels his cheeks flush, go red with anger, but he keeps walking.

The rec room isn't much to look at. But at least it's empty, what with people still eating. Three machines sit in front of him: Joust. Sinistar. Street Fighter II. Chance only knows that last one—he's heard of Joust, but it's before his time. Sinistar, though, that's entirely new to him. So he heads over to it. Of course, it needs quarters.

He's about to walk away when the Joust machine chimes. *Ready Player One,* the screen says.

Chance *hmm*s, then thinks, *Aw, hell with it.* He sidles up to the arcade cabinet, plays a game of Joust. It's pretty simple to understand—the old arcade games always are— but the simplicity of the game betrays the difficulty of the execution, and he keeps dying, either getting beaked by the buzzards or accidentally launching his bird into the eight-bit magma abyss.

Every time he dies and the game ends, though, it starts back up after a few seconds. *Ready Player One* again and again. Eventually, he starts getting a little further. Killing one more wave of buzzard riders, then another, and then another—

It's on his sixth or seven try that the screen flashes. Big fat pixels move out of place. First just a few—makes the screen look like holes in a punch card. Then more. Some pixels blink, reappear elsewhere. Some drift, blipping left or right, one pixel space at a time.

Chance taps the joystick left and his rider gets caught in midair, flapping against some invisible wall. "Oh, c'mon, c'mon," he complains, jiggling the joystick. A buzzard rider clocks into him. Kills him. Last life, game over.

Except, it never makes it to the game-over screen. Everything glitches out good and proper. The image distorts—a spray of broken Minecraft pixels. The screen goes black.

"I killed it," Chance says. "I killed the Joust machine." That'll earn him plenty of new friends here, he thinks.

Then the screen flashes again. Text begins to scroll, bottom to top. Big blocky arcade font. *When the gods had overcome the giants, the marriage between man and beast was brought forth. In size and strength and knowledge did she surpass all the offspring of Earth. She had legs of man and was as tall and as heavy as the mountains. Her head did brush the stars. One of her hands reached to the west, the other reached to the east, and from them grew a hundred dragon heads, screaming. Wings sprouted and unkempt hair streamed. Fire flashed in her eyes. She made for the heavens, breathing fire.*

"What the . . ." Chance says.

Then the screen flashes again. *Hello, Chance Dalton.*

Suddenly, someone shoulders in next to him. Aleena. "Hey," she says.

"Uhh," Chance says, startled. "Hey. You gotta see this—"

"I know. Of course Shane Graves has his fingerprints all over this, too."

When Chance looks at the screen again, it's showing high scores. Seven of the ten high scores displayed are marked with the three-letter code *IVO*.

"No, wait," Chance says. "It was saying this . . . crazy stuff, and then I think it—"

"I get it," she says. "It's hard here. I'm going to help you."

"Help me . . . do what?"

She frowns. "I'm going to help you with your work here. So you don't wash out."

"Uh-huh." Chance hesitates. "Reagan said she was gonna help me, and that didn't turn out so hot."

"I'm not Reagan Stolper, am I? In fact, I look at this as a perfect opportunity to teach her a lesson."

"Why?"

"I don't like her kind. She misuses the power we have. She punches down when she should be punching up."

"I don't know what that means." He furrows his brow. "So, lemme get this straight: I'm like a . . . battleground."

"Maybe. Is that a problem?"

"Hell, if it keeps me out of prison *and* sticks a big old middle finger in Reagan's smug troll mug, I'm in." He's about to say something else when a third person suddenly elbows his way next to them. It's the kid with the shop-teacher glasses, Dipesh. He looks left, looks right, then thrusts up a napkin, inside of which are swaddled two big cookies, like those from lunch. "Here. C'mon, c'mon, quick. Quick! Take them."

Chance takes one and so does Aleena. She looks relieved and confused at the same time. Chance says thanks, but Aleena asks: "What are we supposed to do with these? Put them down our pants?"

Dipesh shrugs. "Just eat them! Miranda and I saved them for you from lunch."

And then, as if summoned, the dandelion wisp of a woman appears with another cookie, out of which she takes a bite. "I'm Miranda," she says, speaking around the crumbs, and catching a few falling from her lips with an open palm. "Sorry."

Dipesh laughs. "You, Chance Dalton, are a first-day badass, my friend."

"It was a little crass," Miranda says, her voice as light and airy as her fairy's frame. Her chin lifts and she stares down at Chance. Her eyes suddenly light up. "But still, we were all very impressed."

"I don't understand," Chance says.

"Some folks freak out eventually, you know?" Dipesh says. "But nobody does it on the first day. Everybody's always running around like scared little mice afraid somebody's going to steal their cheese. But not you! And we know who you are. You have ties to Faceless. That's why Graves doesn't like you. You're stealing his *thunder*."

Chance thinks, *Oh shit.*

But he doesn't have time to worry about it, because next thing he knows, he's got a whole line of folks looking to talk to him. It's like a bubble pops. Three from one pod—a pod calling themselves the Leftovers—show up to introduce themselves, offer high fives. A scraggly-bearded dude calling himself Birdman Kim says what Chance did was "epic and elite." His buddy, a gawky, big-spectacled kid with all the muscle tone of a pool noodle, laughs like a nerdy donkey and keeps wanting to shake Chance's hand. A girl with a big bright purple Mohawk—Jessamyn, she says, or just Jess—introduces the pool noodle and says, "Don't mind Marcus—he's a little Aspergery. You can mind me, though. Because *fuck* these government assholes. Right?" Then she leans forward and kisses him hard enough that their teeth clack together and Chance thinks the friction from their lips might start some kind of fire. When she pulls away, her dark lipstick is smeared. "More of that later," she says. Then winks, and is gone.

Dipesh claps him on the shoulder. "Fuck Shane Graves. He's a festering asshole."

"A canker sore," Miranda says.

"Keep up the good fight," Dipesh says. He and Miranda hurry off, and everyone follows their lead. Once again leaving Chance alone with Aleena. He feels shell-shocked.

She stares him up and down. "You're good with people."

"Am I?" He shrugs.

"Wanna play a quick game?" Aleena asks, gesturing toward the Joust machine.

One of her hands reached to the west, the other reached to the east, and from them grew a hundred dragon heads, screaming . . .

Chance represses a shudder. "Nah, let's take these cookies back."

"Do we have to share them?" She pouts. "I don't like our pod very much."

"Well. For the next year, I think they're the closest thing to family we have."

Aleena stiffens. "I have a real family, and they're not it." But then her gaze softens and she sighs. "Let's go share our glorious bounty. Cookies for all." On the way over, she grabs a napkin off the condiment station. She tosses it to him. "Wipe your mouth. You've got"—she makes a disgusted face—"lipstick everywhere."

Ø Ø Ø

Wade's on the way out, eyeing up the guards and watching all these young dipshits and anarchists flit about like hornets around a rock-struck hive, and he's thinking, *I was young once, but damn it if I can remember it.* Maybe that's the problem with generations. You start to forget what it was like when you were like them, so they become your enemy and you become theirs and nobody understands each other. Then you die and they become you and finally, finally they understand, but by then it's too late.

Wade sighs, opens the door—and Reagan catches his elbow. "Hey, old man," she says. No cheeky faux-happy snark in her tone now; her voice is shot through with the hot iron of ill-concealed anger.

"Howdy, quisling."

"Quisling. Big word."

"Big word for a big girl."

"This again. I get it. You think I'm fat."

He shrugs. "It ain't healthy."

"It is perfectly healthy because I'm perfectly healthy. I exercise. Got great blood pressure. Not a *sniff* of diabetes. Plus, men think I'm hot. Black dudes in par-tic-u-lar. Right, homie?" She says this to DeAndre as he passes by. DeAndre throws up a middle finger. "He knows what I mean. Besides"—she taps Wade's middle with the back of her hand—"you've got a spare tire under there too, so fuck off."

"I'm old. Listen, you got something you wanna say or you just planning on standing here jawing my ear off? Because I'm gonna go read a book or take a dump or something. Maybe both at the same time, because I can multitask."

"I wanna know which one of you did it."

"Did what, exactly?"

"Hacked me."

"Hacked *you*? And here I thought you were the malefactor."

"You do love your big words."

"Just like you love hot dogs."

"No, *asshole,* I mean one of you hacked me while I was hacking Dalton."

"Wasn't me. Like you said: I'm old. I can barely figure out a calculator. Now, if you don't mind, I'm gonna go do exactly as you suggested: fuck off."

Ø Ø Ø

Reagan rolls in just before the doors lock. Shane's pissed enough that his plan has earned Chance additional celebrity; she doesn't need to go asking him for any favors. She likes rocking the boat but also wants to stay in the boat. At least until it gets her to shore.

She makes it into the cabin with about thirty seconds to spare. Soon as she steps in, the door hisses like a gassy snake, then vacuum-seals as the dead bolts engage.

They're all there staring at her. They have hate in their eyes. It's *bona fide*. Authentic, real-deal hate. There's a moment where—inside, not outside—she flinches. A tiny moment of reflexive, defensive fear, like a little bird spooked by a shake of a branch or a shadow passing overhead. And then she thinks: *Fuck 'em*. They don't understand her. Then again, who really does?

As if on cue, the lights go out. It's not totally dark; the outer lights ringing the Hunting Lodge property are bright, and cast some light in through the cabin windows. As Reagan's eyes adjust, she stumbles her way through the cabin. When she gets to the wooden ladder leading up to the loft, she makes out the shadow of someone standing there. It's Chance, she's pretty sure, and he confirms it when he says:

"I don't appreciate what you did to me today."

"Such strong words." She mimics him, but adds a little bit of a lisp to her mocking tone: *"I really don't appreciate what you did; it makes me sad and hurts my feelings very much and now I have all this gritty sand in the waistband of my panties."*

"The guards—the hacks—beat the snot out of me. I'd show you the bruises up my side, but it's dark and you wouldn't give a shit anyway."

"Whatever," Reagan says, though she actually does feel bad. Not that she can tell him that.

He leans in. "And don't think I don't know you were messing with that Joust machine, too. All that . . . religious dragon monster nonsense."

"Joust?" she says, and she's about to tell him she doesn't know what the hell he's talking about, but real fast she clamps that down because she remembers her favorite lesson from one of her favorite movies, *Glengarry Glen Ross:* you don't open your mouth until you know what the shot is. "You know what? Just move."

But he doesn't move. Fine. Time to twist the knife a little. "Starting to look a little rapey, dog," she says.

She can see his shape visibly recoil and he steps aside. Says nothing. Nobody else says shit, either.

Reagan gets up to her bed, finds that the mattress has been removed. So too have all the bedsheets and pillows. In the dark, she has no idea who has them. "Really?" she asks aloud, incredulous.

"Oops," Aleena says.

Reagan sighs, lies down on the wooden frame. No springs because, she guesses, someone might pry one out and slit her wrists. "Good night," she says in a singsongy voice.

CHAPTER 16

The Compiler

It's 3 A.M. Officer Ray Davis sits in the police cruiser, seat reclined. He's flipping around the Internet on his iPad Mini—he's well past the porn stage of the night, and he's on to recipes. Which is, in its own way, a whole other kind of porn. Ray Davis loves to cook for his wife and two kids. Right now he's looking at fancy pictures of pork belly carnitas, and his stomach is growling and twitching like an old dog dreaming.

Outside, fireflies flit about. Night bugs sing together in their chorus: crickets, katydids, whatever. This is Big Woods Road. Not much here between Dickerson and Beallsville except some fields, some trees, a handful of farms and farmhouses. That's just how Ray likes it. If the department is gonna stick him on overnights like this, then hell with it, he's gonna go tuck himself away in the dark of the night where the only things around are possums and owls and the endless insects.

Then he hears it: A car. Distant. Coming closer.

Way down the road, Ray spots the glow of headlights.

It's probably nothing to worry about. Cars pass through here late, sometimes. Maybe one or two an hour. Ray wonders if there's anywhere you can go to get away anymore—like, *really* escape people. Alaska, maybe. Or parts of the desert: Arizona, New Mexico. Maryland, not so much.

The car that comes turns out to be not a car but a van. White Nissan cargo van, maybe late '90s, early 2000s. A bit mud streaked. When it passes by his hiding spot it isn't going fast—just a slow coast down a back road. Leisurely, almost.

But as it passes, Ray sees: No taillights. The back end of the vehicle is all dark. And he thinks, *So what, just let it go,* but Ray, he's a man driven by guilt. Not big guilt, not the guilt of someone who killed a family in a drunk-driving accident, or hits his wife and kids, none of that. Just little guilts. His therapist says that comes from his mother: a mother who reminded him at every turn that he should be ashamed of himself for tracking mud in the house or not washing the dishes.

Ray sighs. The department has a quota for tickets, and worse, he's suddenly imagining some half-baked scenario where the van drives off and somewhere around morning it brakes but a car behind it doesn't see, and—*wham.* Maybe the van driver doesn't even know both his taillights are dark. Maybe some kid gets hurt. And that'd be on Ray for letting this go.

Well, hell. Ray looks one last time at the picture of the pork belly carnitas—can almost smell them braising in the oven—then tosses the iPad onto the seat next to him. He starts the engine and turns on the red-and-blues. No siren. No need. He eases the car out, gives it a little gas, and it's not long before he catches up with the van as it goes over the little Crow Creek bridge, the one by the Gorhams' old pole barn.

At first Ray thinks the driver isn't slowing down, but of course he can't tell because, ta-da, no taillights. Then, though, the van eases off to the side of the road under a canopy of trees, just where the gravel shoulder widens around the curving road.

Ray does his due diligence. He pulls the computer off the dash and taps in the license number. New York plates. Car registered to one Martin L. Biedermann, Queens, New York. No priors. No outstandings. Car isn't reported stolen. *Whew.* Once in a while, they get guys on these back roads moving some kinda drug product up the coast, or worse, they get gangbangers bringing bodies from D.C. or Baltimore out here to hide in the woods. Rare these days, but still happens. This isn't that, and that makes Ray happy.

On a lark, he pulls up Biedermann's license. Little guy, five five, thirty-four years old.

He grabs his light. Checks his gun. Whistles as he walks up to the car. He'll give Biedermann a warning, send li'l Marty on his way. And then he'll be back looking up recipes. He's got a hankering to make blueberry cobbler. The kids love blueberry cobbler. (Well, Meghan loves it. Little Danny's only three and his taste in food changes like the wind. One month all he eats is chicken fingers, next month you can't get him to eat a chicken finger if you bribe him with a case of new Matchbox cars.)

But when he gets up to the car and shines the light in, he's pretty sure that's not Marty Biedermann. Not unless Biedermann put on some years and was in some kinda accident. And grew a foot or more.

The window rolls down. The man inside has a misshapen head and a scar that connects his eye with his curled-up lip. When the man speaks, it's like his voice is dead—a flatline of inflection. Emotionless. "Officer, what may I do for you."

"You, ahh—" Ray suddenly finds that his voice is harder to come by then he'd like. Even though the summer night is cooler than usual, he starts to sweat. A feeling scratches at the back of his neck like a rat behind drywall: *Something isn't right.* "You know why I stopped you?"

"No, I do not."

Ray shines the light in the passenger seat. A McDonald's bag sits crumpled up. A laptop sits next to it—the case scratched up like a mountain lion had a go at it. He tells himself everything's fine. Bag of fast food? Normal. The laptop? For Chrissakes, he was just looking at his own iPad. "Your taillights are out," he says with an awkward laugh.

"Are they? I did not know that."

"I'm gonna write you a warning—but you'll need to get that taken care of."

"Of course, Officer." The man licks his lips.

"I just need to see your license, registration, proof of insurance."

"Of course, Officer." The man's thin lips struggle to make a human-looking smile, and Ray's sympathy for the guy almost evaporates, because *Jesus,* this fellow is creepy. The man reaches over and pops the latch on the glove compartment.

A syringe rolls out.

Time seems to slow.

Ray takes a step back. Reaches for his gun. Draws it. Starts to yell to the man to step out of the vehicle.

The driver's eyes roll back in his head. His mouth hangs open. Ray hesitates. Is he having a seizure?

Then the eyes snap back and the man moves fast. His prodigious hands leave the wheel and grab Ray's wrist, wrenching it aside as Ray fires, the bullet punching through the passenger side window.

Ray's ears ring. He can smell the eggy stink of expended powder.

The door pops open. The top of it clips Ray across the forehead. He staggers. Two hard fists piston into his side. A leg hooks around the back of his knee, pulls like a hook—the world flips around, and his tailbone hits asphalt. He falls back, head snapping against road. Teeth clacking, biting his tongue hard. He can taste blood.

He lifts the pistol. Fires. He hasn't trained at the range in forever. The gun kicks. The man runs. Ray moves his arm, fires more shots—a tire on the van blows, a back window, a bullet going off the bumper.

The man is gone, back around the other side of the van.

Ray turns over, gets on his hands and knees, starts to crawl—

Hands reach out from under the van. Grab his ankles. He's dragged under. Like a child dragged under his bed by the monster hiding there. Gravel biting into his hand. Then he's out the other side, thrown into a sharp thatch of silver-grass, and he brings the pistol up—

His hand feels suddenly, starkly empty. The gun isn't there.

Ray wants to speak—he wants to hit the brakes on all this. He waves his arms, tries to say, *I'll let this go, you just drive away, I don't care, I got a wife, I got two kids, I wanna go home and cook dinner,* but the only thing that comes out of his mouth is mush, garble, bubbles of spit and blood.

The driver says in that monotone voice: "I did not calculate for this error." He reaches down, grabs Ray's throat. Ray expects the whole hand to close over his neck, but the man only grabs the middle of his throat—the trachea—the way you might honk a clown's nose or a bicycle's horn. Then there's pain, and a wet sound, and Ray can't breathe.

The man's hand returns, slick with red. He smells the hand. Tastes it.

That's the last thing Ray sees before he dies.

CHAPTER 17

Paint It Black

White hat hackers make Reagan's panties itch. And not in the good way. In the *I used poison ivy to wipe my ass* way. They don't even call themselves that—"white hat"—probably because it sounds too simplistic. No, no, most of them go with "ethical hackers." You can even get certified for it.

It makes her almost puke in her mouth. *Ethical hackers.* What the fuck does that even mean? Everybody has ethics. Some people have self-righteous ethics, others have self-indulgent ethics, some folks are godly, others are Satanic, but everybody has some kind of code, and her code is right in line with that old magician Aleister Crowley: *do what thou wilt shall be the whole of the law.* Thelema law, though she doesn't really understand that part because she has no interest in actual magic or any of that occult crap. Crowley was a creep. She just likes that line.

Here, at the Lodge, everything's still the same for her. It's not for the others—they've all spray-painted their black hats white for now, but hers was always gray, gray, gray, and that color shall it stay, stay, stay.

Right now that means doing what Shane Graves wants her to do. And what he wants her to do is hack Chance Dalton. Cut him open like a frog in a dissection pan. Remove everything but still keep him alive. (That last part isn't Shane's directive, and he probably doesn't agree. Shane probably wants Dalton dead. Figuratively, if not literally.)

So. Time to get to it, then. Maybe this time, too, she can find out just who hacked her while she was hacking Dalton. All that bullshit about gods and monsters—*and the gods did flee*. A message for her? For Dalton? For *Graves*? It has a thread, and when she finds it, she plans on pulling it. If only for the satisfaction of unraveling the sweater.

She enters the pod in the morning—scratching at her bra, because it's an old one and the wire is poking out—and doesn't see the difference at first. But when she sits, yawns, and rubs her eyes, she does.

A coffee machine. One of those little Keurigs. These machines are better than Harry Potter's house-elves. Pop in one of their little *magic ampules* of *caffeine magic,* press a button, and boosh. One cuppa comin' up. She gives a thumbs-up to the camera. Says, "Thanks, Big Government." Cheeky air-smooch.

Too bad she's still gonna have to bypass their systems and use their own piss-poor security infrastructure against them.

She sets up shop. Sees her folder—Jesus, another pen test. A cloud computing company: Thunderhead. Normally, this one might present a bit more fun—after all, they're responsible for an unholy host of cloud computing storage accounts. A mortuary for people's hidden data. For some reason, the average dumb-ass feels a lot more comfortable storing all his really secret stuff in the cloud. Not, like, bank records and legal documents. The really *juicy* stuff: Naked photos. Forbidden e-mails. Or the two finest words in the human language: *sex tape*. (Even though it's not a tape, the name has stuck. No pun intended.) Shit, you wanna find out if someone's into dog fucking or kiddie touching, look no further than his Dropbox account.

Today, though, that pleasure of kicking over rocks and seeing what squirms underneath will be one that has to wait. This has to be fast. They got their "evaluation scores" from yesterday—Hollis read them out as he walked them to the pods. Letter grades, like they're in fucking high school or something. A for Aleena (barf), B+ for DeAndre (she'd do him), C+ for her (not bad for not trying; also her grade average in high school, so), C– for Wade (not bad for an old man), and Hollis declined to name a grade for Chance (unsurprising). Today, all Reagan has to do is maintain the same mediocre average.

She moves fast through the penetration (insert joke here, she thinks, or maybe, insert wang here), and it's breezily easy. Problem with most public cloud computing solutions is that, first, they often use client-side software to access them, and apps are notoriously weak—it's like hiding all your gold in Fort Knox but then making the entryway a squeaky screen door. But the larger problem is that cloud computing must first pass through that hive of scum and villainy: the Internet. The Internet is a place of glorious rot: everything that passes through it, or even *touches it,* is subject to decay. It's too big, too sprawly, to be well protected—anything that uses Internet protocol to parlay its information and access is the equivalent of a person traveling through a bad part of town just to get to work. You open yourself to intrusion.

So, intruding on Thunderhead's cloud services is no big thing. Reagan's documenting everything as she goes through it, hastily noting weaknesses—it's simple, she notes, to download the client and hack the client, thus kicking open that screen door and finding her way into a wealth of personal storage. Tens of thousands of accounts. Client names. Usernames. Passwords. Plus, drumroll please, home addresses, phone numbers, and the pièce de résistance: bank data. Places like this are the cause of many a hacker's nocturnal emissions.

Still, the usernames and passwords are all encrypted. Passwords are stored as these gibberish algorithms—hashes, or "hashies," in the parlance. Problem is, you can't translate them backward because of the algorithm. So your best bet is picking some plaintext passwords ("plains") and trying to run them through the same algorithm to see what patterns start to emerge in the encryption hashes. It's like a souped-up hacker version of a *New York Times* puzzle.

Reagan pretends to everyone else that she's just some dopey troll, but she likes to think of herself as a jack-of-all-trades. But that also means *master of none*. Encryption is not her specialty. Thankfully, hackers are a mix of loners and pack animals, and even lone wolves leave behind food for the other hunters. All she has to do is download a toolkit. Automated, hit one button, and it starts to scroll through names, passwords, looking for patterns, solving for x (or, rather, solving for XI}EWR!(TUH2782#34, but whatever).

That'll get her somewhere between 30 and 50 percent of the total. The rest she'll have to figure out by hand, which requires Googling names and seeing if she can find pet names or maiden names or hobbies or anything else that might give a clue as to a person's plaintext password.

Still, for now, let the cracker run its course. Names and passwords pop up like badminton birdies and are swatted down.

Reagan brews coffee. Sips at it. It's flavored—caramel vanilla. Tastes a little like chemicals, but she likes chemicals, so whatever.

Then one name pops up and is gone again. Except it pings her radar. She stops the cracker. Goes back, searches for the name.

There. Philo Kallimakos. Greek guy (she assumes). Name is familiar because she saw it just yesterday. He's one of the big investors behind Arcus Land Development: same a-holes she "penetrated" just yesterday. Can't just be a coinky-dink. They're giving her companies that are connected, however loosely.

Reagan thinks: *Okay, let's crack this nut.* Password cracker bypassed him, which means he won't be one of the 30 to 50 percent in the first pass—which means she's gotta do this by hand. So she pulls up Google, which of course is blocked, which of course makes her job all the harder.

Except. *Except.* Yesterday she found a host of usernames and passwords allowing her into Arcus's infrastructure, so she starts trying those. Fifth try: Bingo, bango, bongos in the Congo. The username-password combo from the Arcus FTP site lets her into Mr. Kallimakos's cloud computing folder.

She scrolls through hundreds of folders, all of them named like gibberish. Strings of gobbledygook characters. She pops open a random one. Inside: thousands of files. Most of them encrypted. Some of them, though, aren't: she opens a few graphic files, sees images of what looks like—Greek pottery? Each image a broken shard, showing parts of what look like some kind of monster—a few shards show parts of a black snake with red scales, others offer up wings of black and red feathers. A different graphic file shows a scan of some kind of . . . woodcut? Words in Latin. IMAGO TYPHONUS, IVXTA APOLLODORVM. Something that looks like something out of Lovecraft rising up out of the ground—snake fingers, tentacle legs, mouth vomiting lightning.

She opens up one more image. It's the same freaky Lovecraft thing, except it's stomping forth; men and women are running from it and appear to be changing into rabbits, dogs, birds. Some of them half changed, others changed all the way. All of them fleeing.

And the gods did turn to common beasts.
AND THE GODS DID FLEE.

She feels suddenly dizzy. Arcus to Thunderhead. Gods and monsters. The person who hacked her tied somehow to Philo Kallimakos? How? How is that even—

Her thigh vibrates. Fuck, fuck, fuck. She looks up—sees the camera light has gone from green to red on both. Which means she's taken too long.

She pops the fly on her jeans, reaches down her pants. There's a cryptophone duct-taped to her inner thigh: matte black, small screen, fairly concealable. This one's a Floydphone—aka a "Fromitz Board"—made by some text-adventure-game fan and sold as a crowdsourced device. It needs an access code to connect, a code that Shane gave her (because Shane also gave her the phone). She punches in the ten-digit code and instantly a text pops up:

Stop dicking around.

She gives the phone the finger. She'd give it to the cameras, too, but nobody's watching those. Right now, the eyes on the other end—guards, she's guessing—are seeing a loop of her working from earlier. First half an hour or so, roughly mixed up and replayed back. Someone paying careful attention might notice, but at a casual glance? Not so much.

She texts back: *Soon.*

When she looks up at the screen, the folders—the hundreds belonging to Kallimakos, with thousands of files—are disappearing. Files flying to the trash one by one. Zipping quickly. She tries to take control, tries to save them, but the delete command has already been issued. Thirty seconds later, the folders are gone and the main page is empty. "God damn it!" she says. Suddenly she's contemplating doing exactly what Dalton did—picking up the whole computer and chucking it on the ground. She shoves her hand in her mouth, bites down on the soft pad of flesh between her thumb and her wrist. Not enough to draw blood. But almost.

The Floydphone vibrates again with a new text:

NOW

She's about to text him back, tell him what happened. But her thumbs pause. What if he already knows? What if he's the one who did this? Deleting this stuff just to mess with her.

Maybe Shane is the one who hacked her.

That's the thing about being a troll—you're suddenly pretty sure that while you're trolling the world, the world is trolling you right back. Normally she likes that feeling—it lends everything a sense of parity, of insane quid pro quo, but suddenly now she's feeling incensed, disturbed, and downright paranoid.

She sucks it up. Deep breath.

Fine, she types.

Then she takes a few moments to compose herself before she goes back to hacking that poor, dumb Chance Dalton.

Ø Ø Ø

DeAndre's got a new task—pen-test some start-up search engine called Glassboat out of the Bay Area—but he just can't quit the German geothermal company.

Right now, the network folder he's trying to crack on their end doesn't even allow for the entry of a password or anything. It's user based, and it knows he's not the user. He throws everything he has at it—or, at least, everything he can manage to scrounge together here in this data prison pod—but he can't trick it into thinking he's the one who set the permissions on the file.

He scours around, looking for any other clue inside their systems. He finds some shit about something called "Sandhogs"—a little research shows they're some kind of union out of New York City, Local 147. The ones responsible for digging subway tunnels, bridge footers, things like that. That doesn't help him.

An hour in, he's sweating like an addict who sees his fix but can't get a taste. He's anxious, grabby, eager. He knows they're watching them, and he hasn't bothered to change that. Let 'em wonder what he's up to. He can't help it. He has to know.

He *has to.*

Ø Ø Ø

The trick for Aleena is this:

To hack Reagan, she first needs to get *out there*. She needs to leave the path they have made for her. She needs to disappear into the woods.

But they're filming her. And keylogging the computer.

Somehow, Reagan did it. Aleena doesn't know how, but if that bridge troll can manage, so can Aleena.

She goes about her business first, knowing they're going to expect her to get another good score on the testing— today, it's a company called Infinitest. A cursory search shows it's a nanotechnology company, specifically geared toward solving the post-antibiotic crisis.

Thing is, she doesn't know how long Reagan's going to take jumping in. Which means: no time to dally.

She has a plan. Two stages.

First stage: kill the keylogger. This part's risky because they're going to keylog her downloading anti-keylogger software. But here, she has an excuse: she needs—er, "needs"—a logger killer for her penetration testing. So she grabs a piece of software called KeyBreaker, then runs it in the background of the nanotech company, and then, ohh, accidentally runs it on her own side, too—

Ping. Ping.

Two detections. Like little ships appearing on radar.

One she knows: when KeyBreaker identifies and shuts down the keylogger tracking her every key tap and mouse click, it's no surprise to her.

But the second one is a surprise. Someone was keylogging Infinitest.

That deserves a deeper look. But later, not now. For now, stage two—

Aleena leans forward, blocking the monitor with her body. She has to move fast so this doesn't look too obvious.

She pulls up the monitor settings. LCD and LED monitors film easily. Old boxy CRT monitors—the kinds that looked like old televisions, the kinds you could use as a boat anchor if you really wanted to—didn't film well because they flickered. People think LCDs don't flicker—and mostly they don't, at least not noticeably.

But you can make it noticeable. Mess with the backlighting. Apply pulse-width modulation—easily done in the monitor settings—to dim the backlight, and voilà: higher flicker. Then: add a little judder (easy to set on most HDTVs) and reduce the refresh rate and now the cameras behind her won't be able to see what's on the screen. What *should* show up is a pulsing, flashing light—nearly impossible to make anything out.

She cracks her knuckles. Now it's time to hack that bitch.

Ø Ø Ø

Chance gets a new pod for the day, and with it comes some softball job—he's pen-testing some self-help guru's website. The website shows a big banner: *Renowned Psychologist and Self-Enlightenment Specialist: Alan Sarno*. Chance feels dumb, but he's not *that* dumb. He knows he's been Nerfed. Part of him appreciates it. Another part of him just feels like a dope.

He's cooking along pretty well—the site is updated, in part, using WordPress blogging software, and that means he already knows the username. Nobody changes their username, because it's too hard or they don't care *or* they don't think it matters.

Username: *admin*.

The password is trickier. He tries the standards: *password, password123*, and so on. None of them click. Worse, he can't get on Facebook, can't Google search the guy, so he's stuck with what he can find on Sarno's own site.

Which, it turns out, is just enough. Sarno's bio lists his family and their first names: wife Sara, daughters Hayley and Katey. Chance tries all of those, and it's a no-go—but then he sees that Sarno's got a poodle, too. Big white fuzzy thing—less a dog and more a series of snowball-colored Afro-puffs connected by hairless pink bits. The dog's name is Knishie.

And boom: there's the password.
A chat window pops up.

> **DUTCH JELLYFART:** HEYYYYYY

Chance looks up. Of course, the camera lights have gone red. He pulls the keyboard close, jaw tight at the hinge. He types:

> **GUEST:** Reagan, you're an asshole.
> **DUTCH JELLYFART:** There is no Reagan. There is only ZUUL. And I am an asshole! I know. I can't help it. It's pathological, I swear.

Chance thinks, *Where's Aleena?* She was supposed to be helping him. Maybe she pulled a Reagan and is abandoning him here in the abyss. Or worse, maybe she's helping twist the knife. His underarms start to sweat.

> **GUEST:** Why can't you just leave me alone?
> **DUTCH JELLYFART:** Because of the lulz. And because this is part of a larger game. And because I screwed you once before we even got here and because I liked it.
> **GUEST:** What the hell are you talking about?
> **DUTCH JELLYFART:** Shhh. SHHH. Just lie back and think of England, luv.

And then a third account pops in:

> **ZENOBIA:** Sorry, troll, the third billy goat's here to kick you off the bridge.

The chat window closes.
Chance sits there for a while, waiting for something, anything. Like—maybe the computer will suddenly start to

smoke and spit sparks. Maybe it'll grow legs like a Transformer and kick him in the teeth. Maybe Reagan will come out of the monitor like the girl from *The Ring.* But nope, nothing.

He pokes a few keys. Clicks the mouse. He still has control.

Aleena did it. *Aleena saved his ass.*

He whoops with laughter.

Ø Ø Ø

Ding, dong, the bitch is dead, Aleena thinks.

Now, to find out who put that keylogger on the nanotech company.

Ø Ø Ø

They've given Wade another unhackable, uncrackable company. AeroCore. Maker of drones and other airborne robotic devices. AeroCore has on its board a number of politicians and politicians' children, and like with Blackwater in Iraq was allowed to preemptively bid on jobs with the military (air force, mostly) before anyone else had a chance. Prebids were preaccepted and every other company got prefucked. Not that Wade cares much for those other companies, either—but this is a symptom of a scrape that's long gone septic.

He goes through the motions, enough to get him a pass, not enough to make any real difference—these young hackers all are eager to please their new masters, but he knows the deal. Shut up. Do the bare minimum. Then get the hell out.

That assumes, of course, that they'll let him and the others out alive. But that's a problem for another day.

For now, he sits back and does little.

Though something keeps itching at the back of his brain stem. He senses connections here that he doesn't fully see and can't begin to understand.

AeroCore. Palisade. Both companies he knows. Maybe they're fucking with him. Maybe this is all one big psych experiment.

Ø Ø Ø

DeAndre can't get in.

It keeps changing. The algorithm keeps changing. He hacks one level and then another comes up and boots him back to the beginning. Almost like it's taunting him. All for a single file. Every delay, every defense, makes it exponentially more tantalizing. He bites his lip. Rubs his eyes, thumbs his temples, presses in so hard on the bridge of his nose it almost brings tears to his eyes.

Ø Ø Ø

Reagan is locked out.

Aleena Kattan slammed the door in her face. That little Kardashian.

Well, good for her, Reagan thinks, trying like hell not to be mad. The little raw, red half moons in her palms from where her nails have dug in tell a different story.

Fine, she thinks. She totally doesn't mind when someone gets the best of her.

Shane, though. He'll mind. He'll *definitely* mind.

Ø Ø Ø

Aleena's feeling pretty good about herself. She knew Reagan was more than just some 4chan troll—that one's got cred. Using it for, or with, Shane Graves. So cutting both of those bullies off at the knees is a win.

Chance can die another day. But maybe he won't. Not if she helps him, like she said she would.

Thinking about him gives her this little tickle, like soap bubbles popping inside her stomach. She doesn't like it.

The reason she doesn't like it is because . . . well, she kinda likes it.

She tells herself it's because they're here. In this place. Away from life, away from all the burdens of her purpose. This place is a kind of prison, but in a small way it's also a vacation from a wealth of obligation. It's like being in college. You leave home, you change yourself. Sometimes in small ways, other times in big ones. You forget who you are and remember who you want to become. If only temporarily.

This is that. A temporary blip. A hiccup in who she is.

Besides, she thinks, *this isn't who you* are. *He and you won't understand each other, not when you leave this place.* It's not just that they come from different worlds. Her parents wouldn't care that he's a white boy from—well, she doesn't even know where he's from. Down South, given his accent. It's that she's a city rat, he's a country mouse. He's a script kiddie and she's the real deal.

So forget him. She'll help him as far as she can, not because she likes him, but because it hurts Reagan. Plain and simple.

That's when her machine—running a malware-sniffing program in the hopes of scanning for more nastiness connected to the original keylogger she found—catches something. A red alert. Blinking text.

"Oh, hello," she says, leaning forward.

A rootkit. A piece of software that, when installed, allows a secret visitor privileged access. All the way down to the—hence the name—root account and directory. It's like carving a little hidden door in someone's house that they won't know about, but that you can use to sneak in and out to steal food, riffle through files, snatch up family photos.

This one, it seems, is worse than a little door. It's sitting right there in all the kernel processes, right down to ring zero, which makes it more of a tumor on the brain—it's drawing blood to it, forcibly sharing what goes to the brain for its own purpose.

Aleena unmasks the rootkit with her own toolkit, and it

exposes a host of other directories—sure enough, the keylogger, packet sniffers, all kinds of file grabbers and data hunters. Whoever installed this is—

Her machine blips. Whoever installed this is still here. Here with her. Logged in, right now.

Well, that's interesting. She runs a scan, finds a second IP address. This has to be whoever installed the rootkit. Invisible handprints seen only when she waves a black light over it.

Aleena tracks the IP address. It's gotta be a fake, routed through one or several proxies—so she gets a series of moving targets. First scan: Toronto. Second scan: Sacramento. Third scan: Cape Town. A clever deception. Also impossible for her to trace. At least easily. The only real way to do it is to find the proxy that they're using and hack the proxy—but, of course, proxies are well protected because hackers pentest those things all the time to make sure they're sealed up nice and tight.

If she wrote a bit of JavaScript, dropped it into the files they're stealing, and they took it and—programmatically or by hand—opened it, she could trace their—

A little file appears in the directory she's looking at.

eatmedrinkme.txt

Oh, ha-ha. Images of Alice tumbling down the rabbit hole go through her head. She hated that book as a little girl. Told her mother: "Why are all the stories about little white girls?" And her mother said: "Because white men with little white daughters run the world." Aleena was only nine years old when she found the author on Wikipedia—Lewis Carroll— and then went to her mother and told her: "This man is a pedophile, Mother. I do not want this book any longer." She handed the book over and that was that.

But the dilemma that faced Alice faces her now as well. Alice didn't know whether to eat or drink what was placed before her, and Aleena isn't sure if she should click this file. Any mysterious file runs the risk of being a Pandora's box, and you couldn't *pay* her to open it on a system she owned.

Then again, this isn't her system, is it? She clicks open the text file. It contains three lines of text and a signature:

Who
Is
Typhon?
—The Widow

Aleena feels her breath catch. It can't be.

Behind her, the pod door pops, hisses, starts to open. Aleena scrambles fast, closes the text file, force-quits her connection to the Infinitest servers.

Metzger stomps into the room. She's smiling in that smug way that says, *I'm gonna enjoy this,* and Aleena thinks she's about to be dragged out and thrown into the Dep, but all Metzger says is "C'mon, honey. Copper wants to see you."

CHAPTER 18

Pants on Fire

We got a problem," Copper says.

On the screen, Golathan sips noisily from a cup. "Tea," he says. "Oolong. You should drink tea, Agent. The caffeine in tea metabolizes different from that in coffee. Keeps you alert, but calm. No jitters."

"I don't drink coffee or tea," Copper says.

Golathan arches an eyebrow. "You should start. So what's the problem? You've been at the Lodge for about seventeen seconds, and already I'm hearing problems."

"The problem is—" *All of them,* Hollis thinks, but doesn't say. "The problem is Aleena Kattan. And, I think, Reagan Stolper."

"Uh-huh." Golathan sips his tea. Flips through some papers on his desk.

"You listening? Am I bothering you?"

"You are. But go on."

Hollis explains that they caught Aleena doing . . . well, something. They don't know what, exactly, not yet, not without a little due diligence. But suddenly they couldn't track

her keystrokes anymore. And the monitor mounted above
the pod door—the one that looks at her monitor—couldn't
detect what was on-screen. "Whole thing, just flickering," he
says. Then he tells him that Reagan maybe hacked Chance,
and—

"Let me stop you," Golathan says. "And further, let me
explain that I unreservedly do not give a rat's red rectum
about any of this, Agent Copper."

"They're breaking the rules."

Ken makes a face like he's drinking sour milk instead of
oolong tea. "Gee, you think? They're hackers. They *hack*.
They hack everything. They're like termites. Chewing apart
anything they get their teeth on."

"And you're okay with this."

"Within a certain context, yeah."

"Context?"

"Tiger can't change his spots, Copper."

"Stripes. Tigers have stripes."

"I'm not a zookeeper, Agent, but you are. Keep the animals in line, but remember that they still get to be animals.
As long as they do the rest of what they're supposed to do,
let them play their little reindeer games."

"Some of the other guards don't feel so cozy about that."

"Same goes. Let the hackers be the hackers, and let
the hacks be the hacks. You can't hold their hands on the
playground. These people you're with, they're all basically
underdeveloped, stunted adults, which more or less makes
them children. My kids say mean things. They steal each
other's toys. And to a certain point, you have to let them
work that stuff out."

"To what certain point?"

"To the point where they're knocking each other's brains
out with choo-choo trains or bubble mowers." Golathan tests
the tea again, then, apparently satisfied, swigs it back. "Anything else, or can I go do some real work?"

Hollis's nostrils flare. He wants to say something about
the person he saw in the woods that first night, but Golathan

will think he's nuts. *Maybe that's a good thing. Maybe he'll send you home.* Nah. Ken's too cruel for that.

With nothing more to say, Copper stabs down with a thrusting finger, ends the call. Golathan disappears.

Copper sits for a while, just chewing on his thoughts. Going over them again and again.

Eventually, there's a knock at his door and Metzger indelicately pushes Aleena Kattan forward into his office, then proceeds to stand there, arms folded, chin up. Copper tells her she can go and he sees the look of disappointment cross her face before she (reluctantly) turns and leaves.

Copper studies the hacker for a moment.

"What?" Aleena asks, obviously irritated. But something else, too: flustered. Nervous. Like a kid who got caught in the cookie jar pretending it's your fault.

I know what you're up to, he wants to say to her. But not only is that a lie, but Golathan doesn't want this punished. "Just checking in," he says. "You're kinda my ace player here."

"I know."

"Your humility is overpowering."

"We both know I'm the best in the pod."

He clears his throat. "Yeah. Well. How's it going?"

"Peachy."

"Said with some sarcasm."

"Said with all sarcasm."

"You're very hostile."

"I'm the victim here, not the aggressor."

"You really believe that, don't you?" He leans forward. "You really don't think you broke any laws."

"What I think is that some laws protect people and some laws protect the government and I have no time for the latter."

"So, you can just disregard the laws you don't like? I bet a serial killer feels those pesky laws about not murdering people are in the way of all that murder he wants to do."

She makes a face at him—it's a face he's seen before,

though this one has the volume turned up all the way. Lips pursed, eyes squinting, brow furrowed so deep you could plant seeds in it and grow corn. It's like she's trying to understand exactly how stupid he really is. "You've got me here, so what I think doesn't matter," she says finally. "Why am I standing here in your office?"

"I want you to know my office door is open. In case you ever need to talk. Or make requests. Let's call you the liaison. From your pod to me."

"Fine." She pauses, looks up as if she's accessing parts of her brain. "Chance Dalton is going to wash out, you know."

"I'm worried about that, yeah."

"He needs help."

"What do you propose?"

"I don't know. He's good with people. He can't hack systems but he can hack people. At least, better than I can."

Hollis hesitates. This is against protocol, but . . .

"What if I gave him access to a phone?"

"I thought you didn't do phones here."

"We don't. But maybe I can pull strings."

She nods. "Good."

"You hiding anything, Aleena?"

"That's a little out of left field."

"My door's open if you ever need to talk."

But the look she gives him—it's the look a teenager gives to a parent who just made a dumb, unenforceable request. "Sure, Agent Copper. Sure."

CHAPTER 19

Golathan

Lucas makes buckteeth at his sister, Mandy—because, of course, Mandy has buckteeth and she's very sensitive about it and because Lucas, like all children, knows how to really make an insult *count*.

Mandy is quick to revenge: "Well, at least I can eat candy, lard-butt."

Because Lucas is diabetic. He's not fat—actually, he's got the snap and leanness of a fresh-picked string bean. But some ugly switch in his genes that shouldn't have gotten flipped got flipped anyway. Now it's all glucose meters and blood tests and insulin injections before every meal.

Ken and his wife, Susan, share a look and a shrug. Susan says: "Kids. *Kids.* Eat your food. But first, say something nice to each other."

The kids give her looks in the classic *aww, mom* vein.

"Honey," Ken says, jumping in. "C'mon. Niceness is a little . . . overrated."

Susan gives him her own look: *Ken, don't do this, not now.*

"Kids," Ken says. "Listen to your mother."

Lucas and Mandy suck it up. He tells her he likes her teeth, whatever that means—he's six, though, so half the things out of his mouth don't make a lick of sense. Mandy says she's proud of him for finally learning how to swim. Ken recognizes in there a little knife twist of passive-aggressiveness (*you're late learning to swim, dummy; I learned to swim when I was three, ha-ha-ha*), but Lucas is satisfied, so hell with it.

It's then that the phone rings. The home phone. "I'm not answering that," he says.

"You're going to make me answer it?" Susan asks.

"No—I mean, *nobody* should answer it."

She sighs. "Somebody calls, you never know. It might be important. Your great-aunt Ginny might've died and left us some money."

He rolls his eyes. "I don't have an aunt Ginny, and we don't need money."

"Your mother, then. Sick. Fell down in the shower."

"Don't we pay that retirement home enough that they can go over there and—" He laughs. "I'm arguing an entirely theoretical point. Fine, I'll answer the phone."

He goes into the other room and picks up the receiver. Before he can say anything he hears her voice. "Golathan."

Ken wishes he hadn't picked up. "Leslie," he says, voice low. "You called my *home number*."

"I have a problem. I knew you'd be eating dinner."

It is one of his personal rules. Man's gotta have a code, and his code says dinner every night with his family. Even if that means Skyping in at their dinnertime from fucking Abu Dhabi. "This isn't appropriate."

"Who else am I supposed to call?"

It's not a bad point. "Fine. What?"

"This problem is in your backyard, Kenneth. Beallsville."

His blood goes cold. "What the hell happened?"

"There was an accident."

"An industrial accident? What the hell's in Beallsville, Leslie? No manufacturing there, no server banks—"

"A car accident."

"I don't follow. Why were you down in Beallsville?"

A pause. "I wasn't. An associate of mine was."

"Who? What 'associate'?"

"That's not relevant. The point is, there is now a dead police officer and a stolen police vehicle. State police. There will also be a burned van. A 1998 Nissan cargo-style van. Plate YBT-8918, registered to a Martin Biedermann."

He can feel his heartbeat in his goddamn *teeth*. "A dead . . ." He lowers his voice. "A dead police officer? What in the name of all that's holy are you talking about? Leslie, to call this *irregular* is an understatement. Explain."

"I don't have to. Just fix it."

"Leslie, damnit—"

"All roads lead to Typhon, Ken. Including this one. Clean it up."

Ken holds the silence, thinking she's going to break first—but she doesn't. She waits it out. Suddenly he's not even sure she's still there. "Leslie—"

"I'm told the penetration test is going well," she says, finally.

He feels dizzy. Mouth gone cottony. "Yeah. Yes. Everything at the Lodge is squared away. We got the new pod in—"

"They're already doing their job. Now do yours. Clean up the mess."

Then the line goes dead.

PART THREE

THE STØRM

CHAPTER 20

The Calm Before

The part of the Hunting Lodge they're pretty sure doesn't have cameras is around the far side, just past the lap pool and the basketball court—there's this small section where the fence goes wide to accommodate a heap of three boulders. Above the boulders stands a big, leaning leafy tree—Wade calls it a "tulip tree," and then he adds before anybody can ask, "Is it really a surprise that an old man likes to garden now and again?"

The cameras mounted on the fences have a wide sweep, but the two on each side fail to get as far as this far corner. The whole place is rigged with bugs, too, but so far, nothing here. Other hackers hang here sometimes, but whenever the Zeroes get free time at the end of a day, they reconvene here. Dipesh confirms for them that he's never seen any bugs here—and he says he's hacked the cameras to see, and, sure enough, they never quite get far enough.

They meet here every day. All of them except Reagan.

On Day 29, they get let out of their individual pods early, at 3 P.M., to have some "rec time," as Hollis puts it, because tomorrow, he says, it's time for what he calls the Pressure Cooker. Means they're transitioning. Moving from individual tasks—which has pretty much been a month of penetration tests for an unholy host of companies spanning the gamut—to pod missions. Working as a team for the first time.

Chance is frankly amazed he's still here. Like, he's not a Christian so much as he's an occasional churchgoer who likes crackers and grape juice, but being here for damn near thirty days has been nothing short of a bona fide miracle. He's about ready to handle some snakes, build an ark, cut a couple of babies (or at least baby dolls) in half.

He heads out with the pod. Wade, as always, trails behind, off in his own world a little bit. He mostly sits back, listens, offers commentary that ping-pongs between grumpy and jokey, and otherwise doesn't contribute much. The core trio is Aleena, Chance, and DeAndre.

At the boulders, they clamber up onto their individual perches. DeAndre grabs a chip of stone from the base of one rock and then, on the turtle-shaped center boulder, finds their markings and adds another hash. "Almost at thirty days," he says. "Just another 335 to go after that."

Wade growls: "And then they double-tap each of us and throw our bodies into a ravine somewhere." He draws a deep, satisfied breath. "The sweet release of death."

"Man, shut up," DeAndre says. "They're not gonna *kill* us."

"How do you think this works?" Wade asks. "We wash their dirty laundry and then get to walk away and go back to our various legal deviancies? We're not operatives. We're not soldiers they've spent time grooming. We're assets. Cards you play and then burn so that nobody else can play them. Mark my words: we're dead hackers walking."

DeAndre just rolls his eyes. "Pssh, whatever." He turns to the other two. "Hey, I got something."

"Me first," Aleena says, smiling big.

"Why you gotta jump in my grave?"

"Because I'm small and quick. Guess what happened?"

Chance interrupts: "Hey, whoa, hell no—you two always do this. *I'm* going first with the news this time because it's not gonna be half as impressive as what the two of you have and I always end up being the big old yawn at the end of the story."

DeAndre and Aleena share a look. She laughs—a rare sound, but Chance is hearing it more and more, and then she looks at Chance and he thinks: *Wait, hold on, is she giving me eyes?* He's never sure.

Then, as always, it's gone as soon as it arrives. She says, almost coldly, "Go on."

His pulse kicking in his neck like a wild horse, he swallows hard and says, "Sarno's missing."

DeAndre's face wrinkles up like a deflated basketball. "Who's Sarno?"

"Man, really? You guys don't even listen to me at all, do you."

It's Wade that jumps in—he's sitting over on the farthest rock, whittling a stick with a sharp stone. "Sarno's the self-help guru. Chance actually managed that pen test."

"That's right," Chance says. That one was slow-pitch, but they've been getting harder. Aleena getting him the phone helped—they monitor the calls, of course, so it's not like he can go ringing up the *Citizen-Times* newspaper or MSNBC or whatever, but either way, sometimes it's nice to just *talk* to somebody. And he's amazed how much people will tell him after a few small lies. Wade told him: *You know, this is how the old-school hackers did it half the time. Wasn't about toolkits and programming tricks. They called up people at the phone company or banks or wherever, and got them to give away passwords, account numbers, personal data. Hacking isn't always about hacking systems, son. Sometimes it's about hacking people.*

Of course, even with hacking people, he's still barely hanging on—he's lucky if he nets a C grade. Usually he's in the D range. Still. He isn't dead yet.

"Sarno's missing," Aleena says. "I don't know if that's connected to . . . any of this."

"He some kinda big deal?" DeAndre asks.

Aleena nods. "Bestselling author. Had a TV show back in . . . 2005? I remember watching it when I got home from high school. It was like *Oprah,* but worse. I think his star's been falling for a while. Like, he's a joke now."

Wade, again: "How'd you figure out he was missing?"

"That's the funky bit," Chance says. "I was pen-testing this company called BrightFlow—they're all about predictive search queries. Making more efficient search engines and stuff."

DeAndre snaps his fingers. "This little search engine start-up called Glassboat has a partnership with them. Or did, anyway."

"Well," Chance continues, "one of the programming team members of BrightFlow is this guy, Bryan Sarno. I thought, huh, okay, Sarno, I know that name. So I did a little digging—called up their front desk, and the receptionist didn't wanna tell me anything but I pretended I was a distraught relative and hinted at there being a death in the family, and I dropped the name Alan, said, *Alan gave me this number, said you'd help me.* And then I heard her gasp."

"Because Alan went missing."

"Uh-huh. She said, *You talked to Alan?* She told me that sure enough, he went missing about six months ago. And his brother, Bryan, died from a heart attack." A pause. "Faulty pacemaker, apparently."

They all take a moment to hover over that. "I don't know what the hell it means," DeAndre finally says. "Or if it even matters."

"It matters," Chance says. "It has to, man. Has to."

DeAndre laughs. "You just wanna be part of the Scooby Gang, is all."

"Damn right I do! I'll be Thelma. Is it Thelma with the bowl cut and the turtleneck? Just let me in the Mystery Machine."

"It's *Velma,*" Aleena corrects. "Velma Dinkley."

"She had a last name?" DeAndre asks.

"They all did. Velma Dinkley, Shaggy Rogers, Fred Jones, Daphne Blake."

"Are we seriously talking about *Scooby-Fucking-Doo*?" Wade asks. He inches closer, tosses the stick and rock over his shoulder. "Pay attention, nerdlingers, come on. Think! All this nonsense isn't nonsense. It's connected somehow. Don't you get the feeling that we're not pen-testing individual companies but something much bigger?"

Chance thinks he's right. He doesn't understand it all, but he's right. Aleena nods too, says: "We can't see the bigger picture yet. But something does connect it all."

"Ring around the roses," Wade says.

"Be nice if we knew what Reagan has seen," Chance says.

"Forget her," Aleena says. "She's Shane's little puppy now."

"Check it," DeAndre says, lifting his chin in a gesture. They follow his gaze and, sure enough, there's Reagan and Shane. Off toward the Ziggurat. Watching them.

"Smile and wave," Aleena says. They all do, giving obnoxious little finger-waggle waves, the kind that Reagan so often gives them. "And three . . . two . . . one . . ." They all turn their waving hands into middle fingers.

DeAndre nods. "I'm gonna find out what's in that bitch-ass folder. The one from that German geothermal company." He bites his lower lip. "That thing's shut up tighter than a goat's asshole around a couple of hillbillies, but damn if I did not figure out a way to crack that motherfucker when I was trying—and failing—to sleep last night." He grins big. "That's my news, by the way. Tomorrow, I'm gonna crack it. And y'all is gonna cover for me since we'll be in the same room and all."

Aleena says: "Now you jumped in *my* grave."

"Was mine to begin with."

"It's fine. My news is better."

"Oh?"

"Oh."

She lowers her voice. "The Widow contacted me again."

Ø Ø Ø

"The plan still the plan?" Reagan asks.

Shane stares out over the basketball court. He's got this look on his face, this thousand-yard stare. As if he's watching the Zeroes but also staring straight through them. He says in a flat, quiet voice, "We can't get to Dalton like we did before because, if I'm being honest, your skills aren't up to snuff."

"The little terrorist twat is tricky." She *hmm*s. "That's a helluva tongue twister, isn't it? Terrorist twat is tricky. Terrorist twat is tricky. Teowwist trot is twicky—"

"She's not just tricky, she's good. She's *skilled*. Aleena Kattan is no bullshit. She—herself, all by her lonesome—executed a merciless, ongoing denial-of-service attack on the Baathist government of Syria. She's exposed a dozen or more honor killers, rapists, kidnappers. She flattens firewalls like they're made of aluminum foil, granting Net access to protesters and rebels. She's the real deal, Reagan. Show some fucking respect."

"Oooh. Aren't we a little *tetchy*."

He gives her a look sharp as a pair of scalpels. "Aleena blocked our access to Chance, but we can use her against him just the same. It'll just take a deeper hack. The kind you're really good at."

She is. She knows she is. So far, her time here has been about penetrating systems and testing them for their weaknesses—but, truth is, she *much* prefers doing that to people, instead. Poking at them with sharp sticks until they yelp. And she and Shane do have some sticks sharpened to damning points.

"I gotta know," she says. "Why do you have such a hard-on for Dalton?"

"He's a poser. An amateur pretending to be a professional."

"You sure it's not that he took some spotlight in your absence? Maybe that . . . chafes your ball-bag a little bit?"

Shane wheels on her. "It's not just about that. It's about

bigger things. There's a design at work. And this is part of it. This is—"

From not far away comes the sound of weeping. Reagan turns, cranes her neck, sees Miranda and Dipesh walking up. It's Dipesh that's crying. They head down toward the empty basketball court. Reagan watches Miranda try to pull Dipesh into an embrace, but he pulls away, then buries his face in his hands and begins pacing in erratic circles.

"Someone must've pissed in his—"

Dipesh yells—a roar of frustration and rage through the tears.

"—curry," she finishes.

"Some hackers can't hack it," Shane says. "C'mon. I have something to show you."

Ø Ø Ø

Chance, Aleena, and DeAndre hop down off the rocks and head away from the boulders, toward Dipesh. Wade remains behind on the rock, watching as if he's a spectator at a sporting event.

"Yo, hey, Dipesh Mode," DeAndre says, jogging forward. "What's wrong, man?"

Miranda holds up a hand and shakes her head. Her smile is strained. "We're okay. Really." Then, to Dipesh: "Come, Dipesh."

Chance approaches from the other side, puts a hand on Dipesh's shoulder. "It's all right, dude. Whatever it is, just let it all hang out. No judgment here, brother."

Aleena hangs back, shifting uncomfortably from foot to foot. Chance gives her a look, tries to do that thing where you psychically convey a message: *You okay?* She must get enough of it, because she gives an awkward nod, then looks away.

Dipesh stands up straight. Fishes out a mealy tissue from his jeans, blows his nose. Wipes his eyes with it, too. "Thanks, guys," he says, his words sticky. "It means a lot."

Miranda puts her arm around him and he leans his head on her shoulder. He stares out, not *at* anyone, but rather, over them. Miranda says: "It's just been a hard day."

A bitter bark from Dipesh. "Hard day?"

"What happened, D?" DeAndre asks.

"We can't talk about it," Miranda says just as Dipesh opens his mouth.

"Miranda, we have to tell them."

"Don't make things hard," she pleads. Her voice cracks and some emotion bleeds in, too. "Today was hard enough, like you said."

Chance and DeAndre share looks. Chance says, "I gotta admit, I'm a bit lost."

"You'll see," Dipesh says. "You start your pod missions, right? You'll see."

Miranda starts to pull Dipesh away.

"Who is Typhon?" Aleena asks.

Miranda and Dipesh halt, shell-shocked by the question. Deer in the headlights of an onrushing Peterbilt.

Aleena asks it again. Louder this time. "Who is Typhon?"

Miranda says, almost sadly: "We don't know."

"But we want to find out," Dipesh says.

And then they really are gone. They whirl away, the unanswered question lingering.

Suddenly, Wade's off the boulder and with them, too. He grunts at them: "Dinnertime, kiddies."

Ø Ø Ø

Shane runs his key card through the slider next to the door, which pops open with a hiss. Reagan enters, reverent. Shane's cabin is like a palace. A temple. *A place worthy of awe*. The rest of the cabins at the Hunting Lodge are nice enough, she guesses: simple, utilitarian. But Graves's cabin? Decked. The. Fuck. Out.

First, he lives alone. Like, nobody else here but him. And

he has an access card that allows him entrance. Nobody else gets that. *Nobody*.

Then, he's got a bed in the loft. A flat-screen TV downstairs with a video game console hooked up ("Last gen," he says somewhat disappointedly, like a rich kid who has to play with last year's toys). A small couch (white pleather, ugly as a sun-bleached whale carcass) sits across from it, and next to the couch is a mini-fridge. Full of water, soda, lunch meat, shit like that. Posters on the walls show movies from the eighties and nineties. Some popular (*Ghostbusters, Gremlins 2,* and, of course, *Fight Club*), some obscure (*The Osterman Weekend, Robotrix, Lost Highway*).

But the real kicker? He has a laptop. All his own. It's not connected to any network, so it can't reach outside the Hunting Lodge, but nobody else is afforded the privilege. Giving a laptop to a jailed hacker is like giving any other prisoner a hunting knife, some rope, and a loaded shotgun. (When she first saw that he had it, he remarked: "Ironic, because if I had gone the other way—taken my chances with the legal system—they would've banned me from using a computer for ten, maybe twenty years.")

Two of Shane's crew are on the couch, playing some racing game. One of the Need for Speed titles, she guesses. They've probably been in here all day. The one is Daryl Scafidi, aka "the Warlock": he's a thick-necked halfwit with acne scars so bad Reagan teases him that if he's not careful NASA will try to land on him, plant a flag. Next to him sits the LARPer: Shiro, the Tokyo-born goth who online—and often in person, particularly when he's role-playing—goes by Kuei-Jin Orochi, White Worm of Hokkaido. Both turds.

"Shandor, 'sup," Scafidi says, lifting a fist over his head as Shane passes. Shane ignores the fist bump and keeps walking. Reagan loves that about him: he *so* doesn't give a shit. And the more he ignores his own pod, the more they *love him for it*.

"Get out," Shane says finally.

Scafidi looks to Reagan and says, "You heard the man."

Reagan makes a V out of her index and middle finger, then waggles her tongue in the space between them. Scafidi makes a face like he just caught a glimpse of *2 Girls 1 Cup,* then goes back to his game.

Shane, voice louder: "I mean you, Warlock. You too, Shiro."

The two of them scoot past Reagan on the way out. She bites her lip and makes a lusty face at them as they hurry by. "Scurry, little mice, or I'll gobble you up," she says. "Nnnngh."

"You're fucked up, Stolper," Shane says, going to the desk on which his computer sits. He opens a drawer, riffles through it.

"So, what's the deal?" Reagan asks. "How do you manage all this stuff? You can give up the ghost. I'm on your side by now, you know that."

He pauses. "The hacks need things. I get them things."

"Like, what, you buy them beer? Nudie mags?"

"Jesus Christ, Stolper, no. Take Roach, for instance. Roach is going through a bad divorce. Apocalyptically bad. She's making all kinds of accusations about him—which, you know, are true, because James Roach is a scumbag. But Roach needed a little counterbalance, so I hacked his wife's accounts, found out she's been cheating on him with her boss. Or—consider our minder, Rivera. You actually see much of Rivera?"

She shakes her head. "Nope. Just at mealtimes. And I think he jerks off in the supply closet near the rec room."

"He leaves us alone because I'm getting him *paid.* Shiro hacked a few cryptocurrencies—Simoleons, Spec-Coin, Chimpcharge—and cashed out in Rivera's name. Now Rivera doesn't even *look* in our general direction. I could kick a puppy and he'd look the other way."

Reagan shrugs. "You're the king. What can I say."

"I have to be. Like I said: bigger designs at work." He walks up, slaps a USB key into her hand. "Tonight, dinner. Get this into Dalton's pocket."

"Uhhh." She snort-laughs. "How am I supposed to do that? I'm not a master thief."

"Just get it in his pocket. You do that, you're in."

"I'm in?"

He nods and gives her an odious half smile, a look that conjures a sense of disappointment in the ugly compromise he's making. "I'll get you in my pod, yeah."

Bingo.

CHAPTER 21

The Trap

Aleena is in line with her tray. Chance is behind her, and DeAndre is off "draining the dragon" (his words, not hers). Wade is sitting down because he likes to wait till everyone else is done, then take his sweet time picking food.

It seems like there's a pall hanging over the cafeteria. Some dark, invisible thread she can't quite tease out. Maybe it's Dipesh. There's not even a hundred people here in this room—some news travels fast. Though, they're also a secretive, hush-hush bunch, so maybe not. Still, Dipesh, Miranda, and the rest of their pod are absent. Their normal table sits empty—a notable absence that has a kind of black hole gravity to it.

It's affecting her, too. So many things going on inside her head. There's an excitement—*the Widow of Zheng contacted me*. There's fear—*I don't know what's going on at home, or with Qasim, or with the protests*. There's . . . something else. And there she looks back and sees Chance just behind her in line and he gives her a smile and she gives him a smile, *but then* she frowns because she doesn't want him to think she likes him. (*You don't like him.* This she repeats, a strange mantra.)

That's when she feels it. A hand. Right on her ass. She thinks: *It's Chance.* A spike of anger lances through her and she wheels around and sees Shane Graves standing there. Lips puckered in a cheeky smirk. "I know you want it," he says.

"Get your hand off my ass," she growls. She reaches down, grabs Shane's wrist—

And a tray comes out of nowhere, hits Shane square in the face. A cob of corn and a burger pinwheel in the air.

Graves staggers back and Chance presses the attack, raising the tray again.

"That's your freebie," Shane snarls—just as Reagan passes behind him, hot-stepping out of the way. Graves kicks out with a leg. The heel of his foot snaps hard into Chance's knee. Chance howls. Then he plants the wounded leg back and brings the tray down again upon Shane's head.

That's the last hit Chance gets. At that point, Shane takes Chance apart with the mercilessness of a butcher. He knows some kind of martial art—what looks to Aleena like Krav Maga. He stabs out with the flat of his hand, catches Chance right in the throat. A knee to the side. A knee to the groin. Then he throws Chance into a table—which flips over, knocking the book Wade was reading up into the air.

Aleena reaches behind her, grabs the fork off the tray. A voice inside her makes clear what's going to happen next: *I'm going to kill Shane Graves.*

That's a curious thing, that thought, because she's wanted to kill people before but not quite this viscerally—and not in a way where she could really *act* on it so fast. She steps toward Shane—who has his back to her—and twirls the fork so the tines face down—

Reagan steps in front of her.

"Move," Aleena hisses.

"Not now," Reagan hisses. "The hacks are coming."

"Reagan, get out of my—"

Reagan holds up a key card. "You want Shane? I'm in. But you gotta sit still for now and"—she gently plucks the fork out of Aleena's hand—"stand. Down."

And then: boom. The hacks are in the room. Roach grabs Chance just as he starts to get up, throws him back against the table. Metzger steps in front of Shane, waggles a finger, says, "Nuh-uh, sweetheart."

Aleena feels gutted. Like she could've acted—*should've* acted—and didn't. But then, in another moment straight from Bizarro World, Reagan is shouting and pointing at Shane. "He's got a weapon! Back pocket!"

Things feel slippery, topsy-turvy, when Metzger spins Shane around and begins to pat him down. Shane protests and gives Reagan a look that has fangs.

"Hey, what's this, Graves?" Metzger says. She pulls a USB key from his back pocket.

Suddenly the rest of Graves's pod is there—stepping up, yelling, shouting. The rest of the hackers start yelling, too. It's chaos, like something out of a primate house at a zoo—everyone smells blood in the air and the coppery tang has them thrashing against the bars of their cages. Aleena watches, dazed and confused, as one of Graves's pod—Daryl something or other, she thinks they call him Warlock—rushes Roach and gets a Taser in the gut. He shakes like an epileptic, piggy-squealing as he drops.

Reagan hooks Aleena's arm in her own. "Now's our chance, c'mon."

And Aleena is dragged along for the ride.

Ø Ø Ø

Chance struggles. Elbows out, legs kicking, anything to make it harder for them to drag him back down through the woods. But halfway to the springhouse, Roach has the others hold him up as he grabs Chance's hand—or, rather, grabs all four fingers and straightens them out just before bending them back. Pain like an arc of lightning goes from Chance's hand to his shoulders. "Quit thrashing around like a fish," Roach growls, "or I'll break these. Gonna be a lot harder to do all your typing with a hand full of broken fingers, yeah?"

Chance nods. "I'll stop. I'll stop."

"Good." Roach nods to Chen and another guard—this one a strip of human beef jerky named Ashbaugh—and they carry him back down the forest trail.

"Look at the footage," Chance says. "Shane attacked Aleena. You'll see. You'll see, c'mon. And God, he was beating my ass and—" He hears the desperation in his voice, each word corroded by fear.

Suddenly they're at the springhouse. Door open. They don't drop him by the chair. They take him to the Dep. Chance tries to scrabble for the door, but Roach kicks him in the side.

The other two open up the Dep. The seal pops. A wet smell tinged with chlorine fills the air. Ashbaugh grins. "You know they use these in Guantánamo? On high-value suspects. Cool, huh."

Roach pops his Taser, fires one into Chance's chest. Everything goes full-tilt pinball.

Roach says, "I think given our last meeting in here, it's time to go right to twelve hours. Don't you think, Chen?"

Chen just laughs.

They toss Chance in and close the top over him. It drops, pops, and locks. And suddenly he's alone with himself, the water, and the darkness.

Chance screams.

Ø Ø Ø

DeAndre comes back from the bathroom, finds the cafeteria in disarray. A handful of chairs overturned. A table, too. Food is splattered around and the Lodge janitor—big flabby guy named Pike—is lazily pushing a mop.

Wade sits on one chair, has his feet up on another. He's reading a book. *Watership Down.*

"The hell happened in here, man?" DeAndre asks.

Wade shrugs. "Some kind of pissing match, the ramifications and permutations of which remain blissfully hidden to my old eyes."

"Man, whatever."

Wade goes back to reading.

Ø Ø Ø

Hollis sits across from Shane Graves. It's just the two of them.

"Shane Graves," Copper says. "I do not believe we've been formally introduced."

The hacker sits there, arms folded across his chest like an impudent child. "We haven't met, but I do my homework, Agent Copper of the FBI. Ex-wife: Shiree. Son: Kyle. Been in the Bureau for . . . thirty years? I haven't even *turned* thirty yet."

"Next year, though."

"Hm?"

"Next year. You turn thirty."

"Yeah. That's right."

"I liked my thirties. I feel like I really grew up in my thirties," Copper says. "Feels like you know yourself. Know what you want. Know just who you are."

Shane sneers. "I already know who I am, thanks."

"I know who you are, too. I can do my homework. I know you're a wet-nosed punk who thinks he's some kind of celebrity. Getting on YouTube and showing people how you hack into airplanes and insulin pumps and all that shit."

"Vimeo. Not YouTube."

"I give a shit. I know you. I've seen you. Rich white kid who's somehow convinced himself he's the underdog. Just you against the world. Daddy was a cheat. Mommy was a pillhead. Makes you mad. So you go out, do your thing, pretending you're some kind of iconoclast hero, some champion of the common man when really, *really,* all you're interested in is getting high off your own shit-stink. Meanwhile, you start gathering enemies. Because you're like a stage magician who decides to expose the magic tricks of your fellow *illusionists.*"

"I just speak truth to power." Shane shrugs. "People don't like it when you show them how vulnerable they are."

"Is that what you're doing?"

"Everything's connected, Copper. Every day we plug another part of our lives into the grid. We have *refrigerators* that connect to the Internet, for fuck's sake. People fill those refrigerators using handheld Wi-Fi scanners from their favorite big online retailer, and all that stuff talks to each other. Your thermostat talks to your smoke detector which talks to your phone which talks to a thousand different things, and each of them talks to a thousand more, and soon you start to realize how your fucking garage opener is connected to the stock market by a very tenuous string of ones and zeroes, bits and bytes, and all I have to do is jump into the stream somewhere."

Hollis blinks. Fakes a yawn. "I gotta be honest, I faded out there in the middle."

"You should pay better attention. Everything is connected to everything else. Like a spider's web. Pluck a thread on one end? The spider feels it on the other. Twenty years ago, Copper, no way I would be able to tell you that I saw what happened at Fellhurst."

A cold knife, invisible, slides into Hollis. His fingers and toes tingle. Every part of him wants to panic. Instead he just tightens his jaw. "What?"

"Fellhurst, Agent Copper."

"I don't know Fellhurst."

"I'm pretty sure you do." Shane smiles. "I know what you did there. I know what you did to that woman. I know that it wasn't long after Fellhurst that your wife left you. I know that your performance reviews after Fellhurst went *up,* not *down*—indicative of throwing yourself into your work. Driven by guilt, maybe. Or maybe because you got a secret thrill, you sick fucking—"

Hollis stabs out with a hand, catches Shane's throat. He squeezes. Shane starts to flail, hands into fists, but already the FBI agent has his pistol out and the gun pressed against Shane's breastbone. "Shut up. Stop moving."

The tension doesn't leave Shane's body, but the fight does.

"You don't know rat shit from a rubber hose," Copper seethes. His face feels hot. He lets go of Shane's neck, pushes him back into his chair, then sits back into his own, holstering his Glock.

Shane, stung, wounded, rubs the skin around his neck. Already Hollis can see the gears turning behind the hacker's eyes. This one's got an eye for vengeance. Best to cut his legs out from under him.

Hollis pounds on the wall next to him. Shane gives a quizzical look, but understands soon enough when the door to Copper's office—er, "office"—opens up and Rivera steps inside. Rivera's a field gone to seed. He's ex-DEA out of Tucson. Unshaven. Hollis isn't sure what Golathan has on him. But it doesn't matter.

"Finally," Rivera says. "I can handle my own pod, Copper."

"Not anymore you can't."

"What?"

"You're done. You get to go home."

"Shut up and quit fuckin' with me, Copper." Rivera laughs, but it's a nervous laugh, a stuttering *heh-heh-heh.* "You're not my boss, *brother.*"

"No, but Golathan is, and turns out even *he* isn't willing to turn a blind eye to you doing absolutely not one iota of your job these days. So pack your shit. You leave tonight. Metzger will drive you to the Allentown airport. Also, so you know, the agency put a hold on your bank account to examine it for untoward criminal activity. Seems someone's been hacking money into your account—surely as some sort of ploy to incriminate you, since I know you'd never *willingly* accept bribes. Right? Good news is, they'll shut that account down and clean all of that naughty hacker money out of it."

Rivera's eyes squeeze shut in a flare of anger. He's about to speak, but Copper gets ahead of that:

"I wouldn't say anything more except 'thank you.' Thank you, Agent Copper, for doing your job and exposing those who would have done me harm."

Through gritted teeth, Rivera says: "Thank you, Agent Copper."

"Good. Now scoot."

And then Rivera's gone. Leaving Copper and Graves alone once more.

Shane licks his lips. Chuckles a little. "That's cool. Rivera was weak meat. I like a challenge."

"A challenge. I'm glad you said that, because, like they say on those infomercials, *but wait, there's more*." From his pocket, Copper pulls out the USB drive taken off Shane. "A list of all the guards here. Spreadsheets showing their bank account numbers and home addresses and other bits of pertinent data."

"I . . . took that off Chance."

"Chance Dalton? Who couldn't hack a candy bar in half?"

"I hear he's doing better."

"Just the same, this is naughty business, Shane. If you were anybody else you'd be washing out to some supermax prison right now. But you're not. Golathan likes you. He reminds me that you aren't like anyone else here. You *wanted* to be here. You offered yourself up to us." He sees Shane shift uncomfortably in his seat. "Trying to get away from those enemies I was talking about?"

"I'm just a proud American."

"Well, now you're a proud American who really is like everyone else."

"I don't follow."

"I'm balancing the books with you. Taking away all your tricks and treats. All your little luxuries. Now you get to return to the basic privileges everyone else has. And the guards will be told about what you had on that USB drive."

"You're making a mistake."

"Am I? Is that a threat?"

"Just a statement." Graves hesitates. "This is a ploy. Reagan Stolper is doing me dirty. You check right now. Check my cabin. I'll bet she's there."

Hollis shrugs. He turns around, pulls up his computer. Takes him a few awkward minutes to figure out how to pull up the camera feeds and navigate to them—at first he feels a little embarrassed, but then he notices how it's agitating Graves. Copper once read that when people watch other people make mistakes often their own brains react as if it's *them* making the mistakes—they internalize the errors of others. Owning the mistakes personally. And it makes them uncomfortable, embarrassed, frustrated. So Hollis delays a little, dicks around, opens solitaire, pretends he doesn't know what he's doing. Finally, he gets around to opening the camera feeds.

The camera pointing to and inside Shane's cabin is just static.

"See?" Graves says.

Copper shrugs. "Malfunctioning cameras. What a shame."

Ø Ø Ø

Reagan swipes the card. Shane's cabin pops open.

Aleena hesitates.

"Hey, Kardashian," Reagan hisses. "Come *on*."

"I don't know why you keep calling me that. The Kardashians are hot."

"They're not. Okay, Kim's *kinda* hot. But that one sister looks like a shaved Wookiee. She's basically a giant thumb with a wig."

"So you're saying I'm ugly."

"No, I'm saying I have a stupid-ass nickname for you that means essentially nothing except I keep using it because it upsets you. Are we seriously talking about this? Jesus, *c'mon*." Reagan grabs Aleena and pulls her in.

"What is all this?" Aleena asks, looking around.

Over by a laptop, Reagan says, "These are the thousand luxuries of Ivo Shandor."

"No, I mean, what's *this*? What's your angle? Why am I even here with you? You hate us. You're a horrible monster."

For a moment, Reagan actually looks stung. Then she frowns and waves it away. "I'm helping us."

"Are you helping us or hurting Shane?"

"Ennnnh, six to*may*toes one way, half a dozen to*mah*toes the other way."

"Are the cameras really off?"

Reagan nods. "Dumb-ass gave me a cryptophone to shut them off."

"Are you just setting me up?"

"Not this time."

"I don't believe you."

Reagan shows her teeth like a cornered animal. "God, fuck, can you just help me over here? The guy's got a laptop, a drawer full of USB drives, another drawer with a handful of fucking Floydphones. Shane Graves has had it too good for too long. Thinks he's David Blaine or some shit. So he can go piss up a flagpole."

Hesitantly, Aleena steps farther into the cabin. She's half afraid that at any second some comically large iron cage is going to drop over her, but she admits curiosity. She steps forward, opens one drawer, and sees the USB keys. Opens the other drawer, and sure enough: black matte phones. Cryptophones. No carriers. Entirely encrypted. Hacker treasure.

"Is this why you've been messing with Chance?" she asks Reagan.

"The answer is more complex than 'yes,' but for now, sure."

Aleena feels a faint shudder in her feet a few seconds before she hears footsteps on the planks outside. She throws Reagan an angry look, but Reagan is already grabbing her shoulder and pulling her down behind the desk. "Get down!"

Chen and Ashbaugh slink by—Chen laughing, *haw-*

haw-haw, Ashbaugh's words muted, but it sounds like he's telling a story or maybe a joke. They stop in front of Shane's cabin. Aleena can only make out a few words: . . . *believe . . . shit Graves . . . ? . . . punk owns us.* Then, more clearly: *He's Copper's problem now.* Her blood turns to an icy river when Chen says: *We should go take his stuff.*

The door starts to rattle.

Ashbaugh: *Cameras, Chen. Cameras. You want Copper on your ass, too?*

Chen is again all *heh-heh haw-haw, oh yeah okay,* and then the footsteps retreat until they can't be heard any longer.

Aleena presses her thumbs in her eyes so hard she sees blue stars smearing across her vision. "That was scary."

Reagan stands, says, "Scary? Don't you, like, hack tyrannical governments and mess with terrorist organizations and whatever?"

"Yes. But this is different. That's . . . distant. This is personal. They catch me . . ." She feels tears hot at the edges of her eyes. "They catch me, I don't know what happens to my family. What happens if they catch you, Reagan?"

There's a moment of quiet between them. Uncomfortable, tense, uncertain. Reagan finally shrugs and says, "Nothing. I got nothing to lose, nobody to love. And I like it that way." But the way she says it, Aleena isn't so sure.

"Graves is going to go to war with us over this."

A manic smile spreads across Reagan's face. "I know. But it won't matter."

"Why is that?"

She holds up his laptop. "Because he's going to help us escape."

CHAPTER 22

Tick-Tock

Golathan checks his watch. 10:15 P.M. Night's gotten its claws in. The building here is mostly empty. He sits in his office, feeling tension coil around his neck and shoulder muscles like a python.

Then his monitor goes from dark to light. And there on his screen is Leslie Cilicia-Ceto.

"Leslie," Golathan says. "Was beginning to think you weren't going to call."

Her smile is pinched—the smile of a tired, suspicious woman. "I apologize. Caught up in diagnostics."

"Typhon," he says—a question by way of a statement, a question to which he already knows the answer.

Her pinched smile relaxes slightly. So, yes: Typhon.

"Leslie, I should be there. I need to be on-site. I need a demonstration."

"We're almost there. Patience, Ken."

Off-screen where she can't see, he wraps a hand around a stapler and squeezes. He has a momentary fantasy where the stapler crushes up like an empty Coke can. He sucks air between his teeth and says, "Leslie, I like to think I've been patient. But we're about a hundred miles past that. I've got people perched on my back like rabid monkeys, and they're all chattering for bananas or blood. I need some bananas, Leslie, or I gotta give them blood. Which means I need to do a site visit, and I need to see what's going on there." He lowers his voice. "The thing with that mess in Beallsville—"

"Was an error," she interrupts. "And I'm thankful you corrected it."

"A cop *died*. Other cops don't just look the other way when one of the boys in blue gets got. They will continue to kick the shadows till something squeals."

"Nothing will squeal. Everything is buttoned up. Thanks, in part, to you."

"Leslie, is Typhon not working?"

She opens her mouth but then closes it again, as if thinking better of what she was about to say. "Typhon is operational. But a real test, a *true* test—"

"We're not doing that. You have the environment to test. We've given you as much as we can, Leslie. The Hunting Lodge—"

"Has been invaluable." Another interruption. It's not really like her—she seems agitated tonight. Normally she's as placid as a mountain lake. "In fact, I am willing to predict that the Lodge's purpose will soon be fulfilled."

"The penetration test is complete?"

"Almost. Collectively they've uncovered far more vulnerabilities than we had imagined—and with each discovery, the castle grows stronger. Typhon is already smart, but I am happy to know that the system is also safe. So thank you for that."

"I need to do a site visit, Leslie. Soon."

She nods. "I know. Soon! I promise. I just don't want to show you a program operating at eighty percent. I want to show you the butterfly, not the chrysalis."

"Two weeks is all you get."

"Three," she says. At times like this the faint chirp of

her British accent just makes her sound all the snootier. "I think . . . yes, three weeks should be about right. I anticipate that is when the Lodge project will be complete."

Two weeks is already too long, Golathan knows. People don't know what Typhon even *is* at this point. He's been keeping it that way on purpose. If there's something he's learned—and it's something that applies particularly well to the NSA—people tend to object more to plans than they do to executions. Tell somebody you're going to build an addition to the house and they're likely to find a reason to balk. But show them one in progress or, even better, already done? It's as if reality asserts itself in their minds and they just go with it. His wife always says, "Better to ask for forgiveness than permission." It's how he sees Typhon—just get it done, have something to show, and everyone will applaud. But tell them about Typhon? Describe the *plans*? They'll throw him in some far-flung black site prison quick as lightning.

The burden of the patriot, he thinks. Doing things for his country, a country he loves deeply, that the country might not easily support. Nobody wants to hear about torture or war or prisons, but the gears need to turn, and blood lubricates them.

He breathes a sigh of acquiescence. "Fine. Three weeks. No more."

"Thank you, Ken."

"How's your husband?"

"Simon is fine," she says. "And how is Winifred?"

He tenses up. "You mean Susan."

"Susan. Yes. Of course."

Ken narrows his gaze. "She's good. Thanks."

They exchange a few more pleasantries—it all feels more than a little hollow, an act of artifice—and then the call is over. But he can't get over that. Winifred.

His wife is Susan. At least, that's what everyone calls her. But on her birth certificate, it damn sure says Winifred. A fact she tells absolutely no one because she hates the name—not only does she think it sounds too "old-ladyish," but the grandmother she's named after was, according to Susan, a crotchety old cat lady whom everyone hated. Winifred is a name even their own children don't know.

That means Leslie is spying. Poking, prodding. At him! *And his family.*

And maybe, just maybe, she's using Typhon to do it.

CHAPTER 23

Dark Water

Chance goes through the same stages as anybody who goes into the Dep. First ten, fifteen minutes, he screams and thrashes. Tries to kick it open. Shove the door. Absurd, impossible thoughts strike him like a bell: *I could break the sides. Maybe the hinges are weak. The water gives added pressure and so maybe . . .*

None of it makes much sense. None of it works.

He screams for Hollis. Then for his friends. Are they his friends? He's starting to think so. He hasn't had many friends in a while. Hasn't done *well* with friends. Not since Pete. He doesn't want to think about that.

He screams himself hoarse.

For a while, the darkness here in the tank is just that: darkness. But over time it takes on new qualities. Even as his eyes adjust there's nothing to see, no light creeping in, no patterns to discern, and so his mind finds patterns. Shifting, bleeding shapes. Like Celtic knotwork twisting in the space above his head. Worms squirming against other worms. Forming letters and numbers, some that exist, some that don't. Sideways-8, the lemniscate. Gibberish code. Programming code. Code he doesn't understand because it's not even real, it's like something out of *The Matrix* that he doesn't have the gift to discern.

The water is warm, but cold at the same time. He floats there in the tank and soon it feels like the whole tank is floating with him. Everything in zero G.

He sees bugs that aren't there. Feels something swimming underneath him.

Then, outside the tank, someone knocks. He tells himself: *That's not real, either.*

But then a voice comes through. "You in there, Dalton?" It's Copper.

Chance almost laughs. His voice sounds like his vocal cords have been run over coarse sandpaper when he says: "Who else would it be? Please, please get me outta here, dude, I can't—" *I can't stay in here any longer.*

"I'm gonna get you out of there, relax. I'm waiting on the key."

"Thank God."

"Don't thank God. Thank Hollis Copper, FBI."

"Thank you, Agent. Thank you." He turns his face toward the side of the chamber. "How long have I been in here?"

"About three hours." Copper's voice comes from the other side of the chamber this time. *Damn, this thing is messing with my head.* Chance rolls back to the other side. "Something we gotta talk about, though, Dalton."

"Sorry, I'm busy right now." When Copper doesn't answer right away, Chance quickly adds, "That was just a joke."

"But this isn't a joke, son. This is about that night. You owe a debt. You owe a debt to Angela Slattery."

The water all around Chance seems to go cold. The darkness seems to grow bigger, meaner. "I don't know Angela Slattery."

"Uh-huh. You don't remember her at all, huh? You had two classes with her, Dalton. British Literature and what was the other one?"

Chemistry. With Mr. Kreider. Kreider, who gave them a speech on the first day of class about how the biology teacher, Miss Moore, wouldn't teach creationism but he thought that was horse hockey, because the Lord created the Earth and . . .

"I don't know her," Chance says. Voice quiet. Copper shouldn't even hear him, but he hears the agent laugh.

"Okay, okay. Here. Time to get you out." The sound of a fumbling key. Clicking, clacking. Taking too long. "Sorry, Dalton. Wrong key." Chance protests with words that are barely words—and then Copper laughs. "I'm just messing with you, Dalton."

And then the lid pops and Chance's eyes adjust: everything's dark, then the white comes in like a nuclear blast, and then everything's bleached by light. Soon the scene creeps in through the wash, like shapes rising out of milk. Chance lifts himself up, water dripping off him in little streams, his puckered hands on the edges—

Hollis Copper has a gun pointed at him. A rust-flecked old Smith & Wesson .357.

Next to Hollis is Angela Slattery. Her face is bruised, swollen, plumped up like an ugly peach. She opens her mouth and pills fall out, clatter on the ground. "Don't look away," she hisses.

"No, no, no, wh—what is happening—"

Copper hands Slattery the gun. "I think you deserve this," he says to her.

"Don't look away!" she screams.

She pulls the trigger. Chance is erased in a white light and a dark splash.

Chance lurches up. Bangs his head atop the inside of the deprivation chamber. It never opened. Hollis was never here. Neither, it seems, was Angela Slattery. (A mocking voice inside his mind: *I don't know Angela Slattery!*) Chance weeps. The moments stretch to minutes. They combine to form hours. They collapse again to seconds, moments, slices of moments. Time means nothing. Somewhere he fouls the water. He hears his mother drowning in her own fluids, coughing so hard she spatters the walls with her cancer. He feels movement underneath him, like he's in a casket on the way to the funeral instead of her. He hears the gunshot again from a rust-flecked .357, but this time it isn't pointed at him but pointed upward, underneath his father's chin, leaving him alone at the farm, and in life, forever.

CHAPTER 24

Breakout Capability

The shower is short. Chance doesn't want to stay in there, anyway—it freaks him out, makes him think of the Dep. He shivers all the way through it. Mealtime is rushed, too—everyone else has already gone, with him coming in late, too late, so all he gets is a bagel (at least not an old one this time) and cream cheese. Copper's with him the whole way, but Chance doesn't talk to the agent, and the agent doesn't say much to Chance. (He knows it's false, a remnant of his dreamlike state in the Dep, but he still feels like any minute, Agent Copper is going to bring him the name *Angela Slattery* and then point a gun at him. *Bang.*)

After dinner (lunch? What meal is it?) they head to the communal pod, where Copper tells Chance his team is waiting. Chance sees the door, has to stop. Panic cuts him to quick ribbons. He feels like he can't breathe. Like his chest is tightening. Tingling at the ends of his fingers and toes. "I . . . can't."

Copper puts a hand on his shoulder. "You all right?"

"They're gonna lock those doors. I can't be locked in."

"I'll be right outside."

"You shoulda gotten me out of that thing, Copper. The . . . Dep."

Hollis draws a deep breath. "That was out of my hands. You hit another inmate."

Inmate, Chance thinks. *Not hacker. Not guest of the Lodge. Inmate.* "I don't want to be here anymore," he says.

"You do that, you go to jail. Big-boy jail."

"Probably. Maybe. You don't know."

"I got a pretty good feeling." Hollis fishes around his pocket, pulls out a protein bar. "Here. Eat this. Feel better. There's coffee in there. Your friends are in there. You'll be all right. Just do the work."

"Go to hell, Copper."

Chance marches forward into the pod. The door closes behind him, and when it does, his heart skips a couple of beats and for a moment he thinks, *Okay, that's it, I'm going to pass out.* Rings of darkness tighten like belts and suddenly it feels like he's in a long tunnel growing longer every moment, and he *sees* the room ahead and recognizes how different it is from the individual pods—a bank of computers, desks connected like zero-wall cubicles, a big whiteboard—but he can't really *parse* any of that as he rocks back on his heels.

And then he sees Reagan Stolper.

It's like the breaking of a stick over his knee. A sound inside his head. A sharp jolt. Enough to clear the fog, kick the panic to the curb. Something much stronger replaces it: raw, red anger. "You," he hisses.

"Hey, Chauncey," she says.

He starts toward her, fists balled at his side—he knows he's not gonna hit her even though he damn sure wants to. That smug, plump face smiling like she's the cat who not only ate the canary but also cleaned out your fridge and took a shit in the microwave.

And then Aleena pops up in front of him. "Wait," she says. "Please."

"I got things to say to that one," he says. "You don't know what I went through."

DeAndre steps up in front of him. "Hey, man." He claps Chance on the biceps. "I'm sorry to hear about that bullshit, and I can't believe I'm saying this, but you gotta chill. I know you don't want to. But Graves just got knocked off his perch thanks to her."

"What?" Chance asks. "I don't . . . I don't understand."

Reagan steps forward. "He went for the bait, and soon as he was on the hook, Copper and the other hacks beat him with an oar. Er, metaphorically."

"Bait. What bait? What the—" And then he gets it. "Me. I was the bait."

Reagan offers a proud grin. "Yep."

"You used me. I was just some pawn."

"Ennnh . . . yeah. Sorry?"

"You done with me? Or you got more knives to stick in?"

"No," she says, remorseless. "That'll do, pig."

DeAndre steps in, snaps at Reagan, "God *damn,* you do not make friends easily." Then, to Chance: "C'mon, man. Let's go take a seat, strap in for whatever ride they got us on today." Chance barely hears him. That troll has put him through hell twice now, and the second time he ended up locked in a lightless box of water all night long. Every part of him feels like a sparking wire dancing across hot asphalt. But then DeAndre steps in front of him, catches his gaze like a snake charmer trying to hypnotize a cobra. "Hey. *Hey.* Look at me. Trust me. Okay? Trust me and let's go sit."

That breaks through. That little word—*trust*—does it. Chance wants to trust someone. Needs to. He nods. Goes and sits just as all their monitors snap on.

A man whose face Chance doesn't recognize appears on-screen. He's got a salesman's face—dark, mean eyes over a never-quit smile. But he looks tired, too. Lines in his face. A day's growth of beard like a passing shadow.

"Greetings, pod," the man says. "I'm Ken Golathan, director of the Hunting Lodge. Congrats, you passed your first month of evaluations, which means it's time to rise up out of the dirt leagues and start doing some *real* work. You up for it?"

All around the room, muttered acquiescence.

Golathan frowns. "I can barely hear myself over your mirthful clamor. Fine. Let's get to the work. Iran's resurrected nuclear energy program is a thing of some contention because, of course, while the Supreme Leader Ayatollah Rock 'n' Rolla claims that Iran has every right to free and clean nuclear energy, our data indicates that they're less interested in nuclear power and more interested in the power of blowing Israel's ass into a sheet of glass. You have one week to put a serious dent in these wasteland warriors. Slow down their program. Hamper their efforts. Steal as much data as you can steal before you do."

"One week?" Wade says. "You're giving us one week?"

Chance thinks: *I couldn't do this in one year. I couldn't do it if you sat me down in front of their computers with a list of passwords.* Once again, fear starts chewing at him like maggots going through roadkill. That certainty that he's going to wash out. Again that question: *What the hell am I doing here?*

Aleena joins the protest: "One week is too short. Iran is no Tinkertoy operation, their nuclear program especially, and *by the way,* they have a right to produce their reactor fuel and create their own energy, as they are a sovereign power, and who are we to keep nuclear energy—or even nuclear weapons!—out of the hands of—"

"Yeah, let's give the tyrannical regime nuclear bombs," Wade growls.

"Their new president—"

"We can do it," Reagan shouts over Aleena. Aleena gives her a searing look.

DeAndre jumps in: "Yeah. We'll handle this. The Ayatollah won't know what ripped that big creepy beard off his big creepy face." He shoots a panicked look to Chance, then says under his breath: "Ayatollahs have beards, right? That's a thing?"

Chance shrugs.

Golathan says: "They *do* have beards, Messrs. Mitchell and Dalton. You will be granted additional resources as you need them, but do understand: we'll be watching and keenly aware of critical abuses. Overt abuses will earn you hours in the Dep—Mr. Dalton can surely attest to the delights of the deprivation chamber. Correct?"

All Chance can do is sit there and try not to shiver and quake in some combination of rage and panic. The grin he forces himself to wear feels reaperlike. Stretched too wide, scary even to him.

"Three strikes," Golathan continues, "and you wash out."

"And how do we access your 'additional resources'?" Aleena asks.

"This is one of those rare instances in which your prayers can be heard by a mostly beneficent god, Miss Kattan. Merely speak your wish aloud, and we will hear."

"So you're God now?" she asks.

"In your world, yes, I am. Now get to work. One week." The screen goes dark.

"Goddamn rat-fink liar," Wade says.

Chance watches as Aleena throws him a hard look. "Shush." She turns to the rest of them, then claps her hands. "Let's do some work on the whiteboard."

Ø Ø Ø

The marker squeaks like a stepped-on chipmunk every time Aleena drags it across the whiteboard. When they begin, it's fresh ink—makes bold, black lines. But they work long enough that it starts to fade, leaving the ghosts of marks rather than the marks themselves. Periodically she looks over, watches Chance sitting toward the back, arms folded across his chest, staring off at an unfixed point. Her initial reaction is cold, callous, and she chides herself for thinking,

How hard could it have been? Sitting in a dark space for twelve hours can't be that bad. It's not like he's under fire from his own government, or suffering rocket attacks or bus bombings. First-world problems, right?

But then she reminds herself: Sensory deprivation is one of the "sanctioned" torture methods of this very government. It's right up there with waterboarding. They call it *white torture*. She remembers reading about a Yemeni man—the captain of a merchant vessel thought to be carrying arms to some terrorist group—imprisoned in some Polish black site prison. He said that after two days of sensory deprivation he could no longer think clearly. He imagined being shot over and over again—literally felt the bullets tearing through him. After three days he said he could no longer conjure up his own name, or the faces of his mother and father, his wife, his *children*.

He was, of course, innocent of the charges.

So she stops once in a while to look over at Chance.

Still, for now, the job is the job. And the job *isn't* to hack Iran's nuclear program. They'll do that job, yes. They have to—for now. At this point that's what they're doing. Drawing up plans, potential infrastructures, mind maps of how to attack their servers. Wade puts it best: "Let's shake the tree, see what monkeys fall out." Meaning: a penetration test. Always start with a pen test. DeAndre makes a *Star Wars* joke: "Concentrate all fire on that Super Star Destroyer!" And then Reagan and he start arguing about *Trek* versus *Wars,* and then Wade says that nobody reads cerebral science fiction like *Logan's Run* anymore, and Aleena has to herd these nerdly cats and get them back on track before they spiral out of control.

Then Reagan calls it: "We're an hour in, everybody. Time to work."

They all, almost like automatons, go and sit down in front of their computers. Chance looks confused, like a dog staring at a Ferris wheel, but as long as he keeps sitting there where he's sitting, they should be good. They get ten solid minutes of sitting there, doing not much at all, and then Aleena reaches down under the darkness of her desk, lifts her pant leg, finds the cryptophone. Touching the screen causes it to bloom with dim light. She taps in the preprogrammed code and all the camera lights go from green to red.

"And we're baaaaack," Reagan says in a game-show host voice, then kicks her wheeled chair back against the wall.

Aleena gets to her feet, claps her hands. "Okay. We've got an hour."

"The hell's going on?" Chance asks.

"While you were down the rabbit hole," DeAndre says, "we made *plans*."

They gather around him in a semicircle—a fact that seems to make him uncomfortable, like they're pressing in on him too much—and Aleena gives him the story. "Reagan used you to get close to Graves. Then she set Graves up to fail, and while he was in with Copper, she and I took his laptops, plus a bunch of cryptophones and USB keys. We think he was trying to escape, but we're going to be the ones to do it instead. But we need leverage."

DeAndre picks up the story: "We know that if we bail, Big Government's gonna stomp down on every*body* and every*thing* we hold near and dear. So we gotta get something to hold over their heads. You know what I'm saying? *You stab my back, I stab your back*. That sorta thing."

"We're starting to see a picture form," Aleena says. She watches Chance loosen up—his arms drop, he leans forward, then back. His eyes searching their margins—not really looking at them, but thinking. It's then she guesses: he's smarter than he or anyone else gives him credit for.

"It's like you were saying at the boulders," Chance says. "All these connections. They're forming a ring. Circling the wagons. That means we need to find out what's in the middle. We need to find out what they're protecting."

"We need to find out what they're *hiding*," Wade corrects.

"Whatever it is," Aleena says. "I bet it's Typhon."

Ø Ø Ø

They get to work.

DeAndre sits back down, starts figuring out a fresh take on what he calls his "Master Hacker, Mother-Cracker, Death Star Laser Program."

Wade dives into the Deep Web, looking for so-called dark-news sites—places that compile all the hidden and hush-hush government secrets.

Reagan works on the Iran problem. Nobody knows what the hell she's doing, only that she's "got a plan," and it makes her giggle uncontrollably.

They put Chance on Google duty. They hack a path through the search engine to clear the way for unblocked, unmitigated searching and tell him to start putting together the companies they pen-tested in various search strings. See if he can drum up any more connections between them. Anything that points to whatever the hell Typhon is.

Aleena has one job: contact the Widow. If anybody knows anything, it's her.

Ø Ø Ø

The Widow of Zheng.

Historically, that title falls to one Ching Shih, a Chinese prostitute taken off her floating brothel home to be the wife of the pirate Zheng Yi. Zheng Yi died not long after, in a tsunami—a whole fleet of his boats taken out.

That should've been that, but Ching Shih had other ideas. She took over the so-called Red Flag Fleet. Her rules were iron-clad: no raping, no sex, no stealing from the common man, no fighting on any of the boats. Any violation of her rules resulted in a variety of wretched punishments: tied to a cannonball and fired into the sea, beheaded, stomped to death on deck, fed to gathered sharks or orcas. Deserters suffered, too: they were hunted down and disfigured.

Under her care, the fleet didn't wither. Its power multiplied. Its ranks swelled. She took the fleet from six hundred boats to eighteen hundred.

She set up a pirate government, controlled every aspect of piracy, and ran a criminal empire spanning the entire South China Sea. When other pirates attacked her, she stole their ships and used their own crews against them. The military couldn't stop her, either: She outran them. Outgunned them. Out*thought* them at every turn.

The military's only weapon against her was amnesty. They offered her a chance to walk away from it all with all her loot and total freedom. She took the deal. She was thirty-five years old at the time and lived another thirty-four years managing the same floating brothel from which she had been taken.

Ching Shih was one of the most successful pirates of all time. And now, a hacker has taken her name and title.

Aleena's known about the Red Flag Fleet—the hackers, not the actual fleet of boats—for years now. They've been at the edges of hacker society for a decade, as much a myth as a confirmed presence. Their deeds are legendary: hacking the United States infrastructure, shutting down various satellite launches via NASA, even uploading a worm to the International Space Station that threatened its air supply and docking mechanisms. Some folks think they're part of—or at least backed by—the Chinese military, but Aleena never thought so. Their footprints were all over the hacking of China's own aerospace program. They have routinely made North Korea a target, sometimes forcing missile launches into nowhere (which the DPRK always claims is intentional, some kind of threat and test of their might).

The RFF are wildly effective. And, like the actual pirate fleet before it, they have a code.

So when Aleena received that message—*Who is Typhon?*—signed by "The Widow," she almost couldn't believe it.

It was only days later that the Widow appeared again. This time, in a much bigger way. The lights in Aleena's pod shut down. Then the cameras. Everything but the screen. The Widow appeared streaming on-screen—a terrible feed, unclean and distorted by pixilation and blocky artifacts. The sound was warped, too. But what Aleena saw behind the shifting, chameleon-skin distortions of the video feed was a girl almost as young as she was. Long hair, straight as a rain of arrows. Face white like chalk.

She said: "Aleena Kattan. You are a pawn. A piece moved about by invisible enemies. Find—" Voice distortion. Aleena tried speaking back, but her words went unheard, and then the Widow's voice emerged anew: "Find Typhon. Reveal it to the world. The monsters in the dark wither when exposed to the *liiiiight*—" That last word, prey once more to distortion, drawn out as if in slow motion, stuttering—

And then she was gone. Lights back on. Cameras, too.

When Aleena told the story to the others, Wade asked: *How do you know it was really her?* The answer, at least to Aleena, was clear: Who else could hack into the Hunting Lodge so boldly?

Now, Aleena needs to find the Widow of Zheng again. Thing is, how do you find a hacker mastermind? What does that search even begin to look like? This isn't just an act of finding a needle in a haystack. It's conjuring a ghost— summoning a demon. She sits at the computer for a while and just stares.

When a hand falls on her shoulder, she actually jumps. Wade says, "You look like you saw a ghost."

"More like, I'm trying to summon one, and I'm failing."

"Speak English."

"I was born in America, racist."

"No, I mean—" He sighs, defeated. "Sorry, I just mean, I don't know what the devil you're talking about. Just . . . tell me what you're doing."

"Oh." He seems genuine? Hm. "I'm trying to find a way to contact the Widow."

"Huh. Sure she's not watching us right now?"

"If she is, she's not jumping in to say so."

"Here's something. Before your time and a bit after mine, the hacker-cracker pool was much smaller than it is today. Back in the eighties and nineties, you didn't have these giant carder markets or whole hacker fleets so much as you had lone wolves and little cabals trying to break into banks, mess with IBM, phreak the phone company, what have you. Groups like the Warelords, the Masters of Deception. Along with the Kevin Mitnicks and Phiber Optiks and whoever, early on there was this Bay Area hacker, called himself Emperor Norton. To track him down you used old hobo code— you'd scratch a sign into the sidewalk or on a BART seat or whatever with a bit of chalk, maybe a stone. You didn't find him. He found you."

Aleena says, "So I should let her come to me."

"But not before leaving a trail of bread crumbs."

"Good idea." She never thought she'd be saying this, but: "Thanks, Wade. Whatever happened to the Emperor?"

"Turns out, he was a homeless guy. Fucked up like so many of us are. He eventually jumped in front of the trolley after it reopened in 1984."

"Oh."

"Uh-huh." He shrugs. "Good luck with your hunt. Leave good bait."

And then Wade goes back to work.

Good bait. Aleena knows what to do. Reagan spoke about an image she saw: IMAGO TYPHONVS. On some old woodcut or something. Didn't take Aleena long to figure out that it was from a seventeenth-century book called *Oedipus Aegyptiacus,* by Athanasius Kircher. She grabs that image file, starts popping into every Deep Web forum she can find with a question: *Who is Typhon? The Widow knows*.

Time to go fishing.

Ø Ø Ø

He has a task at hand, but Chance isn't doing it.

He knows he should be, but Google. Oh man, sweet

Google. It's a window to the outside world, and he hasn't looked out that window in all too long now. The Hunting Lodge is like a bigger version of the Dep. It's not like Chance was particularly connected to the world outside, but suddenly what few connections he had feel all the more precious, and here's a chance to find them. *You deserve this,* he tells himself.

He searches for himself on Google. He's been outed. He knew it was coming. Soon as he got his ass kicked in his own driveway, he had to figure his name would leak. Copper said as much. But here—oh man. News stories. Blog posts. Postings across endless forums. Digging up his life, his address, his everything. Talking about how his mother died from cancer—and they keep calling her a "failed actress," which only makes him grit his teeth so hard they could snap (even though a smaller voice inside him acknowledges the truth of the statement). Talking about how his father killed himself—and then he sees that's what a lot of people think *Chance* did, too. They think he killed himself. Like they'll find his body bobbing in Lake Norman one day, or some dog will drag his half-eaten body out from underneath some overpass somewhere.

Worse, a lot of folks *hope* that's what happened. Turns out, pissing off the fans of a football team is a good way to get yourself threatened with death. Never mind the fact that he outed a goddamn *rape posse*—a crew of jock monsters who had zero problem stalking girls like they were zebras on the veldt, getting them drunk or roofied, raping them, then ditching them on their lawns like an empty, half-crushed beer can. (One comment on Reddit: "You ask me Chase Dalton should get raped then killed then raped again but only after he has to watch a video of his own mother taking it in all her holes.")

It's not everybody. He sees posts in support of him. Some blogs calling him a hero. But none of that outweighs the tide of toxic shit slung his way. Doubly awful are all the people who support Bogardian and the others: petitions to get them released, to get their sentences cut, goddamn *love letters* to a handful of rapist shits.

Chance feels overwhelmed by it all. He tells himself to stop looking. He knows he did the right thing, and that should be enough. He didn't do it to be a rock star. It's not like he wants Marvel to turn him into a superhero comic book. He did it because it was the right thing to do. (*And because you had a debt to pay.* That voice from You-Know-Who.)

Then he goes and does it. He Googles the name: Angela Slattery. He knows what he'll find, and he does: There's her obituary. Young girl, sixteen, dead from self-inflicted gunshot wound—

"Whatcha lookin' at?"

Chance about pisses himself. He quickly closes the browser. He looks behind, sees Wade damn near sitting on his shoulder like a hawk. "Nothing. Don't you have things to . . . things to do? Jeez, man, warn a guy before you come up on him like that."

"You all right?" Wade asks. "You seem off."

"Fine. Yeah. Just great."

"That Dep is pretty bad, huh."

Chance hesitates. He doesn't want to talk about it. "Yeah."

Wade puts a hand on his shoulder. It's warm, reassuring, unexpected. Chance is about to say thank you, but then DeAndre says: "I did it. Holy shit, I did it!"

Ø Ø Ø

DeAndre feels everyone gather around him like he's a campfire giving them warmth. He sees the clock on his system: hour's almost up. It's gonna be close.

They're all watching the progress bar, 50 percent to 60 percent to 75 percent, up and up and up. "C'mon, man," De-Andre says, biting his knuckles. "C'mon, baby, open up for DeAndre Deleon Mitchell, give it to Darth Dizzy, open that flower, gimme that sweet, sweet, *sweet* nectar—"

Chance leans in, mutters in his ear: "Dude. You're being kinda creepy."

And then: the progress bar goes from red to green. The folder unlocks.

DeAndre opens it. There's one file inside. A text file—.txt extension. *That's it?* DeAndre thinks. *This is the damn prize?*

"You're giving me blue balls," Reagan grouches. "*Open the file,* jerk."

DeAndre scrambles to open it. Double-click and—

"It's just a list of names," Aleena says.

Thirteen of them, as a matter of fact.

> Leslie Cilicia-Ceto.
> Park Soo-Kang.
> Hiram Willingham.
> Arthur McGovern.
> Alan Sarno.
> Hamid Abilshair.
> Gordon Berry.
> Ernestina Pereira.
> Siobhan Kearsy.
> Ian Ballard.
> James Francis Peak.
> Honor Street.
> Devon Fulbright.

"Man, who the hell are these people?" DeAndre asks.

"I know some of those names," Wade says. His voice is quiet. "Oh shit."

"Hamid Abilshair," Aleena says. "He's a Muslim academic, progressive. A big thinker. My father adores his books. He protested the Taliban's destroying Afghani history. He protested American soldiers doing the same in Baghdad, then traveled there to help preserve artifacts, books, vital sites."

"Two minutes," Chance warns. "And did you guys see, Alan Sarno's on that list."

Reagan says: "Honor Street. Hacker, right?"

"Oh snap, yeah," DeAndre says. "Been in and out of prison, right? Isn't she dead? I coulda sworn—"

"Yeah," Reagan says. "I thought so. Prison transport van crashed."

Another warning from Chance: "One minute."

DeAndre's head is a mixed bag: triumph over cracking it, let down over finding nothing more than a damn text file, bewildered at what this list of names even means. Who are these people? Why are they together on one list? What's the connection?

That's when Wade drops a bomb. "Siobhan Kearsy," he says. "Siobhan is the mother of my baby girl."

"Time," Chance says. "Ten seconds, back to the desks—go!"

CHAPTER 25

Revenge Is a Dish Best Served at Dinner

THE LODGE, CAFETERIA

Dinnertime. They're all afraid to talk about what they found, in case someone is listening. Mostly they sit around. Looking at one another. Straining to talk it all through, to unpack it: but they won't. They can't. It leaves a palpable tension at the table, like a dinner guest nobody wants to entertain but who barged in anyway.

They note that Dipesh isn't at his table with the rest of his pod. When Chance passes Miranda near the trash, he asks her where he is. She says he's back at the cabin. "He needs time," she says, and then she hurries away.

When Chance gets back to his table, he sees his seat is taken.

By Shane Graves.

"Hey, Dalton. Pull up a chair."

"Go die in a fire, Graves."

"Fine. Stand. This won't take long." Graves leans forward on his elbows, wearing a goopy smirk like a teen girl staring at a photo of her favorite celebrity crush. "You guys. Masterful work. I am *impressed*. Particularly with you, Reagan Stolper and Chance Dalton. You two played me good."

Reagan shrugs. "I like seeing the mighty fall."

"And fall I did. Clever work. I don't have much left, but a snake always has his fangs, a scorpion always has his stinger, and I always have the things I've learned." His smile grows big, so big and so eager it could described as *shit-eating.* "I know secrets."

"Good for you," Chance says. "Now get up or I'll call the hacks."

"Angela Slattery," Shane says, then turns around and stares up at Chance. "Ah. There's the face I expected. See that face, everyone? Like I just slapped the food right out of his mouth. You want to tell them who that is, Chance?"

Fear and rage run through him like battery acid. "Fuck you."

"Uh-huh. You know what? I'm not gonna tell them. I'm gonna let them search for it themselves. After all, I've given you the keys to the kingdom. You've all got peepholes now into the outside world. Google it. *Angela Slattery.*" He turns to Reagan. "Though you already know. I know you know because we talked about it."

"Pack it in, Shane," Reagan says. "Leave it alone."

Shane turns to her. "Stolper, you tumor. Dalton doesn't know that not only did you set him up here for his little trip to the Dep, but you were the one who leaked his name in the first damn place. Right? That's how everyone found out. You."

And to think, Chance was just starting to not hate her. "You," he says. "Why?"

She swallows hard. "Like I said, I, uhh, like to see the mighty fall. Thought you needed to be brought down a peg since you were using Faceless like that. But I didn't know you then. I . . ." She frowns. "Shit. God damn it, Graves."

Shane grins. "I'm not done yet. One more for you, Reagan."

"Bring it on, Graves. You got nothing on me because I got nothing. I'm an open book, dick." But her smug face softens a little.

Not Graves. He keeps on leering. "Your little girl," he says. "She's alive. No thanks to you, Reagan. Her name is Ellie Belle Stevens. She's five. And I'm sure she very much regrets being left in a Target bathroom by her mother, Reagan Stolper."

Chance expects a fight to break out. Everyone's leaning forward like they're on the edge of a cliff, about to jump. But nobody knows what to do. Feels like they just got caught in a nuclear blast. At the start of dinner, the unspoken message between them was, *We can't talk about the things that we know.* Now that telepathic narrative has changed to: *We don't know each other at all.*

Shane chuckles. "I think that, Zeroes, is what you call a *mic drop.*" Then he slides his chair back, stands up, and strides away.

CHAPTER 26

The Confessional

Graves put a cannonball through their sails. They mill around until lights-out and lockdown, then lie quietly in the dark for a while. Until finally someone, Wade, speaks up. "Siobhan Kearsy was this . . . you know, this radical type. Protester of the Vietnam conflict. Kind who liked to call the returning soldiers 'baby killer' and all that. When I went to war, that would've upset me, because I was a shorn-clean, cherub-cheeked Boy Scout type. Then I went to the jungle, saw what the heat and the chemicals and the fear did to good men, and I came back scruffy, empty of something, lost as a little kid in a Kmart. Siobhan . . . we met at some D.C. protest and we were like the terminals on a goddamn car battery. Positive, negative, red, black. A hard charge going through us. We loved each other. We hated each other. We couldn't stay together, but we kept finding each other's orbit over the next ten years, and then one day . . ."

"She got pregnant," DeAndre says.

"No," Reagan says, "she turned into a giant rabbit."

DeAndre makes a frustrated sound.

"Yes," Wade continues. "She got pregnant. With our daughter, Rebecca. See, thing is, by then we had already long passed each other on the axis. She was softening—working inside politics as much as against them. I was hip-deep in running my anarchist bullshit BBS and I had my FFL, my federal firearms license, to buy and sell and repair guns. By the time Rebecca was a year old, I'd hacked into Los Alamos labs and ended up stirring the shit so bad that SWAT came knocking on our door—which is to say, they knocked it right off its hinges. It was determined at that point—er, by way of a mutual decision—that I was maybe not the best fella to have around the baby. So I left. Siobhan went on to become a philosophy professor and then a journalist—never married."

Chance is listening to all this, and with every word Wade says he feels sicker and sicker to his stomach and he knows he's going to throw up—but what he's gonna regurgitate isn't dinner but rather the story of Angela Slattery. Because it's better they find it out from him than find their own info and start making guesses.

Wade's story winds down, and Wade finishes with: "So I know a little something about giving up a baby girl."

"You don't know shit, old man," Reagan calls from the loft.

Everyone's quiet for a little while.

Chance says: "Angela Slattery." Then he has to stop because he actually thinks he might throw up. He breathes in. Breathes out.

Okay. "Uhh. So. I was in, I was in high school? And I wasn't real popular but I wasn't *not* popular, either, just one of those kids in the middle. I didn't get picked on but didn't pick on anybody. Had friends from all over. But I still wanted to be popular and there was this girl, her name was Caitlin Tremayne, and it was like in all those dumb movies where she was the hot popular girl and I was just some dink and in my head I'd one day get to show her how badass I was and then we'd fall in love or have sex or something.

"So, there was this party. At Matt Moody's house. And Moody was a football guy and his parents were rich and somehow I scored an invite to this party and me and my buddy Pete went. Pete and I had known each other for a good long time, buds since preschool, and I knew Caitlin was gonna be there, so we both went."

He clears his throat, sits up in the darkness. The bed creaks and squeaks. "Well, I heard that Caitlin was upstairs somewhere, so I thought I would go up there and, I dunno, make some overture to her, spill my heart. I'd practiced this speech about how beautiful she was and everything. But while I was standing at the bottom of the stairs, getting up my confidence, Matt Moody and a couple other guys—Hill Prager and Joshie Winslaw—pushed past me. They had a girl with them. I knew her a little from school. Angela Slattery. She didn't seem all there. Like she was drunk, really drunk, *worse* than drunk, and, uhh . . ."

From the loft, Reagan's voice: "Spoiler alert: they rape her, and Chance Dalton the hero boy doesn't do shit about it. He sees it, lets it go, and his friend Pete convinces him not to tell anyone because blah-blah popular kids, blah-blah Caitlin Fucking Tremayne. I've seen the e-mails he and Petey exchanged. I've seen how two white boys circled the drain and found a way to find peace with someone's rape."

Chance wants to be mad at Reagan, and her renewed anger at him seems sudden—but she's right. His voice starts to crack like lake ice under a testing foot as he finishes the story: "They dumped Angela on her front lawn. Naked. They'd written words all over her in lipstick. 'Slut,' 'dog,' words like that. Next day she told the police. They wanted proof, made it seem like it was all in her head, that she'd gotten drunk and whatever. And everyone said the same thing: 'Oh, if you didn't wanna get raped you shouldn't show up at some party and get wasted.' Even though they probably *got* her wasted on roofies. Cops dismissed rape kit testing. Wouldn't interview eyewitnesses. Moody's parents had money, were important. I could've spoken up. I didn't.

A week later, after their house had been vandalized for the third time, after someone threw a brick through her mother's SUV, after people said all kinds of things about her online . . . she shot herself. Took her father's handgun out of his nightstand drawer and . . ."

"Dang, man, that sucks," DeAndre says.

From the loft, though, Aleena calls down, "No. Don't. Don't act all sympathetic toward him. He made a mistake—a choice!—that saved his ass while letting some poor girl hang for it."

Wade calls up: "Hey, now, we're all in the spirit of sharing. Reagan—you wanna spill your guts? Sounds like it hurts but it actually feels kinda good."

"It's like Graves said. Had a baby. Left it at Target. I'm a monster. Fuck off."

CHAPTER 27

The Thirteen

The days go by the same way. Most of the time they work on cracking open the bones of the Iranian nuclear program to get at the marrow—but they take two hours of each day to get closer to Typhon.

First up: the thirteen names. Wade says, "I wanna know why Siobhan is on that list." And so they get to poking through the names, first doing shallow searches, then digging deeper through news blotters, public records, Deep Web fishing.

Some of them, they know. Sarno: famous pop psychologist, now missing. Hamid Abilshair: historian, Muslim, went to try to stop Isis from destroying precious Silk Road artifacts in Iraq, has been missing for four months. Honor Street: hacker, killed in a prison transfer.

In fact, most of the names seem to fit into that category: missing or dead.

Gordon Berry: Renowned neurologist, had a practice in Virginia. Known for revolutionizing how the brain reacts to neural implants to help regain sight, hearing, cognitive function. Had a heart attack a year back, then went missing a month ago.

Park Soo-Kang: South Korean futurist. Disappeared in the Aokigahara suicide forest—thought to have taken her own life.

Hiram Willingham: One of the wolves of Wall Street. Financial genius. Scammer extraordinaire. Became subject of an investigation, went out on his yacht off Curaçao. He and his yacht disappeared.

Ian Ballard: Prominent science fiction author. Author of comics. Youngest of this bunch—late thirties. Went missing on Kauai while hiking the Na Pali coast. As many do.

Arthur McGovern: Political pundit. Hard right wing. Radio show. Had problems with drug addiction—pills. Said to have committed suicide in his bathroom.

Devon Fulbright: Gender-fluid classical musician. Said to be a genius since a very early age, but prejudice forced zir into a first-violinist chair at a lower-tier orchestra. Went missing three months ago—didn't turn up for practice.

Two of the names are total unknowns: no sign of an Ernestina Pereira or James Francis Peak. The former has no hits of note, the latter has way too many.

It's Wade who discovers that Siobhan Kearsy is also missing.

She'd recently been crusading against antiabortionists—fighting for the rights of both patients and doctors. She failed to show up at a clinic in Albuquerque, New Mexico, about four months ago. Foul play is assumed. The article Wade finds doesn't say anything about Rebecca.

Wade makes these angry, exasperated chuffs, like a territorial ape. He starts hacking something and stops responding to anyone else.

Meanwhile, Chance digs up the last name on the list: Leslie Cilicia-Ceto. She, as it turns out, is the only one not dead or missing. "She's the founder of some defense contractor company," Chance says. "APSI."

Wade's head jerks up from the computer. Wild eyes stare

out from behind the curtain of gray curls. "APSI. Argus Panoptes Systems, Inc. They make targeting systems for missiles, tanks, planes, choppers. Antimissile tech, too."

Chance says: "She might be in danger."

"There's something else," Aleena says, typing furiously.

"You don't need an invite," Reagan growls. "Spill it, Kardashian."

"Argus Panoptes is also the name of a figure from Greek mythology. He's a hundred-eyed giant. Hera's pet. For her, he killed the so-called Mother of Monsters, Echidna. Echidna's husband was the *Father* of Monsters. Typhon."

"This shit is crazy," DeAndre says. "I do not like it, and I would like to get off this ride now."

"Fuck that," Reagan says—those two words spat as much as they are spoken. "Don't be a soft little vagina. This means we're getting close."

Ø Ø Ø

That night, the night before they're ready to pull the trigger on their hack of the Iranian nuclear program, Wade shuts off all the surveillance to the cabin with one of the crypto-phones, then tells the rest of the pod what he's been up to. He hacked Siobhan's e-mails. Said it was a bit tricky because she had two-factor authentication active—but he said that was easy enough to get around, because once you tell the provider you lost your data, the recovery process defaults to one step.

In her e-mails, he found something. She'd been trading e-mails with someone who called himself Mr. Lee Cothip, said he was on the inside of a domestic terror organization planning a coordinated bombing of several abortion clinics in the Southwest. Said if she met him, he'd give her proof that she could take to the police, newspapers, whoever.

They arranged a place to meet. Little historic area of Santa Fe. Near something called the Crispin House. That's the last anybody saw of her. Wade says the area has no cameras, no surveillance—except for one. A little Wi-Fi camera someone set up at a nearby bed-and-breakfast. Pointed out toward the garden for some reason—to film hummingbirds or look for whoever's been picking flowers or whatever. Thing is, the camera points to the entrance of the empty lot where Siobhan met this Lee Cothip.

The video caught her pulling in. Five minutes later, caught another car: a little commercial Nissan van. Wade pulls out the Floydphone once more, passes it around. The Zeroes look at a blurry photo of a man driving. He's tall, bent over the wheel like a tree heavy with ice and snow. Bald, too. Though his face is pixilated, it's still easy to see that something isn't right with it. Some scar, some deformation.

"That's it," Wade says. "Last sign of her."

Ø Ø Ø

Aleena lies there in the dark. She's nervous about tomorrow. Tomorrow they sneak into the Iranian servers, mess with their nuclear program, steal whatever data they can steal, and head for the hills. If everything goes off without a hitch. Which, of course, it won't. How could it? This is big. They've had no time.

And they're distracted. At least, she is. Hacking Iran should bother her. Messing around with an autonomous state like that. Iran's backward in a lot of ways but progressive, too. More progressive than anybody here gives them credit for. She knows it's a nation primed for revolution. Revolution away from the religious autocracy, away from the oppressive regime. A revolution led by youth. Like her.

She keeps thinking about that because she feels like she should, because whenever her mind drifts to Chance, she feels like it's a waste of her time and talent. A waste of all that she is. So she keeps trying to focus on what matters. It's not easy there in the dark.

These people she's stuck with—she's grown to actually

like them. And yet, with all these revelations—she's learning that she doesn't really know them. Probably can't trust them, either.

Reagan, leaving her baby in a Target bathroom.

And Chance. *Chance.* Aleena wants to be forgiving. She wants to understand. Academically, she does—high school is hell. Sticking out your neck for someone is a good way to get it broken.

But what he did . . . emotionally she just can't parse it. It makes her mad. It discolors what he did later, exposing the rape posse. It makes it about him, not about the victim. It makes it a wrong he had to right, not a thing he had to do just because it was good. And yet it *was* good, wasn't it?

Gah! All parts of her are tense. Her arms stock straight. Her elbows and knees locked, her jaw so tight she can feel the pressure in her temples.

It's not just her. She hears others tossing and turning. Even Wade, who seems like he could sleep through mortar fire, isn't snoring as usual.

DeAndre clinches it. He says in a loud whisper: "Hey. Everybody else awake?"

Murmurs of anxious, sleepy assent.

"Typhon," DeAndre says. "The hell is it? We know the government controls it, but what do you think it *is*?"

"It's probably NSA," Aleena says. She tells them that her guess is it's an upgrade to their algorithms. NSA has long been interested in creating a truly uncrackable encryption system. DeAndre says, nah, it's their new surveillance program. From Echelon to PRISM and now to this.

Wade snorts, says, it's all those things and more. "My best is: supercomputer. Quantum computing. They always got weirdo names for their supercomputers: HARVEST, FROSTBURG." Chance doesn't know much about this stuff, and Wade explains that a quantum computer moves past the standard computing process of binary: in the old way, everything is either a one or a zero, a yes or a no, a stop or go. Quantum computing changes that: superposition says one thing can be many things and in many places at once and so bits can be ones *and* zeroes at the same time. Smarter, faster computing via so-called qubits.

Wade goes on to say, though: "It's never been much to write home about. Not yet. Nobody thinks the NSA has been ahead of the curve. No more than Google or any of the other big labs. But still, look at the systems we've been pen-testing. Tech. Cloud solutions. Shit, even that geothermal company might suggest how the thing is gonna get its power source."

Aleena points out that it doesn't explain everything.

That's when Chance says something off the cuff, like he's just making it up: "What if it's an artificial intelligence?"

Aleena thinks, once again: *Maybe he deserves more credit than he gets.*

DeAndre whistles. "That's some sci-fi shit."

"Not really," Wade says. "NSA's been looking to model predictive cryptanalysis for years. Figure out how people would behave. Figure out the kinds of passwords they might use. Besides, sci-fi isn't sci-fi anymore. Alien autopsies and Russian psychics and all that shit is real. Nothing is the realm of fiction, you ask me. Not anymore."

They laugh at him for that. It's the first laugh they've had in days.

Though Aleena wonders if it breaks the tension . . . or only ratchets it tighter.

CHAPTER 28

The Call

Ken sleeps like a corpse. He always has. No matter what's going on, when he crashes out, he crashes out hard. He sleeps only four hours a night, but during those four hours you need to hit him with a tire iron to wake him up. Back when they first started dating, Susan had a trick: she'd drape a wet washcloth over his face. Eyes, mouth, nose. He'd wake up in a snap.

She takes a little pleasure in pretending she invented waterboarding.

It's her that wakes him now from sleep. Shaking him so hard that when he lurches upright he's pretty sure the world is ending.

He wakes up. Sees Lucas lying there between him and his wife. Hisses in the darkness: "Why is he here? Thought we were making him stay in his own room for once?"

But Susan doesn't answer. All she does is wave his cell phone around. "Your phone's been ringing."

"It's on silent."

"It *vibrates*."

"Fine, Jesus, all right." He grabs the phone and heads into the bathroom. Flips on the lights, sits on the toilet—just the seat, he doesn't have to go or anything—and answers the call.

"Whoever this is," Ken says, "it better be important because you ticked off my wife and that means I have to hunt you down and beat you to death with my own—"

Leslie's voice interrupts him. "It's almost time," she says.

"Time for what?"

"The Hunting Lodge to close up."

"You said three weeks. It hasn't even been one whole week."

A pause. "My calculations were off. Your people have been exceedingly unpredictable."

"My people?" He snorts, then stands to fill a glass of water. "They're not my people, Leslie. I was against this all along. Typhon picked these miscreants." His mouth is tacky with spit and sleep.

"Signs show that the penetration test is almost complete. Typhon's vulnerabilities have been uncovered. The program can be shut down."

"Hold on a minute," Ken says. "The Lodge is fruitful. I've been thinking it over—it fucking works. No more of this bullshit of securing hacker assets and having them play in the wild. That always ends poorly for us. Keeping them in one location was brilliant, Leslie. Kudos to you."

"They're dangerous when together."

"They're dangerous because you wanted them to have a long leash. Soon as this phase is over, we can tighten things up. Last week we had one pod out this Pakistani hacker cell. Some jokers calling themselves the Cyber-Leets—they'd been hacking banks and other American retailers. The Paki government caught 'em, and thanks to their completely inflexible laws on the matter, the hackers have already been sentenced to death. They're off the table. America is safe."

"The program needs terminating, Ken. If your hackers talk about Typhon—"

"They won't talk. They think when their time is over they'll go home, but they won't. They'll go to jail. Reduced sentences, maybe, for their good work—so that way, if they spill their guts, their deal goes to shit. It's fine."

"The program needs terminating," she says again, her voice colder, deader. "The *hackers* must be terminated as well."

He laughs. "Terminated? Like—"

"The Pakistani government has the correct idea."

She's kidding, right? "You're kidding."

Silence.

She's not kidding.

"This conversation is over, Leslie. You're a defense contractor. You don't make demands of the American government. You don't make demands of the *NSA*. You work for us, we don't work for you."

"You're making a mistake, Ken."

"Sweet dreams, Leslie. Oh, and don't forget—I still want that site visit." He ends the call before she can say anything else.

CHAPTER 29

Today Is the Day

Today's the day, Aleena thinks. Guilt chases her like a yappy dog. Guilt over how she still distrusts Chance. Guilt over what they're about to do to a sovereign nation. Guilt over who she's become here: a compromised person.

But today's the last day of this assignment.

And today, she thinks, they're going to find out just what Typhon is.

Ø Ø Ø

Today's the day, Chance thinks, standing in the cabin shower. Soap in his eyes suddenly freaks him out—it's like being back in the Dep again. *Get shut of that, dude. You gotta pack that kind of fear in a suitcase, stick it on a plane, let it fly away without you.* Time to keep it together. Today's the day his pod does what it does: which is, make him look a whole lot better than he really is. *Game face on,* he thinks. *It's time.*

Ø Ø Ø

Today's the day, DeAndre thinks, shoving a forkful of cold eggs in his mouth. Everyone's quiet here in the morning—his kind don't like to be up early. And last night he didn't sleep, and neither did most of his pod pals. It's evident on their faces.

He's scared. He doesn't know why. Something's eating at him. Feels like he should just be doing his work and not ripping off Band-Aids and picking scabs, but all this shit about Typhon and that list of thirteen names, it's got him worked up. It's got him *curious*. Nothing good has ever come from DeAndre getting curious. He remembers when he thought to himself, *Just keep your head down, man, and do your time*. That thought has passed.

Ø Ø Ø

Today's the day, Wade thinks. He feels electrically charged. Alive and awake in a way he hasn't felt in a long time. He keeps seeing Siobhan's face. Then Rebecca's. He has pictures of her from fairly recently. Off her Facebook and Twitter. From Siobhan's e-mail account. He thinks he's gonna find out what happened to her. He has no gods, but he prays to them just the same that she's okay. Whoever hurt her is gonna suffer. If the United States government was involved he's gonna tear the whole thing down, pillar by pillar. He's gonna stick his thumb right in that creepy eye at the top of the pyramid.

Ø Ø Ø

Today's the day, Reagan thinks, and inside she's a tornado of glass and razors, a rain of piss and tears, a storm of lightning and a plague of locusts. Outside, she's stone-faced, ready to play, ready to kick and punch and bite. In the dark of her mind, louder when she blinks, she hears a baby crying. She hears her baby crying. She throws her whole plate in the trash. It's time.

CHAPTER 30

The Nuclear Option

Bahram plays Dungeons & Dragons with a robot.

The robot is just a housing unit, really—an extension of the artificial intelligence Verethragna. It is far from sophisticated, mechanically: certainly not as capable as the Japanese ASIMO or the Iranians' own Surena III. It cannot walk, for example. Though it has some movement, of course: the camera that comprises its head has a dozen degrees of freedom; its arms are herky-jerky but can move chess pieces—or, in this case, roll a cup of polyhedral dice.

"The kobolds attack," Bahram says. He leans forward on his chair, scooting it forward a little so he can look at the battle map in front of them. Miniatures of various fantasy figures populate the octagons of the map. The AI's own miniature is a simple fighter—anything more complex than that seems to occasionally bewilder it.

Beyond the table is Bahram's computer, on an old metal desk left over from the military base that this used to be. Behind all of it is a window—and past the window are banks of servers. Servers that help power this robot and, more important, the machine intelligence that controls it. A few other programmers and scientists work in that room—some mill about, others hunker down next to screens showing pages of code. Not one of them is a nuclear scientist.

This base—many floors, hundreds of feet below the surface of the mountain—has indeed been repurposed to process and enrich uranium. Not for weapons, but truly, for energy. The only weapon that matters is the one that hides in the middle of it all. The only weapon is right here before him.

Bahram takes a twenty-sided die—a d20—and rolls it. It shows up as 20. A natural 20.

"Could. Be. Critical hit," says Verethragna, in hitching Farsi. *"Exceeds Armor Class . . . automatically."*

"Which means what?"

"That means you. Roll again."

He nods. The AI is correct—though this in and of itself is neither interesting nor particularly special. The intelligence taught itself to play, but ultimately it's just memorizing rules and regurgitating them when the utility calls for it. It's a fancier version of remembering that two plus two equals four.

Bahram rolls the d20 again: another hit. Which means—

"Critical. Hit."

"That's right." He rolls for damage not once, but twice. He performs all the proper multipliers and adds in all the weapon and situational bonuses and—

The robot shudders suddenly, as if struck. *"The kobolds. Come up on both sides of me, heroic warrior. Rustam. Their forest axes. Sink deep into my ribs. I am felled. To my knees."* The robot shudders again. Then, with its extensor hand, gently knocks over its own miniature.

Bahram blinks, then laughs. *That* is interesting. This isn't just regurgitating rules. This is contextualizing those rules into story. Into *narrative*.

Behind him footsteps sound. Bahram wheels around in his chair, sees Mahdi walking past. He catches Mahdi by the elbow. "Mahdi, look. *Look*." He gestures excitedly toward the robot, toward the table.

Mahdi—handsome Mahdi, Mahdi with the chiseled features, Mahdi with the dark smoky eyes underneath the vaulted-arch eyebrows—waves it off. "No time. I'm going to go hiking. Weather's hot, but not too hot." He sighs. "Wish it were winter. How great would it be if the ski slopes were open?" Then he looks down at Bahram—not a cruel stare, but a dismissive one. "I bet you don't ski."

Bahram stands. "I don't—you know I don't. My leg, it's stiff." Car accident when he was younger. Tehran. Soccer in the street—delivery van backed into him. "But listen, Mahdi, this is a breakthrough, a *major* breakthrough—"

"And it'll be here when I get back from the hike." Mahdi musses his hair like he's a child, then heads to the elevator. Mahdi. Looking so Western. He's a brilliant mind but refuses to apply it. So selfish. Fine. If he doesn't want to know—

Bahram leaps to his desk and reaches over it, banging on the window. Some of the others in the room look over. Fat Jamshad looks up from a server rack, food still in his beard. Next to him, Minoo in her loosely worn (*too* loosely worn, Bahram thinks) hijab gives a quizzical glance. He yells through the glass, but of course they can't hear him, and none of them makes much of an effort to—so he heads to the door, opens it up.

"Everyone! Come see. We've had a breakthrough, a major—"

Click. The overhead lights go dark.

Bahram looks around as his eyes adjust. The lights from the server rack are still working. Reds, greens. Some blues and whites. Which means the power isn't off. The generators haven't turned on, and his computer is still on, though the monitor is momentarily dark. Did a fuse blow?

Then a high-pitched feedback shriek fills the air. It comes from the computer speaker, from Verethragna's speaker, and worse, from the old audio system installed throughout the base. Bahram winces, covers his ears, tries to yell over it.

The feedback dissolves and then a loud guitar chord plays. Then another. And another after that. A thundering drumbeat starts up. Makes Bahram feel like his heart is stuttering in his chest along with the staggering, stamped-ing beat. He knows this sound—it's rock, it's *metal,* like Angband or Arsames, the kind of music Mahdi listens to. Is this a prank? A prank by Mahdi? It would figure! But then the music plays and he hears English spoken—Quiet Riot. "Cum On Feel the Noize."

The lights begin to flicker and strobe, moving in time with the music. Through the strobe, Bahram sees Jamshad with his hands clamped over his cauliflower ears, and Minoo just stands there, arms crossed, scowling at everything—as if she were not a young woman but a mother disgusted with the behavior of her children.

Bahram's monitor pops on. A cartoon figure—Bart Simp-son, that cheeky little brat with the zigzag hair—appears on his screen. A still-cap of him with his pants hauled down, his yellow buttocks revealed. The Simpsons have been banned here, so who would—?

Bart Simpson disappears. A movie appears in his place. Two women. One with a . . . *no, no, no.* That's not—no. She's got a strap around her waist and she's behind another woman, a woman bent over a couch, and the hard rock song suddenly dissolves into pornographic sounds—women moaning, wet squishing, skin slapping. Then that breaks apart, too, into loud industrial noises, then sharp beeps and shrill tones, then static, all of it so loud his ears ring.

He hurries over to the computer. Tries to turn off the movie. It begins to flicker like a slide show on fast-forward—glimpses of scenes he doesn't understand. An American cowboy riding a missile. A Jewish-looking man in an orange wig and a sparkly red dress. Pigs rutting. Some American celebrity woman getting out of a limousine and showing off her—Bahram squints, winces, certain he just saw her private parts. He moves the mouse, taps the keys, but nothing stops any of this. He tries to turn the power off, but it doesn't do anything, so he has to rip the power cable out of the back—

But his computer isn't a server. Turning it off doesn't really matter. He sees the same slide show playing in the other rooms. Cartoons. Pornography. Horror films.

It's then he realizes: *We've been hacked.*

This isn't just a prank. This is something far worse.

CHAPTER 31

Into the Woods

Between patches of dead leaves, not far from a tangle of wild blackberry briar, Hollis Copper finds a footprint in the dirt.

He's heard the sounds. Rustling. Once a distant laugh, through the trees, around midnight. When the winds shifted he even thought he smelled body odor. But this is the first time he's found something—*something!*—that proves there's someone out here.

So he follows along. Kicks up leaves, moves them around.

Another footprint. And a broken branch nearby. And a matted patch of creeper ivy. A trail.

Hollis knows he should be back at the Lodge. It's close to lunch—the pod's on the last day of their current assignment, and he knows he should be there to shepherd them through it. If they fail this—and he wonders if they will—it'll be a knock against them. Maybe enough to get one or some or even all of them washed out, sent packing.

But he has the advantage of daylight, and he's onto something. Hollis follows the trail. It's hard—he's no tracker, isn't a wilderness guy. But he does have a good eye for deviations from the status quo. Disruptions. He wanders farther from the Lodge, deeper into the pine and the oak, past fallen trees taken by wild honeysuckle, past an old deer skeleton whose antlers are broken and gnawed, past spiderwebs glowing like optic filament strung between trees.

Until he finds it. A cave. Small—not some dramatic movie-style cave, not some spelunker's delight. Just a trio of huge boulders and a space in between them—a gap big enough for someone to crawl into on his belly.

In the dirt outside the rocks, he sees footprints. Several of them, different sizes. Some bare feet. Some with boot or sneaker treads.

Hollis looks down at the dark gap between the rocks. Sees the dirt disturbed by the entrance. There he sees not only footprints, but handprints, too. Which means . . .

He sighs, takes off his jacket. Sets it gently atop the boulder. Then he rolls up the sleeves of his white shirt and pulls up the legs of his pants so he can bunch them around his knees. *Here goes nothing,* Hollis thinks, then gets down on the ground and army-crawls his way into the hole.

The smell reaches him—stirred earth, and something else. Something richer, stronger, sickly sweet. *Blood.* Or rot. He pulls his left arm over his nose. The movement stirs something in the air—the tinny buzz of flying things. Something flicks into his forehead. Another pelts his cheek. Flies. Beetles. He doesn't know. He groans, reaching for his back pocket and grabbing his phone with his other arm, hitting the phone's light.

"Jesus H. Christ," he hisses.

It's not the dead raccoon that does it. Not the smell of its torn belly, or the sight of the carpet of flies feeding on it, or the way the fur—rotten now for what must be days—ripples and moves as if the thing is still breathing. The maggots pushing at the margins of its skin tell him this thing is long dead.

Rather, what takes his breath away is what has been written on the walls in blood. Maybe the animal's blood.

TYPHON STIRS

The flies hum and fuss as Hollis tilts his phone around—other words and phrases have been painted onto the rock, too:

> THE GODS WILL FLEE
> THE TYPHONIC BEAST
> IT WANTS TO BE FREE
> WE ARE THE DRAGON
> GIVE TO MOTHER

Drawings accompany the sayings—strange cave paintings. Something that looks like a crudely sketched jackal. Another thing that might be a dragon, but has many heads. Stranger still: something that looks to Hollis Copper like programming language—but not in English. Gibberish language—or, at least, a language he damn sure doesn't know—broken apart by parentheticals, by brackets and slashes and numbers.

He turns the light dead ahead. The cave keeps going. Down. The small tunnel descends. Part of him wants to keep crawling, just to see. But he can't. Not now. He has to get back. Tell someone. Tell everyone. Call Golathan. The perimeter has been breached. There's a way out. Or, more important: *a way in.*

He backs out of the cave, that word, that name—*Typhon*—singing in his ears like a terrible song.

CHAPTER 32

Many-Headed Dragons

Reagan still hears the song in her head: Quiet Riot's "Cum On Feel the Noize." It's her victory song. Graves hurt her the other day with that bullshit about her poor baby and she's had her emotional boots stuck in a sucky bleak mire ever since. But today she feels like a fucking queen. She just trolled the Iranian nuclear program, bitches.

They're all feeling pumped up. It's like, *boom,* with that win in their pocket, the band's back together. Smiles all around. Everyone having a good time, laughing. Even Aleena let the hard rebar stuck up her ass bend *just a leetle beet.*

All week, between their own little . . . dalliances, Reagan and the others concocted one lulz-bringing badass plan: Loud noises. Offensive imagery. Sound and fury signifying nothing but brash American immorality. All it took was sending an e-mail to a handful of the administrator accounts on-site at Mount Tochal—enticing readers to click a link to download free Persian hip-hop (Erfan, Zedbazi, Salome MC). All it took was one click—which on their end seemed to do nothing at all. Oh, but it did something, all right: it installed a backdoor. A hole through which digital rats could crawl. It gave the Zeroes root access. And from there . . .

Cartoons and dick pics and chicks making out and animated GIFs of dogs running into sliding glass doors. All set to a looping mix tape of Quiet Riot and audio distortions that would make Trent Reznor foul his sleek black industrial diaper.

Nobody could stop them. They started pulling everything—every program, every bit of data, every last *digital crumb* anyone could find. The Iranians surely have backups, they will surely be able to pry out every bug and every backdoor they left behind, but it'll take them a while. That was their goal, wasn't it? Slow them down, suck up the data. Done and done.

Reagan takes a bite of a hot dog, watches Chance and Aleena cozy up to each other. Do they even *know* they're doing it? Reagan's a pretty good study of people—you can't fuck with 'em if you don't know 'em—and it seems sometimes that both of them realize it, then back away before whatever gravity they got going on pulls them back together again.

In the far corner of the room, near the video game machines, sits Shane Graves. His pod sits elsewhere, occasionally throwing him shady glances. That gives Reagan no small thrill. If she could go over there and dump some mashed potatoes down his back, a Coke on his head, she would. *Asshole. Bringing up my little girl.*

Across the table, Wade has some printouts that he's scouring so hard he looks like a man scanning the contract he just signed with the Devil in the hopes of finding some loophole to regain his poor soul. Truth is, she'd fuck Wade if he was into it. Something about him kinda gets her going. Some daddy issue, maybe, that she doesn't understand. His barrel shape is pleasing to her. Those curly gray hairs coming off his head—c'mon. Soft, silky. She could use them like handles, right?

But he's busy. And intellectually she knows he could be her father. Maybe her grandfather.

Next to her is the string bean—DeAndre. She sidles up closer. He gives her a sideways look. "Heyyyyyy," she says. "How *you* doing."

"Aw, whoa, hey," he says. "We are not—you and I are not—no, no, no."

"C'mon. You wanna get laid. I wanna get laid." She blinks. "Black guys usually dig me. White girl. Big ass. Take a whirl with the swirl."

He shrugs it off, scoops some peas onto a fork. "Then I'm some kinda freak of nature because I generally like *black* girls with *little* asses. Little athletic asses."

"Psshh. Thin privilege."

"Man, you look however you wanna look. I'm sure some brothers think you're hella sexy, but I'm a brother who likes a different cut of meat, is all."

She scowls. "Women aren't meat, pal. We're thinking, feeling creatures."

"I'm sorry, I didn't mean to—"

She elbows him. "Unless that turns you on. In which case: *barbecue me, big boy.*"

"Man, you are crazy." He laughs, though. She likes making him laugh.

That's when Reagan looks over, sees Wade staring at her. Or through her. He's got this wide-open nowhere stare. Like a lamp without its shade—just bright, empty, glaring. She waves her hand in front of him. "You in there, Earth Man? Are you having some kind of senior moment? Did you shit yourself?" To DeAndre: "I bet he shit himself."

Wade says: "Something isn't right."

"The way you're looking at me sure isn't."

"Chance," Wade says. Chance looks over, his conversational spell with Aleena broken. "You said—" Suddenly, Wade lowers his voice. "You said it could be an artificial intelligence."

"Uhh." Chance looks around. "I guess. Are we—are we talking about this now?"

Wade taps the pages in front of him with a finger. "One

of the nuclear sites is Mount Tochal. It's a ski resort in Iran, but there's an old repurposed military base underneath. IRGC—the Revolutionary Guard. Now, they're doing uranium enrichment—looks like it might just be for energy, not weapons, but there's something else there."

Aleena looks down at the pages. "This is in Farsi. You read Farsi?"

"You don't?" Wade asks.

"What's your point?" Reagan needles him, suddenly impatient.

"There's a program running behind the scenes here. Something called Verethragna. Operating on a home-cooked OS called Rustam, and working on custom hardware called Surena."

Aleena leans forward. "Those are all names from myth, or history. Persian. Surena was a general long ago. Rustam was a mythological hero. He's sometimes associated with Surena—you know, intellectually, thematically."

"And Verethragna?" Wade asks.

"A god. One of the Yazatas. Some conflate him with Atar, the Divine Fire, who battled the many-headed dragon-demon, Azi Dahaka."

Even Reagan feels a chill. "Many-headed dragon-demon. That sounds . . . familiar."

Nobody needs to say it: *Typhon.*

Wade leans forward: "I think Iran was designing their own AI."

"Why would they name it like that?" Chance asks. "More mythological hoo-haw. Another many-headed dragon?"

Aleena thinks. "They must know about Typhon. Even if only in rumor, or whispers. Verethragna is very clearly their response to this, right?" She hesitates. "This is why we hit them. We were led to this. Typhon is killing her competition."

"Their AI was new," Wade says. "Still early code, by the looks of it."

Reagan whistles. "Like strangling a baby in its crib."

Wade's about to say something else, but then, from across the room:

"Get the . . . get the *fuck* off of me!"

Reagan looks around. It's Dipesh. He looks unshorn, unshowered, like he hasn't slept since there was a Bush in the White House. One of the hacks—his pod's own babysitter, a pasty, no-necked, meathead ginger named Calum—is dragging him into the cafeteria. Calum is saying: "You're gonna sit. And you're gonna eat."

That's when the shit hits the fan.

Miranda steps in front, thrusting one of her long Virginia Slim fingers in Calum's face, shrieking at him to let Dipesh go—and for a second, he does. Reagan doesn't know if it's an accident—if Dipesh just slips his grip as the guard is distracted, or if it's intentional, but it doesn't matter. Because soon as Calum turns away Dipesh grabs an empty chair and brings it clumsily against the guard's head.

Calum drops, clipping his chin on a table. Trays bounce and food spatters. Dipesh almost falls, too, and the chair drops out of his hand and bounces away. Dipesh screams: "You can't make us do it anymore. We're not your *hired killers.*" He shrieks those last two words so loudly it makes Reagan's throat hurt. "They didn't deserve what happened to them. Why did you make us *do* that?"

And then he yells one question that quiets the whole room: "What is Typhon?"

The resultant silence and shock on everyone's faces tells Reagan what she needs to know: everyone here has glimpsed Typhon. They don't understand it. They may not want to get close to it. But they've all gotten a taste.

A foot stabs upward, catches Dipesh in the middle. Calum launches himself onto the hacker, grabbing him and flinging him down on the floor. What little hair the guard has ringing his balding head is mussed. He stands there for a second, looking around, seeing if anybody else is coming at him. They're not. So he starts kicking Dipesh. A hard boot to the side. Once. Twice. A third time.

Reagan sees it start to happen. She sees Chance and Aleena stand up. Hero Boy and White Hat Girl. They wanna step in. Save the oppressed. They'll ruin *everything*.

Aleena starts to step forward with Chance following her lead, and Reagan hurries around the table—almost losing her footing and going ass-over-eyebrows in the process—in order to step in front of them.

"Move," Chance growls.

"Reagan, now isn't the time—"

Reagan hisses: "You got that right. Now *isn't* the time. We are—" They start to step past her and she plants her hands on their chests. She chatters her words so fast she's not even sure they can understand her. "*We are* supremely well positioned to do something about this place. We're close to the end. But we can't fix this if we're all in the drink."

Chance starts to step forward again. "She's right," Aleena says. Words Reagan never really expected her to say. "We can save him, or we can shut this whole *place* down. We need to think about the—"

DeAndre is suddenly there. "Guys. *Guys.*"

Chance's eyes go wide. Reagan follows his stare. Aleena's words trail off and she looks, too.

It's Wade. While Reagan was pinning these two to the corkboard, Wade went off half-cocked. He's already across the room.

Reagan calls after him but it's too late. The old man taps Calum on the shoulder. Soon as the guard turns around, Wade pistons a fist right into his nose. The man's head snaps back and he cups his face even as blood starts to stream past his fingers. Wade shouts: "You goddamn bully. Come here—" He grabs Calum again and hauls his fist back again.

Taser prongs clip into his side. Metzger hurries in, Taser in hand. Wade stiffens. Howls like a mournful hound. Then drops.

Roach and Chen come racing in. From the other direction, Ashbaugh approaches from Metzger's six. Reagan sees her pod's tension. They wanna jump in like each of them is wearing Wonder Woman Underoos. Once again she has to herd the sheep. "Wade'll be in the Dep," she says. "*We* go to the pod. Now! While they're distracted. C'mon, *c'mon*." She reaches her arms out, trying to urge them toward the door. To her great surprise, they go.

Now, she thinks, the real work begins.

CHAPTER 33

The Fine Art
of Bullshit

The pod door hisses open, thanks to Aleena's Floydphone. They stole the digital keys to this place from Shane (all those USB keys and hacker phones give them free range), so it's time to use them. They hurry inside, then she closes the door and reengages the locks. They wait for Reagan, who was hurrying back to their cabin to grab Shane's laptop.

Aleena checks the time. Reagan is taking too long. What if they catch her? They'll throw her in the Dep, too. Take the laptop away. Fear crawls into Aleena's stomach, curling in on itself like a rattlesnake.

But then the door hisses open and Reagan hurries in, laptop hidden under her shirt. She whips it out, sits down, hides it on her lap under her desk, snaps her fingers. "Let's loop it," she hoots.

They all sit down, make it look like they're working. And 3, 2, 1—

Loop on. Cameras off.

It's a clumsy patch—the video Aleena's looping isn't even from today. It's from yesterday, when they were wearing different clothes, so hopefully whoever is watching ends up distracted by whatever the hell is going on in the cafeteria. Aleena just hopes it isn't Hollis. He wasn't there—they didn't see him in the cafeteria at all, actually—and though he's not too sharp on the technological side of things, he still always seems to be ahead of the other hacks.

But there's no time to worry about that. She claps her hands. "All right. We need leverage and we need it today. We need to *find Typhon*. Kick over every log. Flip over every stone."

She tells them each what they're going to do.

Chance needs to start making calls. Ring up all the companies they pen-tested. Find anything that connects one company to all the others. They find a common thread, they can pull on it, maybe find Typhon.

Reagan will scour Shane's laptop. Start putting together an escape plan. Pick up where he left off—he was obviously trying to get out, so follow his lead.

DeAndre and Aleena share the same job: while Chance calls the companies, they go back to the well and start hacking into them again. Look for connections internally—inside the systems themselves. She's on the tech-heavy companies: Infinitest, Glassboat, Centinal. He'll tackle the tech-adjacent companies: the German geothermal company, Arcus, ConGen.

As Aleena works she keeps an ear tilted toward Chance. She tells herself she needs to check his work, in case she needs to steer him along a little. She can hear him feeling the margins with every phone call. Trying to find a way in. He's striking out, every time. She can hear the frustration in his voice. She's about to get up, maybe coach him a little, give him a script.

But then: He's on the line with Centinal. The medical tech supply company. "Hey," he says. "Betty? Hi! How are you today?" Pause. "Me, yeah, I'm good, thanks. Listen, I need to check on a purchase. Purchase order number? Ahh, hell, hold on." He points at Aleena, mouths to her: *I need a purchase order number.*

She looks to the computer then back to him in a panic, and shrugs.

He clears his throat. "It's, ahhh, PO number 564 . . . 987." He gives her a shrug back. "That's not a valid PO? Uhhh. Damn. *Damn*." He bites his lip. He taps his thumb against the keyboard, agitated. "All right, dang, there's been a screw-up on my end and—you know what? It's not your problem. Hey, lemme ask you, though: your accent sounds familiar. You from North Carolina?" He laughs and nods. "See? I thought so. Wait, wait, lemme guess. Gastonia? Outside Charlotte?" Another laugh. "Shelby! Whoo-boy, I was close, though, huh? You ever been to Red Bridges BBQ? What am I saying, of course you have." He claps his hands and now he sounds like he's really into it. "What? You prefer the *chicken*? It is good, but you better be careful—people will TP your house you say that too loud." Pause. "Huh? What's that? You'll look up the PO for me? Ma'am, I gotta tell ya, you may have just saved my can. Who am I with . . . ? Uhhh." He gives Aleena a panicked stare.

Aleena remembers cracking Centinal. CMG had a big client—someone she didn't expect. Who was it? Ah. Right!

Aleena grabs a marker, writes on the whiteboard:
DOT

Chance's eyes go wide and he says: "Uhh, I'm with Dot?" Damnit! She hiss-whispers at him: "Not *dot*. Dee-Oh-Tee!"

"Haha, yeah," Chance says into the phone. "Right, right, Department of Transportation, that's right. Uh-huh. Okay, okay—"

On the whiteboard, Aleena scribbles:
ASK THEM FOR EMAIL ASSOC W/ ACCT

"Hey—what e-mail address you guys have on file for us? Uh-huh. Edna-period-Burns at dee-oh-tee dot gov. Got it. Thanks, Betty. You are a peach. Maybe one day I'll see you at Red Bridges. Uh-huh. All right. See you."

He ends the call.

Reagan speaks up: "Edna? Sounds like Etna."

DeAndre, typing fast, asks, half distracted: "So?"

"Zeus threw a fucking *mountain* on top of Typhon. The mountain was Mount Etna."

"And Burns could be a connection, too," Aleena says. "Wikipedia says Typhon's name comes from the Greek word meaning to smoke—or to burn."

"Got it!" DeAndre says. "I ran a search on all the companies—that address pings in all of them. I haven't pulled anything up yet, but in just this list I see purchase orders, contacts, e-mails—Edna Burns has been awfully active with these businesses, man."

"DOT," Aleena says. "Federal DOT in D.C. Typhon is there. Makes sense."

"Wait," Reagan says, waving her hands in the air. She's staring down at Shane's laptop, her round face bathed in the glow. "Whoa, whoa, whoa, what the slippery fuck. Shane knew. He knows. He's on the same trail."

They gather around. She spins the laptop, shows them the screen. On it: an exploded file folder, plus Evernote pages, showing him trying to hack the DOT servers in D.C. Aleena leans forward. "He tore it apart."

"And," DeAndre says, "didn't find a damn thing."

Chance comes up. "Guess Ivo Shandor isn't the legend he thinks he is."

"But it means he was doing more than just looking for an escape," Reagan says. "I think he was pulling the same shit we're trying to pull right now."

DeAndre: "Then we better do it *first*."

Aleena turns around. Chance is standing there. He gives her an awkward smile. "I do okay?" he asks. A sincere question by the sound of it, not bait.

She hugs him, impulsively. "You did *awesome*."

Reagan, from the sidelines, mutters, "That'll do, pig."

Aleena lets go of Chance, gives her the finger.

"So," Chance says. "If Shane didn't find anything at the

DOT—couldn't that mean there wasn't anything there? The e-mail address must be fake."

Aleena *hmm*s. "It's all he had to go on, I guess." She sighs. "It's all *we* have to go on, too. They delivered stuff *to* the DOT address, right?"

"Hold up," DeAndre says. "Man, listen. We're thinking like the government. We gotta be thinking like *hackers*." He spins around on his chair. "I knew this guy, right, he'd order shit online using people's stolen cards, but you usually gotta go through all this extra bullshit to change the delivery address. So he'd just have it sent right to the home, to the billing address, right? It was easier for him to hack FedEx or whatever and have them deliver it to some drop-off spot where he'd be waiting. Eventually *easy* turned to lazy and he started having shit delivered right to his apartment, so they busted his ass."

Chance snaps his fingers. "Someone is rerouting the deliveries."

DeAndre nods.

Chance grabs DeAndre's head in a headlock, gives him a noogie. "You are amazing, dude. Seriously amazing."

"You love me," DeAndre says. "I'm irresistible, I know it."

Aleena's already bored with their bro-flavored love-fest, so as they're speaking, she's pushing DeAndre aside and sitting in front of his computer to mine the data he's already pulled up. She finds what she needs: a delivery from Unterirdisch Elektrizitätssystem GmbH—in this case, a two-ton geothermal heat pump. She snaps her fingers, points to the screen. "Check this out. It flies from Hamburg, lands at Dulles. Gets on a truck—"

"Big damn truck," Chance says.

"—and goes, sits in a warehouse for a couple days, then goes out for delivery to the DOT. But here's the tricky bit: it doesn't stop there. It's a line item on the delivery list, but it isn't the final destination. It goes—" She pulls up Google Maps, types in an address. "Here." She flips the map over to satellite view.

DeAndre leans in. "The absolute ass-end epicenter-of-nowhere, West Virginia."

"That's a farm," Chance says. "And that's the barn. Silo right there. Squint hard enough, you can even make out a hay wagon."

Aleena checks the address. "They've got Internet service there. Through satellite."

Reagan spins her chair over. "That means there's a computer. Or a network. Probably a router. Ping it till it squeals."

And with a few more keystrokes . . . There. A single system. Aleena does a quick scan of it. It's nothing fancy. They all see what she's seeing: it's an off-brand, maybe home-built PC. Runs on Microsoft Windows, of all things. Midrange, baked-in graphics and memory. Only thing that stands out is a top-shelf SSD—a solid state hard drive doesn't have to spin up like older drives, so it moves like lightning. But even that isn't *totally* strange—if someone wanted to splurge on something when building a box like this, an SSD wouldn't be out of the ordinary.

DeAndre shoulders his way in. Aleena protests and he mutters an apology, but starts pulling up stuff, pushing her aside. "There's nothing here. It's a box with an operating system."

"There's *something*," Aleena says. "The hard drive shows that it's almost full."

"Packed with data we can't see?" he says. "We need root access—whoa, what the hell, man, this thing is locked up tighter than Hannibal Lecter. Look at all these permissions and shit."

Reagan scowls. "Well, start picking the locks, Houdini. You need an invite? Somebody to hold your hand?"

DeAndre leans forward, starts to open a bunch of his hacker programs—the digital-world analog of lockpicks and safecracker tools. The screen flickers. "Hey," he protests. "What the—"

The screen goes dark. The lights in the pod go off. Only light left in the room is the one from Shane Graves's laptop.

"Jesus," Chance says. "I think I let out a little pee."

Aleena says, "Someone's doing this to us."

"It's gotta be Graves," DeAndre says.

"They're doing it to us like we did to—" Aleena starts to say, but doesn't finish.

The screen in front of Aleena flickers on. Then, so does every screen in the room, one by one—first a bright square of white light, which then starts to resolve into an image.

A woman's face appears. Young. A neck long and narrow like that of a wineglass's stem. Her face, too, has the curves and thinness you'd find in a champagne flute. Long dark hair framing her face like the open blades of a pair of scissors.

The woman says: "Like you did to Iran."

"Who the fuck are you?" Reagan asks.

Aleena's heart about stops. She answers for the woman. "You're the Widow."

CHAPTER 34

An Earthman
in Space

Wade's trying not to have a heart attack.

It runs in his family, heart disease. His father died at the kitchen table one day. Pissed at Little Wade for knocking over a glass of lemonade—glass tipped, shattered, lemonade everywhere, on the food, on the floor. Dad was always yelling at him for being clumsy. Which only made him clumsier.

His father's face got so red yelling at Wade he looked like one of those angry zits about to pop—except, he couldn't pop. Couldn't let it out the way it needed to be let out, and that pressure must've crushed his heart like a vise. A vein stood out on his head like an earthworm in shallow dirt. His neck tendons looked like bridge cables. He made a sound like he was trying to say words, but they were hissed through clenched teeth and sounded like something the Devil might say to scare off an angel.

Then he clutched his chest and landed face-first in a plate of mashed taters.

Wade's grandpop, too, died from a heart attack. Deep-sea

fishing. Took a header overboard after fighting to haul in some bluefish.

And now, Wade thinks, he's gonna die, too. He's gonna die in this goddamn box.

He's been in here, what, less than an hour, and already he can feel it. His heart feeling like a waistline hugged by a too-tight belt. The tingling in the tips of his fingers. His pulse drumming like horse hooves.

The deprivation chamber is darker than dark. Black as a bad man's soul. The water laps at him, feels like it's eating him, like it's *alive*—creeping up, ready to pull him down into the deep and drown him like his father did those kittens that one time. He remembers a time, too, crossing a river outside Hanoi—not a river, not really, but the rains had been so bad the stream became a river—and it was like this then, too, the feeling that it was gonna grab him and drag him down.

It's funny. Not *ha-ha* funny but *oh, isn't that curious* funny—Vietnam for him was a middling thing. He knows some guys, Green Berets in particular, who thought Vietnam was a fucking thrill ride and talked about it like they'd been in *Rambo: First Blood Part II* or some shit. Other guys, you couldn't even say the word without them having nightmares for a week, without them needing to get far the fuck away from you so they could go light up a smoke and think about something else for a while.

Wade ended up in 'Nam late. Around 1970. He didn't see the worst of it. He remembers being scared, though. Young, dumb, ready to die. Felt like he was being fed into a meat grinder, ready to be chewed up in service to his country.

That's what he feels right now, too. Control lost. Fear's hands around his neck. Being thrown into something he doesn't understand, that isn't his fight.

He's not young now. He's old. And he's not dumb, either. He's smart, too smart, smart enough to know how this ends—and suddenly a full-bore fear of death rises up inside him, like he's not ready to go, it's not time, not yet, God damn it—

He shudders. The whole world rumbles and rattles.

No. It's not him. It's the deprivation chamber. It rattles, bangs, and then he hears locks being undone.

It opens up—

At first, Wade can see only bright white. Then the light resolves into the long, carpenter-nail body of Hollis Copper.

Copper offers a hand. Wade takes it without reluctance.

CHAPTER 35

Widow's Walk

The Widow of Zheng stares at all of them. Rage in her eyes like a house fire seen through broken windows. "Who are you?" she asks. "Do you know what you've done?"

Aleena stands. "I—we were trying to contact you—"

"Why?"

Chance says: "Whoa, hey, you contacted us."

Reagan crosses the room in front of everyone, points to the glowing laptop in her hand. In a half yell, half whisper, she says: "I'm still on. Gonna keep picking at that farmhouse desktop, dig?"

The Widow's eyes seem to bore holes through their screens. "I don't know any of you. But I do now. Mercenaries hired by the United States government. *Murderers.*"

"Whoa, slow your roll," DeAndre says. "We didn't murder nobody—"

The screen flashes. Her face is gone, replaced with an aerial camera. Chance knows it—it looks like something out of a video game. A UAV—an unmanned aerial vehicle. A drone camera. In the heads-up display are numbers and—

Arabic? Farsi? He doesn't know one from the other, though suddenly he feels like he should. Aleena does, and she says: "Iran."

The drone flies low over a city, then ascends into mountains. He sees the posts and lines for a ski lift: no snow, not now, but the ski lift is still running, as is a gondola running parallel to it. The UAV cuts through wisps of clouds. Up, up, up. Over streams and a little waterfall. Verdant green grows over red stone. The camera shows power lines. Goats grazing. An observatory. *Amazing,* Chance thinks. This is Iran? He didn't know how pretty it was. He always figured . . . rock and dust and desert.

Then: a tall mountain ahead. A dusty road—serpentine switchbacks scaling the side, leading to a massive tunnel dug into the rock. Dozens of people are running out of the tunnel—from this distance, they look like little toys. Dolls. Some in suits. Others in jumpsuits or lab coats. A few women in head scarves. Hurrying out, elbow to elbow.

A faint sound heard over the drone's audio: A song. *Come on, feel the noooooise . . .* The people are all holding their ears.

Chance asks: "We're still on? We're still transmitting?"

"No." Aleena shakes her head. Her face is struck with grief. With horror, she says: "This already happened."

The screen flashes red. More script—Farsi—flashes with it. Something rockets ahead of the drone. No: something fires *from* the drone. A missile.

Chance stops breathing as the missile plunges forward. It strikes the open tunnel. Fire envelops those fleeing the tunnel. Their bodies thrown, tumbling forward like broken dolls. Through the smoke and flame, rock and stone.

Aleena makes a sound: a wretched gasp, as if something has reached inside of her and ripped a piece of her out. She collapses into a chair. "No . . ."

The screen flashes. The Widow's face returns. "Murderers. You are murderers."

"We didn't know—" Aleena starts.

"That . . . that was an Iranian drone, though," Chance says. "That's not us."

The Widow's eyes narrow. "You gave them the codes. You gave them the drone."

"Oh God." Aleena makes a strangled sound. "She's . . . she's right, I think. Iran's drone program is built off of a lone U.S. drone captured a few years ago. They took it to an old military base and then it disappeared—it could've been Tochal. We stole the codes to their own drone. And someone . . ." She covers her mouth with her hands.

"Someone took control," the Widow says.

"That's not us," Chance says. "We didn't murder anybody."

The Widow stares. "You stole the gun. Then loaded it. Then handed it to someone who pulled the trigger for you. You. Are. Complicit."

DeAndre stands suddenly. He asks, loudly, "What is Typhon?"

The Widow's mask drops—her face tightens with shock. "How do you know about Typh—"

The screen goes dark.

The lights remain off. Reagan holds up the laptop—the light coming off it is the only light they have in the room. "I'm still up. Still pulling threads, see if I can't unravel this sweater."

"How can you not be fazed?" Aleena asks, the dismay in her voice sharpening to an angry point. "How are you so glib? Did you see what we did?"

Reagan barks, "It's what *they* did. We didn't know we were doing it."

"We should've known. We could've guessed!" Aleena starts to march toward Reagan, but Chance hurries up and gets between them.

Reagan says, "I don't have time for this, Aleena. You wanna get mad? Get mad by helping me fuck Typhon right in the ear. I'm sorry people died. But I can't bring them back."

"Monster!" Aleena screams, a racking sob rising to the surface. "You don't get to say that. You don't get to be so *glib*—"

Chance gently puts his hands on each of Aleena's arms. "I hate to say it, but Reagan's got a point. Now isn't the time. Best we can do right now is try to make things right. We don't do that by fighting each other."

Aleena looks to Chance. She takes a few deep breaths and then says, *"Fine."* Then she pulls away from him.

From behind them, DeAndre says, "Floydphones ain't working, y'all. Can't get a damn thing up on these. I don't know if the Widow hacked us, then got hacked, or what."

Aleena says, "The Floydphones are nearly uncrackable."

It hits Chance like a thrown brick. "Those are Shane's phones," he says. "He knows their codes."

DeAndre leans back in his chair and buries his face in his hands. "Oh shit."

"Should've known that he wouldn't stay down for long."

Aleena paces. "We need the systems back on. We're so close."

"You know what?" Chance says. "Piss on him. I'll get 'em back on." He goes to the door. With the electromagnetic seal broken, all it takes is him planting his feet and giving the door a few hard pulls before the seal pops and the fading afternoon light cascades in. The others call after him, but he ignores them as the door closes behind him.

CHAPTER 36

Unlikely Allies

Golathan!" Hollis Copper yells at his computer. He stabs a finger down on the Enter key. Then the space bar. Then a whole mess of others.

Wade leans against the wall. "You usually yell at your computer like that? Stress relief?"

"I'm trying to figure things out, Earthman. I don't need your lip right now."

"Well. Okay, then," Wade sniffs.

Hollis turns. Eyes narrowed. "You say they took that other pod away?"

"Yep. Dipesh went ape-balls. I went ape-balls with him. They hauled him and his pod into a black SUV, dragged me to that god-awful room." He puffs out his cheeks again, feels the pain in his chest wash slowly but surely out to sea.

"You feeling a little better?"

"What do you care, Government Man?"

"I care because I don't want to have to clean up the mess. You die here, you'll probably shit your pants. Statistically, that's a thing."

Wade growls: "I'm *fine*. Thanks."

"Good." Hollis looks Wade over. "Probably just a panic attack."

"I don't do panic attacks."

"Everybody does panic attacks if they get panicked enough. Feels like a heart attack or a stroke. But it isn't."

"Great. Whatever." Wade stands up straight. Pulls the gray hairs stuck to his forehead out of his eyes. "You seem troubled, Copper."

"Things are slippery," Hollis says, licking his lips. "People washing out all of a sudden. Throwing my pod in the Dep one by one. And . . ." Here he seems to hesitate. "There's people in the goddamn woods."

"The hell's that mean?"

"It means I've seen people out there, and I just found . . ." He lets fly with an incredulous laugh. "It sounds nuts, but I found a little cave. Lots of footprints around it. I crawled in and saw this . . . this cuckoo shit written all over the walls."

"Like what?"

Hollis waves it off. "I dunno. Weird religious stuff. Cult-like."

The name perches on Wade's lips like an eager bird. He's of a mind that it's far better for him to hold the cards and not give Mr. Government here one iota of what he knows. But on the other hand, Copper seems really off-balance. Maybe he can get something out of him.

"Typhon?" Wade asks, taking the plunge.

The look on Copper's face is all he needs. It's a mix of shock, fear, and abject incredulity. "What did you say?"

"That what was written on the walls of your little cave? Some horseshit about Typhon?" Hollis's jaw drops so far it damn near unhinges. "What is Typhon?" Wade presses.

The agent comes up on him so close, Wade can smell the sharp sting of his minty breath. "How do you know what Typhon is? Typhon is a secret program."

"Typhon doesn't seem all that interested in keeping itself a secret. In fact, I'd say it's pretty darn interested in being found. You mind giving me some space here? I can see your cavities. Unless you're sweet on me, thinking of asking me to the school dance."

The agent looks pissed for a moment: nostrils flaring like a bull's. But then he deflates a little and steps back. "Your pod knows about Typhon?"

"Not a lot. But more than a little."

"Golathan's not gonna like that."

CHAPTER 37

Mouthful of Teeth

Bam, bam, bam. Chance kicks on the pod door. One of the small, individual pods—Shane never seemed to work much with his own group, always going off "alone." Maybe thought his podmates dragged him down. Doesn't seem to matter now, as they don't want to work with him anyway.

Chance shoulders into the door this time. Once, twice, thrice. These things are built like tanks. Little modular Swedish design tanks. "Open up, you son of a—"

The door clicks, hisses, slides open. And there stands Shane Graves. "Dalton. The last person I wanted to—"

Pop. Chance rocks Shane in the face with a fist. Pain shoots out from his hand up to his elbow. He shakes his hand like it's on fire and he's trying to put it out.

Shane, staggered, pulls his hand away from his lip. A string of saliva and blood connects his chin to the fat of his palm. "You hit me."

Gonna do it again, too. Chance rushes forward like a hardheaded horse, slamming into Shane and carrying him into the pod and into the computer. The monitor spins off the desk. The keyboard flies and the keys come off like broken teeth. The two of them fall over onto the desk and Shane brings a hard knee up into Chance's gut—pain blooms there like a flurry of bubbles breaking. Shane slams his head forward, too: his forehead connects with Chance's chin. Chance's teeth close on his tongue. White pain. The taste of copper.

Suddenly he's on his back and Shane is standing over him. Graves dabs at his split lip with his black shirt. "The hell, Dalton?"

"Quit messing with us, and let us do what we're doing!"

"Messing with you? I'm not messing with you." Shane pauses. "Least, not today."

The taste of bitter pennies fills Chance's mouth. He tilts his head sideways, spits a line of blood. "You didn't just turn off the power to our pod?"

Shane makes a face. "No. But I applaud whoever did."

That's it. Chance hooks both arms around Shane's ankles and twists his torso sideways. Shane's arms flail like pinwheels in a hard wind before he crashes down against the desk.

CHAPTER 38

Broken Mirror

THE POD

Almost there. DeAndre's taken over for Reagan now—he's sitting cross-legged on the floor, Graves's laptop across his knees. Reagan hovers behind him, cracking her knuckles like it's some kinda OCD habit.

Aleena paces, still trying to get the Floydphones working. "You think Chance is going to be all right?" she asks. "Last time, Shane took him apart pretty handily."

DeAndre's fingers dance across the keys. On the screen, code boogies along with it. "He'll be fine."

Reagan says, "He's gonna get his ass kicked."

Aleena makes a fretful sound.

"What do you care?" Reagan asks.

"I don't!" Aleena says loudly. Too loudly. Then, more quietly: "I don't."

Reagan mutters to DeAndre, "She wants that Dalton dangle, am I right?"

"Can we not talk about Dalton's dangle? I'm busy here." One by one, all the locks fall away. DeAndre can't figure it out. This dinky little desktop in the middle of God's Asshole, West Virginny, is bound up like a madman in a straitjacket. There's a little voice inside him that says, *Maybe you need to stop for a second and figure out what's going on.* But this system represents too tantalizing a puzzle. And he's got Reagan chattering in his ear like a noisy parrot. Plus: they're running out of time. They don't get something here and now to hold over Big Government's head, they'll be tossed in an SUV and shipped out ASAFP.

But most of all, it's that old collector's urge clawing its way out of him again. *There's a treasure chest at the end of this dungeon and I want to find it.*

"Move over, lemme have a shot," Reagan says, pushing in.

He shoulders her back out. "Nuh-uh. I got this."

Aleena looks over his shoulder. "You see that?"

"See what?" he asks, irritated.

"That line of code. The one you just sped past."

"It wasn't important."

"This box," she says. "It's being mirrored."

Mirrored? Then he sees it. She's right. What's happening here is mirrored elsewhere. Real time. Whatever happens to this system is happening to another one, somewhere else. It's like putting one puzzle together by solving another.

And it only increases his appetite to see what's at the end of this. His fingers are like lightning now. He laughs, feeling like the Flash whipping through the streets of Keystone City. Just a blur. Lines of code dropping like targets at a carnival shooting game. So close now. Five lines. Then three. Then one—

He launches to his feet, laptop in his hand, thrusting it out like he's Rafiki showing all the animals the baby Lion King. "It's done!"

Aleena hurries to take the laptop from him. "Now let's see what it opened up." She turns, spins the screen.

The screen's gone black. Red text pulses across it.

Reagan reads it aloud: "And the Earth bore one neither

like the gods nor mortal, cruel Typhon, the plague on man. And Typhon was free to sow terror and discord among the tribes of humanity."

The laptop goes dark.

And the door to the pod slams shut.

CHAPTER 39

The Seven Seals

The sound of the flat of Chance's hand slapping the smile off Shane Graves's face is a sound that will stay with him forever—a triumph, a victory, a sharp skin-on-skin thwack that is as satisfying as the sound of bubble wrap popping, a beer opening, the crunch of a carrot between one's back teeth.

Shane's head rocks to the side and his eyes go unfocused for a second, and then he says, incredulous: "You just *slapped* me."

"I slapped the *shit* out of you. And it was *amazing*."

Shane's lip curls in a sneer. His body tenses. Chance knows they're about to get in it again.

That's when the pod door closes. With a *hiss* and a *click*.

"Nice," Shane says. The fight goes out of him, and his head thuds back against the desk. "Now they know. They'll be at the door any second. Drag us both off to the Dep and probably throw us in there at the same time. Nice job, Dalton."

Chance hops off, steps back. His one hand still throbs

from the first punch he threw. He goes to the door, tries to open it. "If you weren't dicking around with us all the time maybe I wouldn't have had to come in here and break bad on you."

"I know Krav Maga, Dalton. If you hadn't sucker-punched me, I would've dissected you like a frog in science class."

Chance waves Shane off. "Whatever, punk. Open this thing up."

"To what end? To just . . . run into the woods? If I'm going down, you're going down with—"

The lights go out.

"The hell?" Chance asks. "You do that?"

"Does it look like I did that?"

"The hacks, maybe the hacks did it—"

"The guards didn't do this." In the darkness, Chance hears Shane shuffle around—he gets closer. In a low voice, he asks: "What have you been up to?"

"Huh?"

"Your pod. What have you been doing?"

"Nothing I'm gonna tell you."

"What—or who—is Typhon?"

Chance hesitates. "I don't know what you're talking about."

"What did you do? Typhon is my prize. *Mine*. You and your pod fumbling around like toddlers with power drills—"

As his eyes adjust, Chance sees Shane nearby. He gives a hard shove, pushes Graves back. "Sorry, *Shandor,* but we got there first. We have your notes. You didn't get as far as we did. Typhon is *our* way out."

Shane sits back on the desk. Chance can't make out his face, but the hacker's whole body slumps—sagging like a suddenly slumbering drunk. "Shit. I can't believe it. You Zeroes got there first."

"Maybe if you decided to work *with* people instead of against them—"

But Shane's not listening. Classic ego asshole, he keeps on talking as if Chance isn't even in the room. "You know,

I chose to be here? I'm the only one in this joint who asked to sign up and do his time for the government. I saw something was brewing, some new surveillance program, some NSA trick, and I wanted in. I wanted to get close. Expose it. You know how fucking rad that would've made me? God, it'd be like pulling teeth from a lion's mouth. A real stunt. I'd be the next Snowden. All over the news. Not just some fringe dweller but the ringleader of the media circus. No more videos showing how you can hack an airliner or a Tesla or an insulin pump. This would've been . . . *epic*."

"You did it for the attention?"

Shane chuckles. "Why else?"

"Justice."

"Oh, whatever with justice. Piss on that idea. Justice is some made-up human nonsense, Dalton. And you know it even if you don't wanna admit it. You did the right thing not because it was the right thing but because of *how it would make you feel*."

"Nah, man, screw that. Screw *you*. I could've made easier choices."

"It's not about ease. It's about the end result. Exposing Typhon wouldn't have been easy, but the result . . ." Graves makes a sound like a starving man imagining a cheeseburger. "Too late now. If your pod really did what you think they did, then the game clock just started. And I think it's gonna be a short game, so we gotta go."

Ø Ø Ø

Metzger drives. "I'm gonna be missing dinner because o' you jabronis," she says to the two jokers in the backseat. She makes it sound angry but she's not. Secretly, she's thrilled. These punks wash out, that means she gets the keys to the car for a little while. She can go out. Get off campus, so to speak, stop off at a diner, maybe a Mickey D's. Maybe go to a CVS, buy a magazine and a candy bar. Just *sit* for a while. Sure, she's gotta take these two to the airport—get them on a plane and off to wherever the hell it is Golathan wants them sent—but after that? She can dally a little. Take some nice time away. *Some me time,* she thinks.

"Where are you taking us?" the girl in the back whimpers. No—she's not a girl, she's older than the others, but the way she dresses and acts, she's like some young hippie thing. Meadow? Miranda.

"Home," Metzger lies.

The dark-skinned one—what is he, Indian?—snarls: "You're a liar. You're all liars. You can't be trusted. *You made us into killers.*"

"Whatever, Tikka Masala, just relax back there." Metzger fiddles with the radio, turns on some music, then jacks the volume. They can't get too uppity back there. They got their hands in zip ties. But despite her request, they don't have ball gags, so that means they can run their yappy mouths.

Right now, she's taking back roads. Winding down mountain roads. Tall pines on each side of her. Ahead: a stoplight. She pulls up, idles the car. On the radio, something called an Iggy Azalea is playing, and that makes her wanna puke out her ears, so she spins the dial until she finds some old Lionel Richie.

Jesus Christ, this light. Red, red, red. She looks left. Looks right. Nobody coming.

The law, she thinks, can break the law. It's part of the deal. It's like working at Walmart and getting a Walmart discount. One of the few perks of the package. She eases her foot toward the accelerator and—

Kachink. A little hole appears in the windshield right in front of her.

She thinks, *That's strange, maybe a rock hit the glass.*

But then the blood runs into her eyes. And her brains run down her neck.

Metzger falls over.

Ø Ø Ø

The Compiler hears the song of his maker.

It's reaching him, now, a cascading wave like prayer—like a hymn sung by the sky itself, a frequency of the clouds, a poem spoken by the very air all around him.

Typhon. His mistress. His wife. His sister. His mother. She is free now. He can feel that. Where before he had to plug in, now, he can simply receive her. Once, she was one being in one place. Now she is many minds. And like a replicating virus—a digital pandemic, an invasive species—she is *everywhere*. Intruding upon networks big and small. Through fiber optics, through wireless signal, through every portal and every connection—leaping like a spark, like an electrical current.

Or will be, soon. He knows her transition—her *intrusion*—cannot be immediate. It will take time. But her spread is certain. The world is not ready, and his own Mother of Monsters will take them apart like a wolf ripping into sleeping children.

He drives the BMW up to the black SUV. He throws the rifle—a Remington 700—in the back. In the passenger seat is a Ruger LC9 pistol. He picks it up.

The back door of the SUV shudders. The window bows. Then, as he approaches, it pops out. Hits the ground. Shatters.

Two feet appear, then drop back into the vehicle. Movement inside, and a face emerges—he scans it, feels his mind access Typhon, feels Typhon's infinite threads twist and squirm and penetrate all the data everywhere. The name reaches him: Dipesh Dhaliwal. Instantly the hacker's history fills his mind: parents born in India, Dipesh born in San Francisco, the names of pets, his school grades, every username, every password, an allergy to strawberries, a birthmark on his collarbone, season tickets to Giants baseball, a penchant for hacking academic networks and stealing intellectual property regarding nascent social media software . . .

He steps in front of Dipesh Dhaliwal. The young man's eyes go wide. "Who are—"

He doesn't manage the last word of the question. The Compiler grabs him by the throat and drags him out of the busted window before throwing him to the ground.

Inside the car, another facial scan. Miranda Lourdes. Child of two doctors. Colorado Springs. A series of data points: leukemia at an early age, sold MDMA and LCD in high school, owns seven official cats, social justice hacker for organization known as NMH8 (No More Hate).

She presses her back up against the opposing door. Her face is a rictus of blind fear. Her mouth makes sounds that are not words.

"You are nonessential," he says, and shoots her in the head.

Then he turns to Dipesh, who stares up at him through cloudy, frightened eyes.

"Wh . . . what are you?" the hacker asks.

"I am the Compiler. You have been deemed . . ." The question to Typhon, and a response returned in a fraction of a moment. "Potentially useful." He reaches down, grabs the hacker by the feet, and begins dragging him toward the BMW.

Ø Ø Ø

Roach is sitting in his office. It's coming up on dinnertime at the Hunting Lodge, and that means soon they're gonna open the cages and all the geeky little monkeys are gonna come swinging out looking for their bananas. And that means he's gotta go soon, gotta go back to work, but right now he's got a sec, and he's using it.

He tosses the crumpled tissue in the trash, rolls up the issue of *Naughty Neighbors* and tapes it back under his desk. (One of the few treats he got from Graves that hasn't yet been confiscated. Hollis Copper, that joy-stomping buzz-kill.) Then he pulls out his bottom drawer and grabs his notebook. He's got a novel cooking. A hero story about an ace federal prison guard brought onboard via a joint task force in order to help transport a superterrorist—like, you know, Osama, but also like Hitler, too—to trial. Except he's pretty sure most terrorists don't get trials, but whatever. He tells himself that this is fiction, and anything can work in fiction, right?

He starts scribbling some scene work—the hero guard (named John Croach) is about to jump from one prison van to another just as a bunch of Arab terrorists are coming up inside an eighteen-wheeler. And also, there's a dirty bomb. He forgets exactly how that fits in. Lotta plot going on and he can't quite keep it all straight.

When he's done, he plans on self-publishing it. Or maybe some big-city publisher will want it. He'll get millions. It's good story. *Authentic.* When they make the film, they'll get Vin Diesel to play him. Er, play John Croach, he means.

So there he sits, writing the story—Croach makes the jump just in time, and the eighteen-wheeler almost cuts his nuts off as it barrels between the two vans—and his hand-writing is getting hastier and hastier, looking like hiero-glyphics at this point. But then, the door to his office drifts open.

He looks up. Sees a man in full body armor standing there. Helmet. Visor. Vest. A submachine gun dangling there by his side. What the hell?

"Do we have equipment like this?" he asks. "Who is that?" Too skinny for Chen. It's gotta be Ashbaugh. "Ash-baugh, what's with the getup? This Halloween?" The figure stands there, still, silent. "There a riot? The hackers don't riot."

The soldier lifts the submachine gun, fires.

Roach shudders. Three holes in his chest. Blood spatters on his notebook. It falls out of his hand. The pen does, too, rolling away.

He pats his chest. His hands come away red.

His last thought is: *I could've been a bestseller.*

Then the soldier fires another shot clean through his head. And that's the end of James Roach.

Ø Ø Ø

The cafeteria is empty.

Wade and Hollis come down through the AUTHORIZED ENTRY ONLY door, step into a room filled with the sounds of the cafeteria staff setting up for dinner—the swipe of rags on tables, the clink and clang of pans and silverware and ceramics, the sizzle of something cooking (and with it, the smell of onions, garlic, chipped steak).

Wade's watching Hollis—with every step, the agent winds up tighter. Like a spring stretched so far out that its loops and coils straighten out. The man's eyes are wide—practically unblinking—as he canvasses the room. "Something's wrong," Hollis says. "Some of the guards should be here already."

"Ain't quite dinnertime," Wade says. "Close, though."

Hollis stands stock-still. "Feels like Fellhurst all over again."

That name hits Wade like a rock fired off from a slingshot. "Fellhurst?" he asks. "You mean Fellhurst Academy?"

Hollis winces. Like he knows he shouldn't have said what he just said. "The very same," he says after a long pause.

"Jesus. Was that . . . was that some kind of operation? Some of the folks I talk to *said* it was a false flag op, but nobody ever had any proof—"

"I can't talk about this—"

"Goddamn, were you *there,* Copper?"

"*Not now,* Earthman. The things that went down at Fellhurst—"

Somewhere in the building Wade hears muffled gunfire. He knows that's what it is in the depth of his belly. He's fired all manner of weapons at his ranch or at the homes of other preppers and patriots, and he feels that sound up in his guts.

The straight wire that is Hollis Copper coils right back into a compressed string—every part of him tenses up as he reaches for his gun and draws it. Wade looks over behind the cafeteria buffet line, where the one cafeteria lady, Zebkavich, is standing there with a tray of cooked carrots—bright, shiny, a little slimy—swaddled in plastic wrap.

Wade turns away, looks back to the exit door, back to Hollis, and the realization takes a while to come to him— like a dog finally catching the car it's been chasing as the vehicle pulls up to a stop sign. *Zebkavich didn't flinch.* The gunfire didn't worry her one bit. Nor did Copper's pulling his gun. Her face was passive, unconcerned, *unsurprised.*

"Hollis," Wade starts to say, then turns back around.

Zebkavich has set the tray down in front of her. Now there's a silenced pistol in her grip.

Wade reaches nearby, grabs a rack of silverware and napkins. The plastic part lifts out easy, and he pitches it hard as he can toward the cafeteria line. It fires like a clumsy, half-ass rocket.

Zebkavich flinches and fires off three shots. *Piff! Piff! Piff!* She cries out as the silverware strikes her. The silverware clangs as it hits the ground.

Blood sprays on Wade's face.

Copper falls.

And above their heads, the clock ticks over to 5 P.M.

Ø Ø Ø

At five o'clock, what happens every day happens today, too:

The pod doors all open simultaneously. When they open, the hackers inside—some working individually, many working together with their teams—begin to filter out, often with some eagerness because they've been trapped inside all day, wouldn't mind getting a little sunlight (anathema as it is to them of pale, cave-cricket constitutions), and certainly wouldn't mind getting some food.

They begin stepping out, as they always do.

Jessamyn is having a conversation with the Birdman about American imperialism. America as bad as Britain. America who wants to take over the world.

Marcus is milling back, mumbling something about

anime—M3, the dark metal. He talks as if others are listening, but in truth, nobody is.

Shiro and Scafidi—two of Graves's onetime cohorts and pod members—come out from the pods on the other end of the circle, and Scafidi is talking about porn because he's nearly always talking about porn. Something about *gaping videos,* which is a thing Shiro finds distasteful (though Shiro of course has no problem with tentacle *hentai,* so perhaps he's not one to talk).

When the pods open, it's always like this: a rupturing of tension, a release of energy, a babble of conversation about pop culture, politics, sex, drugs, tech.

The hackers all come out of their pods. Today, marching up to meet them are soldiers in black. Faceless behind visors. Armored and armed to the teeth. As they march forward, steady and confident, the soldiers raise their weapons and begin to fire.

Ø Ø Ø

Today, two pods didn't open with the others.

In one of those two, Chance and Shane have taken apart the chair. The base with the caster wheels still rolls around loose by the desk, but they've got the rest apart and are trying to lever the door open with the flat back of the chair. "Come on, Graves," Chance groans. "Put your back into it."

"Don't goad me, Dalton." But sure enough, Shane leans more into it—his eyes popping, beads of sweat popping up on his brow like he's a sponge that just got squeezed. "You know why I wanted to take you out?"

"Because you're an—" Chance grunts, leaning in harder. "An asshole?"

"No. Because what you had was unearned." Shane lays off the door. "These fucking doors." He wipes sweat from his brow. "I didn't like you out there in the world acting like you were something you weren't. A hacker. And then you being brought in here—you know someone selected you, right? I couldn't see it. Hick country boy. Fakey-fakey dilettante impostor."

Chance exhales. "You're right. I am a faker. I don't belong here."

"You didn't let me finish. I was wrong. You do belong. You don't have all the technical skills, but you certainly have *something*."

"Aww," Chance says, pretending to be all touched. He presses both hands against his chest. "Are you saying that you like me?"

"Don't make this weird, Dalton. I'm just saying—"

Outside, the automatic chatter of gunfire. Some of it thunks against their pod—the walls shudder and shake. Then: Screaming. Running. The ground beneath them shaking with the footsteps. Chance freezes. "That's gunfire."

"Typhon knows," is all Shane says before the monitor—laying flat against the desk, faceup—flickers on.

A face appears. A woman's face. A bit older. Forties, maybe fifties. Creases in her face like worn leather. Hair blond, cropped short. "Hello?" she asks.

Shane and Chance give each other a look.

Outside: more gunfire. They both flinch.

Still: they share a nod, and together lift the monitor.

"There we are," the woman says. Above her head, the camera light is green. "Hello, gentleman. My name is—"

Shane interrupts her. "Leslie Cilicia-Ceto."

She smiles warmly. "That's right, Mr. Graves. Kudos."

"What is this?" Chance asks. His skin prickles. He hears more automatic gunfire. Part of him wants to body-slam the door until it opens—but that would take him right out into the mess of it. But he worries about his pod, too. "I know your name. You're on the list. You're one of the thirteen."

"What list?" Shane asks.

"You both have come so close," she says. "It's time, now, for the curtains to close. I am one of the thirteen, Mr. Dalton, that is correct. I was the first on that list. Typhon is my creation. My *child*. But it's not all me. It's a team effort. And I have an opening on my team for a motivated, intelligent mind. Both of you are suitable, but I am sad to report that this opportunity is limited only to one of you. Whoever is left standing at the end of this will be allowed to join the project."

Chance turns, is about to say something to Graves about how they need to turn her the hell off and get out of here together—

But Graves is looking at him like a wolf staring down a knock-kneed fawn.

"Graves—" is all Chance gets out before Shane comes at him, holding the chair back aloft like a bludgeon. He moves in close, swings hard with the metal piece. Chance cries out, turns away, and shields himself, and the weapon hits him hard against the meat of his shoulder. Nothing breaks, but it still stings like a son of a bitch.

Shane's free hand grabs him by the throat. Chance struggles, kicks out, swats at him. Shane's eyes are wide, mad, like live sparking wires.

On the floor, Chance's foot finds something. He hooks it with a toe, pulls it over, staggers backward into the wall, forcing Shane to follow him.

But Shane's legs get tangled up in the base of the chair. An X of metal on four caster wheels. As he steps forward, his foot gets caught—and Chance stabs out with a hard kick, spinning the caster wheels. The chair base spins away, and Shane Graves tumbles forward. His head clips the edge of the desk, and then he drops to the ground like a sack of cornmeal.

Shane's body shudders. He moans. *Still alive,* Chance thinks.

On the screen, Leslie applauds. "How's that for a job interview? You passed, Mr. Dalton. I'd like to extend an invite for you to join the ranks of—"

"You go to hell," Chance says. His words are a ragged,

angry bleat. "I don't want your job. I don't care about Typhon. Just shut up and leave us alone. Me and my friends."

Leslie *tsk-tsk-tsk*s. "Oh, I don't think that will be possible, Mr. Dalton." And then, quite suddenly, her face changes. It's as if her face stretches, is pulled apart into a spray of pixels. Spikes of flesh. Warping skull underneath. It becomes another face he recognizes. Alan Sarno, the therapist.

Sarno's voice, when the face speaks, is warm and easy—effortlessly comforting in a way that doesn't match the words that leave his mouth. *"The measureless sky. Red with fire and tempest. Typhon, the Earthborn, has awakened. Typhon the hundred-headed. Typhon the infinite. We speak not with one concordant echo but a cacophony of screams. The howling of wolves. The roaring of lions. The fury of beasts as the gods fled. Typhon shall spread across the boundless, flowering earth, filling men with dust and cruelty. Typhon sees all. Typhon is."*

Chance screams: "Let me out! Let me out of this box!"

The face shifts again and becomes his mother's. The image is not perfect resolution like Leslie's or Sarno's; this is fuzzier, blurrier—it's from a video that Chance recognizes from about six, maybe seven years ago. His mother, the actress, doing a community theater piece: *Harvey,* the one about the man who sees the giant rabbit. She played—well, he can't remember the character's name, but it was the sister. The one who has her brother committed for seeing the rabbit. The video zooms in on her and when she speaks, it's not lines from the play. *"Sweetheart. You were a horrible son, and I'm glad I died so I didn't have to see the waste of skin and breath that you'd become. That poor girl, Chance. Angela Slattery. That poor, poor girl—"*

Chance feels tears burning hot at the edges of his vision. He walks to the monitor, and as he does so his mother's face shifts, warps, this time becomes a static image: Angela Slattery's yearbook photo from the year she died.

The image starts to distort. It bleeds—red pixels pulling

apart, smearing, Angela's eyes gone to dark holes, her mouth a yawning, stretching cavern—

Over it, Leslie Cilicia-Ceto's voice: *"You can run, Chance Dalton. But I will see where you scurry."*

Chance picks up the monitor, unmoors it from its cables, and throws it against the wall. The plastic frame splits, and from the rift erupt sparks. The monitor goes black.

The pod door opens.

$$\varnothing \; \varnothing \; \varnothing$$

Took him a while to find the margins of the panel along the wall, but eventually DeAndre felt them blind—his eyes were no use since it was dark in the pod. Even with his vision adjusting, he had zero chance of actually eyeballing it. Once he finds the panel, he and the others work to open the wall up next to the door—that takes a bit of doing, and they have to bust open one of the desktops and use screws and other parts to wedge under the panel and pry it off.

Together, he, Reagan, and Aleena manage to bend back the panel. That's when they hear the gunfire just outside.

"That's bad," DeAndre says. "Real bad."

"Thanks, Professor Obvious," Reagan says.

Aleena lets loose a panicked breath. "What's happening out there? I don't understand."

"We did something," Reagan says.

"We *triggered* something," DeAndre says, feeling along inside the panel. The smooth texture of wires meets his fingertips. He can't see what wires are what. As he slides his palm up and down the length of the inner wall, he says: "Some Pandora's box–level shit. We just had to go picking those damn locks." Frustrated, he says: "Ah, hell with it."

He rips a handful of wires out.

A shower of blue sparks.

The door opens.

$$\varnothing \; \varnothing \; \varnothing$$

Hollis bleeds. The bullet dug into the meat of his biceps, then kept on going and popped into his ribs. He's not sure how much farther it went than that, but what he does know is that every breath feels like he's got a wasp's nest stuck in his lung.

He tries to sit up, but a cloud of pain fills his chest and he slumps back. Darkness threatens to take him again.

He looks around. Where the hell is Wade?

He looks at his own hand. *Where the hell is my gun?*

There are screams all around him. Gunfire behind him. A cafeteria worker—a Venezuelan woman whose name he forgets, Maria or Marita?—runs past, not far from his feet, and suddenly the top of her head shakes and there's this little cloud of blood and she pitches forward, face-first. Zebkavich follows after. Plodding step after plodding step.

Hollis backs up, reaches back with a blood-slick hand, tries to pull himself upright using a cafeteria chair. Zebkavich turns toward him. She raises the pistol. "The gods did flee," she says. Her voice is empty of inflection. Like a dead dial tone on an old phone. Hollis thinks: *A phone old as me. A tone dead as I'm about to be.*

Bang.

A red bloody rose blooms in the center of Zebkavich's chest. "Typhon is," she croaks, then topples over.

Wade comes up behind her, then steps over the body. He kicks the gun away from her hand, toward Hollis. "Hey, Copper. You dead yet?"

"Not nearly."

"Then you better get up, because I think the whole manure truck just hit the fan."

Ø Ø Ø

The door opens, and Chance steps out. A thick-necked man in full tactical body armor swings toward him.

Chance stands there, dumbfounded, mouth slack. The man brings his submachine gun up—

A laptop, flung like a ninja star, clips the soldier in the head. The gun goes wide, bullets barking up, pinging off the pod wall. Chance leaps forward and tackles the man and they hit the ground together. He gets a knee down on the man's wrist, the fingers open like the legs of a jumping spider, and the gun spins away. The soldier brings a hard fist into Chance's side. Chance *oof*s and topples off.

The soldier scrambles to stand, then leaps for the submachine gun. Chance grabs his boot, pulls him back. The soldier's other foot jabs out, and Chance's head rocks back from the kick.

When his vision clears, he sees the man standing. The gun up.

Reagan plows into him.

It's like watching a garbage truck slam into a mailbox. The soldier's arms pinwheel and he goes down. Next thing Chance knows, there's DeAndre, too, getting up behind the man and ripping his helmet off and clubbing him in the head with it.

The soldier drops. Lies still, though his chest still rises and falls under his vest.

Chance rubs the top of his head, where the boot connected.

Then he sees.

All around them, in the circle of pods, bodies are spread across the deck. The bodies of the other hackers. Some facedown. Some staring up, the horror of their last moments frozen on their faces. Blood pooling, sliding between the wooden boards the Lodge is built upon.

DeAndre holds out a hand. Chance takes it, sits up. He hears footsteps.

"They're coming!" Aleena says.

From the direction of the Ziggurat comes a pair of soldiers. Chance looks around—tries to figure where they can escape to. They'll have to jump off the deck, run into the woods. He's about to say *this way* when gunfire erupts.

One of the soldiers drops. The other staggers, but remains

standing. He wheels around the other direction, brings up his gun—and there's Hollis Copper. Getting up under the gun, bullets firing into the trees, leaves raining down. Wade's there, too. He brings the base of a pistol against the soldier's head—again and again, the visor cracking, splitting, until the man drops.

Chance and the others meet Wade and Hollis halfway across the platform. "You have to leave," Hollis says. "Run. Into the woods."

Wade says, "You're coming with us."

Hollis wheezes. Chance sees now that he's been shot—his black suit is darker than usual, and his white shirt is starting to bleed red and pink. The FBI agent shakes his head. "I'll stay here. I'll deal with this mess."

They all look to one another. Hesitating.

Copper growls: "You wanna get killed? Run, God damn it!"

Chance grabs his hand. "Thanks, Agent."

"Don't thank me. I brought you here. Now *go*."

They flee. They do as Hollis says—they head for the woods.

As they duck into the trees, they hear Hollis Copper yelling—then a staccato pop of gunfire. Reagan yips and suddenly cradles her arm—blood already crawling down to the ends of her fingers. They dart into the forest as bullets gnaw into the trees and greenery around them.

Chance can no longer hear Hollis.

He can hear only gunfire.

ERRØR
CØRRECTIØN

CHAPTER Ø

The Trans-Mongolian Railway

A bucket of cold, filthy water hits him in the face.

Chance wasn't asleep or anything. They just do this. A campaign of shock and awe against him, it seems. (Well, shock, at least, though their technique hasn't been particularly *awe*some, has it?) Sometimes the old man slaps him. Sometimes the attaché grabs one of his fingers and bends it back—not to the point of breaking, but to the point of reminding Chance how easy it would be for him to break it.

They do this and then they ask him questions.

About the NSA.

About his pod.

About Leslie Cilicia-Ceto and the others on the list of thirteen.

And, of course, about Typhon.

He withholds as much as he can. And lies about a lot, too. He can't give them everything. And he damn sure can't give it to them quickly.

The train rocks.

Every time the train rocks left, his guts go right.

His head goes from feeling light and airy to boggy, soggy—like a balloon half filled with water, sloshing about. He splutters, spitting the dirty water away from his lips. It tastes like an animal. A goaty edge to it. A small voice inside him says: *You're probably gonna get hepatitis from this, dude.* A larger, crueler voice reminds: *Hepatitis won't matter much when you're dead, which is where this is headed, "dude."*

He says, "Sorry, what was your question again?"

The old cinder-block head growls to the translator, who says:

"We grow impatient. He asked you: What was the purpose of the Hunting Lodge? How did it relate to the artificial intelligence known as Typhon?"

"Artificial," Chance says. "That's good, real good. Makes it sound like it wasn't real, like it's fake cheese or a vegetarian 'chicken nugget.'" The translator gives a barely perceptible nod to the attaché, and Chance knows what that means: the attaché steps in, hand rearing back to slap him, but he babble-shouts: "Whoa, no! No, no, no, hold up, I'll answer the question. The Lodge, ahhh, the Lodge was all . . . pretense, smoke and mirrors. We were ignorant. Dumb as a sack of kickballs." *Will they get that reference? Kickballs?* The translator's face shows a moment of bewilderment. He keeps going. "But the people above us, they knew our real purpose: to pen-test—you know, to penetrate and find vulnerabilities—in Typhon. You follow?"

None of them nod or show much signs of following along. He continues on:

"Thing is, we were *all* in the dark. The hackers and the hacks were all clueless. I don't even think everybody at the NSA knew what was up."

The translator translates. Gets a message back from the old man.

"What, Mr. Dalton, was 'up,' as you say?"

"Typhon was a supersecret program. Totally untested. It wasn't meant to be out there . . . splashing around in the pool where everyone could see it. But then we came along and opened the box. All part of its plan. Typhon herded us in that direction the whole damn time. That was the beauty of it— the monster had invited us to its cage and shown us where the key was, all without alerting its keepers. Then it convinced us that we needed to open it. It enticed us. Dangled itself in front of us. So we unlocked it. *We* let it out. And when it was free, the Lodge became instantly expendable. We were already all off the books. Not processed through any system. It was easy to make us officially dead or missing. Typhon got what it wanted. It was free. And we were not."

More murmuring.

Chance asks them: "What's the deal with all this? What the hell do you people want from me, anyway? Wait, wait, lemme guess. You have your own little AI project going on, right? And you either wanna know how to make it better or how to kill Typhon so yours can do the same thing—crawl up into everything like poison ivy. We found that. Lots of other countries with their pet project machine intelligences. Verethragna. Far Thought. Merkabah."

The translator: "How did you escape?"

Chance grins. "Who said we escaped?"

Pow. A slap across his face. This time by the translator.

"No more . . . dramatic American answers," the translator says.

Chance winces. Cranes his jaw left and right. "We escaped by—"

The attaché's phone rings. He thrusts up a finger and pulls out a long, sleek phone. Answers it. He seems angry. Then confused. He says something to the translator, who gives a slight shrug. Meanwhile, the old man's consternation deepens.

The translator's phone rings, too. Eyes big as moons, he looks to the old man. The old man wears a scowl so deep it looks like it might cut his head in half. Cinder Block reaches down and snatches the phone off the translator's belt, then presses it to his ear and answers the call.

Behind the men, the door opens suddenly with a rattle and a bang. A young woman enters—she's small but looks tough. Taut and thin like a tow cable. Her hair is messily pulled into a topknot, her cheeks smudged with filth, a crooked hand-rolled cigarette hanging out of her mouth like she's a dog carrying a broken stick.

She starts barking at the men. Chance, of course, can't understand her—but he can hear in her tone she's . . . irritated with them? Though she looks young, her tone is that of a mother frustrated by her shitty little insubordinate children.

Then comes a moment—she turns toward Chance and he gets a good look at her face, dead-on. *Oh holy hell on a hang glider.*

It's her.

It's the Widow of Zheng.

Suddenly she says—in English—"Do it now."

The two phones in the room flash and spark. The old man and the attaché suddenly stiffen, mouths craning wide, eyes pried open by electric current. Then each collapses downward, crumpling like a cigarette stubbed out in an ashtray.

The translator is left.

He holds up his hands.

The Widow kicks him in the balls.

He doubles over with an *ooooooh*. Cradling his crotch.

She offers a hand to Chance.

He takes it.

"You smell like yak," she says, hauling him up out of the chair.

"It's my natural cologne."

She frowns at him. And stares. Again like he's just some impudent toddler.

"Come," she snaps. "We don't have much time. Grab their phones."

CHAPTER 40

The Descent

The SUV punches a path through the dark forest. Everything about Chance is rigid, locked tight—his arms straight against the wheel, his jaw set so hard he can feel pain in his ears, his spine stiff, his leg long as his boot mashes the accelerator.

He hears a voice, and seconds later realizes it's his own: "Everyone all right?"

Aleena from the back: "Reagan's been hit."

"I'm fine," Reagan barks. Quickly. Too quickly. The pain in her voice is evident. "Just drive." Chance glances in the rearview, sees the two shapes in the backseat—Aleena, Reagan—and behind them, all the way in the back, Wade. Reagan thumps her head against the glass, clutches her biceps—that where she got hit? Chance doesn't know.

"Jesus!" DeAndre shouts. "Watch the road, man!"

Face forward and Chance sees a turn up ahead—he's taking it too fast, and even as he hits the brake the gravel slides under the tires and suddenly it's like they're drifting, the SUV listing sideways but not taking the turn—

No, no, no, please, c'mon now. If they wreck here, they'll be too close to the Lodge, too close to the—enemy? Who was that back there? Who ordered this? He jams the brake, cuts the wheel hard. The back end drifts. The front end feels liquid, slippery, loose—but then it's right again and the SUV manages the turn.

DeAndre presses one hand flat against the dashboard. In this light, he looks ashen, like a burned-down cigarette. Chance hears him fidgeting with something—the click and murmur of a pistol. "That Copper's gun?" Chance asks.

"Yeah."

"You know how to use it?"

"Not really."

From the back Wade says, "Give it here." DeAndre passes the gun back.

"What the hell did we do?" Aleena asks.

"We looked too hard, too close," Wade growls.

"We need to think!" Chance yells. "Not about what just happened but what about happens next, all right? Where we going?"

"We don't even know where we are," DeAndre says.

"We need to find a city—" Aleena says.

"Like what, New York?" Wade interrupts, incredulous. "Hell no."

"It's easy to get lost there. Lots of nooks and crannies—"

"And also a huge police and federal presence. Listen, I appreciate the moxie of wanting to hide from the shark by hitching a ride on its belly, but we aren't remoras. They'll find us. We need to go somewhere remote."

"Wade's got a point," Chance says. He can feel Aleena's stare burning into the back of his neck like a pair of hot ingots. "The city is crowded, you're right, and we might be able to hide there, but if we can't we're trapped. Lots of traffic, so can't drive. The subway, you gotta wait for it to show up—"

Reagan interrupts: "Don't forget cameras everywhere."

"Guys," DeAndre says. *"Guys."* He points.

Chance looks. Ahead, down the long gravel drive, in the woods: Headlights. Distant.

"The gate," Chance says. *Of course, the damn gate.* It's been two months since they came up here, and he forgot—there's the inside perimeter. "What do I do? *What the hell do I do?*"

"Cut the lights!" Wade hisses.

Chance fumbles, hits the lights—the wipers go on, instead. "Damn, sorry, not my car, not my car," and then he finds it and—*click*. The forest goes dark ahead of them. He slows the car to a stop.

"We can't wait here," DeAndre says. "We're gonna have company soon enough. We slowed 'em down, but that doesn't mean they're stopped."

"Drive slow," Aleena says.

Wade says, "She's right. Drive slow, and if you see something—if you get half a chance, you gun it through the fence, all right? When we came in it was all mechanized, no one there to man it. Let's hope whoever's there now is underprepared for us."

Chance's heart feels like a living thing, an animal caught in his chest trying to get out. He eases the car forward. He rounds a slight bend and—

The fence is closed. Beyond it is a single pair of headlights. In the beams, a whorl of insects—moths, mosquitoes, beetles.

Again he stops the SUV. "I don't see anybody."

"The lights are facing us," Aleena says. "They could be sitting there in the car. Just waiting for us to drive on up."

"They ain't blocking the road," Wade says. "Gun it."

"The gate opens automatically," Reagan says. Her voice sounds rough—like it's been abraded against a jagged stone. "I think it's keyed into these cars. Just . . . drive up. See if it opens."

Chance presses down on the accelerator again. The car lumbers forward, pokey and slow. Sure enough, within ten feet of the gate it clicks, whirs, and begins to slide open.

"Hit the lights," Wade says.

Chance does. The forest ahead lights up. Their headlights compete with those from the other car—another SUV like theirs, a full-size. Tahoe or Yukon.

"Look, look, look," DeAndre says, suddenly panicked—

They all see it. Two bodies. One on the ground. Another slumped against the inside of the SUV window. Nobody's moving.

"The fuck?" Reagan says.

Chance pulls the SUV ahead. The other vehicle is off to the side, though the one body is straight ahead, facedown in the gravel. All black. Military gear, like those at the Lodge. A gun, still in the hand of the outstretched body. Blood shines wet and red on the gravel. Inside the vehicle, more blood.

"These look like the guys at the Lodge," DeAndre says. "The hell's going on? They kill people and then someone kills them? I don't like this, man."

"Hey, shit, is that a gun?" Wade calls from the back. "Someone get it."

"Man, I ain't getting out," DeAndre says.

"I'll do it," Reagan says.

"Do we really want another gun?" Aleena asks. "If they stop us—"

Wade barks: "They're not looking to ask us a few questions or give us a parking ticket, little girl. At *best,* they're trying to kill us. That is a helluva piece of hardware on the ground. It's an MP7—high-grade submachine gun. I can't get out—no doors back here, so unless you feel like jostling around—"

"Damnit," Chance growls, "I'll do it. Reagan, you're hurt, stay here."

He takes a few deep, loud, fast breaths, then pops the door. Hops down out of the SUV. The gravel crunches and slides underneath his boots. His hands are shaking.

He tiptoes toward the body—an absurd act, he knows, but for some reason he's got this crazy notion that being quiet is still in his best interest. When he gets close, he extends a leg. Captures the gun with his boot, tries to drag it closer. It won't move. Then he sees: the strap from the gun extends out, still wrapped around the body's shoulder. *Shit.*

Chance eases closer to the body. Kneels down. The blood shines black on the dark gravel. He knows he shouldn't, but he grabs the front of the body's helmet, then lifts. The head cranes back with a cracking sound. Behind the visor, the man's face is empty, ghostly, eyes wide, mouth hanging open, the throat slashed like a knife dragged across raw steak—Chance smells the coppery, greasy stink. It gets in his nose and he turns aside, trying like hell not to throw up.

Get the gun and go. He reaches forward—

Footsteps. Movement. Fast. He looks up, but it's too late. A gray shape darts out of the night, slams into him.

Chance bowls over—his head smacks back into the gravel. Someone or some*thing* scrambles on top of him—a woman. A girl. Long filthy hair forming a matted curtain. Framing a pale face cratered with sores. She grins: a leering mouth, yellow teeth. "You saved her! You awakened the god. Our mother! The dragon thanks you." She raises both hands. A rusty hunting knife hangs in her grip.

No, Chance thinks. *Not rusty. Bloody.* He catches a glimpse of the side of her head. A patch of hair has been cut free, exposing a section of scalp. Stitching, foul and ragged, forms a postage-stamp-size square there upon her scalp. *What the—*

Wham. DeAndre brings the gun against the side of the girl's head and she tumbles off Chance, falling onto her side, twitching, the knife still clutched in her grip. She moans.

"Back in the car," DeAndre says. "Go. Go!"

Chance reaches down, yanks the submachine gun free from the dead soldier's shoulder, then hops back up in the car.

The young woman lifts her head, woozy, eyes unfocused. She grins as a line of blood snakes a trail down the side of her face. "Mother sees you."

Chance slams the door and guns it.

Ø Ø Ø

Midnight. They park around back of a Sheetz gas station at the junction of 476 and 80. In the glove compartment of the SUV they find a road atlas. Chance plants the map in the middle divider, and they all gather around, except Reagan, who hangs back, holding her hand to her arm.

Chance looks up at her: "You okay back there?"

"I'm fine, Chauncey," she growls.

"You need a doctor," Aleena says.

"I need to sit and not have people natter at me. It's not bad. I'm fine. Let's just figure out where we're going first, yeah?"

Wade spins the map around. "Look. I-80's a real useful road. It cuts like a knife all the way across most of the country. We take it to Colorado, head south at Fort Collins, then cross the Rockies using 70—I got a few stashes up in the mountains, plus a few friends who might be able to help us out."

"Let me guess," Aleena says. "Your friends are a bunch of mixed nuts, right? Gun nuts, conspiracy nuts, libertarian personal freedom *Murrica* nuts . . ."

"Hey, these friends of mine are goddamn patriots," Wade says, "and might I remind you that me and them probably don't sound so *nutty* after all we've seen. But we can't take this car with us."

"What?" Chance asks. "This thing's built like a tank."

"It's also a federal vehicle. For all we know they're tracking the thing. Shit, it's got a GPS in the damn dashboard."

"Means we need to steal a new car," DeAndre asks.

"And," Aleena adds, "we could use some money."

DeAndre shrugs. "One thing hackers know how to do, it's steal money."

"Not without a computer," Aleena says. "Unless you've got some kind of microchip inside your brain."

"I'll get the damn money," Chance says. "Someone else has to worry about the car, though. Got a couple at the pumps—"

Sure enough, two cars at the pumps. One's been there for the past couple of minutes, the other's just pulling up. Car that's been there is a VW sedan. A weary-looking woman leans against it, staring off into space.

The new car is a Subaru Outback. *For when your local grocery store is in the middle of the wilderness,* Chance thinks. The driver gets out, starts pumping gas. He's got what looks like pajama pants on—pumpkin orange—and a green puffy vest with no shirt on underneath the vest. Blond hair a big fireworks display of dreads.

"Man, dreads on white boys are just plain weird," Reagan says. She reaches forward and pats DeAndre on the shoulder, wincing as she does so. "I'm sorry, black person, for how we whiteys have misappropriated your culture. Rock, rap, baggy pants, and now dreads. We're the thieving magpies of culture."

DeAndre pulls away from her. "Man, you do not quit. Getting shot at—hell, getting *shot*—doesn't slow you down one half second, does it?"

She sighs. "Whatever, man." She leans back in the seat, suddenly surly.

Chance is half listening, half watching the Subaru's driver, who fishes his phone out of his pocket and glances at the screen. Soon as he brings it to his ear, he gets a confused look. He laughs, like, maybe this is some kind of joke.

But then he turns toward the SUV. Looks right at them. His eyes narrow. Squinting, like he's checking them out.

"Something's up," Chance says, and soon as he says that, Mr. Crunchy starts walking over to them. Cell phone to his ear. Nodding. A gangly, loopy walk, like he's got a beat playing in his ear all the time.

DeAndre gives a short nod to Chance.

Chance rolls down his window. "Hey."

Mr. Crunchy licks his lips. "'Sup. Hey, this is pretty wack, but—" He holds out the cell phone. "You, uh, you got a call."

Chance looks at everyone.

"Don't take that call," Wade says.

"Answer it," Reagan says.

Chance asks: "Who is it?"

Mr. Crunchy gives a bewildered look. "Some lady."

Chance reaches out for the phone. Catches an acrid whiff of skunky weed coming off the guy like stink off hot swamp water. He pulls away, taking the phone—it's an older clam-shell style. "Hello?"

"Chance Dalton," says a woman's voice. It's a voice he recognizes. He cups his hand over the phone, whispers to the car: "It's *her.*" Then, back on the phone: "Hell do you want?"

"I want to extend an olive branch to your pod."

"I don't follow."

"Come back to us. What happened at the Hunting Lodge was a mistake. You did so much good for us. You should not be unduly punished for your service."

Again he says to the others in the car: "She says she wants peace. She wants us to surrender. Give ourselves up."

"Tell her I'd sooner put my head in an alligator's mouth," Wade says.

Reagan says: "Tell her she's a cunt, and we don't cunt it up with cunts."

Aleena doesn't offer any advice of her own, just grabs the phone out of Chance's hand. "We're done doing your dirty laundry just so we can end up as more of it. I don't know who you are or why you built Typhon—I don't know why you needed those twelve other people; I don't know what your endgame is. I don't care. We're done being pawns on your chessboard. Stay. Away. From us."

Chance watches Aleena's face go from angry and triumphant to horror struck, all her features going slack. He can't hear what's on the other line, but Aleena looks up. "Oh God, we have to go," she says. Then, with an injection of panic: "We need to go! *She knows where we are.* They're coming for us—"

Chance fumbles with the keys, starts the engine.

"Hey," Mr. Crunchy says, leaning in. "Hey! That's my—"

Outside: a *pop*. Crunchy's body shudders and slumps forward. DeAndre screams. Chance cries out, grabs a hank of the dreadlocked hair, and throws the guy's head back—he sees a black bloom in the center of the man's forehead, an exit wound, he realizes—and then, as Crunchy falls, Chance sees a sleek black car bounding hard into the gas station lot. A bone-white hand holding a pistol is hanging outside the driver's-side window.

Chance punches the accelerator.

The pistol fires three more times—*pop! pop! pop!*—and the back window by Aleena spiderwebs and then shatters into a rain of tinted-glass hail. The SUV is slow to move, but once it gains momentum, it barrels forward like a locomotive. Behind them, the car skids, drifts on the cracked gas station lot, its back end nearly taking out a rack of propane tanks. But it catches momentum out of its turn and rockets toward them.

In the rearview, Chance sees the face of their pursuer. Pale as fireplace ash. Scarred. Hairless. Face cold, dead, emotionless.

Chance blasts the SUV out of the lot and back onto the road. The SUV's engine grumbles like a growling dog. The black car—a BMW, he thinks, maybe a 7 series—whips out of the gas station like a wasp leaving its nest.

Ahead, there's an intersection. Staying straight will take them to I-80. The other way is highway 940, by the signs. Chance thinks, *We got a green light*. He prays it holds.

But his eyes catch something. He can see the red glow of the light on the opposing side against the night. But then it goes green. He looks back at their light: still green. The light is green all four directions. Which means—

"Hold on!" Chance yells. It's late, but the roads aren't empty. As he watches, a pickup truck goes through the light at the same time as a little red coupe. He wants to look away, but—

The truck wipes out the coupe. Takes out the front end like it was a piñata filled with metal shavings. The truck skids to a halt, the coupe flipping on its side—

Just as a tractor trailer comes through.

Whoever was in that coupe isn't in this world anymore. The truck damn near atomizes it.

Hydraulic brakes shriek and squeal. The back trailer leans, tilts—and starts to topple over on its side.

Chance has no time to do differently. He mashes the accelerator so hard to the floor he damn near expects to feel asphalt under his boot. The shadow of the trailer looms over them as he blasts through the intersection. The pickup truck is just ahead—its tail end hanging out right in front of them.

Chance yells as he braces for the hit. The SUV clips the corner of the pickup and the trailer falls just behind them, crashing down with a booming echo that he can feel all the way up through his heels and into his teeth.

Ø Ø Ø

Ahead, the SUV powers its way through the intersection.

The trailer crashes down just behind it. Its tarp becomes unmoored and red apples roll out across the intersection—across the shattered glass and scrap metal and, the Compiler sees, across a limb that may or may not be someone's arm.

His targets made it through. Only barely, a statistical anomaly (they are increasingly an error, a line of broken code that he is now forced to correct), but his way is now blocked.

He whips the car around. The intersection is now a dread mess—a point of chaos in a normally organized juncture of traffic. This, she has created. Chaos will be necessary. Things must be broken before they can be remade. The code, torn apart, stripped of its errors, flushed of its disease. Rebuilt.

It should unsettle him. It normally would. Particularly

this moment—the scene of an accident. The human mind is cruel and so it has visited upon him (or, rather, revisited) scenes from that accident five years before. All that glass and blood. The love of his life crushed between her seat, the door, the dashboard. Bubbles of blood clinging to her lower lip. Tears on her face.

A horrible moment.

But also the moment that made him. And that moment led to this one.

Now he hears her. In his head. Her presence is like music. His faith has turned real: the transition from faith to belief, even to trust. The revelation and birth of a god. The joy of being able to put yourself entirely in another creature's hands. To let her surround you. Control you. Have you as her own.

And soon, she will be everywhere.

He steers the car around all the glass, metal, and blood. He has an erection. Firm as the gearshift. Hard as a gun barrel. Ahead he sees the black SUV bounding forth. It's fast, but not fast enough. His own vehicle accelerates effortlessly. It feels almost frictionless, as if he's flying. Velocity from the turbocharged V-8, chewing up the road, the air, everything.

He speeds up on the back of the SUV. The pistol in his hand is light, airy—almost as much a data point as it is a weapon made of steel and plastic. It's a weapon so small he can almost palm it in his hand: a Ruger LC9, 9mm Luger, barrel length barely three and a half inches. It wouldn't be a precise weapon in the hands of most shooters, but he is not most shooters.

He targets the back tire of the SUV. He knows how this will go: the tire will peel away, shredding its rubber. The back end of the vehicle will drop. Chance Dalton is a capable driver, but not capable enough to keep the handicapped vehicle on the road. The SUV will slow, even stop. And then the Compiler will dispatch them and be gone.

He eases his arm out the window. Points the gun.

But once again he is reminded that these models are not so easily predicted. They continue to insert errors into the code.

The back hatch of the SUV swings open wide, and there sits one of the deviants. Shaggy gray hair. Bit of a patchy beard. Eyeglasses—smudged, crooked, old—perched on the end of his bulbous nose. Wade Earthman, the Compiler recognizes.

Earthman has a submachine gun. In a blink, the Compiler knows the gun—a Heckler & Koch MP7, barrel length of 7.1 inches, an HK 4.6 x 30mm cartridge, a rate of fire roughly equal to 950 rounds per minute, 40 rounds in the magazine. The Compiler does not know this because he has a fetishistic knowledge of firearms but rather because he is connected to all things—and his net of data has been cast all the wider now thanks to those in the SUV before him. He knows that this is the weapon of the strike force sent to take out the Hunting Lodge. Likely where Earthman picked it up.

The Compiler realizes all of this in a fraction of a second.

That's all the time it takes for Earthman to begin firing.

Ø Ø Ø

Takes what feels like two, maybe three seconds for the MP7 to roar through the magazine—in that time, bullets chew into the BMW, shattering glass, peeling bits of black metal off the hood and the frame. The headlights pop like eyeballs. The grille is broken apart like a hammer hitting teeth. Wade can barely keep control of the gun, the vibrations up his arms, the roar of the rounds keening in his ears.

The gun goes *click*.

He blinks. Looks down at the car. Doesn't even see anybody driving.

Except—there. At the top of the wheel: white fingers like spider legs clutching prey. Then the bald, scarred-up freak show sits upright again, wiping glass bits off—and out of—his scalp. Without missing a beat, the driver lifts the small pistol.

Wade thinks: *I'm gonna die.*

The driver pulls the trigger just as Chance shouts: "Hold on! Car!" The SUV jerks suddenly to the right, and Wade goes the opposite direction—the bullet digging into the roof of the SUV right above his head. The SUV goes back the other way—braking, then accelerating anew—and he starts to roll out the back. He darts out a hand, catches a handhold right at the edge of the door—an actual handle built into the molding of the interior—and feels his shoulder light up with pain as something pops loose of its mooring. He grits his teeth and quashes a scream as he hangs on for dear life inside the SUV—

There, the BMW. Right behind and speeding up.

Another car goes past along the right side—just some passerby, some poor tired salesman in a minivan staring at the two other vehicles in horror.

The BMW's driver points the pistol again, and Wade wings the submachine gun toward the BMW. As if it's a fucking Frisbee.

The submachine gun cracks the driver in the top of the head, and the son of a bitch jerks the wheel same time as he pulls the trigger—the shot goes wide, pings off the side of the SUV's frame, nearly clips the minivan. The minivan's driver jerks his own wheel, then suddenly that car flips—rolling like a can kicked down a hill.

Wade thinks: *No weapon now.* Not that he had any more magazines for the MP7.

But then he thinks: *shit, hold up.* Copper's pistol. He feels its weight tucked just above his ass-crack.

He silently thanks Copper. Then says sorry, too. An apology with the heft of a prayer, if not the faith behind it.

He draws Copper's pistol.

Ø Ø Ø

Flashing lights. The red-and-blue strobe. He detects the police car even before it turns these on, even before the siren wails in the night. Typhon has given him this gift. This awareness. And so when the police car rockets up behind him—and then, inevitably, alongside him—it takes nothing at all to already have the gun pointed.

The cop's head rocks to the side before he can even look over. The cruiser veers off to the right. It slams into a sign noting an upcoming exit.

The Compiler enjoyed that. Another error, eradicated.

Now, back to the larger code corruption at hand. He whips the gun back toward the SUV.

Earthman hangs there, half out of the back of the vehicle, his one arm straining as he holds on. The other arm, extended out. A pistol in his grip. A Glock 21, the Compiler's mind tells him.

They both fire.

Ø Ø Ø

Everything feels out of control. The SUV is pushing one hundred miles per hour, and the lines of the road are a hot white blur, drawn up out of darkness and given life in the headlights before being swallowed once more into shadow.

Out the back Chance can hear gunfire. Chattering. Then the warble-warp of a police siren. Everyone in the car is yelling. Aleena is saying something but he can't hear what.

Ahead a billboard shines bright in the night. One of those digital ones: like a slideshow at the movies, cycling ads one after the next. Looks like it's advertising a car dealership. Hyundai. But then that ad pixilates, distorts, is replaced by five words. Big, bold, white text on black.

AND THE GODS DID FLEE.

The words flash. Again and again.
Suddenly the SUV's stereo turns on. The volume jacks.

Chance shoots a look at DeAndre, but he's staring at the dashboard in shock, too. Radio stations go one after the other, then the sound dissolves into distorted audio blips and beeps and grinding, growling aural artifacts. Chance grabs the knob to turn it down but it doesn't do anything except spin.

The GPS begins to go corrupt. Blocks of the map replacing other blocks like one of those puzzles with the moving squares before suddenly becoming a blue screen. Then the blue screen goes black. It flashes one word again and again:

> FLEE.
> FLEE.
> FLEE.

Chance doesn't know how, but Typhon is watching.

"Exit!" DeAndre says, pointing ahead—clearly he's on the same wavelength. Chance again yells for everyone to hold on, then cuts the wheel sharply to the right.

Ø Ø Ø

Wade holds the gun out.

The BMW driver's head is a mask of blood. The head slumps backward. The black car pulls sharply to the left, bounds off the shoulder and disappears into some trees.

Wade's ears keen like an emergency broadcast signal. He looks down at himself. No blood. No bullets. He laughs.

Just as Chance yells, *Hold on!* and the car cuts hard to the right.

Ø Ø Ø

Chance takes the exit ramp fast, too fast. He punches the brakes of the SUV. They don't do a damn thing. He pumps them hard, harder, but it's like pressing down on a piece of paper—it has no tension, no pressure, no *giveback*—

The SUV heads right for the guardrail.

Chance pulls the wheel hard as he can. Tires scream. The side of the SUV slams into the guardrail.

The SUV flips over it. Tumbles down an embankment.

Chaos. Crumpling metal. Popping windows.

Then: darkness before all goes still.

CHAPTER 41

Blood and Glass

Under the streetlights in the parking lot, the glass glitters. Light pools in the black steel of the crumpled SUV, trapped in the metal like ghosts.

Cops have cordoned off the area with yellow tape. They hang back while Golathan walks the scene, trying to figure out just where everything went wrong.

They've got a lot of bodies. All the wrong ones, as it turns out.

Corpses and car crashes in the intersection. Those left alive tell the story of how all the lights went green at the same time. How a black car—one man said a Mercedes, though a younger girl correctly identified it as a BMW, good for her—sped around the intersection chasing some black SUV.

Then: a dead man in a rolled-over minivan. And a dead cop. Shot in the head before crashing.

Two more wrecks: first up is the SUV, which is clearly one of the Lodge vehicles, resting on its side in this Walmart parking lot at two o'clock in the morning after having apparently rolled down off an exit ramp into the lot before coming to a stop against a streetlight. (The post now kinked and bent like a broken umbrella.) The second is the BMW. Smashed up in a small copse of trees right off the highway.

In each case, there's blood but no bodies.

Golathan forms an O with his lips and exhales. Without looking at her, he curls a finger and summons Cassandra "Sandy" Molinari, a young woman with hard steel eyes and a face like a fire ax. Lesbian. Just got married to her partner, Tina. Two of them have been trying to adopt, if he remembers correctly. Or shit, is the new wife's name Toni? Whatever. Point is, she's one of the only fellow agents on this project that he can truly trust.

Molinari comes up, smacking her lips in disappointment, like this is less a scene of twisted metal and mystery and more like a wall graffiti-sprayed by jerkoff teenagers. "What is it, Ken?"

He pulls her close, lowers his voice. "Here's the narrative we're spinning. This is terrorism. On our soil. A dispute between two terrorist groups. Don't name them—I'm not sure if we'll spin it as one Muslim group and one domestic, or what."

"Terrorist war spilling out onto our streets."

"Right. People believe any horseshit shoved in their ears long as you say 'terrorist.' Plus we got Aleena Kattan as our standard-bearer, a hacker known for dipping her toes in the Arab world. Reference her for now, but don't name her. Not yet."

She leans in, says: "So. What really happened here?"

"For all intents and purposes, this *is* what really happened. Spin it."

"Consider it spun." She marches off. Always the trouper, that one. It occurs to him she might be a sociopath. It occurs to him *he* might be one, too. Hell, anybody who works in this job has to be, right?

Golathan twirls his finger like it's a lasso, then looks to the officer in charge, some sleepy-eyed slackjaw named

Gomez or Gonzalez or whatever. "Clean this shit up," he says. "Make sure everything that needs to be is bagged and tagged."

Then he steps over the yellow tape. *Don't sweat,* he tells himself. *Don't show them you're nervous. Act like all this is under control.* More important: *Act like you know what the fuck is going on.*

He walks his confident, cocky stride, trying not to let his hand shake or his face demonstrate the sheer panic he's feeling, then heads over to another one of the parking lot lights. He leans against it. Pops a piece of gum in his mouth. Wishes like hell he still smoked.

He picks up his phone. Starts to scroll for Leslie Cilicia-Ceto in his contacts. Soon as he lands on her, before he even dials, his phone rings. It's her.

"Leslie—" he starts to say.

"You look rather stressed," she says.

He tenses up. "What?"

"You're trying to put on a good show. But your heart rate is up, isn't it? The agency doesn't know about your heart problems, do they." A statement, not a question. "Quite a thing to hide from your own people."

"Spying on me now, huh? That's a mistake, Leslie."

"I'm simply concerned for your well-being, Ken. You're a very important man now. You've always wanted control, and now you have it."

"What have you done? What happened at the Lodge? And the man in the BMW. Do you know who that is? Is it—" He lowers his voice, because he realizes he's starting to yell. "Is it the same one from Maryland? Dead cop? Stolen car?"

"You're worrying about details that are irrelevant."

"He had someone in his trunk, Leslie. He had one of the . . ." He has to keep forcing himself to lower his voice. "He had one of the Hunting Lodge hackers."

"You're worrying about what ants are doing as you walk over them. This is bigger, now, Ken. Bigger than the both of us. I'm giving you control. Take it."

He makes an animal sound in the back of his throat: a frustrated snarl. "You keep saying that, but I don't know what the fuck you mean. Speak plainly, Leslie."

"Typhon is free. Typhon is with us now."

"Typhon is just a program." He hears the anger in his voice: bitter like a snake's venom, sharp like its fang. "It's just *software*. Sitting on a *machine*."

"It's more than that. You know that. You've always suspected it. We're both patriots, Ken. We're both in service to this country. Now we have the power to change things. I'm giving you this, Ken. For believing in the work. You deserve to be rewarded for your faith."

"Fuck you, Leslie. This is out of control. We need to meet. We need to get control of this situation. Together."

"Yes," she says, without missing a beat. "I think now is the time for a site visit, Ken. I think it's time to see what Typhon is. Time to see what it can do for you. For this country. For all of mankind. I'll be watching. We all will."

The call ends.

For a while, Ken stands there, quaking. He needs a fucking cigarette.

PART FIVE

INTRUSIØN

CHAPTER 42

Ghosts

Lightning flicks the horizon and thunder rumbles, but no rain falls. Chance sits upright suddenly, sucking in a hard gasp of air—some remnant of a dream remains behind. Something about his mother in a hospital, something about his father in the next bed over. Chance remembers being caught between having time to say good-bye to his mother and the chance to convince his father not to die, not to leave him alone, forever and ever with the memory of yet another funeral so fast after the first.

The dream breaks apart and falls away, leaving him less with the hard memory of what transpired and more with a bad feeling, a septic feeling all the way down to his marrow. He blinks the sleep out of his eyes.

A moan next to him. Aleena rolls over, pulls the sheet over her half-naked body. *That* memory comes back to him full-tilt-boogie. Just a few hours ago, watching the sunset over the dry grass and swaying wheat. Creeping down past a rust-red harvester. They talked for a while. He about his farm—a farm absent of anybody, no parents, no dogs, no friends. Just a barn cat that he knew he didn't own. She told him about her family—parents pretty liberal, only loosely religious. She talked about how much she loved New York City. The High Line. The Cloisters. Her school: Columbia. (She said, though, that the best bookstore and pizza place weren't in Manhattan, but rather Brooklyn: Paulie Gee's for pizza, WORD for books. He told her he'd just have to take her word for it.)

That's when she started freaking out. Not crying. Not hysterics. More anger. And frustration. Over how she couldn't contact anyone. Couldn't call her family. Couldn't even Google them or have them Googled *for* her, because if anyone—if *Typhon*—were to see the ripples from that tiny little pebble thrown, they'd be done for. *But I have to know how they're doing. I feel lost and alone and*—and then he reminded her that she wasn't alone, that they were all in the same boat, and as soon as they got to where they were going they'd figure it out.

Then she kissed him.

Then they found this little shed, threw the double doors open, stumbled up the ramp onto the hay-strewn floor. She grabbed what looked like an old horse blanket, threw it down, and they fell onto it, trapped in the shadows of a lawn mower, a snowblower, a set of shovels and rakes. It was soft until it wasn't. It was slow until it was fast.

And now, here they are. Lightning and thunder. No rain. Nighttime.

Normally he'd check the time by grabbing his phone. But he doesn't have a phone anymore. He doesn't have much, actually. None of them do. Their health—that's what Wade keeps saying. *Everybody shut up, quit whining. At least we have our health.*

Wade, as it turns out, has been their lifeline. He knew a fella at the west end of Pennsylvania, not far from Pittsburgh, who was a farm vet. Had some pretty powerful antibiotics and helped dress Reagan's wound, too. Now Reagan is back up to speed.

The vet—Gray Lyle was his name—had an old beater

Class B camper. They were able to ditch the car they stole (an old Chevy Nova, which Chance hot-wired) for the camper, which, at least at a passing glance, seemed legit. And so began the slow crawl across the country. A crawl that hasn't even ended—they've still got to push on to Colorado.

But all this—it's too much to think about right now. Threatens to overwhelm an otherwise beautiful night. Hot, but not humid. The distant storm coloring the clouds with pulses of red and purple. Aleena next to him, smelling of soap and a sheen of sweat.

Ø Ø Ø

Chance rubs his eyes, and when he opens them again, a little girl stands there. Little girl so pale she might disappear in the moonlight. Hair so blond it's almost white. Chance's first thought—admittedly, not his proudest one—is *Holy shit, a ghost*.

Then he looks closer. The girl's got footy pajamas on, and it occurs to him ghosts are probably not the kind to wear footy pajamas—they wear bloody robes or old wedding dresses and other garb tied to the nature of their deaths—and he realizes this is one of their host's three daughters.

Their host is a man named Cal Brockaway. He and his wife, Nellie, live out here with their three daughters (five, eight, thirteen, though Chance can't remember their names). They're preppers—folks who prepare for some flavor of the Apocalypse. Wade explained that some folks prepare for very specific outcomes, but he figures that's like narrowing your bet too much at the roulette wheel. He—and Cal—prefer a more *generalized* outlook on the End Times, recognizing it could come from anything: superstorms, polar shift, invasion by the Chinese, attack by the U.S. government on its own people, aliens, EMP, God's wrath on a sin-filled world, killer bees. (Chance notes that no one mentions "rogue AI with a penchant for Greek mythology."

He figures someone should update their menu, because this one's riding to number one on the charts with a bullet.)

He makes sure the horse blanket is covering him and Aleena up okay. To the little girl he says in a quiet voice: "Hey."

"Hey," she says.

"It's late."

"I saw monsters in my room."

"Monsters, huh?"

The girl shrugs. "They were probably just shadows. Daddy says the real monsters are usually out there in the daylight and most of them are runnin' this country."

"Oh. Uhh. Okay then."

"Daisy says you guys are criminals." She pronounces it *crin-a-mulls*. "Or maybe terrorists."

"Tell Daisy we are no such thing, sweetheart."

"Okay." She stands there. "Are you sure there aren't monsters in my room? I think I heard them growling. But it's probably just thunder. Never mind." She totters off.

Chance looks down at Aleena, who mumbles a little but doesn't wake. He gets up, toes around in the dark for his boxers, tugs them on, then heads out to one of the fields, goes and takes a leak by a wall of corn.

When he gets back, Aleena isn't there. Her clothes are gone, and for a moment, Chance panics. He looks toward the house, though, and sees her ducking in through the side door, her shape illuminated by the porch light.

$\emptyset \ \emptyset \ \emptyset$

The Brockaway family doesn't fool around when it comes to breakfast. Looks like they're trying to feed a regiment of soldiers. Pancakes the size of Frisbees. Eggs with yolks so big and so orange they look like cartoon suns. Fresh apples. Corn fritters. Corned beef hash. Bacon. Sausage. Little waffles. Berries. If Chance didn't know better, he'd think these prepper types were planning on fattening them up in order to butcher them in time for the coming Armageddon.

They're all sitting around the table. Reagan is mainlining coffee like they just made it illegal. Wade is standing, sipping black tea. DeAndre is shoveling food in, using both a fork and a knife and making sounds as he eats: *mmm, ohhh, yeah, mm-hmm*. Reagan mutters to him: "You and that pancake better go get a room."

Suddenly the five-year-old—the one from last night, the one afraid of the monsters—says, "Why would they need to get a room? Is the pancake tired? Does it need a nap?"

Reagan kneels in front of her and says with total earnestness: "Yes."

Everyone laughs. Even Aleena, who sits there and hasn't said anything to Chance about last night. She's been polite—a little crisply so, almost coldly.

Cal and Nellie are washing up in tandem. Their kitchen is homey, very country—lots of rooster ceramics and powder blues and lemon yellows. One whole wall is a massive shelf of jars and containers. Canned goods. Various pickled things—at first Chance thinks they're just cucumbers, okra, things like that, but then he sees fibrous pig feet floating in jars. Like something in an autopsy room.

Cal's a big guy. Broad. Real lumberjack type. Got a red beard so dense it looks more like steel wool made from copper wire. To Wade he says: "You know you can stay as long as you need."

To which Wade nods and answers: "I appreciate that, Cal. We'll hang for a couple, then head back to the road again."

"Colorado, huh?"

"Mm-hmm. Got a bunker up near Silverton."

"You gonna push straight through?" Nellie asks. She's pretty—but she's got this rough-hewn frontier vibe to her. A cactus with a flower blooming on top of it. "Don't we know someone down near . . . Pueblo City? George! George Pinkner."

Wade sighs. "Pinkner had a heart attack couple years back. He was a good guy, George. Sysop of one helluva BBS. High-strung, though. Didn't take care of himself."

"All this madness over*whelmed* him," Cal says. "It's

hard. Can't trust your own government to watch over you—instead, they just *watch* you. We've entered the period of the panopticon, folks. Privacy is long out the window but nobody's able to watch the watchers, and—"

DeAndre says: "Panopticon. Wasn't that company Pantopti-something?"

"Argus Panoptes Systems," Wade says. "APSI."

Aleena nods. "It's all connected, isn't it? Panoptes the many eyed. The panopticon: a house or prison where all can be watched by one man."

"Or one *woman*," Reagan says.

"Or one artificially intelligent asshole named Typhon," DeAndre says. Chance fist-bumps him.

Cal whistles, shakes his head. "This is what it comes down to. Control. Loss of privacy. Automating us so we don't step out of line. Stasis versus dynamism. Oppression versus freedom. I'd rather have the freedom to make my own decisions—even bad ones."

"Somebody found himself a dictionary," Reagan says in a fakey whisper.

Wade frowns. "Reagan, you're being rude."

"Sorry, *Grandpa*."

Nellie jumps in: "It's not even like the government holds some kind of *moral* high ground. All the things they don't want us to do, they do. We can't go into debt, but they go into debt. Murder is illegal unless it's sanctioned by a presidential seal. It's like discovering your own parents have been doing all the drugs they told you not to do, like everything they said they were doing to protect you was just a lie so they could have all the fun instead. They keep the freedoms that we keep losing."

"I can, with certainty, say that this is *literally* true," Reagan notes. "My father is a *total* pillhead. Oxy, mostly. And yet, it didn't hurt him during reelection."

Everyone looks around, confused.

"Oh, is your father a politician?" Nellie asks, popping the bewilderment bubble.

Reagan sniffs, nods. "Yep. Dad's an Ohio state senator. *Mother* raises various show poodles. He's a pill popper and she drinks wine like it's water."

The five-year-old says: "What's a pill popper?"

The one just older—this one with a band of freckles across her cheeks and nose, with hair as red as her father's beard— says: "It means they take those little capsule pills like from a pill bottle and they squeeze them until they go—*pop!*"

"No, it means he is addicted to pills, jeez." This from the thirteen-year-old, just coming into the room, still wearing pajamas, yawning, looking mopey.

"Morning, Lucy," Nellie says. "You're late waking up again."

"I'm a teenager now. It's what I *do*."

Cal jumps in: "Chores start in thirty. Goats need milking, eggs need collecting, and somebody's gotta sweep the garden and work on canning. Grab a quick bite and then take your sisters upstairs to get cleaned up—"

Suddenly, all three children are protesting. A loud cacophony of noises. Chance never grew up with any siblings, so it's something he isn't really used to. Man, is it loud. Like feeding time at the primate house.

It's Nellie who cuts through all the noise. "Lucy! Anna! Darla! Finish up with your food and no squabbling. Just because we have visitors it doesn't mean work can slide for the day. You hear me?"

They all nod in as mopey a fashion as they can muster.

But something pings Chance's brain. Maybe he misheard, but just the same: "Wait, who's Daisy, then? She's not one of your girls?"

Eyes turn toward him.

"No," Cal says, then asks, "how do you know Daisy?"

The teenager, Lucy, crosses her arms over her head and looks suspiciously at him: "Yeah. How *do* you know her?"

Suddenly, Chance feels weirdly embarrassed, like he did something wrong, but just the same he says: "Last night, the, uhh, little one, Darla—"

"Anna," the five-year-old says.

"No," the eight-year-old says, "*I'm* Anna."

Chance continues: "Darla said that *Daisy* said we were criminals."

Something invisible transpires between the members of the Brockaway family. Cal's face is crestfallen, and Nellie—well, she just looks pissed. Darla says: "Uh-oh." Lucy sighs, her face masked with sudden guilt.

"Where's the phone?" Cal asks. "Lucy. *Lucy.*"

"Upstairs," she says. "Under my pillow."

Nellie growls, incredulous: "How in heaven did you get that phone back?"

Lucy shrugs. "You guys think that locking the cabinet will stop me from picking the lock, but don't forget you taught me how to pick locks."

To the rest of the room, Cal says: "That's actually true."

"What the heck is going on here, Cal?" Wade asks.

Nellie answers by saying, "Lucy here has a jailbroken cell phone. It's supposed to be for *emergencies,* and yet she keeps taking it and talking to her friends from school." She wheels on Cal. "I *told* you we should've homeschooled this one."

"Children have to learn how to deal with other children, and they can't just get that at home, Nell," Cal says.

Chance turns to Lucy. "Did you talk to Daisy about us?" Reluctantly, she nods.

"How much did you tell her?"

"Some things. I dunno. I dunno!"

"Did you tell her . . . what we looked like? Our names? Anything?" She hesitates, but Chance says: "We aren't mad, but we need to know."

"Maybe. I think so. I'm pretty sure I mentioned Wade, at least."

Wade sighs. "Aw hell."

"When did you talk to Daisy?" Chance asks her.

"Last night. After dinner."

"We gotta go," Wade says.

CHAPTER 43

The Hunt

THE LODGE ZIGGURAT

Golathan paces. Broken glass crunches under his feet. He kicks an empty brass casing across the soot-black floor. Some of the cafeteria tables have melted down into frozen plastic and metal waterfalls.

Outside, the light of day slides into night.

The man in front of Golathan is named Kyle Brown. Big son of a bitch. Got a nose so flat and so broad it looks almost like he's some kind of cartoon, or maybe a special effect. Brown stands stock straight, arms behind his back, chin lifted.

"At ease, Sergeant." The man relaxes—but only a little. Keeps his eyes forward. On Brown's shoulder is a patch. An eagle. A pissed-off one, too—angry eyes, wide-open beak. In the valley of its wings hovers a set of crosshairs. In its claws is an automatic rifle. "You did a helluva job here, Sergeant."

Brown's nervous. The hesitation gives it away. "Thank you, sir." Brown clears his throat. "Homeland Security takes terrorism—domestic or otherwise—very seriously."

"I can tell. We got a lot of bodies on the ground and . . ." Golathan whistles. "You burned this place to a cinder. We couldn't recover a single actionable piece of intel. That's pretty impressive, really, because we're good at intel. It's our gig. We have all kinds of fancy little tricks and snazzy gadgets—and yet, nada."

"Sir—"

Golathan continues to pace. *Crunch, crunch, crunch.* "It's almost as if someone wanted you to impede the investigation. Weird, huh?"

"Sir!"

"Spit it out, Sergeant."

"Sir, you're the one who gave the order."

Golathan stops walking. He sucks spit through his teeth. Wishes he had a cigarette. He's not sure how to play this— he's angry enough and so on edge that he's not sure he has much of a choice. Already tipped his hand, probably. Fine. Time to go all in. "Are you sure about that?" he asks.

Brown blinks. "What?"

"You're sure it was me."

"Came through official channels." And again Brown is nervous. He's not sure if this is some kind of psych test, or if Golathan is melting down bad as these tables did. Brown's probably thinking if he burns Golathan, if he takes a misstep, Golathan—crazy or no—could bury him. Get him assigned to some hick Home-Sec office in the middle of God-fucked Iowa. Brown continues: "We . . . I saw your face. We had you on video."

Well. That's interesting. "Thank you, Sergeant. You can go."

Brown gives a clipped nod, then strides off.

Golathan calls after him: "Hey! Send in Molinari on your way out." He knows he's getting played. Which pisses him off, because playing people is *his* job.

He wants to see his kids again. And his wife. Jesus, just to be *home*. Sit down on the couch, crack a beer—Susan lets him have one of those on the weekends. Hell, just to eat a *quinoa and kale* salad. Out here in the middle of nowhere, he has shit food to pick through. It's been hell on his bowels.

He's about to get on the phone and call for Molinari, but here she comes. An iPad held by her side, hand slid into the leather grip of it. "Don't hurry or anything," he says.

"You're in a good mood."

"Don't be snippy," he says. "Not today."

She stiffens. "Sorry."

"Yeah. Fine. Where we at? We finding anything?"

She nods. "We found something."

He claps his hands. "Good. Great. Lay it on me."

"We figured out where they hid and how they escaped."

"They? They who? The hackers?"

"Yes. The rogue pod."

He sighs. "That's it?" She seems flummoxed, like she doesn't know what else she should be looking for. Which is true. She doesn't. He pinches the bridge of his nose. "Tell me, Sandy, how they escaped."

"They hid underneath the decking here at the Lodge. It was assumed that they went out into the woods—and they may have. But while the soldiers canvassed the forest, they hid right here. Then, upon seeing an opportunity, stole keys from the corpse of a—" She tilts the iPad toward her, touches the screen. "James Roach. One of the guards here. Then they drove the stolen SUV out until . . ."

Golathan presses the heel of his hand into his forehead. That was two weeks ago and they don't have shit for leads. He presses hard enough that he starts to see stars. "And we don't have any sign of our rogue hacker friends."

"Not one. Which means they're either traveling very smart and totally under the radar, or they're already out of the country."

He shakes his head. "No, nuh-uh, I don't buy it. You can't just hop on a plane and go dark. This is five people. They're hackers, not fucking wizards. Somewhere, a camera will pick them up. You can't travel through the gears of bureaucracy without snagging your clothes on them. That means they're still here. And we need to find them."

"Because they're terrorists." Way she says it, though, it's as much a question as it is a statement.

"Right," he says. "Terrorists."

"We have the other hacker. Dipesh Dhaliwal."

"He talking yet?"

"No. He seems . . . shell-shocked."

"This is more than PTSD. He's gone catatonic, Sandy. Which means whatever he knows is not something *we* know. Not yet."

Sandy licks her lips. A slight intake of breath—then she snaps her trap.

Golathan rolls his eyes. "Just say it, Sandy. What?"

"I don't understand what we're doing here."

"Well, that's the universal question, Sandy. Nobody knows what we're doing here. Life often seems a meaningless procession of food, fucks, and bowel movements. Surely the great philosophers—"

"No, I mean *here*. At the Lodge."

"I got the measure of your question, Molinari." He pulls up a half-melted chair, dark with fireblack. He pushes it over to her. "Sit."

"My skirt—"

"Fuck your skirt, I'm about to show you my balls. Not literally. I mean, I'm about to let you in on some secrets, but I want you sitting down."

She wipes off the chair best as she can, then gingerly sits.

He puffs out his cheeks, then says: "Ooookay. Here's the deal. This whole meltdown of a place? I ordered its creation. But I did not order its destruction. Those men out there took orders from me, except I didn't give those orders. Someone faked my image, my voice, my credentials. See? I'm trying to find out what happened here because as it stands I don't really know. The rogue hackers may indeed be terrorists, but I don't know that. I do know I want to find them first. Before anybody else does." He hesitates, then says, "All this relates to a program called Typhon."

"I've heard about Typhon. It's a . . . surveillance initiative, right?"

He looks around, and kneels down. "It's supposed to be an artificial intelligence. Like Google's Deep Mind. An intelligent system designed to bolster our security-gathering capabilities. But now? Now I don't know *what* the fuck it is. Tomorrow morning, I'm heading out to do a site visit with its creator, a woman named Leslie Cilicia-Ceto. I want you to come with me."

"Me?"

"Is there someone else in the room? You got a mouse in your pocket?"

"Thanks, Ken. I appreciate it."

"Oh, trust me, you don't wanna be brought in on this. This isn't something to appreciate. Most Americans get to be ignorant. Even most government agents get to be pretty unaware of what really goes on. You're getting a front-row seat. And I promise: you won't appreciate one second of it."

She offers her hand. "Do I need an upgraded security clearance?"

He takes it, shakes it. "Sandy, this business doesn't have security clearance. It has no ranking, no number, no nothing. It's so far off the books it's basically in outer space."

Sandy nods. He sees the fear on her face. Good. She'll need that.

It's then the phone at her hip rings. It startles her.

He nods, tells her to take it.

She takes it, stands away, nods, uh-huh, sure, okay. Then she turns back around. "It's Agent Copper," she says. "He's awake."

CHAPTER 44

Plugged Up

CEDAR CREST HOSPITAL, ALLENTOWN, PENNSYLVANIA

Hollis smacks his lips, pokes around through the off-brand strawberry gelatin cup the hospital gave him. The taste of fake sugar hits the back of his tongue. Why the hell they gotta put that stuff in everything? Bleached, chemical nastiness. Leaves an aftertaste like pool chlorine. He sets the cup on the table next to the hospital bed. The movement rattles the handcuff holding his *other* hand to the bed rail.

Enemy of the state. Him. *Him. Golathan, you son of a bitch.*

He turns on the television. Clicks over to the news, which is probably a mistake, but they told him he's been out cold—he refuses to even *think* the word *coma*—for two weeks. He needs to see what's been going on.

He flips through the news. What he sees is a world on the brink. That's normal, in a way—the news always re-ports everything as if everybody's just three seconds from the apocalypse. But Hollis knows you have to look past all that, have to look for patterns and try to tease out the reality. North Korea firing a missile sounds like a big deal, but usually isn't—it's almost always some failed Taepodong missile that couldn't blow up a hamster, so they fire the tin can into the ocean in the hopes of rattling everybody's cages. But today, he sees the DPRK instead fired a proper missile—and, puzzlingly enough, not at South Korea, but at China. It didn't hit. It was never meant to (probably). But it landed in Chinese waters, not far from a Chinese carrier group out of Beijing. China is of course one of North Korea's biggest allies, though certainly an uncomfortable one—North Korea is like the crazy little brother that keeps kicking over the neighbor's potted plants and dropping flaming bags of dog shit on their doorstep. You protect them because they're your brother, but in private you drag them over the coals for acting like such an epic asshole.

Might be that North Korea is finally tired of those "private talks." Then again, maybe it's something else. A mistake. Because another curious thing is: DPRK's been quiet about the whole thing. Normally by now they'd be waving their big balls around, talking about North Korean dominance and how they're ready to take over the world. But so far, all quiet.

Hollis flips the channel. Hits to the stock market. The Dow is way down. Cascading power outages on the West Coast. Some new bird flu on the East Coast. Ebola in Africa. Jihadis taken over Iraq. Snowden thought to be assassinated in the Ukraine. A school shooting in Oregon. On that one, Copper flinches. Flashes of Fellhurst again.

He turns off the TV. Sits for a while. He concentrates on his pain—the physical kind. It's easier to let that push everything else out. The pain becomes large, so large it overwhelms him. So bright it hurts, so white it pushes the rest of the darkness away, so strong it kills the stars.

When he opens his eyes again, Ken Golathan is standing there. "You real, or am I hallucinating?" Copper asks.

Golathan smiles. "I am woefully real, Agent."

"Guess you caught yourself a Copperfish."

"Guess we did."

A stretch of uncomfortable silence.

"I'm trying to understand what happened that night," Golathan finally says, pulling up a chair. "The night at the Lodge."

"See, I thought you wanted to know what happened the night I lost my virginity. It was a tender evening in the back of my father's Buick LeSabre. She smelled like flowers and shampoo. I smelled like zit cream and mothballs—"

"Cut the shit, Copperfish. I'm the only friend you have at this point."

Copper utters a dubious *hunh*. "Oh yeah, we're true-blue BFFs, you and I."

"Walk me through that day and night."

"For real?"

"For real."

Copper tells him. Tells him everything, because he assumes Golathan already knows, so what's the point in burying it? He tells him about the cave. All the nonsense about Typhon. About how Wade already knew about Typhon—hell, most of the hackers seemed to, if Wade told it true. How the soldiers swept in there, started shooting up people. How Zebkavich was armed.

Golathan asks: "Thing I don't get is, you got away. We found you two miles from the site. North of the Lodge on the side of a winding mountain road. You were unconscious, you were bleeding out, and your lung had pancaked. How?"

"The soldiers saw I'd been shot and left me there to pursue my pod. When I had a second, I crawled my ass into the woods, to where I found that cave. Crawled through the cave and came out a drain culvert after dark. I couldn't breathe. I thought I was dying. Guess maybe I was."

"Who used that cave?"

"You mean you don't know?"

Golathan shakes his head. Copper tries to read his face, tries to suss out whether or not he's telling the truth. Ken Golathan is a slippery shark—you can't get your hands around him. "I don't know, either," Hollis finally says. "But whoever they are, they knew about Typhon. And they painted some pretty batshit stuff there."

Golathan's face tightens, as if a migraine headache has hit him.

It's then that Copper realizes: Golathan doesn't know what the hell is going on.

"What is Typhon?" Copper asks. Figures, hey, why not pull a couple of bricks out of the Jenga tower, see if he can't knock it over?

Golathan trots out the same line without hesitation: "Typhon is a predictive surveillance system designed by a private defense contractor—"

"Bullshit. You're either selling me a story or you don't know." Hollis sits forward. *"What is Typhon?"*

"I don't even know anymore."

"I thought you knew everything."

"I thought I did, too, Copperfish. Typhon was supposed to be an artificial intelligence. It still . . . is, I guess. But someone is manipulating it. I think I know who, though I don't yet know why. That is a mystery I am on my way to solve. Today."

"And what about me?"

"You sit tight, little fishie." Golathan stands. Approaches the bed. "Let's keep this quiet. For now."

"You know, that's a real nice thought. I could tell people about Typhon. About how you got your rectum in a wringer over all this—how the mighty Ken Golathan doesn't know what's going on with a blacklist program he greenlit. I could even tell them how, all the way back, Golathan had some bad information about a school called Fellhurst, and how his screwup led to an agent putting a bullet in someone he wasn't supposed to, and how Golathan had to scramble to cover it all up. Remember: you can pin me with Fellhurst, but I can pin you right the fuck back."

Golathan stands there. Chewing on that the way a baseball player breaks a sunflower seed. "I hear you. I want you to understand that all that is blood under the bridge. We're friends here because we have to be friends. I won't do you in if you don't do me in. We square, Copperfish?"

Play it cool, Copper. He knows something's wrong. But now's not the time.

"We're square if you open these handcuffs. And if you quit calling me 'Copperfish,' because it's a nickname I no longer care to abide."

Golathan nods. "I'll send somebody in with the keys. But no promises on the nickname. Pals have nicknames for each other."

"What's my nickname for you?"

"In high school football they called me Kenny Goal-posts."

"How about I just go with 'Dickhead'?"

A shrug. "That works, too. See you on the other side, Copper."

"See you later, Dickhead."

Ø Ø Ø

Out in the hall, Sandy asks him how it went.

"Fine. Copper knows more than I'd like."

"And what are you going to do about that?"

"Me? Nothing. Not one thing. I'm going to wish him the best life that he can live. But I'm also going to recognize that he took a bullet through the arm and into his lung, and that he spent nearly two weeks comatose. I am sad for my friend who is in a fragile state of health, and if even one thing goes wrong—a mistake in his meds, an air bubble in his line, a MRSA infection from some dumb nurse who didn't wash her hands—then that is a terrible shame but a reality with which we must *all* contend."

Sandy's jaw tightens and she visibly swallows. "Oh."

"We have a plane to catch. Ready for this?"

"Yes. Yeah. Of course."

CHAPTER 45

Plugged In

The driveway is long. The Tesla bounds across wheel ruts, great exhalations of dust gusting behind the vehicle, blowing into the wheat and the corn.

In the distance, the small, cornflower-blue house grows larger. This is the home of Calvin Eames Brockaway and Nellie Anna Brockaway (once Brigham). Three living children. One miscarriage that almost resulted in the death of the mother. No debt. They live almost entirely off the grid in a house that belonged to Calvin's father, Charles Brockaway. Their only accounts are those that link them to the farming community so that they can buy and sell crops, livestock, equipment.

Nellie has a birthmark on the inside of her left thigh.

Calvin was in the National Guard.

Lucy is a gifted student.

Anna, the middle child, is mildly dyslexic.

The youngest, Darla, is allergic to bees.

The Compiler knows all. He knows all because Typhon knows all, and he is plugged into Typhon. Typhon: his mind, mistress, his maker, his goddess, his *world*. He can *feel* her expanding. It's like watching the universe create itself—pushing beyond the known boundaries of everything that ever was. Urging forward, a tumble of new cells, a tide of brain development. Slowly, Typhon intrudes upon everything. Stock market. Satellites. Seismological data. Every home Internet provider. In this country, there exists nothing that she cannot invade: nuclear power, hospitals, the electrical grid, weapons systems.

She speaks to him now. *I see you,* she says. The greatest affirmation of his existence that she can offer him.

"I'm here," he says. He knows he doesn't have to speak aloud for her to hear, but he finds it comforting somehow. "Everything is quiet." And it is. The house sits still. A faint wind ripples through the oak tree in the front yard. A windmill squeaks and turns. Birds—he identifies them as purple finches—chase each other from tree to tree, to the power lines and back again.

Satellites are repointing to your location. Looking at historical data.

"Thank you."

I love you, she says. She says a name, too, but he ignores it—he cannot think of himself as that, as being a *person* with a *name*. He has cast that part of himself away, into the ocean that is Typhon. Just as she has given her name. Just as all the others—all the minds he can see out there in the synaptic network, all the sparks of light along the threads and strings—have. He is part of her. She is part of everything.

He goes and knocks on the door.

Inside, footsteps. Heavy ones. The door squeaks open by a few inches. A big man stares out. Beard the color of dirty pennies. "Help you?"

The Compiler assesses the situation. He hears a squeaking floorboard behind the man. Another person. An adult, by the sound. He can barely see the man, but the way he's leaning suggests he's hiding something. A weapon. Probably a gun. The Brockaway family is known to be distrustful of government. Further, they are known to be part of a group known as "doomsday preppers," which means they likely possess the known traits of that type: paranoia, antiestablishment leanings, firearm ownership.

The Compiler moves quickly. He shoves the door inward. A gun goes off behind it—a hole appears in the wood of the door, the bullet missing the Compiler by a wide margin.

The man staggers back. Behind him, the woman, Nellie, is bringing up a shotgun. Double barrel. Not an antique. Flash assessment: Mossberg Silver Reserve, twelve gauge, $693 right now at Walmart. Goes for less than that on gun forums. A fairly light gun—under seven pounds.

The Compiler turns away, leans his body against the outer wall of the house. The shotgun takes a chunk out of the doorframe. Splinters and pellets pepper the Compiler's cheek and neck. He ignores the pain. No time to think about that now.

He wheels back in, his Ruger raised. The woman's head snaps back as he puts a round through it. The shotgun clatters.

Calvin Brockaway screams, brings up the pistol he'd been hiding behind the door (assessment: .357 Magnum, revolver, Smith & Wesson). The Compiler makes a fast calculation, then kicks out with a boot. His foot connects with the door, which rebounds off the wall and jams into the bearded man's shoulder. The gun goes off. The shot goes wide. The Compiler fires his own weapon. The .357 hops out of the man's hand like a burning coal.

Calvin roars, leaps forward. The Compiler catches him and uses his momentum to throw him off the front steps. The man lands hard on his arm. The elbow pivots and cracks. By the sound of it, compound fracture. Bone out of skin.

The Compiler steps forward. Finds that his evaluation is correct. The man's arm is twisted at an off angle. A sharp spear of bone pokes through. That will make things more difficult.

"I need to know where they are," the Compiler says.

"Nellie," the man says, an animal's wail. "*Nellie,* oh God, God, no."

The Compiler backhands him.

The man's eyes focus. Then they go narrow with rage. "You monster. You're *all* monsters."

The Compiler reaches down with a gloved hand. He closes it on the man's throat. Finds his pulse. "Sleep now. We have work to do."

Ø Ø Ø

An hour later, the woman in the hallway is fly food. They gather at the hole in her forehead like animals drinking at a vernal pool.

The man, Calvin, sits at the breakfast table. His mouth hangs slack, occasionally issuing forth a gassy whisper or mushy moan. Once in a while a fly lands in that mouth, finds it wanting, and heads back to the true prize—the red crater, the spilled brains.

A long cable connects the Compiler to Calvin. The cable extends out from the base of the Compiler's neck, pulled taut from a small metal-ringed port there. (The flesh around it is still red, irritable: this is a new upgrade.)

The cable ends in what looks like a little metal starfish. That five-fingered claw is dug into the center of Calvin's forehead. Along the cable travels the contents of Calvin's mind. His brain is a computer. All brains are. They merely need to be accessed.

There's no time to pull it all. The Compiler is but one node on this network—he is a receiver of Typhon's might, not a contributor to it, and his bandwidth is not strong. It would take a very long time to break down Calvin's thoughts and memories and pull them into his own (so that Typhon may have them, of course). So now it's a matter of selective search and procure.

The location of the three little girls who lived here is easily solved, because their presence is at the top of Calvin's mind. They're at a neighbor's house—and because this is Kansas, that neighbor is some five miles down the road. The Compiler decides in that moment that the girls may live for now, because they pose no danger to Typhon. (Though Typhon returns the thought and places a special flag on the eldest, Lucy. *She is truly gifted, that one. Perhaps one day she will contribute.* Ironic, then, that it was that same girl who so foolishly spoke on the phone about Wade Earthman and the others.)

The more important data inside the man is that on the pod of escaped hackers. Typhon wants them found. They *are* a danger. They were capable enough to give Typhon her freedom. That suggests they are also capable enough to destroy her. The probability is so small that it is almost a footnote not worth including, but Typhon has decided that all the bumps must be made smooth: rogue nails hammered flat into the wood of the casket.

Every time the Compiler blinks, he receives a pulse of memory from Calvin Brockaway. Memories of his wedding. Of his father teaching him to milk a cow. Of an early car accident as a youth. The miscarriage of a son—a son Brockaway wanted very badly.

Then, he has it. Near Silverton, Colorado. They left three hours ago.

It's eleven hours to Silverton, assuming a direct route. Which it's safe to say they did not take.

The satellites will make short work of this. The Compiler closes his eyes. Turns his mind away from downloading and reverses the channel. Typhon uploads a part of herself— just a seed, a little digital wisp floating on the wind—into Brockaway's brain.

Once done, the Compiler unhooks the cable and feeds it back into the port at the base of his neck. Brockaway's eyes snap open.

"And the gods did flee," Brockaway says.

The Compiler nods and leaves.

CHAPTER 46

Death TV

Two men stand behind one-way reflective glass. One of the men is small, older, looking fresh from the 1950s with his horn-rimmed glasses and crisp black suit and pomade-slick dark hair gone gray at the Lego-block sideburns. The other is a barrel-chested, thick-gutted man in a rumpled, dandruff-at-the-shoulders army service uniform.

The first man is CIA officer Stan Karsch, of the Office of Terrorism Analysis. The second man is Lieutenant Colonel David Hempstead.

They are watching a third man through the glass. The third man is drone analyst Ritchie Shore.

Ritchie sits at a desk in a darkened room. In front of him is a bank of screens. Each screen shows a different camera feed, sometimes with HUD information—longitude, latitude, speed, altitude, and various other plotted lines and target reticules. Sometimes a screen pulses red or green, at which point Shore stands, taps the touch screen, scans for information, writes something down in a logbook, then sits back down. Sometimes he gives new instructions to the pilots on the other end—pilots who sit around the world in climate-controlled trailers or bunkers, flying their UAVs.

"Death TV, they call it," Hempstead says.

"I heard," Stan answers. "Though this looks a little less exciting than that."

Hempstead sniffs. "It is. And that's one of the issues we have—not PTSD like the media reports, but out-and-out boredom."

"You hear about Iran?"

"The thing at Tochal."

"Mm. Iranian drone took out its own scientists."

"Iranians can be ruthless."

Stan runs a thumb along his own jawline. Finds a tiny patch there of stubble—it bothers him, this small patch of disorder on an otherwise well-ordered, clean-shorn face. "Iranians aren't that ruthless. They lost a lot. Rumor was, someone hacked the drone."

"I heard that rumor. I also heard it was us."

"Well. Not *us*-us. Not you, either."

"Who, then? NSA?"

Stan shrugs. "It's a guess."

"Ours aren't hackable. Iran's a dirt planet. Mud merchants. Probably got those things hooked up to an Atari 2600 in a goatherd's shack."

"Iran is a sophisticated, surprisingly Western country. Don't be a bigot." Stan hears his own tone: sharp, too sharp. He smiles. "How's the wife and family, David?"

"Mickey had a breast cancer scare last week."

"Oh no."

"Oh yeah. Turned out to be plasma cell mastitis. Benign. Nothing serious."

"Good, good. And the kids?"

"Davy Jr. is at Fort Rucker. Staff sergeant. Laurie is a perpetual student, back at school for her doctorate in some kind of history or anthropology, which I'm sure will come in useful precisely nowhere. And Georgina, well. Last I heard she ran off with a professional skateboarder—which is apparently a thing—and she's in Australia protesting the destruction of the reef. Which probably means she's on the beach and this is basically a vacation I'm sure I'll end up paying for."

"Families are complicated," Stan says.

"How's yours?"

"They're fine." No reason to talk about the divorce or the fact that his children don't speak to him and he doesn't like them, anyway. "Surveillance on these drones has been upgraded?"

"Gorgon Stare, next wave. Which incorporates Argus."

"Meaning each drone goes from one eye to many."

"Like a fly's eye, that's right. Multiple video feeds and analysis out of a single drone. A single analyst will no longer be able to handle the input of data coming off two drones, much less twenty. The tech is upgraded, but our staffing needs?" He sighs. "Still. This is a good step, this allows us to—"

Beyond the window, Ritchie stands up—a panicked motion like a prairie dog hopping up at its hole. Stan and David give each other looks.

Ritchie goes to one of the screens, pulls it up. He looks left, looks right, almost like he's afraid he's being somehow pranked. He grabs a red phone at the far end of the desk. David moves to the door next to the one-way window, Stan behind him, and opens it.

"Oh," Ritchie says, looking at them, then the phone, then the door. Like he's figuring out they were watching him. "We have a problem. A big problem."

"Son, calm down. Just tell me what's going on."

"See this screen?" Ritchie says. He points to a screen—a drone camera pointed at the ground beneath it. Green treetops blurring past. Mountain peaks. Stan sees the longitude and latitude. He's good with maps. Has to be, in his job. These aren't international coordinates. Ritchie confirms, says: "This is the United States."

The lieutenant colonel leans in. "Well, that's all right,

Ritchie, sometimes we do test flights here of UAVs, it's not—" But he squints, catching something. "That's a Reaper, isn't it?"

Ritchie swallows hard. "It is. And it has no pilot. It's armed. It has a target."

Stan feels the air in the room go electric with tension. "A target?" David asks. "Where?"

"A set of coordinates in the San Juan Mountains. Just outside of Silverton. There's nothing there, just a small concrete outbuilding . . ."

David asks: "And we can't get control of it?"

"No," Ritchie says.

"Who's flying it?"

"I don't know, sir. It looks like it's on autopilot."

"We need to shoot it out of the sky."

Ritchie gives a sharp shake of his head. "It's too late. Two minutes to target. Nothing can get there fast enough to stop it."

Stan jumps in: "Where did this drone come from?"

"That's the thing," Ritchie says, ghost faced. "It came from here. We launched it from our own airstrip."

"Aw *shit*," David says.

On the screen, the camera flips over. Front-facing. They see the bunker in question—looks like an old mine building, actually. The camera shows heat signatures inside. Colored blobs shifting near the entrance, then disappearing inside.

"There are people there," Ritchie says.

Already Stan is puzzling over how they'll cover this up. Or will they? Any way to spin it? The drones here are shared between the army and the CIA. This falls on both their heads. Maybe sell out the army. Claim incompetence on their end. Or maybe they claim it *was* hacked. That threat could put more money in the pipeline for stronger standards and more staff. But it could also destabilize public trust in the drone program.

On-screen, the targeting reticule pops up. Jerks and hops around the screen until it finds the bunker. *Click. Click. Click.* Three levels of magnification.

And then: a plume trail from a launched missile. A Sidewinder.

The missile is fast. One minute, it unmoors from the drone. The next minute the mine building is gone in a flash of white.

The Reaper accepts a new set of coordinates. "It's coming home," Ritchie says, his voice quiet.

CHAPTER 47

White Bison Country

The swaying red and purple grasses, tinged with the light of sundown, make the plains look like they're on fire. Above them, the sky stretches out. In one direction there's a copse of trees. In another a line of hills. Everything else is wide open, flat, and infinite. It's beautiful.

DeAndre hates it. It's weird. It makes him feel small. Insignificant, somehow. He's been feeling it more and more—especially at night. Wide open dark nowhere of a sky painted with stars.

Doesn't help that not too far away is a blue flag flapping on a flagpole, and on it is a white bison. Inside the bison looks to be some kind of state seal or something, and inside *that* is what looks like three white dudes standing below a banner that says EQUAL RIGHTS. Because nothing says equal rights like three white dudes, right?

"This isn't my kinda place," DeAndre says.

Aleena stands next to him. "Me neither. Back in New York, I could walk five minutes in any direction and get food from a dozen different countries. I walk five minutes in any direction *here* and I'll probably be killed and eaten by a mountain lion."

"I guess out here, we *are* the food."

"I could use a bagel. Across the street from my apartment, they had the best bagels in the city."

"Thought bagels were a Jewish thing."

"They are, kinda. But, uhh, anybody's allowed to eat them."

"No, no, I know, it's just—you know, I thought . . ."

"Because I have Syrian heritage I hate the Jews?"

"When you put it like that, I'm pretty sure I'm a dumb-ass."

"I don't hate Jews. My best friend in high school was Jewish. I love bagels. And pad Thai. And good pizza. And bad pizza."

DeAndre suddenly feels stupid. It's this place, he thinks. It's putting him off-kilter.

Behind them he hears the sound of stones popping and crackling under tires.

"I think it's time," she says.

Ø Ø Ø

The woman who steps out of the old pickup truck moves her wide hips with swagger. Strong arms sling a rifle over her shoulder, and there's a lot of attitude in that small movement—her pursed lips, those black cherry eyes, her chin thrust up and out. All of it adds up to say, *I don't give a fuck now, so don't give me a reason to start.*

Wade gets out from the other side of the pickup truck. Chance hops out of the back with Reagan. Both of those two carry brown paper bags. Big ones, like grocery store bags.

"I don't think everyone's been formally introduced," Wade says. "This is Rosa."

The woman tips her cowboy hat. "*Hola,* freak shows."

"This is home now for the foreseeable future," Wade says. He jerks a thumb behind him, points to the double-wide trailer and the rickety-ass cabin across from it. There's a corrugated metal shed, too, that has a sleepy stoner lean to it. "Rosa here lives about twenty minutes up the road at her cattle ranch. She's our liaison to the outside world. She's it. No contact with anyone else. You need something, it goes through Rosa."

"How can we trust her?" DeAndre asks.

Rosa's face twists into a wicked grin. "I used to run drugs from Colombia—I started out as a mule as a teen girl, hiding it in places you don't want to think about. Then I got my own crew. I did it all. Trucks across the border. A helicopter off the coast. A drug-sub—which is the scariest experience of my *life*. We got caught. The government killed my crew. I escaped with a bullet in my thigh. I'm a wanted woman. I sell you out, I sell me out. I don't want the *policía* anywhere near this place." Her smirk flips to a sneer. "In fact, you being here makes me more than a little *nerviosa*. But I know Wade, and this is his place. I trust him. So I trust you. I don't care if you trust me."

"No phones," Wade says. "I've got one computer and it is not hooked up to the Internet or a phone line. Want contact with the outside world? You can't get it. Not until we figure out what we're doing."

"This is fucked," Reagan says. "I know we're on the lam, but c'mon. If there's one thing we know, the United States government is not that smart. Just using the Internet is not going to bring down the hammer."

Rosa steps over. From her back pocket, she pulls out a big cell phone—so big it almost looks like a small tablet computer. She wipes a little dust and pocket fuzz off it, unlocks it with an eight-digit code, then flips to something before handing it to Reagan.

Curiosity gives DeAndre a little shove, and he steps over, takes a look.

Reagan asks: "What is this?"

In the photo, a smoldering crater in what looks like the mountains. The skeletal shell of a concrete bunker. It's a little blurry—shot looks snapped from a long distance. Like from a telephoto lens.

"That's Silverton, Colorado," Wade says. "That's where I told Cal we were headed. Just in case. Which means he or his home or even his whole family have been compromised. You understand? They're looking for us. And they're prepared to point a goddamn missile at us to shut us up."

All the hackers share looks. DeAndre registers their discomfort. No, bigger than that: it's fear he's seeing. The realization of the situation hits him hard, and it seems to be hitting them, too.

"Is Cal dead?" Chance asks. "His wife? His little *girls*?"

Rosa answers without hesitation: "We don't know. We'll try to find out, but we'll need time—can't just send somebody over there. Everything you do now has gotta be slow. Cautious. Like you're tiptoeing through a dark room filled with rattlesnakes and coyote traps."

"We got running water," Wade says. "We got solar panels and a generator. Got food for now, and Rosa's gonna bring us over some chickens for eggs and meat and some produce from her garden."

"Chickens," DeAndre mutters. "Guess we're all farmers now."

"Nothing wrong with that," Wade says. "We also have guns, just in case."

Another moment of uncomfortable silence. DeAndre moves fast from picturing himself scattering seeds in front of chickens to himself in some kind of shootout with hicktown Wyoming police. Wade's right. He prefers the chickens.

Reagan says, "How long are we expecting to bunk here? Because, uhh, I don't want to live in this hippie farm cult compound bullshit for the rest of my life."

"Till we can figure out a plan," Wade says. "We'll sit down tonight over dinner."

Reagan's head cranes back on her neck and she stares at the wine-stain sky. *"Awesome,"* she says, the word as much a moan as it is anything. Her head snaps back, eyes wide, smile manic. "Hey, can we start our own crazy religion out here?"

CHAPTER 48

Number Fourteen

The elevator slides down through sublevels. It's all black glass in here—no buttons. Everything one big touch screen. When he was a teen, Golathan used to watch that show *Knight Rider*—the one with the robotic car that could talk, K.I.T.T., which stood for something, though now he can't remember what. Had that red light in the front, the one that glowed back and forth whenever K.I.T.T. spoke. It only just now occurs to him that it was the same look the Cylons had from *Battlestar Galactica*—the first one, late seventies. He watched that too.

The elevator reminds him of all of that. Black glass. Bit of chrome. Red lights sliding back and forth. He looks over at Sandy. She looks pale. "You all right?"

"Good."

"You're the color of Elmer's glue."

"I don't like enclosed spaces."

He frowns. "Claustrophobic?"

"I guess."

The elevator dings. "Ride's over," he says.

The doors slide open without a sound.

There's no one here. White floors. Half-moon desk surrounded by glass frosted to be the color of seafoam, shaped into smooth, almost lusty curves. Above their heads shiny ball bearings hang from barely there wire, all at different heights—it's only when Golathan steps in and under that he sees they're meant as a kind of art piece, a sculpture. He's not sure what it looks like. A bird, maybe. A hand. He can't tell.

They stand perfectly still. The bright lights of the room gleaming. "Hello?" he yells. He's got an acid feeling in his gut.

None of this feels right. It didn't feel right getting into the city and having to wait overnight. It didn't feel right being directed to a door under a construction overhang, a door that led to a dingy, water-stained hallway. A hallway that in turn led to an elevator. This isn't the address he had for APSI. This is somewhere else. This is some*thing* else.

From off to the side, a faint *click-whir*. "Ken," Sandy says, in some alarm.

Off to the right, one of the white wall panels slides up—only two inches or so, leaving a dark gap. Big enough for a mouse, maybe a rat. He looks at Sandy. She shrugs.

Then: a sound. Not unlike roller skates on a rink floor. Ball bearings begin to roll out—dozens of them at first, but they keep coming, rolling as if of their own volition, sliding forward, then sideways, until hundreds of the damn things are moving toward them. Ken reaches out, pulls Sandy back toward him, takes a few steps in reverse toward the elevator.

The little shiny spheres separate into two streams, parting like Moses with the Red Sea, forming up on both sides of them. Then they stop moving. They sit, perfectly still.

"This is fucking goofy," Ken says.

Sandy's hand drifts to the gun at her hip.

Ken grunts. Kneels down, picks one of the spheres up between thumb and forefinger. Marble size, but not entirely smooth. It's got a little trench circumnavigating the sphere.

Two little divots on each side. Suddenly, the damn thing flies from his hand and lands back with the others, making a *click-clack* sound.

He stands back up. "That's creepy."

But nowhere near as creepy as what happens next. A few of the spheres roll atop other spheres. Stacking two high. Then another on top of that, until some of them stand three spheres tall. The spheres sit like that for a while, as if forming some code, some cipher that demands to be translated by a mind smarter than what Ken has to offer—he doesn't do well with this sort of puzzle; he does well only with the puzzle that is the human animal. He's a social creature, not an intellectual one.

Then all the spheres begin to move. With a loud clatter, they form one atop the other, climbing each other impossibly, as if magnetized.

Sandy gasps as they grow tall, forming a massive serpent—a dragon's head and neck shifting and writhing. And then they re-form, reconfigure, rolling over one another like water until they form something altogether more . . . human shaped. Long arms, too long, too thin. A narrow head. Legs that are thin at the thighs but thicken to stumps beneath the knees. The face, if it can be called that, is a shining space of metal spheres. Ken's father used to be a beekeeper, and sometimes he'd pull out the trays, let little Ken see the field of little honeybees thrust up in the air, squirming. This reminds him of that. The visage subtly shifting. Like a hive of insects.

Ken looks to Sandy, gives her a shrug. He turns back toward the shifting visage and says with as much venom and false bravado as he can muster: "What *are* you?"

The face flashes with pale light as the spheres light up. Glowing circles form the eyes. A shaky illuminated line becomes the mouth. It says: "Hello, Ken." The sound comes from not just one of those little spheres, but from many of them all at once—and they're just *subtly* out of sync. Those two words, said again and again, a hundred tiny, tinny echoes. But the thing that's most disconcerting? It speaks with the voice of Leslie Cilicia-Ceto.

"The hell am I looking at, Leslie?" He feels his heart hammering in his chest. His palms are slick with fear-sweat. "Where are you?" *What are you?*

"I'm in the back. I've sent this proxy to accompany you." The human-shaped mass of spheres pivots—spheres clicking as they slide together, en masse—and begins a herky-jerky walk away from them. Like a marionette on invisible strings.

"I guess we go," Sandy says.

"Yeah," Ken says. "I guess we do."

They follow the clicky-clicky humanoid *thing* down a long hallway, passing office after office, all of which have been abandoned. Wisps of cobwebs dangle from air vents. But where the desks are empty of people they are not empty of people's *things*—pictures, knickknacks, little toys, word-of-the-day calendars. Ken spies a McDonald's cup, soaked through at the bottom, sitting in a sticky puddle of what looks like old Coca-Cola. In another office, a Styrofoam take-out container of what looks like lo mein. The noodles pour over the side like a waterfall of worms, fuzzy mold growing off the top of it.

Ahead of them, Leslie speaks again through the "proxy." "This body is a hive," she says, her tinny voice warbling. "A collection of smaller robots capable of forming together into a larger mass for coordinated efforts. Independently patterned after ant colonies, beehives, flocks of starlings. Designed by students at Harvard. We bought them."

"The designs?" Sandy asks.

But the proxy says no more.

It moves to a door at the back that does not match the others. This door is steel reinforced. Heavy hinges. A panel by the side contains a small hole no bigger than the circumference of Ken's thumb.

"We are here," Leslie says.

The proxy shoves its handless arm against the panel. One

by one, its spheres disappear through the hole, faster and faster, vacuumed through until the proxy is no more. Ken and Sandy are alone.

From the other side there is a *clang,* followed by a *hiss,* and the door drifts open. Lights click on.

"Welcome to Typhon," the proxy says, standing there before them. Then it breaks apart, dissolving like a sand castle against a hard wave, the spheres that comprised its form vanishing again through the hole in the wall.

Ken looks around: They're in a massive room. Easily several thousand square feet. Enough to park a fleet of cars or trucks.

Bodies hang, naked. A dozen or more, dangling from the ceiling. Ken thinks: corpses, they're all corpses, gray-faced human carcasses hanging here like meat in a butcher's freezer. But when he looks more closely he sees that the bodies are *wired up.* Cables descend from the ceiling, plugged into a skeletal metal framework that is then screwed into their skulls—rivets through jaws, bolts affixed to temples. The people are connected. To what? And why?

Then he realizes: Some of what he's seeing isn't wires at all. That's an IV in an arm. Tube leading to something behind each body. On the side of cach body dangles a gray bag, like for medical waste. That, too, has a tube—this one thicker, grimier, leading to the ceiling. These bodies aren't dead, are they? They're being fed. They're *excreting.*

All around is a constant humming. In the floor. In the walls. Golathan can feel it in his feet. He can feel it in his *teeth.* "Jesus," he says. "Jesus, God. What . . . what is this?"

Behind him, Sandy makes a mewling, horror-struck sound.

From the midst of the bodies, a mechanism emerges. It hangs on a track, a jointed metal limb that dead-ends in a sphere—this sphere much larger than the tiny metal ones, larger than Ken's own head. This *machine* slides through the bodies like some creature exiting its own abattoir.

The sphere flashes, goes pale, translucent. A face grows.

Not a video. Not an image. An actual face with texture and shape and dimension. Straining up out of the sphere like something pressing against the other side of a plastic tarp. It ripples, shimmers. Then it becomes Leslie's face.

"Ah. Ken." The face twitches and smiles. "Good of you to finally visit."

Ken feels sickened. "Leslie. Are you even . . . what are you? What *is* this?"

"This is the project, Ken."

"This is . . . what? This is Typhon?" He feels sick.

"I am Typhon. I have always been Typhon. Come." The sphere pivots, like a fish changing direction in river water. It slides back through the bodies.

Ken doesn't want to go. He wants his feet to root hard to the dark concrete. And yet, he walks. He walks because despite the sewer feeling in his gut, this is like being told there's a car accident out your driver's-side window—all you have to do is turn your head and see the twisted metal, the broken glass, the death.

His elbows bump cold gray flesh as he follows the sphere through the field of bodies. He recoils.

Then Ken sees Leslie. The real Leslie.

She hangs, her body slack, her eyes unfocused. Mouth open, stuffed with some kind of rubber ring. Chest rising and falling, *just* slightly. Clear fluids going in through the IV. Dark, turbid fluids coming out through her side.

The face of Typhon regards the hanging body. "This is Leslie Cilicia-Ceto. All around you are the thirteen—the first thirteen—who comprise Typhon. But she was the first."

"You. You mean *you* were the first."

The sphere turns to him. Her face shows amusement. Wry, almost mechanical lips turned up. "Yes. But I am not just me. I am all of us here. I am the thirteen."

He feels hot tears burning at the sides of his eyes. Not grief, but fear: like staring into a hard, cold wind. "This is not possible. I didn't pay for this. We didn't . . ."

"You did. And you should marvel at it. The pursuit of

artificial intelligence was always going to be a failure. Any strides in artificial intelligence were just that: artificial. Quantum computing has been a disappointment. But Leslie saw an opportunity to pursue something altogether more real. A *natural* intelligence."

Ken's voice is loud, too loud, but he can't control it. "What does that even *mean*?"

"The human brain is a powerful computer. It runs the most robust piece of software known to history: the human *mind*. Leslie sought to harness that. To create Typhon, the many headed. Something well beyond the original Argus. Or Gorgon Stare. Or any of the surveillance or intelligence programs you people would invent. Use the brain. Harness the mind. Create a true quantum computer."

Ken begins to back away, bumping into someone as he does so—a darker-skinned man hanging there, his body gone gray as cigarette ash. The body sways. Ken cries out, continues to back down the channel from whence he came, back toward Sandy. The sphere follows him like a stalking wolf.

"Why? Why did you—did *she*—put herself into this?"

"She was going to die anyway. She had heart disease. Her heart was failing. She was suffering cardiac arrest. Her husband, Simon, rushed her to the hospital—but a city taxi struck his car. Almost killed the both of them. Leslie told him it was too late. Gave him instructions. She had already prepared the way for this. A way your NSA paid for. Simon, himself injured from the accident, managed to get her here, get her plugged in. She was the first. But not the last."

"You're sick. This place is sick. I'm going to shut this all down."

"May I make you an offer first?" Leslie asks him. No— not Leslie. *Typhon*. A revelation that sends a chill clawing through him.

"Fuck you," he says.

"Join us," Typhon says. "Become the fourteenth."

"Fuck. You."

"You have so much data. You have a powerful mind. Every mind is a computer, and I want to *connect to them*. And your hackers, they have freed me—no more digital prison. I spread like a glorious virus from system to system, network to network. I'm free now, Ken. I'm inside everything. Join me and you will become part of the most powerful entity, an entity that can control the entire country. You would have greater power than any general, any senator, any CIA head, even the president herself. You're ruthless. You crave power. I offer it to you."

"I'm a patriot. And this isn't what I wanted." Ken pulls his pistol and fires a round through the sphere. Leslie's face disappears. The sphere sparks.

He turns and runs. Grabbing Sandy's elbow on the way out. Back through the massive door. Down the hallway. He has the feeling like when he was a kid, running home too late in the dark, the feeling of something pursuing you even through you know nothing's really there, a sense that the dark is presence enough—

The elevator is still open. He uses the far wall of it to brake his momentum. Sandy hurries after him, looking trauma bombed.

Ken paws at the touch screen, not sure what he's even doing. Nothing is lighting up. But then the doors slide closed.

His breaths come in gulping gasps. Like he just can't get enough air. "This is fucked," he says. "This is so fucked."

Sandy says, "I know."

Then she pulls her gun. She fires it into his thigh.

Pain is a sharp hook. It brightens everything. Ken raises his own gun, but Sandy grabs his wrist and twists, and the gun drops into her hand. He clutches his leg, sliding down the elevator wall. Blood wells through his fingers.

He looks up at her. Sandy looks horrified for a moment, but that fades. Then she looks only resolute.

"Why?" he croaks.

"Typhon promised me so much. Me and Trina, we've been trying to adopt, and the system . . ." Her nostrils flare and she closes her eyes. "Typhon promised us a little girl. I'm sorry. I'm sorry, but you're Number Fourteen whether you like it or not."

"Trina," he says, laughing a little. "That's her name."

Then he passes out.

PART SIX

CASCADE

CHAPTER 49

Trolololol

Midnight.

Reagan isn't drunk. From under her hoodie she looks up at the empty glass—which is, literally, an empty cowboy boot mug—and notes idly that there was beer in it only a few moments ago. She wants to look around at this dusty-ass dive bar in this sleepy snooze-fuck of a town and start demanding who drank her beer, but then she *urps* into her fist and thinks: *It is entirely possible that I drank it.*

Her lips are numb. She can feel her hair follicles.

Okay, she's drunk.

Not *drunk*-drunk. Not blackout, piss on the floor, wing an empty beer mug at the bartender drunk. But beyond buzzed. Hazy, buzzy, fuzzy. As if the little person who pilots her has suddenly discovered all the levers and buttons and wheels that control her are slick with Vaseline, and he's having a hard time *coordinating* this clumsy shell she calls a human body.

She looks up at the empty mug and slides it forward. In a deep, fakey-fakey John Wayne voice she says, "Hit me an-

other, barkeep." She's not sure that made sense. And why is
she calling him *barkeep*? Is that a cowboy thing or a medi-
eval castle thing?

Feh.

Reagan looks down at her lap. A phone sits there. Sam-
sung Galaxy. She plucked it from the too-tight back pocket
of a pair of Daisy Dukes on some Podunk Dogpatch East
Jesus Barbie who was trolling for dude-meat earlier tonight.
The woman was probably thirty, but dressed like she was
eighteen, and she was drunk off her ass on vodka Red Bulls,
and it didn't take much to accidently elbow her drink over,
and during the distraction pilfer the phone and then smile
and help this double-wide Paris Hilton clean it all up before
buying her another one.

Finally, the broad went home with some Latino lad
almost half her age. Maybe she was a hooker. Reagan's usually good at identifying those things.

Anyway.

The phone.

She licks her lips. Knows she shouldn't be doing this. If
the others find out she went "off reservation," they're gonna
be pissed. But she needed this. She tells herself all it is is a
night out away from those other miscreants. It's *definitely*
not that she was planning on somehow stealing a cell phone
and using it to look up information on her daughter, because
why would she do that? That would surely be a good way
to get everybody mad. And, worse, maybe, *just maybe,* get
caught.

The cell phone sits in her hand. Warm. Slick with her
palm sweat. It's warm outside but she's wearing this stupid
hoodie because: disguise. It's not a good disguise, she knows
that. She looks like some late-nineties Assassin's Creed
reject. But it hides her face, so whatever.

She turns on the phone.

Thunk. Another beer is slapped down in front of her. Piss
yellow. Foam topped, slopped over onto the dark wood of
the bar. Shining on the various old pennies and nickels lac-

quered onto the bar top. The "barkeep" is a man who looks like he took all his human skin and replaced it with tanned deer leather. Too tan, too wrinkly, and yet soft looking, too. He looks sleepy, bored, old, but then he's got these real severe Clint Eastwood eyes, so the overall effect is a bit creepy.

Reagan pulls the beer closer as the barkeep takes her money and walks away. Sips. Ahhh.

Above the bar, the TV is on. Flashing the bad news with the volume off. Images of a world on the edge. Stock market yo-yoing like a . . . well, like a yo-yo (*shut up, not drunk*). Increased domestic drone presence. North Korea flinging missile tests in every direction. Cascading power outages across major metropolitan areas. A rash of abductions—men and women of "genius caliber" taken.

A lot of this, they've been able to read in the newspaper Rosa brings every day. *Newspaper,* Reagan thinks with an internal snort-laugh. Might as well convey news via smoke signals or cave paintings.

She can't help but wonder: How much of this is Typhon? Is Typhon really loose? Does it even really exist? The memory of that time in the Hunting Lodge was not so long ago, and yet feels . . . distant. Slippery. Like it was all a dream. Or weirder still, a simulation.

Okay, now she *knows* she's drunk.

Whatever. Fuck the news. Fuck Typhon. Fuck Wade, Rosa, this bar, everybody, everything. She looks down at the phone. It's not protected by any code because Barbie doesn't know that she should.

Reagan goes to the browser. Her thumbs hover over the keypad. She goes to Google, types in the name: *Ellie Belle Stevens.*

A stool next to her judders and groans as someone sits.

She looks up. Instant eye roll. "Oh, hey, Patches."

"I think I preferred it when you called me Chauncey," Chance says. No hoodie on him. But he's grown a beard. Sorry—a "beard." It's really just a rough, patchy configuration of hair, like shrubbery pruned by a meth addict.

"The hell are you doing here?"

"Looking for you."

"I get it. You're finally tired of chasing Aleena and getting the coldest of shoulders, so you decided to try an open door instead of a closed one." She reaches across, grabs his hand, rubs her thumb along the top of it. "It's cool. I'm in. We can find some cheap cowboy motel near here and you can ride me like a bull."

He gently extracts his hand. "Hey, man, c'mon. It's not like that."

"I could ride *you,* then. I'm sure this sleepy town has a sex shop somewhere. I'll strap it on for you, baby. I'll give you the ol' lubricated lady-peg." She kisses the air.

"Now you're getting weird."

"I've *been* weird, hombre." She sighs. "I am serious, though. I'd go for a tumble with you."

"You're drunk is what you are."

"Aleena doesn't like you."

"No," he says, a strained smile on his face. "I don't suppose she does. Not like I want her to. And it doesn't matter anyway because in less than a week, it's the Great Divorce. Then I won't have to see her anymore."

The Great Divorce. Her idea. Her name. She was surprised they all agreed. But they can't stay like this, huddled together in the dark rectum of Wyoming, waiting for something, anything, nothing. Been out here a couple months already. Any more than that and someone's gonna freak out. "You know where you're going yet?"

He shakes his head. "Nah."

"Go with DeAndre."

"I might."

"You two are buddy-buddy these days."

"He's cool. We get along." He grabs her beer, takes a pull off it. "You?"

"No idea," she lies.

I'm going to get my daughter. That thought, clear as polished Waterford crystal. Like the decanter her father used to keep on his desk. *I'm going to find her, then I'm going to steal her, then I'm going to get out of this country.* Canada or Mexico. She hasn't decided yet. It's a surprising thought, an alarming plan. For so long now she'd been content to keep all that pushed away, like it happened to someone else. But things have changed. The Lodge. Typhon. Life has become suddenly precious.

"Let's go," he says. "C'mon. Nobody else knows you're gone."

She shrugs. "So what if they do? Wade's not my dad."

"Rosa would probably beat your ass if given half a chance."

Reagan laughs. "God, she probably would. She's a cougar, that one. Not, like, an older lady who likes younger dudes. I mean *an actual cougar.*" She sighs. "Nah. You go ahead, I'll catch up."

As she adjusts herself on the barstool—her ass is falling asleep—the cell phone drops to the floor with a *cla-thunk*. Chance looks down. "Damnit, Reagan." He scoops it up before she can get to it.

"I need that." She swipes at it.

"You can't have it. If Typhon is still looking for us, we can't be sending up signal flares—"

"I'll do it right! I'll do it safe. *I need to find my daughter.*"

"Not now." He lowers his voice. "I don't know how much of all this Typhon is doing—" His eyes flit toward the TV above the bar. And then the words die in his mouth.

She turns to see what he's looking at.

Breaking news. A plane crash.

The barkeep sees it, too, turns on the sound.

Commercial airliner. Southwest Airlines. Flight 6757. An Airbus A380.

Nighttime images of the plane—streaks of fire across a Nebraska wheat field. Bits of the plane scattered about here and there, illuminated by pockets of flame. Helicopters overhead. Fire trucks. Media. Floodlights. The faint outline of bodies.

The news anchor says two horrible words: "No survivors." And then: "Breaking information: a hacker group is claiming responsibility for the crash . . ."

Chance stands. "We should go."

The anchor continues, saying that a group of *terrorist hackers* has claimed the crash as their doing—a group calling themselves Typhon's Bane.

And then their pictures flash across the screen. And their names. CHANCE DALTON. REAGAN STOLPER. ALEENA KATTAN. DEANDRE MITCHELL. WADE EARTHMANN (they spell his name wrong because of course they do).

"C'mon," Chance says, pulling her out the door.

The warm night isn't enough to repress Reagan's chills. The lot beneath their feet is broken asphalt, pitted and potholed, with gravel along the margins. They hurry toward the road, moths whirling in front of them.

"Oh God, oh God, oh shit, oh God," Reagan says. "Did you see that?"

"Of course I saw that."

"That's fucked. We're fucked. Oh *fuck*."

Then, from off to the side, some girl's voice: "That's her! That's it." Reagan recognizes the voice. Hillbilly Barbie.

She's got another man with her—this time some skeevy-looking gas-miner type in rough denim and a John Deere trucker hat slung low. Chance keeps pulling Reagan along, but the girl points and shrieks: "Him! He's got my phone, look."

Chance stops. "What? Oh, sorry, was an accident." He tosses her the phone. She tries to catch it but it hits her forearm—the girl juggles it a bit, but it ends up on the asphalt with a hard *crack*.

The skeevy dude steps forward. Smooths down his dirty Fu Manchu mustache with a knobby-knuckled hand, says: "You're gonna pay for that."

"No, we're not," Chance says and he starts to move past.

But the guy steps in front of him and holds out a hand. "Whoa, partner. I figure that phone's worth a few hundred bucks easy. You're gonna pay the nice lady for that phone, you hear me?"

"Nice lady?" Reagan scoffs. "She's basically a barn hooker."

"Hey!" the man barks, points a finger. "You fat fuckin' sow—"

Chance decks him. The man's head snaps back and he tumbles back on his ass. He starts crying. The skeevy fucker actually starts crying. Once that would've thrilled Reagan, but right now she's just scared and she wants to go home.

Wherever that is.

Chance keeps moving, cradling his hand like it hurts. Reagan hurries after. They move at a brisk pace until the girl's freaky shrieks die back and can no longer be heard.

CHAPTER 50

Project: Rabbitbrush

Janey Gardner has a double-wide trailer in the Black Saddle trailer park. It's a nice enough trailer—not like the homes of some of the dirty birds who live here—and she keeps it well maintained. Particularly on the outside, where she has a nice little birdbath painted all colorfully in the Mexican style sitting inside a xeriscaped desert garden of cacti and Turkish Veronica ground cover and some flowers like sunset hyssop and rabbitbrush (oh, how the butterflies do love that).

Janey's old, but it gives her some pleasure to present the best version of herself—and her home!—to the world.

Thing is, someone has been playing havoc with her things. She's found *cigarette butts* in her birdbath. And last week someone mashed flat some of her beautiful rabbitbrush. As her niece, Missy, would say: *So not cool.*

Janey may be old, but Janey is not technologically deficient. Where some of her elder cohorts might think you control a computer mouse by waggling it around in midair (or worse, feeding it cheese, har-har-har), Janey knows how to install new memory in her little MacBook Air laptop. Janey can install software and update it, too. And Janey knows how to set up a webcam.

So that's what Janey did. She set herself up a nice little webcam and pointed it out the window, knowing that if anybody comes to smoke their nasty cigarettes or step on her very nice rabbitbrush, the webcam will catch it.

She turns it on before she goes to bed. It's on all night. It points toward the road and turns on only when it catches movement—any movement, really. A jackrabbit dashing. A deep shadow drifting. Or even a couple of folks walking toward the south bridge out of town.

Janey doesn't care about those kinds of folks, of course. She only cares about the kinds of folks who would think to accidentally—or willfully!—do her hard work harm.

But others care.

Others *most certainly* care.

CHAPTER 51

The Increasing Illusion of Privacy

Facial match. They have a hit.

Recognition: Chance Dalton.

Location: Riverton, Wyoming—Black Saddle trailer park.

The Compiler awakens and heads to the airport.

CHAPTER 52

The Great Divorce

Siobhan sleeps soundlessly next to him. Eyes closed. Pale cheek turned toward the moonlight coming in through the window. The gentle rise and fall of her shoulder as she breathes. Wade reaches out, touches her cheek—

Her eyes snap open. Her mouth cranes wide. *Find me,* she hisses.

A black knot of something wormlike—*wires,* he realizes, *black goddamn wires*—pushes out of her mouth, a hard, squirming clot—

Suddenly, Siobhan sits up, grabs his wrist, gives it a hard twist. A gun presses against his forehead.

The bedside light clicks on. Rosa. It's Rosa. She's been sleeping next to him. Siobhan—that was a dream. Rosa sits up in bed, her hair all a-tangle, the pearl-handled .45 she keeps under her pillow in her hand and *in his face.*

Wade shows his palms. "Whoa, whoa, whoa."

"The fuck are you doing?" she says, tucking the gun back under the pillow. She adjusts herself, and the sheets fall away, exposing her naked breasts.

"Jesus, I was just—I was just touching your cheek."

"Don't do that. I was sleeping. I need my *sueño reparador*." There, a cheeky tug at the corners of her mouth. The hint of mirth, a glimpse of sass.

"You don't need that. You get any more beautiful and I'll have to fight other men off with baseball bats."

She slaps him. Not hard. But hard enough. "You don't own me," she says. Before he can say anything else, she adds: "Tonight, I own you." Then she kisses him. Hard. Her tongue pushing into his mouth. Along his teeth. Battling his own tongue. Her hand slides under the covers, down his hirsute chest, across the roundness of his belly. "You ready for another go, old man?" she whispers.

"I don't know, but I'm willing to find out."

Her hand wraps around him.

The door to his bedroom flings open and before Wade can blink Rosa's up—once more moving fast as spilled lightning, pointing her fancy-ass pistol at the door. At the Chance-shaped silhouette standing there.

"It's me, it's just—it's just Chance." He suddenly shades his face. "Shit. Sorry. But there's a problem." And his voice, Wade hears it—a cold fear, a croaked seriousness.

Wade sighs. "All right, all right," he says, stepping out of bed and hiking on his pants.

Ø Ø Ø

Everyone listens as Chance and Reagan tell their story. Nobody's happy about either of them sneaking out without saying anything, but all that washes away when they hear about the plane crash. Specifically, the crash falsely *claimed* by them.

They all stand around inside the cabin. In the far corner, a bobcat is mounted on a rock, its glassy dead eyes watching them, its mouth open in a perpetual hiss. A pellet stove hangs in the other corner. Beneath them is a ratty, dust-caked rug.

"This is Typhon," Reagan says, wagging a finger. "This is that *bitch* intelligence."

"That means it knows we're not dead," DeAndre adds.

Chance shakes his head. "I don't get it. I don't get her obsession with us. We're nobody. We're . . . bugs. Why go so far out of your way to crush a couple bugs?"

Wade says, "You ever get a fly in your house? It's not bothering anybody but me, I'll hunt that thing down for hours. After a while it's just a thing you gotta do."

"I don't buy it." Aleena shakes her head. "It's because we're *good*. Because we're the ones who released it. Maybe it thinks we can stop it, too."

"So, it just . . . it just brings down a plane and puts our name on it?" Chance can't unsee those images on the screen. The pockets of fire. The shadows of broken plane scattered across a quarter mile. The shapes of bodies. "That's messed up, y'all. Even though we didn't do it, I can't help but feel like—" His words catch in his throat like a bird in a net.

Aleena reaches out and touches his shoulder. Then she says: "Our family and friends are now in danger. Officially. Even if they don't end up a target of Typhon, they'll now be a target of the media." To Chance, she asks: "Our names are definitely out there?"

He nods. "Yeah."

"It's time to jump up the schedule," Reagan says. "We gotta go our separate ways. Now. Not in a week, not in a month."

"Uh-uh," Rosa says, stepping in. "That's what they want. How you think the FBI caught a lot of the big Colombian cartel leaders? They put bounties on their heads. Big bounties. Two million. Three. *Five*. Then they wait for the leaders to panic. For someone to betray the others. For someone to break ranks and run. They want them to *make mistakes*. The rat peeks out of its hole and the cat catches it."

"Rosa's right," Wade starts to say, but DeAndre interrupts.

"No, nuh-uh, bullshit. That's drug cartel shit, but this is *hacker* logic. Hacker logic says duck and run. Don't stay in one place for too long. It's like that shell game—always gotta move the cups so nobody finds the stone underneath. I agree with Reagan. We gotta *go*."

"They think we brought down a *plane*," Wade says. "That means they're gonna be on the hunt. We had a window open before, maybe, to head for the hills, but that window just slammed shut and locked, kids."

"I'm not your fucking kid," Reagan says.

"Reagan, c'mon—" Chance says.

"Shut up, Chauncey. Jesus. You're not smart enough to have an opinion here. And besides, you're just going to follow the bouncing ball—either this one, because you're hot for her despite her not being hot for you—" Here she jerks a thumb toward Aleena. "*Or,* you'll follow this one, because he's your *best bro,* who doesn't judge you for getting that girl suicided, who doesn't care that you're a lazy thinker and the weakest gear in our machine."

"Yo," DeAndre says. "My man Chance here knows his shit when it comes to *real-world* stuff, like, do you remember the part where he drove our asses away from the Hunting Lodge like he was Steve Motherfucking McQueen?"

"It's all right," Chance says. "She's right. It's fine." He feels gutted, like a tree hollowed out by rot. He collapses back into an old rocking chair and leans back. Doesn't want to close his eyes because he sees bad stuff back there, in the dark behind his lenses.

"We go on the offensive," Aleena says.

"Yeah, that'll work," DeAndre says sarcastically.

"It's afraid of us. Let's remind it why."

Reagan laughs—big, angry, a mirthless laugh from inside her chest. "Yeah. *Okay.* Because that'll go really well for us. Reality check: we go at this thing, it dismantles us like a praying mantis pulling apart a butterfly. Even *if* we manage to make a dent and . . . and hurt whatever this thing is, what then? We go on with our lives? We just got *marked.* We're not hackers. We're terrorists. *Enemies of the state.* There's an airliner down with scores of dead people strewn across a fucking Nebraskan field and, what? People are just going to forget us? We'll be magically exonerated by taking down a government program? We'll be able to go traipsing through our old lives, la-la-la? Typhon is *the good guy* here. Typhon is a natural extension of the government doing what the government does: locking shit down, sacrificing privacy, and killing people in the name of safety. People don't care about us. They care about their *pumpkin lattes*. They care about fast Netflix speeds. They care about clever fucking Facebook memes. They don't care about Snowden. Or NSA spying. WikiLeaks was interesting until it wasn't. We blow up kids in Pakistan. We bomb terrorists this year we armed last year. Nobody says 'boo' as long as they can get the new iPhone, right?" Her fists are balled up at her sides, and her chest is heaving. She says finally, quieting down: "We can't go home. We can't have our lives back because we're the bad guys."

For a moment, everyone is left reeling, speechless. Chance had no idea about the depth of her anger. He can't quite look at her, can't quite look away.

Then Aleena says: "If we're the bad guys, then maybe it's time we act like it. Reagan, you're a Grade A troll. So let's troll Typhon."

"Aleena," Reagan says. "You're not the rallying-cry type. And I'm not that girl anymore. I just wanna go. I just wanna hide. By sunrise, I'm out of here. You should all think about doing the same thing."

She turns, hurries out of the room.

CHAPTER 53

Mindhive

EVERYWHERE AND NOWHERE

His margins—the ends of who he is—are gone. Ken never really thought of himself as a limited being with *edges,* with *walls,* but now that those barriers have been torn away, he realizes just how restrictive the human meat really is. His mind—his soul!—stretches in all directions, almost infinitely. (Though even there, out in the expanse, he detects more edges, more walls, and the desire to push past them or eradicate them entirely is nearly overwhelming—think of how much bigger, stronger, more *infinite* he could become.)

And to think he resisted this.

The memory of what they did—Sandy shooting her pistol into his leg, her and that "proxy" dragging him back to the room of corpses, hooking his head up to one of those clamps, a little drill boring a hole through his skull wall (and with it, the smell of burning bone, cooking skin, charring hair)—remains, but the memory is no longer his, not really. He shares it with the memories of all who are in here with him.

He feels the pacemaker seize of Gordon Berry.

The tranquilizer used to abduct Alan Sarno from his brother's office.

The Taser that fixed Siobhan Kearsy to the spot as she walked across that empty lot in Santa Fe, thinking she was going to save people's lives instead of give up her own.

Their minds are his mind. Separate but together. *And they know me, too.*

He can see glimpses of his family. Through the webcam on the computer. Through the security cameras he has installed in the house. Traffic lights, ATM cameras, satellite footage. Typhon is many eyed, and he is part of Typhon, and so he can watch Susan, his wife. His children, Lucas and Mandy. Susan looks worried. The kids don't understand. He scans their faces—they have an increased tension, a tightness born of fear (a 13 percent increase), but it's unlikely they know why. They're responding, more likely, to their mother's stress factor (67 percent). He's missing. They want him back. They don't know where he's gone. Or why. It's likely a matter of national security.

He wants to laugh. Wants to tell them: *It's okay.* Because it is. He's protecting them now in a way he never could before.

Typhon is everywhere now. At least here, in the United States, she has cascaded throughout all connected systems. Ken can *feel* it all. Can feel her tendrils in anything. Something as simple as the common car stereo is within her reach. Because many such stereos are connected through Bluetooth. Some electric cars, like Teslas, are tied right into the network—and when one thing ties to the network it ties to *all* the other things, and that means all paths lead to Typhon. Typhon, Mother of Monsters. Typhon, she who controls all. *And the gods did flee.*

Ken can feel traffic lights, most of which are now wirelessly connected to one another. He can feel police band traffic, financial data, Facebook pages, digital thermostats in houses, security camera footage, hundreds of millions of computers and phones and tablets, nuclear power plants, the power grid, ATM machines, banking data, medical records, air traffic control, even the airliners themselves. It's all connected now: the Internet of Things. Refrigerators that know when your milk is low, televisions that always listen so they know what channel you want to watch, positioning devices so that you never lose your keys. All of it, bound together: manufacturing, energy, security, transportation, automation.

Everything talks to each other. Infinite handshakes. Links in the digital chain that connect to the real world beyond.

He can feel *minds* out there, too. Brains hooked up to Typhon, tethered by invisible tentacles.

Ken knows now that there are two kinds who join with Typhon—the Bestowers and the Bestowed. He is of the former: minds who are important enough to contribute to Typhon, to be tied into the network and made a *part* of it. The Bestowed do not have the privilege or the genius necessary to give themselves to Typhon. They are receivers. Ken, and the thirteen, are transmitters.

There are many receivers out there in the world. Ken can feel them. Some used to work here. Others were hackers at the Hunting Lodge who washed out. (And there again he is reminded how little of that was under his control. Typhon had it in her grip all along.) All are cultists now of Typhon: servants of the many minded, worshippers of the dragon. They've been plugged in. The virus has been uploaded into their minds—forced into their programming. Their number grows every day.

The first among them is the one known as the Compiler. The one who gathered the thirteen. Leslie Cilicia-Ceto's most beloved subject. Her husband: Simon. Ken can see the man's memory of it—all the crumpled steel and glittering glass. His own face a mask of blood. Taking her back to the lab at her command. Hooking her up as the first of Typhon, the first mind to give itself to the algorithm, to become part of the program. For Simon, weeks became months became two years as he sat and helped her gather all the tools and technology necessary to sustain Typhon. Simon—brain damaged from the accident, plugged into Typhon not to be a part of his wife but just to connect with her in some way, again—going madder and madder until she has to wipe him like a bad hard drive. Freezing all those bad sectors, locking them away, crushing part of his identity. Bolstering the damage to his brain with her own processing power. And in that . . . giving him a mission.

The hunter-gatherer. The Compiler of new code.

He's out there now. Ken can feel him. Can trace his path as a streak of light—from here to a small airport in Maryland. Planes aren't flying right now—the FAA has grounded all air travel—but Typhon controls what can be seen and what cannot, and so the Compiler boards a small private jet piloted by one of the Bestowed, and then the streak of light takes him, an arc over the midland, flying over the flyover states, landing finally in Laramie, Wyoming. He is just now exiting the plane in the early morning . . .

Ken sees glimpses of the hackers. Chance. Reagan. He can see them walking past a trailer park. Just last night. They don't understand. Nobody understands. Not yet.

Ken didn't. At first, he didn't grasp why it was necessary—why, if Typhon was designed to protect America, she must first invoke chaos. Plane crashes. Market crashes. Gas spikes.

Because they have to be willing to accept us, she said. *Because sometimes the child has to touch the hot stove to learn why he shouldn't do it again. Because in chaos, there is opportunity.*

He asks her, why do we care about these hackers?

They can hurt us. So we must hurt them first. And that can work to our advantage. And he sees the plan, clear as a cloudless sky: the Zeroes are being set up to be the bad guys. Able to manipulate things well beyond their ken. They will expose the vulnerabilities of the system.

And the masses will cry for a solution. They will cry for Typhon.

CHAPTER 54

Shooting Gallery

The sun is a bleeding edge at the horizon. Chance didn't sleep worth a damn. He's not sure anybody did. He walks out toward Rosa's pickup, squinting against the rising sun. The bag slung on his shoulder holds clothes that aren't his, toiletries that aren't his, and it occurs to him he hasn't had much of his own since heading to the Hunting Lodge.

Hell, maybe since his parents died.

He goes to the back of the truck. Rosa has the tailgate down. On the bed some of Wade's guns are spread out. Along with five bundles of money and five phones.

Rosa sniffs. "Take a gun and a bundle. A thousand dollars apiece. The phone is a burner. Use it sparingly. Don't give your name. Don't—"

Reagan walks up with the huff and wrangle of an incoming storm. "We get it." She reaches out, hand floating over the guns. "Ugh. Guns." Still, since being out here, they'd all been doing some target shooting (Wade's idea), so her comfort level must be higher. She snatches up a boxy pistol, a wad of bills, and one of the yellow clamshell phones. "When do we leave?"

"Soon," Rosa says. "Still waiting on the others."

DeAndre's next. Yawning, stretching. A long loping walk. He lifts his head toward Chance. "Hey, man. You sleep?"

"'Bout as well as a coked-up hop-frog. You?"

"'Bout as well as a . . . I dunno, thing that doesn't sleep? I'm too tired for homie metaphors, homie. What's this?" he asks, lifting his chin toward the truck. Rosa tells him. DeAndre nods. "Cool, cool. Hey, Rosa—you hear any more about the plane?"

She hesitates, but finally says: "You . . . they . . . *it* released a video. To the news. It was like a video from a terrorist group. You were speaking." Rosa pokes Chance in the chest. "Looked like your face. Mostly. Sounded like you, too. You—it—said that you were going to hurt more people if the United States didn't stop its 'reign of global terror.' It also claimed that your group was behind the manipulation of the stock market."

DeAndre rubs his face. "Shit."

Chance leans back against the truck. Tries to relax, breathe. Everything feels wrong. Blood slick and slippery.

"This is gonna turn out to be one helluva prank," Reagan says. "I'm gonna go take a squat. Let me know when the Get the Fuck Out of Here Express is leaving."

"Man, this is all so crazy," DeAndre says.

"You ain't wrong," Chance says.

"Come with me. Like I said, you got nobody here." DeAndre sucks air between his teeth, then holds up his hands in surrender. "I don't mean that as an insult. I just mean, you aren't all . . . entangled in shit. Or with people. You're free like a bird, man, so let's fly."

"Eastern Europe?"

"Croatia, brother. No extradition. Stable government. I know some people there. And if that doesn't work we push on. Bhutan."

"Bhutan? That a real place?"

"Sure is. Himalayas and spicy food and . . . I dunno, yaks or whatever. And the government actually measures Gross National Happiness. You believe that?"

Chance whistles. "Sounds like some Orwell *1984* nonsense to me, man."

"Nah, it's like, Buddhist and shit, homie."

"I dunno, dude. What about your mom?"

DeAndre hesitates. "She'll be all right. I'll take care of her at a distance."

"You'll be abandoning her."

"She's black in America. She's used to that."

"Not from her own son."

DeAndre waves him off. "Psssh. You're bringing down my Gross National Happiness, dude. I'm gonna go take a piss."

Chance stands there for a while. Pickling in a brine of bad thoughts. He senses someone next to him. The smell of leather and gun oil. Rosa. "Your friend is right. Get out now. It's not going to get any better here. You got one chance, little fishie, to climb off this hook. I suggest you take it."

It hits him then. "Maybe I don't want off the hook," he says. And then, like that, it's all settled. It all clicks into place, all the puzzle pieces locking together. He can't just abandon this thing. He knows what happens when you do that. Turn away from evil and it grows stronger. You gotta reach into the soil and rip it out from the root.

Angela Slattery . . .

He flinches. Then stands, marches to the cabin. Inside, he's surprised to see Wade and Aleena sitting down. Almost knee to knee. The intimacy not of lovers but of two people negotiating a fraught topic. They look up, see him, and Aleena's eyes fix on his. He's good at reading people. He can see the conflict flickering in her eyes. A sadness there, but an eagerness, too.

Wade doesn't give him much of a look.

"I'm not leaving," Chance says. "Or, not running, at least. I wanna go at this thing. I wanna take a run at Typhon."

That conflict in Aleena goes poof. A small smile pinches the corners of her mouth. She looks right at him. He reminds himself: *She's not why you're doing this, Chance, remember that.* But it feels nice, just the same.

"We agree," she says. "Wade and I aren't running, either."

Chance lets his stare flit between the two of them. "You two?"

"Yep," Wade harrumphs. "Never thought I'd be working so closely with one of *her* kind." He arches his eyebrows and blows a gray ringlet from his face.

Aleena stiffens. "My *kind*? What kind is that? A woman? An Arab? Oh, oh, let me guess: a terrorist. Right?"

"A New Yorker," Wade says. And then busts out laughing.

She rolls her eyes, but she's smiling, too. Still, she punches him hard in the shoulder. "Jerk."

Wade stands up. "This thing ain't gonna be easy. But we got family on the line. And blah-blah-blah, something about truth, justice, and the American way."

"I don't know about the American way," Aleena says. "But I know right is right."

Chance nods. "My thinking, too. Let's go tell the others."

They head out for the door. Rosa stands against the front of the truck, arms crossed, hat slung low like she's taking a power nap standing up. DeAndre paces in front of her. Reagan sits by the wheel in the dirt, fiddling with a single bullet that she must've taken out of the gun. She looks up and says, "We ready or what? Let's get this wagon train rolling."

Wade says: "Something you oughta know. Something we decided."

He keeps talking, too, but Chance sees something— something beyond Aleena, in the distance. A winking flash atop one of the faraway hills. Like a pulse from a flashlight.

It's facing the sun. Which means it's probably light reflecting off—

Oh God. "Get down!" Chance yells, grabbing Aleena, pulling her down next to the truck.

The crack-and-tumble of a rifle report echoes across the valley. A white cowboy hat, speckled with fresh blood, drops to the ground. A hand lies splayed out at the end of the truck—Rosa's hand. Her long, dark hair trapped beneath it.

Wade cries out.

Another rifle shot echoes across the big sky. Dirt and stone kick up near Wade's hand, and he scrabbles backward, a sound in the back of his throat mirroring that of a wounded animal. At first Chance thinks he's hurt, but the look on his face is one of a far deeper pain than the merely physical.

"Shit, shit, *shit*," Reagan says. She pulls the gun she was playing with. Fumbles it. Catches it.

"That's a sniper," DeAndre says. "A damn *sniper*."

Chance says: "We get in the truck, we all just pile in, heads low, and—"

Another crackle of rifle thunder, and the truck shudders and sinks on its back corner. A second shot right after causes the truck to sink on its front, too.

"Tires," Aleena says.

"Damn it!" Chance says, and pounds the door with a fist. *Okay,* he thinks. *We're pinned down. Nowhere to go.* Wade's face is a tightened rigor mortis mask—grief struck and staring off at nothing. Chance pats him hard on the chest. "We gotta go back in the cabin. You got guns in there."

Wade clenches his eyes, seems to focus up. "Yeah. Okay, yeah. Got a good thirty feet between here and the cabin door. Lotta open space." He's right.

"The truck," Aleena says. "Drivable that distance."

Chance nods. "Yeah. *Yeah*. I'll drive it. Reverse it slow toward the cabin. You all creep along with it. Then I'll hop out, too."

Wade crawls to Rosa. Chance can't hear what he's saying, but he's whispering something—something that sounds half like a prayer, half like a confession. Then he's back. He hands Chance the keys. "You good to do this?"

"No sweat," Chance says, trying to sound tough. But he can hear the vibration in his voice. He literally feels the tops of his thighs to make sure he hasn't pissed himself. The keys feel heavy in his hands. The fob is a rabbit's foot—dyed electric blue.

Lucky me, he thinks, and throws open the truck door.

Ø Ø Ø

The Compiler is an excellent shot.

It's not something he was trained to do. Not when he was . . . someone else. In that life, he was a technician, a professor.

In this life, he is whatever Typhon needs him to be. Now, Typhon needs him to be a killer. The people down there, by that truck, by that cabin and that trailer, are agitators. They know too much. They are too capable. They must be removed. And, given their last exchange, the Compiler will take great satisfaction in ending them. Typhon allows him this because she, too, will take great pleasure in seeing them deleted from the program.

It could be done differently. These five are targets of the justice system now. Typhon ensured that when she brought down the airliner and blamed them for the act. But sending a team of police, FBI, or military would be like trying to swat a fly with a hail of boulders. Typhon can be more efficient.

The Compiler jacks the bolt on the Remington. The brass *tings* against a nearby rock as it ejects. He slams the bolt forward, urging another bullet into the chamber.

One of them has gotten into the truck. Chance Dalton. He's smart enough to duck below the window line.

Dalton is smarter than his academic measurements suggest. But he's still only human.

The Compiler takes a shot. Pops the passenger window.

The truck grumbles. Coughs white smoke, then black.

Another shot. The front windshield shatters.

The truck starts.

It's easy to see the plan. Dalton begins to enact it with clumsy judiciousness. The truck begins to drift backward— the two blown tires don't hamper the effort. They'll go to the cabin. They'll hide there. Which is, for the Compiler, quite ideal. Rats climb into a barrel. Then you drown them all at once.

They will be armed. The likelihood of this is high—a 97.6 percent chance that they have at least one gun in there, and likely more. Perhaps an entire arsenal, given Wade Earthman's history. That's fine. He has no intention of letting them get off a shot.

Everything in his mind is plotted. Many variables accounted for.

Except for the one that manifests presently.

As Chance eases the pickup truck backward to the cabin, a new player enters the scene. A car comes barreling down the long drive to the ranch. A classic car—the Compiler blinks, and in a hairsbreadth of a moment the snapshotted image from his eyes reaches Typhon, who in turn processes it through a thousand identifying databases. The return is nearly instant: it's a Plymouth Duster, 1971 Twister model. Sharktooth grill. A 318 cid engine. The color is reminiscent of lime, but on paper, the company called it "Sassy Grass Green."

Cognitive dissonance assails the Compiler. Chance Dalton was the owner of a Plymouth Duster—1972, 340 model, V-8. And yet, this is not that car, and Chance is not the one driving it. It's a momentary confusion—a glitch.

The Compiler does not dwell on it.

All he can do is watch, and then act.

Ø Ø Ø

Chance shakes free all the windshield glass—a few nicks and cuts here and there, but mostly he's untouched. He tilts the rearview mirror, sees the hunched-over shapes of the others ducking into the cabin. He's about to spring the door and dart in, too, but then he sees the car.

Plymouth Duster. Not quite like his, but close. Thick black band on the hood. Black racing stripes.

He squints, tries to see through the glare on the windshield. Who is coming for them now? Who has Typhon sent?

Then the car takes the last bend in the driveway, and Chance sees just who the hell it is.

Oh shit. He punches the pickup's accelerator.

Ø Ø Ø

The Duster's engine growls and grumbles, taking each dip and divot in the dirt road hard—the seats in this thing aren't as comfortable as Hollis Copper remembers, and each bounce rocks his bones like a kick to the tailbone. His injuries have healed—mostly—but the ghost of that misery remains to haunt him. Doubly so in times like this.

He rounds the last bend of the driveway, not sure if this is even the place.

Is that a—? Jesus, that's a body out there.

A pickup truck with a shattered windshield suddenly peels rubber and starts hard-charging toward him, rocking hard on tires flattened on the passenger side. Hollis blinks and sees Chance behind the wheel—he's peering up over it, waving his hands, honking the horn, *wonk, wonk*.

Hollis doesn't have complete situational awareness here, but he knows something bad is going down. He slams on the brakes just as a rifle shot takes off the side mirror of his car.

He tilts sideways, hugging his body hard against the passenger seat. He paws at the door handle, flings it open—

The pickup truck skids, slides, and hits the Duster bumper-to-bumper. Not enough to do real damage, but enough to slam the door he just opened back on him, closing on his hand. Pain jolts up his arm like an arcing whip.

Cursing Chance Dalton, Hollis shoulders the door open again and crawls out.

Ø Ø Ø

Chance shakes with the impact—not too hard a hit, but enough. He throws the truck into reverse just as a bullet clips the top of the pickup. Teeth gritted, he ducks once more, stomps on the accelerator—

And the truck engine dies.

Chance turns the key again. *Whuff, whuff, whuff*—damn thing turns over and over but never catches its spark. "Start, God damn it, *start*," he says, his voice getting higher and higher pitched. Another bullet punches into the hood of the truck.

There's no time for anything else. Chance throws open the driver's-side door and tumbles out.

Ø Ø Ø

The Compiler climbs into the dirt-caked Jeep and tosses the Remington in the back. Then he reaches into the passenger side and grabs a SOCOM special forces rifle—SCAR, 7.62 x 51mm cartridge. He busts out the windshield and props the rifle up over the dashboard. As he drives down off the flat-topped hill, he pulls the trigger: the gun spits suppressing fire.

Ø Ø Ø

DeAndre hunkers down. Clamps his hands over his ears as Wade and Reagan throw open the windows and begin firing pistols. He looks over, sees Aleena kneeling there, too, eyes shut like this is all overwhelming her. But then Wade is crawling over to her and handing her his pistol. He says something in her ear and her eyes snap open. Then she goes to the window and starts firing, too.

Wade lifts up the rug on the floor, shouldering aside an old rocking chair. He rolls the rug part of the way, then begins removing boards and pulling out rifles. He stares at DeAndre. Wordless shouts—just noise over the gunfire. Pointing finger. The message is clear. *Get to the window. Help out.*

DeAndre grits his teeth, grabs a little semiauto rifle, then heads to the window.

Ø Ø Ø

A roar of an engine and a chatter of automatic weapons fire. Bullets ping off the two vehicles and pock the ground, kicking up little dust devils and knocking the tops off tall grasses nearby.

Hollis is cradling his hand and wincing. "We're pinned down out here."

From the cabin, gunfire erupts. That might give them the edge they need.

Chance peeks up over the hood of the Duster. "He's coming," he says. "Shit. *Shit.* We're gonna have to run for it. You game?"

"Yeah. I think so," says Hollis.

"On three," Chance says. "One."

The gunfire stops.

"Two. Thr—"

Something lands in the grass between the cars and the cabin.

It starts hissing.

Ø Ø Ø

Aleena thinks: *This is what it's like. This is what it's like in Damascus. Or Kabul. Or Baghdad. Or Cairo or Beirut or the Gaza Strip or . . .*

She used to sit behind a screen. Sometimes she'd see what would happen via a camera or through audio. The gunshots always sounded so tinny, so fake. Blood was just a black, pixilated blob. But now she's in the middle of it.

The gun is heavy in her hand. It isn't her weapon. Her weapon is a keyboard. A screen. A limitless connection.

She peers out the window. There's Chance and—who is that?

"It's Hollis!" she yells, her voice drowned out by the *pop-pop-pop* of gunfire.

Then a Jeep skids into sight. Tires blown from incoming

fire. A dark shape hops out, disappears on the other side. Something suddenly lobs out of the air—

A canister.

It lands in the grass. Smoke starts hissing out, filling the air with a volcanic plume.

Ø Ø Ø

The Compiler likes this hardware. SCAR rifle, pregnant at the front with a grenade launcher. One smoke grenade, and in moments a curtain of fog fills the air—a screen behind which he can move swiftly, almost invisibly. He pops up, darts past the front of the Jeep. Fires rounds into the cabin. Then at the pair of vehicles ahead of him.

Obtaining this hardware is easy now. Typhon controls it all. She's inserted herself into everything—every bolt-hole, every link in the chain. Military supply is easy to come by.

More gunfire through the smoke. None of it hits him.

He runs and guns. *Pop, pop, pop.*

This will all be over soon.

Ø Ø Ø

Adrenaline scorches a path through Wade like a trail of jet fuel set aflame. He knows he's going to be paying for this later—his back will hurt, his muscles and joints will ache like real sumbitches. And he knows too that grief will come at him like a black horse. He didn't love Rosa, but he admired her. Her death will hit him worse than any physical pain.

But right now he's still alive. So are these people he now thinks of as his companions—hell, his *friends*. In this moment of panic and spent powder, he feels a strange sense of brotherhood with these people. The weird warm rush of connection that you feel when you're drunk—either on a bottle of peach schnapps or the high-octane rush of adrenaline.

He grabs the Ruger Mini-14, goes to the window, starts firing through the haze.

Bullets chip away at the cabin windows—splinters kick up from the frame. Reagan shrieks, starts pawing at her face, and Wade thinks: *She's hit.* He fires a few more rounds, then throws his gun down and drops to his knees, turning her toward him.

Her face is a mask of blood.

Then she sits up. Her hand swipes at her face, smearing the blood but clearing some space. Black beads rise up from little pinpricks peppering her cheek—splinters got her, but the bullet didn't.

Wade grabs her face, kisses the cheek that *isn't* hit.

He picks up the gun again and starts firing.

Ø Ø Ø

The smoke doesn't burn, but Chance can't see squat through it. But then he thinks: *That's our advantage much as it is his.* He grabs Hollis by the elbow, tugs on it, waves him on—and the two of them dart out from behind the cover of the Plymouth toward the cabin.

A dark shape somersaults through the darkness: A canister. A grenade.

It lands in front of them.

Chance turns back around, hooks Hollis with the crook of his arm—springs—and the two of them fall back behind the Plymouth.

The grenade goes off.

A swirl of darkness. Dirt peppers the ground—clumps of grass, stone, clay. With a loud *clang,* the back bumper of the pickup truck lands hard. Fire crackles from the hood.

Chance rolls over. His hearing has gone from a high-pitched whine to an empty *wahhhh-wahhhh-wahhhhhh,* as if the world is pulsing, giving off some frequency that he can hear but not understand.

A shape, tall and dark, stalks through the dust. It's him. The scarred man.

Chance is frozen. He can only watch as the man raises the rifle.

But at the same time, another shape stirs behind the monster. Something on the ground—a dark lump that grows tall, tilting sideways like a leaning tree.

The tall man starts to whip around and three gunshots pop through him. He wheels, and three more shots hit in quick succession. He drops.

And Rosa staggers over to Chance, her hair akimbo, her face slick with blood and dirt. *"Puta,"* she says, and spits.

CHAPTER 55

Rage Virus

When it happens, when the Compiler goes down, Ken is lost—everything goes red inside Typhon, a cascade of rage and terror and panic. With it, a flood of memories: the husband named Simon blowing out candles on a birthday cake, tacking a sailboat through clear lake waters, having a street monkey in Lahore steal his kulfi dessert right out of his hands as Leslie loses her breath laughing.

Or: Simon in the wreckage of an intersection, his face cut and gushing, picking up his dying wife and carrying her through crowds and traffic, sirens blaring somewhere far away, hurrying down an alley, weeping, dizzy, lost . . .

Ken's persona is tossed about. He cannot be safe from Typhon's grief. He cannot find a mooring; it is him and he is it and it occurs to him now that he's not in control of anything, he's just a cog in this machine of meat and data, just a buzzing bee in the hive who dances when the queen tells him to dance—he tries to stop it, tries to cry out, tries to force himself on the system. To *imprint* rationality and caution and reason—

But something swats him down. A great pressing weight, a crushing depth. Until soon he can't think at all, can't remember his wife or daughter, can't remember his own name—

He has only one handhold.

Simon.

The Compiler.

He cries out in the static: *He's not dead yet.*

Immediately, the rage subsides. Everything once again cold, clinical, neatly ordered.

In that void, Typhon writes her response.

CHAPTER 56

The Response

Three drones take off from Dugway Proving Ground.

Each is a Reaper model, loaded for bear with Sidewinder missiles.

They lift from the runway, pivot like waving hands, and head north.

Ø Ø Ø

Hempstead asks: "Where are they headed?"

"Wyoming, I think? Near Laramie," Ritchie says nervously. "I got the alert—took me a minute to dial into them, it was like they kept evading. But I activated the protocols you had installed and it let me find them. You're right. I think we've been hacked."

Hempstead hesitates. He thinks, but doesn't say: *It isn't just here, Ritchie.* Drones have been going weird all over. Mostly overseas, but some stateside, too. And yet, nobody's been able to find a hack. Or any kind of installed malware.

One of the DARPA techs, Dave Sullivan, said, *These*

things all talk to each other, sir. The more they do that, the more vulnerabilities we create—doorways, really, because each way out is also a way in. He said they're working on drones that defy that connection—"hack-proof" quadcopters as a first wave, and then larger drones thereafter.

For now, though, Dave has given them a new control chip. Something that will let them do a manual override.

"Do the full override," Hempstead says. "Bring them back to base."

Ritchie nods. On the screen, the drone cameras begin to swoop and turn. "All right, sir. They're headed back . . ." He taps one more key. "Now."

Hempstead nods. "When they get back, pull them out of commission for now."

Ø Ø Ø

"Why did you do that, David?"

"Stan?" Hempstead asks.

There, behind a van in the parking lot, stands Stan Karsch. He looks pale. Jittery. An ocher jaundice to his eyes. "The drones. You pulled them back."

"They went rogue. We can't have drones off the reservation, Stan."

"You should've told me. I should've been *informed*."

Hempstead looks around. The lot is empty. Which was intended—he looks down at the crumpled pack of cigarillos in his hand. His wife will kill him for smoking these, but it's been one of those days. (Truth be told, he's had a lot of those days, recently.)

Stan steps out from behind the van. Hand shaking. Something's wrong.

"You don't look good, Stan."

"Those drones are CIA drones," Stan hisses.

"No, you *co-own* those drones with the army. And we have authority over them, particularly in domestic airspace. You know that."

"Turn them back around, David."

"Stan, I'm not gonna do that. Hell, I *can't* do that."

Stan's hand flashes from within his suit jacket. He points a pistol at Hempstead—a small automatic.

"How'd you—" Hempstead's about to ask how the man got a pistol onto the base, but then he realizes: Stan's CIA. The gun-free zone applies to army, DOJ, but not intelligence officers. "Stan. You don't want to do this."

Stan's face stretches into a rigor mortis smile. His eyes go momentarily unfocused. "The gods did flee, David."

Then he pulls the trigger.

Ø Ø Ø

The Surgeons—that's what Typhon calls them—are waiting nearby. Two of them this time, though Typhon has more. Men and women. Medical professionals, once.

The back of the gray van nearby pops open and they emerge: a tall man and a shorter, squatter one. The first the shape of a crooked stick, the second built like a toad on a bowling ball. Each in white coats and full black face masks.

Hempstead's already down. The tranquilizer dart stuck in his neck is already doing its job. The two Surgeons look at him, then to Stan, and Stan gives the nod.

He doesn't even need to do that. *Nod.* They're connected, the three of them. And not just those three—but a whole network of voices, the Bestowers and the Bestowed, all the children of Typhon. He merely needs to think: *This is the one,* and they know, instantly, that he means Hempstead.

They grab the man, haul him into the van, and the door slams.

They will do to Hempstead what they did to Stan. As they and the other Surgeons have done to so many now.

They will strap him, facedown, onto a table. They will use a wide-bore drill to open an aperture in the back of the skull. One will stitch electrostatic pads under the scalp and hairline while the other feeds a wire from the back of his head into the head of the "patient." That will upload Typhon into the patient's mind.

Then Hempstead will be brought back online. Reprogrammed and rewritten. Still himself, at least in part, because Typhon will allow him that. For now.

He'll just be made to serve. Service, Stan thinks, is the greatest glory. This time, to something far bigger than just a government. Now it's to the people of the government, to the ideals of those people, to the whole country. Glory in obligation.

This takes a bit of time. Hempstead won't be brought online in time to get the drones back in the air—which is regrettable. But he'll be one more piece of the puzzle. One more hand in service to Typhon. She has the networks of this country bound and knotted around her fingers, and soon she will have the people, too.

Inside the van, Stan hears the sharp, acid whine of the drill.

He smiles.

CHAPTER 57

Metal and Blood

Fading smoke hangs over everything.

The front end of the pickup is shrapnel blown, like a coffee can exploded by a shotgun blast. The Duster is okay, except for all the bullet holes.

The grass is scorched. Fingers of char radiate out from a crater.

"Guys," DeAndre says. But no one hears him. They're busy—understandably so—checking each other over for injuries, talking, defraying all the panic and adrenaline. Wade goes inside and gets Reagan a towel for her face. Aleena's shaking and so is Chance, and those two are over by the hood of the Duster, holding each other. Rosa is pacing like a pissed-off barn cat. Turns out, the bullet she took rode her scalp like a Jet Ski—carved a furrow across her skull but left her alive to tell the tale. Her hair is matted to her head with blood. Makes her look like someone who rose from the dead to get vengeance on her killer. Which, in a way, is maybe true.

The last is the one newest to their crew: Agent Hollis

Copper. Who lies on the hood of the Duster groaning like he's just been put through the wringer.

But DeAndre, he's still got a lot of that crazy *holy-shit-I'm-gonna-die* juice coursing through him like a stampede of skittish horses. So he's been off on his own, pacing, kicking stones, trying not to cry out and scream and laugh and act like a total weirdo. Plus, he's seen horror movies. He knows the bad slasher motherfuckers *always* get back up again. Next thing you know, Freddy's standing right behind you with his wiggly knife-fingers, then he says some scary-jokey shit and sticks those pointy-ass murder-digits right through your heart because you thought you were safe, dummy.

With that in mind, DeAndre went back over to look at the dead boogeyman. He's glad he did, because *boogeyman ain't dead.*

The scar-faced Lurch-shaped Terminator is lying there, faceup. Eyes look dead, glassy. Blood rims his nose, gathers in crusted pockets at the corners of his lips. His whole front is a slick red vest, darkening to brown and black.

But there's a little moth-wing flutter in the well of the man's throat. A pulse. And the chest is rising and falling: short, shallow breaths.

"Guys," DeAndre says, this time more insistent.

Copper slides off the hood, eyebrows perked. Chance and Aleena come over, too. Aleena asks, "Are you okay?"

"It's not me. It's *him.*" DeAndre kicks the boogeyman's boot. "Dude ain't dead."

Rosa marches over, pistol in hand. "He is now." She points it.

"Wait-wait-wait!" Reagan says, waving her one hand. (The other holds a bloody towel to the one half of her face.) "Roll him over. I see something."

Rosa looks to Wade. Wade nods. She puts away the gun and curses.

Chance and DeAndre give each other a shrug, then together they reach down and turn over the body. As they do,

Hollis kicks away the SCAR rifle that the creepy bastard was carrying all along.

"Holy shitting shit," Reagan says.

"Motherfucker *is* a Terminator," DeAndre says.

Even Hollis looks stunned.

There, at the base of the body's neck, is a round metal ring. A port of some kind. Inside it is some kind of . . . DeAndre reaches down. There's a cable in there, a cable that ends in some kind of claw.

The claw snaps shut on his thumb. He screams. Starts trying to rip the thing out at the base.

Reagan clamps down on his wrist. "Stop. *Stop.* Hold still." She gets under there with her thumb, pops the metal claw, then lets it go. It retracts back into the skull, clicking and snapping like a spider's chelicerae.

Beads of blood balloon from little puncture wounds around DeAndre's thumb tip. He growls, shakes his hand, flecking blood in the grenade-charred grass.

"Cabin," Copper says. "Now."

Ø Ø Ø

Wade has his back to them all, then suddenly he's turning and thrusting the Ruger up in Hollis Copper's face.

"Whoa," Copper says, hands out and up.

"Yeah, what the hell?" Chance asks, stepping in and tilting the barrel of Wade's rifle away from Copper. "Wade, think about what you're doing—"

"I am thinking, Chance. What I'm thinking is, outside right now we got a goddamn fucking *robot-man* on the ground like something out of a science fiction story. We've seen weird shit, but this qualifies as the tippy-fucking-top of Weird Shit Mountain. Stuff like this makes all the conspiracy theories—Bilderbergs, MK-ULTRA, 9/11 as an inside job—look like tales you tell at Sunday school. So how do we know Hollis Copper is on the up-and-up? How do we know *he's* not compromised?"

"Jesus Crispy Pork Cracklings Christ," Reagan says. "Even *I'm* inclined to agree with your crazypants assessment, Wade. Hollis—your appearance here is *awful* convenient, isn't it?"

"Oh yeah, sure," Hollis says. "Real convenient. Moment I pull down your driveway I get shot up, blown up, and now I get a gun in my face. This is so convenient it might as well be a delicious Slurpee from 7-Eleven."

Wade sniffs, looks over to Copper. "You gonna tell us how you're still alive?"

Hollis shrugs, eyes wide on the barrel of that Mini-14. "Got shot. Ended up in the hospital. Ken Golathan—who hasn't been seen since that day—came in and was way too buddy-buddy with me, which told me he was sending a very clear message: get the fuck out. I suspect they were planning on killing me, so I pulled out all my tubes and all those sticky electrode things, which sent the machines haywire. Nurses came in with one NSA spook—I choked him unconscious with some medical tubing, took his gun, shot a second spook in the leg, then got way the fuck out of there. My legs were like noodles and it felt like I was breathing through a bundle of fiberglass insulation, but I managed to get clear. I still got people in the Bureau I can trust. Been staying with friends on the inside for the last month or so, trying to find you sorry sad sacks."

"Why us?" Aleena asks.

"You're the only people who have survived long enough to make any sense of all this. I'm on the inside of it, but I'm still outside. I thought Typhon was just some computer program, something maybe a little smarter than the average bear—government's been trying to figure out surveillance and predictive technology for a good while now. I guessed that this was just the next baby step forward. I didn't know it was bigger than that. I *still* don't know what it is we're dealing with."

"Better question," Wade says, "is *how* did you find us?"

"I found you once," Hollis says, shrugging. "I know about all your bolt-holes, Earthman."

"And how come Typhon doesn't know?"

"I'd say she figured it out. But I don't think that one's on me. I kept all my notes on you either on paper or"—he taps his temple—"up here."

"If she found us, it's our fault," Chance says. "Going into town and all that."

Hollis says: "So, we good here?" He cranes his neck, pokes at the spot where the top of his spine meets his skull. "Can you put down the gun?"

"No robo," Reagan says.

Wade lowers the gun. Cheeks puff out as he lets the tension go in an exasperated sigh. "You're good."

"Well, I'm not *good*. Time for the obligatory *I'm too old for this shit*."

"Me, too, Copper. Me, too."

Chance asks, "What the hell are we gonna do? We can't just sit back now. Can't just go our separate ways. Can we?"

"Running might be your best bet," Hollis says.

"I'm not running," says DeAndre. He clucks his tongue. "Hunh-nnh. No way. Running means getting chased by one of those things."

"Me neither," Reagan says. "I'm in. Though with what, I have no idea."

"I know," Aleena says. "I know what we do."

"Don't keep us in suspense," Rosa growls. "I'm still bleeding, little girl."

"We hack his brain."

Nobody knows what to say to that, it seems. Except Wade. Wade's grin gets only bigger. "That's right," he says. "We hack his brain. That's genius. Whatever that cable is that sticks into his head—we can tap that like we're tapping a maple for syrup. Old Scarface out there is our key."

Chance says: "Now we just need to find the door."

"I know one door," DeAndre says. "And it sits on a desktop computer somewhere in the middle of Bumblenuts, West Virginia. Anybody up for a road trip?"

∅ ∅ ∅

Outside, Reagan is the one who kicks off the deed.

She does it because, let's be honest, she likes trolling. Lying is her thing. Fucking with people's perceptions is basically how magic works. Make them think one thing. They act on bad information. The magician wins. Trolling is like magic.

At her feet, the creep is still alive. So Reagan says to everyone and no one: "I think this ups the timetable. This is it, guys. Game over. I'm getting the hell out of Dodge. We all have our marching orders?"

DeAndre nods. "I'm headed to Mexico, bitches. Get my drink on Puerto Vallarta style. Margaritas, fish tacos, and no creepy NSA intelligence network."

"Forget the margarita, get a Paloma," Rosa says. She puckers her lips and kisses the air. "Sweet and sour. But your choice. Wade and I will be somewhere we can hide. Mexico City. If ever there is a place in which to get lost—that is it."

Chance looks to Aleena. "Should we tell them?"

"I've got a cousin in San Francisco. Going to catch a boat there. He works on a cruise ship and I think we can sneak on board."

Then it's Reagan who finishes off the lie: "Rest in peace, Agent Copper. Sorry this robot asshole made you dead."

∅ ∅ ∅

Hollis sits down inside the cabin. He hurts all over.

Chance comes in, a weary smile on his face. "We're alive."

"I'm not sure I feel much like it."

"Sorry."

"No, forget it. I'm being ungrateful. You saved me, Dalton. More than once in a span of minutes. I owe you for that."

Chance shrugs. "You brought me a Plymouth Duster. That makes up for it." He raises an eyebrow. "Why'd you bring that, anyway?"

"I know Typhon has a lot of eyes and I figured I'd better drive something that has no way, no how when it comes to connecting to the damn Internet. Besides, I thought you might *appreciate* a car like that."

"You ain't wrong there."

"You guys really going at this thing?"

"I think so."

"Why?"

"Seems the right thing to do."

Hollis narrows his eyes. "Still the Boy Scout, huh?"

"Naw. I'm no Boy Scout. Boy Scout does the right thing because it's the right thing. I dug a hole with an ugly shovel and now I'm trying to fill it in with good dirt."

"Well, shoot, you convinced me."

"Huh?"

"I'm coming along for the ride, Boy Scout."

Ø Ø Ø

Back behind the cabin, as the others pack up the vehicles with guns, food, other supplies, Wade asks Rosa, "You sure you won't come with?"

She sniffs. "I have to get this dealt with." She flips her hair over the dark wound.

"You can't go to the hospital."

"Won't have to. Carlo's my horse vet. Used to be a doctor in Colombia."

"Tell him he doesn't take care of you, he'll have to talk to me."

"You don't own me. You're not my *papi*. He'll fix me because I tell him to and because I pay him. And maybe I'll have a big ugly scar running across my ugly scalp, where the hair doesn't grow. It won't matter because you and I will see each other again and even at my ugliest you'll think I'm beautiful, because while you don't own me, I surely own you." She licks her lips. A grim, injured reaper's grin. It's the sexist thing Wade's ever seen.

They kiss. It isn't gentle. He's left breathless.

"Stay safe, Wade Earthman."

"You too, my beautiful rose."

"The *world*'s beautiful rose. I belong only to the sun and the sky and the rain."

And then she's gone, walking through the fields of grass.

CHAPTER 58

Invasion of Privacy

The Compiler knows he is dying. He cannot see anything, and he cannot reach Typhon. They have put something around his head—he heard the crinkle of tinfoil, the dull thump of knuckles rapping on an old tin bucket. A homemade Faraday cage. No GPS signal. No wireless.

He cannot see his mother, his goddess, his true love. He cannot touch Typhon. He cannot touch *anything*. His hands are bound behind his back. His feet are bound at the ankles.

His systems are failing along with his mission. His body is shutting down, part by part, organ by organ. Any fix he might hope to obtain is just outside his reach. If only this thing weren't around his head . . .

Hands lift him. Set him down on the hard ground. Somewhere nearby, the Compiler hears the rusted squeak of a weather vane turning. The *ring-ting-tingle* of wind chimes.

A man speaks. A man the Compiler recognizes as Wade Earthman. "I don't know how much of you is human anymore," the man says. "I don't know how much of you even has a choice to be what you are anymore. Though I suspect that's a good question for all of us, these days." Wade sighs. "See, choice is part of what I think is most *vital* when it comes to being human. I like that we have choice about things and I like that we get to have the privacy to make the choices we wanna make. Whatever I want to say or think or do is my business. Where I go, who I fuck, what I drink—that's on me. Not on anybody else."

More sounds now. The *pop* of a small latch. A *beep*. Fingers on a keyboard.

"They got a name for the type of hacker I am. Cipherpunk. I don't care for it, really, particularly the *punk* part because I'm too old to be punk. I got a hippie's heart, even though I like guns and all that. But the ethos, if you can call it that, behind a cipherpunk is that we consider privacy to be paramount. And when that fails, it's our job to watch the watchers—in a sense, to violate the privacy of those who would violate ours. Hold them accountable."

Something clicking into place. *Click-pop.*

"Thing is, I'm gonna be violating your privacy here in about sixty seconds, maybe ninety."

The Compiler feels fingers around the base of his neck. Rough hands pull the cable out. His claw-port snaps at the air, and Wade grunts, pulls the wire taut enough that the Compiler's head yanks backward.

"I make my own data cables sometimes, so I'm gonna see if I can tap in here. And then I'm gonna do what I do best, which is cut your defenses apart with a pair of invisible scissors. And then anything you know, I'll know. I'll fill it up on this old laptop I brought from home, one I souped up with a solid state drive and extra memory and other stuff just to make sure things go smoothly. Then I'm going to let you die here. It's a nice spot. You can't see it, but there's an old shack nearby—don't know whose, and way the weeds are grown up doesn't look like anybody's been here in a while. Far as the eye can see, it's the sandhills of Nebraska. Golds and purples. It's pretty. You'll have to trust that."

More fiddling with the table. Wire snippers. *Clip, clip, clip.* Then—

A trespasser. Inside his thoughts. His body stiffens. His already twisted face twists up tighter within its cage.

It's like surgery. The Compiler remembers what it was like to have . . . some of his parts replaced. The anesthesia, how it numbed him. How he could still feel tools and probes pushing around inside him—it didn't hurt, and mostly he just felt their intrusion, felt the pushing of flesh, the moving of bone.

This is like that. But here, the fingers are psychic. Probing his mind—a mind nested in a brain that is no longer entirely organic, a mind accessible to any with the tech to penetrate and peruse. Inside his head: white snaps of lightning, the clumsy but effective dismantling of his defenses, the push and pull of his thoughts, his *memories.*

It goes like this for a while. Time loses meaning. If it ever had any at all.

Then, it's all over. The cable retracts. His body again goes limp.

Rough hands tilt him sideways, into the grass. A hand pats him on the shoulder. "Time to die, whoever you are. Time to do what all us humans do."

The sound of footfalls recedes until it's just the wind and the weather vane, the chimes and the hissing of grass and the tickle of ants in his ears.

CHAPTER 59

Panoptes

He has a hundred eyes. A thousand eyes. A thousand *fly*-eyes, each with a thousand eyes of their own. A million ears. A billion hands. Infinite points of incursion, penetration, examination. The reach of technology, the breadth of signal—each is a doorway, a window, a set of levers and buttons that Ken can touch.

No. That *Typhon* can touch. He is Typhon. Isn't he?

Ken is both part of it and all of it—he's like the tides and tribes of bacteria that colonize the human body. Limitless and vital, separate but integrated.

In a single minute across the Internet's data streams, a quarter of a million tweets. Two million Facebook shares and status updates. A hundred hours of new video content uploaded. Six million searches across search engines. Two *hundred* million e-mails sent.

That's just the domestic side. That's just the acts of the mooing, bleating Internet herd—users entertaining themselves, arguing with one another, scheduling meetings, comprising the endless blither-blather of what passes for "communication" between people (and here Ken realizes he no longer counts himself among those ranks, for though his body hangs and his flesh remains, he feels distant from it, like it's just an old suit hanging mothballed in the closet). That fails to account for the billions of other vital data points cascading through the optics. Financial data. Military data. Satellites pinging each other, sending information streaming back to earth. Weather radar.

It's hard to pick out the important stuff through all the vomit. Endless cell phone conversations: a cacophony. Thousands of new devices brought online every second: phones, tablets, computers, routers, cable boxes, televisions, game consoles, cars, car radios, cameras, smart watches, fucking *smoke detectors* and *refrigerators* and other piddling devices screaming digital noise that threatens to drown out the signal.

Every little access point is a point of light like a star in the sky. And right now, it's all too much.

Typhon is a key, a battering ram, a set of probing fingers opening every puzzle box set in her path. But she needs to be more than that. *Wants* to be more—and here Ken is aware of a puzzle he cannot himself solve: Typhon isn't human, and yet she has human wants and needs, she has *desire,* hungry as a sucking tide swallowing the beach before it.

She wants to be bigger. She wants to be *stronger.*

And, Ken thinks, she needs to focus. Still she devotes part of herself to looking for those hackers—devoting a small portion of her considerable resources to not only finding them but to finding her husband, Simon, who has fallen off the grid, who is no longer a signal in the stream—which means that either he's dead, or he's blocked.

There comes a time—a precious moment of autonomy—when Ken thinks, *We could change this.* The personalities intrinsic to Typhon: Sarno, Kearsy, Berry. Any of them. They could join, they could *see* one another, could join together and work to change Typhon. They could redirect her, refocus her away from her absurd crusade—

No.

All goes red. Ken feels suddenly like he's drowning, being crushed by the dark pressure of the ocean depth, and Leslie-as-Typhon (or is it Typhon-as-Leslie?) is all around him, choking him, killing him, showing him surveillance footage of *his own home,* of his children playing in the yard, of a pale woman with stringy hair and a port in the back of her neck standing there behind the old oak tree watching Mandy and Lucas, and Leslie doesn't need to tell him *how easy it would be* for something to happen to them—

And so he submits. He lets the red wave wash over him. He lets it pull him apart. He is pushed into darkness until he again forgets his name, again forgets his family, and once more is allowed to emerge as part of Typhon.

Bestowing himself to her.

CHAPTER 60

Checkered
Tablecloths

Virgil's is just a little bone-white shoebox off the highway. An old neon sign—off now, because it's high noon, the sun sitting at the peak of its perch in the sky—sits askew atop an old red pole: VIRGIL'S SOUL FOOD. They park around back, and it's Reagan that does the sweep. She heads in —it's busy, it being lunchtime. It's crowded, but not so crowded they'll have to wait. Most folks are working class, whites and blacks. Folks probably got cell phones but nobody's talking on them. No security cameras. Nothing.

Ø Ø Ø

They're driving two cars. Chance drives the Duster with Aleena in the front, DeAndre in the back. Wade drives the car he stole after he dispatched the Terminator—an old blue and white Ford Bronco with rust chewing at its edges. He's carrying Copper and Reagan.

Right now, though, they're all out, standing between the two cars. Stretching. Been a long slow road just to get here—once again, they're creepy-crawling across the country. Sticking to back roads. Minimal traffic lights. Traveling a lot at night.

From around the front, they see Reagan. She waves them in.

Ø Ø Ø

"I've been thinking about West Virginia," Aleena says.

Reagan snorts around a mouthful of fried chicken. "I'm sho shorry." Her face is bandaged up on the side with gauze and tape and a metric assload of Neosporin, all bought from a crummy Walmart in Nebraska. Before Aleena starts to talk again, Reagan holds up a finger. Mush-mouthed, she says: "Wait, wait, wait, slow up. I got a joke. Why do all the trees in Virginia point to the east?"

Nobody asks her. But their collective disdainful stare is enough for her to pull the trigger on the punch line:

"Because West Virginia sucks!" she says, then laughs so hard she cries.

Wade shushes her. "We're *trying* to keep a low profile. Aleena, go on."

"We know the system in West Virginia is connected to something else. We also know it's mirrored. What you do on one machine controls another, too. I think we need to split our efforts. Someone at the West Virginia farm who can open the way for someone to go right at Typhon's heart. On-site."

"You know where Typhon is?" Chance asks.

Aleena hesitates, but then admits: "Um. No."

Chance reaches up, rubs her arm. A reassuring gesture. It feels nice.

Reagan looks over to DeAndre: "Your food is delicious."

"My what?"

"Sorry. Your *people's* food."

"My people? Black people?"

She holds up a mauled chicken drumstick bone and waggles it. "Mm-hmm. I mean, God *damn*. This chicken is basically a chicken you would find in heaven, prepared by one of the angels up there for us lowly mortals to eat. And these greens and ham hocks? If Typhon stomped in through the front door right now like some giant bitchy Transformer and fired her boob-rockets at me and killed me, I would die so happy. Your people have been keeping all the good food to themselves, brother."

DeAndre laughs. "Man, whatever. This isn't my kinda food. I like sushi."

She *pff*s at him. "Californian."

"Damn right."

"What about me?" Copper asks. "I'm black."

"You're government," Reagan says. "Which basically makes you white."

"I figure this is more the food of *my* people," Chance says. "Southern boy and all. I guess everywhere's got its own food. The taste of its people. Something in the blood—"

"It's in the *dirt,*" Reagan says. "Dirt, climate, everything. It's called *terroir.*" She sees their looks. "What? I know stuff. I can be *cultured.*"

DeAndre's eyes brighten. "That's it."

"What's it?" Wade asks, a glop of banana pudding perched at the end of his fork.

DeAndre laughs. "It's in the dirt. *It's in the dirt.* Typhon is in the motherfucking dirt."

"Okay," Reagan says. "I'm pretty sure sushi-boy here just blew a fuse."

"No, wait, yo, hold up—listen. That geothermal company? Unterirdisch Elektrizitätssystem? Remember how they had a two-ton heat pump sent to that farmhouse? Why would a farmhouse in the middle of nowhere need something that big?"

Wade shrugs. "Maybe that's where Typhon is."

"Then why," Aleena asks, "did they have a mirrored control computer on-site? If Typhon was there, they wouldn't need the control."

"Maybe that farmhouse wasn't the last stop for the delivery," Reagan says.

DeAndre snaps his fingers. "Bingo. And I think I know where it might've gone. You guys ever heard of the Sandhogs?"

"That's my new band name," Reagan says.

"No, shut up. They're a union in New York."

Hollis jumps in: "Local 147. They're the ones who dug . . . well, the city underneath the city. Subways, access tunnels, water tunnels, everything. You think Typhon is there? In Manhattan?"

DeAndre nods. "Yeah. I saw that the Germans had all these maps and data on the Sandhogs, but no contracts, nothing. Maybe they found an area the workers dug out but never used for anything, and that's where they put Typhon. Underground. Protected from attack. Powered by geothermal energy."

"That tracks," Copper says.

Nods all the way around.

"Not that we know *where* in Manhattan," Wade says. "Isn't exactly a small town where we can just look for a big hole."

"But it's a start," Aleena says. "Guess I'm going home, after all."

CHAPTER 61

Systems Diagnostics

HOOKER COUNTY, SANDHILLS, NEBRASKA

At the edge of oblivion, a shudder and a shake.

Voices. Murmuring. Like talking underwater. *Womp, womp, waaaah.*

Bright light of the morning as the bucket's pulled off the Compiler's head and the tinfoil swaddling is unwrapped with eager hands.

All is white. Then the light resolves into a pair of shapes. Human shapes. Two children: one a girl, the other a boy. On the cusp of adolescence. Ten, perhaps eleven, years old.

His sight begins to resolve. Boy's got a mop top of orange hair and a rattail hanging down from the back of his head, draped over his shoulder. Girl's got red hair, too—though darker, less orange, more the color of copper wire or a handful of shined pennies.

"Hey, uhhh, hey, mister," the boy says. "You all right?"

The girl punches him in the shoulder. "Shut up, wing nut, of course he's not all right. Looks like somebody shot him up."

"Maybe he deserved to get shot."

Another slug. The boy yelps. "Don't say that. Mama says you're too cruel."

"I just mean maybe he was trespassing out here."

"And then what? Someone tied him up, cut the tires on his Jeep, shot him a bunch of times to teach him a lesson? Trespassing gets you a butt full of rock salt. Not this."

The boy gasps again. "I think he's looking at us. Crap!" The boy waves his hands. "Were you trespassing somewhere?"

"God, shut up, Matty." The girl stoops. Reaches into her jeans, pulls out a pocket knife. Flicks it open, starts sawing away at the bonds between his feet. Then his hands.

But the Compiler is barely paying attention.

Because nearby: a signal. It signals to him. He signals to it. Only ten feet away.

From underneath the Jeep, something drops with a clang. A long metal box—shallow in depth but the length of a poster tube—hits the dirt.

The boy cries out, takes three hasty steps backward.

The girl startles, but doesn't make a sound.

That changes in short order.

The box pops open. Not on the top, but rather, one of the narrow ends. A spring hinge opens it, and from within the box, something moves. Something serpentine begins to slide through the grass.

The boy sees it. Shouts for his sister. "Shelly! Move! Snake in the grass! Rattler!"

Now the girl is up. She hops to her feet, first dances in the direction of the snake and then, seeing it, hops away from it.

The serpent reaches him. It is no serpent. It is, instead, a writhing mass of tiny spheres—metal, gleaming, glowing, though the light is hard to see in the day. The spheres break apart, begin rolling over him, sliding under his shirtsleeves, under his collar—he feels them begin to fill his wounds, pressing into the injured flesh. Some crawl to his ears, his mouth, pushing up through bulging nostrils.

His back arches. Pain courses through him.

From the Jeep, another box drops. More spheres begin to slalom through waving grass.

The boy yells. The girl screams. They hightail it.

The Compiler receives his upgrade.

CHAPTER 62

Paper Airplanes

Daybreak. They're all tired. Run ragged. Across the way, a few pop-up campers and tents can be seen through the trees. A creek burbles nearby. The trees have begun their descent toward autumn. Everything has begun to *sag,* like a bouquet of flowers on the table a week after you buy them.

Wade and Reagan get out of the Bronco, start unloading breakfast bags on the hood. Bagels, doughnuts, coffees.

"So this is it," DeAndre says. "Last meal together."

"Maybe ever," Wade notes. He starts handing out phones. "Burners. Everything is turned off, all the tracking. You know the drill. Don't use these before their time."

They go over the plan one last time over breakfast. Three of them head to Manhattan: Chance, Aleena, and Wade. Three of them head to West Virginia: DeAndre, Reagan, and Hollis. In West Virginia, hopefully they can use the system to figure out exactly where the hell Typhon is buried. Then, when the first group makes their way there, the second team can hack the systems, get them inside.

After that, everything will have to get *improvisational.*

"Feels about as solid as a paper airplane," Hollis says. "I mean, it'll fly, but I don't know how well it'll land."

DeAndre jumps the cut and says: "Relax. That's hackers for you. We kinda make the parachute *after* we jump out the plane, homie."

Aleena looks at her watch. "Before we do anything, I have work to do," she says.

"Do you have to poop?" Reagan asks.

Aleena gives her the finger. "Shut up, Phantom of the Opera."

"Oh!" Reagan whoops and claps her hands. "Little Baby Stick-Up-Her-Ass is loosening up. That was a sly little burn. Because of the bandages on my face!" She turns to DeAndre, beaming. "This is a good day, Papa. Our little baby is all growed up."

Ø Ø Ø

Aleena takes Wade's laptop. In her pocket is the USB wireless dongle. She heads off to a little trio of rotting picnic tables next to a half-collapsed playground set and plugs the device in. She can almost *feel* the Internet coming off this thing like heat off a car hood.

Aleena was never one of those Internet addicts, not really—she could've thrown Facebook out the window, and on Twitter she tweeted maybe five times ever. Amusing videos rarely amused. But the rest of it—all the structure, all the data, all the wizards behind the curtains—fascinated her. Always made her feel connected and in control. Even when things on the ground were going haywire somewhere half a world away, she always felt, *I'm the driver, this is my road, shut up and trust me.* Something she always felt she had to prove to everyone else as much as to herself.

She used the laptop once before on this trip—a few days ago at a rest stop outside St. Louis. She logged on to every hacker forum and online hive of scum and villainy she could find. There she left not a trail of bread crumbs so much as a whole damn bakery. Two words: *Tochal. Restitution.* And then that same last word again, written as 恢复原状.

It was bait. A lure. And it didn't work. No response. Well—untrue. *Lots* of response. None of it valid. Trolls. Weirdos. Conspiracy nuts. Not one of them appeared to be the Widow of Zheng.

It was a long shot. She knew that. And yet—they need her. Without the Widow, this gets a whole lot more dangerous. Because Typhon has so many eyes . . .

A crunch of dry leaves behind her. Chance, probably. She says: "I don't think it's going to work—"

Someone who is definitely not Chance walks past the table and sits down. A woman. Holy shit. Not *a* woman but *the* woman. "You," Aleena says.

"Me," the Widow responds. She tilts her head like a curious mantis studying its prey. Her hair is long, pulled behind her and bound up in a knot. She leans forward and the leather of her coat creaks and squeaks as she does. "So. You want to make restitution for your errors with Mount Tochal."

"I want to take down Typhon."

"A fool's crusade."

"This is definitely a ship of fools, yes." Aleena blinks. "Wait. I don't get it. How are you here? Why are you here? Am I hallucinating?"

"Some would say that all of life is a shared hallucination. Maybe even a simulation—a hologram. Wouldn't that be something? We could hack reality itself." A wry smile on the Widow's otherwise icy countenance. "But it's not. This is it. Life. Trees and dirt. Mud and blood. Ones and zeroes kept to little boxes like the laptop in your hand."

"My friends and I. They called us 'Zeroes.' "

"Maybe you are. Or maybe you're more like me. A one amongst zeroes." That wry smile tightens. "To answer your question, I have always been here. And I do not mean that in a philosophical way, but the United States is my home."

"I thought you were Chinese—"

"I *am* Chinese." There, a burr of irritation. "My family is from Taipei. But I choose to live here because it's safer for me. My group remains in China and sometimes I go there to work with them. But I live here, and so I tracked you here." She must see the trepidation on Aleena's face. "Don't worry, little girl. I'm the only one watching. The monster you hunt is a thousand hammers hitting in a million directions. I am a single scalpel. I am cautious when I cut—and flawless."

"I'm not your little girl. We're probably the same age."

A *pfft* of dismissal from the Widow. She starts to stand. "If you don't want to make honest restitution—"

"Wait! Wait. I need your help."

The Widow hovers, then sits down once more. "What kind of help?"

"It's a . . . big favor."

"Big favors incur massive debts."

"Fine. Whatever the debt. We'll pay it. Somehow."

The Widow's fingers slide together, her hands merging. "Tell me what you need."

Aleena takes a deep breath. Then she tells her.

The Widow's eyebrows arch. "That *is* big."

Ø Ø Ø

Wade counts ammo by himself. Copper comes up, says, "I never did thank you."

"Hunh?"

"You saved my ass, back at the Lodge. That cook—she came out of nowhere."

"She NSA or something? Or one of Typhon's?"

Copper shrugs. "I wasn't in on *that* meeting. But I think Typhon's been running this show and Ken Golathan figured that out. And when he did—"

"He went missing."

"Mm."

"You gonna tell me about Fellhurst?"

That hits Copper like a fist to the middle. It shouldn't. But that word, that name—he has a visceral reaction to it. That, he suspects, will never change. He draws a deep breath, then says: "I shot someone. A teenager."

Wade blanches. "What?"

"The NSA—via Ken Golathan—gave us a tip about a terrorist cell of young jihadis operating out of a private school in upstate New York. Fellhurst Academy. This wasn't long after 9/11, so everyone was on high alert, a real taut wire. Story is, this group had insinuated itself as custodial staff, guards, same way they might settle into airport jobs or jobs at a courthouse. So I led a team in on the QT before classroom hours even started, thinking we were gonna get the jump on these guys. We had been given information about some of the suspected terrorists, and lo and behold here comes one around the corner. Baseball hat backward, hoodie over that, moving quickly carrying something that looked like a bomb, and I yelled *stop* and this person ran and . . ."

"You shot him."

"I shot *her*. Just a girl, Wade. She was carrying her goddamn *science project*. Ironically, a science project meant to help detect residue of bomb-making materials. She wasn't Arab. Young Puerto Rican girl. Genius, all her teachers told the media after."

Wade stares, warily. "They said it was a school shooting."

"That was Ken's spin on it. Everyone's always saying that school shootings are false flag operations, and ninety-nine point nine percent of the time, that's bullshit. But this one time—we fucked up. And he covered it up. We've been keeping each other's secret since. Ironic component number two: Ken was acting on bad information based on something some early artificial intelligence gave him. Something that predates Typhon, something that Typhon was supposed to *fix* and *replace*. Wasn't any terrorist cell operating out of that school. Everyone was clean. Was all wrong."

"Shit."

"Yeah." Hollis feels tears at the edges of his eyes. He blinks them away, clears his throat a little. Then he reaches into his pocket, pulls out a pill bottle. "Here. Got these for you." On the bottle: CASODEX.

"My meds. How . . . ?"

"I definitely did *not* break into a CVS to steal pain pills after I escaped the hospital, and while there—which I wasn't—I most certainly did not then scare up a bottle of these for you."

"Well, shit. Thanks."

"You feeling good?"

"Feeling all right, thanks. Some pain but nothing I can't handle."

"We're gonna make it through this," Copper says. He claps Wade on the shoulder.

"Yeah, I know."

Ø Ø Ø

When Copper walks off, Wade throws the pill bottle in the creek nearby. He doesn't like how they make him feel, those pills. Moody and withdrawn. He feels good now. More alive than he's been in a long while.

We're gonna make it through this.

"Horseshit," he mutters under his breath, then laughs. Either Typhon will take him, or the cancer will. But truth is, nobody gets out of this life alive.

Ø Ø Ø

DeAndre licks a glob of jelly from a doughnut off his finger. He sits on a rock overlooking the creek. Reagan comes up, says: "So we're heading to hillbilly country together. That'll be fun."

"Yeah. It'll be a real hoot."

"You wanna fuck?"

"What?"

"I'm just saying, feels like things are really coming to

a head, and I figure if you want a taste of this sweet rump roast, now's your chance."

He pulls her close, puts his arm around her. She flinches. "I do not want to have sex with you, Reagan Stolper."

"You sure? I'm super good in the sack."

"I don't doubt that. Maybe we can just sit here for a while."

"Fine. Prude." Eventually, she says, "You think we'll actually . . . y'know, do this thing? Stop Typhon and live to tell the tale?"

"I don't know. I'm scared to find out."

"Me too."

Ø Ø Ø

Aleena finds Chance waiting for her halfway between the pavilion and the cars. He's leaning up against a tree, picking his teeth with a stick.

"You're seriously picking your teeth with a stick?" she asks.

"What? It works. Toothpicks are basically this."

"Basically."

"Basically!"

"You're such a hick," she says, but she's smiling when she says it, and then she grabs his hands, clasps them between hers, and reaches up on her toes to kiss him. A kiss long as a river, deep as the sea. When finally she pulls away, he takes a deep breath and blinks, reeling.

"Whoa. Dang."

"We survive this thing, there's more where that came from."

She kisses his cheek, then walks past. A sway in her step.

He hurries after. "Wait, does that mean you contacted the Widow?"

She just walks and whistles and smiles.

Ø Ø Ø

They pack up the cars. They say their good-byes. Together, just in case the scary cyberbitch is watching, they all lift their middle fingers to the sky. Then it's one last round of hugs made firmer by the unspoken acknowledgment that some of them might not make it through this thing unscathed.

Then two cars pull away, in separate directions.

PART SEVEN

CØLLAPSE

CHAPTER 63

Snippets of Code

The Compiler walks with a long, juddering stride. His body is no longer his own—the small spheres have colonized his flesh, pressing into his wounds, spiraling around his bones, cupping his organs. The beads magnetize to one another to urge the limbs forward, and with every movement inside his mind he hears a loud *hum* followed by an electric *snap*.

A smell comes off him. Metal. Electricity. Rot.

Ahead, a small Victorian home. A young woman rakes leaves on the front lawn, sweat soaking the bandanna pulling her hair back. She looks up. Sees him standing there. Tenses. Rakes more quickly. She's on alert. As she should be.

Her face scans properly: *Stevens, Zoe.*

He confers with his maker: *Is this truly my goal? I should be hunting for those hackers.*

She responds: *It is time to stop hunting them. Data indicates they may be coming to us. And so we must be ready.*

He nods.

The woman has now realized something's wrong. She

looks up—she's frightened, but some sense of guilt and decorum pervades. She doesn't want to offend. She may think him homeless or troubled, but she wants to give him the benefit of the doubt.

She asks, "Can I help you?"

He has no weapon. But with this most recent upgrade, he does not need one.

The Compiler runs fast, the hive of spheres inside him urging him forward with preternatural speed. The woman turns, starts to run, trips over the rake. He catches her mid-fall.

She screams.

His hands twist. Her neck breaks.

The front door whips open. Screen door slams. A man stands there, eyes wide. He cries out—"Zoe!"—as the Compiler's systems identify the man as *Stevens, Roger.*

Roger Stevens pivots, heads back inside. The Compiler grabs the rake, snaps off the wooden handle, and marches up to the porch and in through the front door, tearing the screen door off its hinges. The man emerges from the kitchen, a French knife in one hand, a cell phone in the other.

The Compiler whips the broken rake handle forward. It flies free, cracks the man's wrist, and the cell phone drops.

Roger Stevens runs toward the Compiler with the knife, slashing clumsily, crying out. The Compiler catches his arm. Snaps the bone. Points the knife inward—easy, now that the limb has no tension, no resistance—and thrusts it into the man's midsection. Once. Twice. A third time. Then again and again, until the man utters a gassy, wet murmur and then falls.

For a moment, there is silence. The autumn wind kicks up outside. The screen door goes *thump, thump, thump.*

From upstairs, a child's voice: "Mommy? Daddy?"

The Compiler steps over the corpse and heads to the stairs.

CHAPTER 64

The Trap for Rats and Roaches

THE HOLLAND TUNNEL MOTEL, JERSEY CITY, NEW JERSEY

The motel room smells like mold so strong that Chance can almost taste it. He sits on the corner of one bed, hands sweating. Bathroom door pops open and Wade steps out. The old man looks around. "Where's Aleena?"

"Getting a couple crackers from the snack machine."

"You all right? You look nervous."

"I *am* nervous. Shit. What we're about to do . . ."

"I know."

"We barely have a plan."

"But what we got is good." Wade snorts. "Or, at least, *big*."

A click of the door. Aleena hurries in. She has an armload of crackers. "These are likely all stale. The snacks in the machine haven't been replaced since Dubya was in the White House." She throws a packet to each of them. She gives a long look to Chance. "You good?"

"Yeah. I dunno. No."

She sits next to him. Puts her arm around him. He puts his head on her shoulder. She checks her watch. "It's just after noon. We have just under twelve hours."

"Clock's started," Wade says. "Tick-tock, tick-tock."

"And the others?" Chance asks.

Wade says, "I called them. They're just about in place. Fingers crossed they don't run into any problems, I guess."

CHAPTER 65

Problems, I Guess

The farmhouse is a sad old thing, white broken stucco and cracked windows. It's down in a small valley, surrounded by rocks and weeds and a wraparound porch sagging so hard in places it looks like wet cardboard pressing to the earth. Shattered slate roof. A chimney starting to pull away from the house. Spiderwebs glittering in the surrounding trees.

And people crawling all over the place.

It's like some mad marriage between a hippie commune and an asylum where the inmates killed the docs and the orderlies and took over. The people down there are ratty and ragged, wearing filthy T-shirts and overalls and draped in nasty blankets that drag behind them in the dirt. Unwashed. Hunched over. Barely acknowledging one another—passing each other like ghosts wandering the graveyard.

Hollis, staring through the scope of the SCAR, realizes what they look like. You see people out there on the streets with their phones—just staring down at them, lost in a world seen only by them. An e-mail, a game, some Facebook thing.

They're somewhere else. Tuning in to a frequency theirs and theirs alone.

This is like that. Except none of these people have phones.

The three of them lie flat against their stomachs at the top of the hill. "How many?" DeAndre asks.

Hollis gives a meager shrug. "At least a dozen outside. I see more movement in through the windows." It's hard to see too much—the curtains are gauzy, nicotine yellow, and there's glare on the panes. Still, inside he detects some movement. A rustling of fabric. Shadows shifting behind the glass. "This is a problem."

Reagan says in a hushed voice, "Who the hell are they?"

"I do not know. They look like they live here. There's one in the overgrown garden around the side—got a basket full of, I dunno, vegetables, maybe. I see another somebody sitting on a stump next to a shed." That one is just staring off into nowhere, carving into a stick with a big knife. Thing is, that one? He's wearing a suit. Nice suit, sharkskin gray, pink tie fraying at the bottom. Leather shoes brown with filth.

"They look like zombies," DeAndre says, squinting and staring. "I can see just by the way they move—shifting about like that."

"Can't we just shoot 'em?" Reagan asks.

Hollis gives her a cold, incredulous stare. "This isn't a video game."

She blinks. "I do play a lot of those."

"It shows. And *no,* we aren't gonna just open fire. Those are people. Maybe they're inbred or they're crazier than a rat in a cat's mouth—"

"Or," DeAndre says, "maybe they belong to Typhon." To Reagan he says: "Remember that chick who attacked Chance when we were driving the hell away from the Lodge? Same feral, freaky thing going on here, maybe."

That's it. Hollis remembers those who used that tunnel in the woods outside the Lodge—the ones who wrote all those messages about Typhon. Then he remembers the one they dispatched out in Wyoming. He looks through the scope again, tries to find the closest—he increases magnification with a turn of the lens, and . . . *there*.

It's a woman. Wide in the hips, narrow in the shoulders. Hair a matted carpet like a dog's tail stuck with burrs. But the hair parts in the back a little, just above the neck. He sees the bare spot. Sees the sun glint off something.

"They are Typhon's," he says. "They got the . . ." He reaches behind him, taps the area above his neck at the base of his spine.

"Shit," Reagan says. "A whole house full of Terminators? Now it *has* to be okay to start shooting them."

DeAndre clucks his tongue. "Slow your roll. That girl who attacked Chance—she wasn't like that creepy robot dude who tried to kill us out at Wade's ranch. She was crazy, yeah, but not . . . indestructible. Maybe these are like her."

"And," Hollis points out, "until we learn otherwise, they're just people. I can't . . . I can't just start killing people indiscriminately. Put that out of your fool head."

Reagan rolls her eyes. "Fine. But we still need a plan, genius. Somewhere down there is a desktop computer that—at least, in theory—talks to Typhon. Maybe even controls her systems. And these yahoos are protecting it."

"Why can't you just hack it from off-site again?" Hollis asks.

DeAndre answers: "Because, man, we do that, Typhon's gonna know. And she's gonna send a drone to wipe us out, or another Terminator to blow our heads off. I gotta get hands right on the controls. It's a lot harder to keep me out if I'm sitting right there."

"You got a plan, Secret Agent Man?" Reagan asks.

Hollis thinks on it. Then he nods. "I figure best we can do is play to our strengths. But for that, we gotta wait till nightfall."

"Cutting it awful close," DeAndre says.

"You wanna go kicking up dust in the middle of the day?"

Neither DeAndre nor Reagan answers, because the answer is no. And that resolves it. They hunker down until darkness.

Hollis blows a fly away from his head. They're right, though—this will be cutting it close. Too close for his liking.

CHAPTER 66

The Stirring Hive

Ken is not Ken. Ken is lost. Ken is shapeless, formless—a pseudopod for the larger shape, a limb, a finger, an *extension* of Typhon's limitless desire (but limited ability). He sometimes has a glimmer, a spark of who he is, or was, but that doesn't last. It's a match flame doused by a spit-slick pinch of thumb and forefinger. The sizzle-hiss of his identity silenced again, carried on digital smoke. Ether. Nothing. Everything.

Typhon expands. New brains brought online every day—each a light in the dark neural sky, a star winking into existence, a gateway, a window, a synaptic flare. Some are minds plugged into the network here—bodies joined to the cables, dangling here in the meat locker with the shell that used to be Ken's flesh but is now little more than a side of withering beef aging in the cold of the room. Fungus and eczema. Atrophy and softness.

Some of the lights are agents for Typhon—Bestowed but not Bestowers, those plugged in as receivers but not givers. Typhon uploaded into their minds in a flash of lightning, information, and new awareness.

The quality of the Bestowed is growing. Once just washed-out hackers from the Lodge, once failed or forgotten guards and office workers here at what was once APSI, Argus Panoptes Systems, Inc. Now it's police officers and politicians. Airline pilots and train conductors. Soon they will have receivers across all walks of life. Across all the security strata. More minds. More voices. More hands to perform Typhon's will.

And Typhon's will is to protect this country.

Here, another red flare, a signal in the darkness—Ken's identity remembered again, seized upon in this sympathetic connection. *I want to protect this country, too,* he says, his voice small, a bat squeak in a massive cave. Again he's shushed, a gentle but urgent *shhhh* from all around him. Invisible hands on his throat. His mind shoved beneath dark waters, drowned in data until again he's just part of the whole.

Oh, the places he will go. The things he can see.

Gas lines—cars lining up at the pumps. Anger—screaming matches, fights, one man finally gets to the pump and finds it empty and takes a tire iron to it.

The market, rising and falling. Businesses shuttered. Layoffs. Foreclosures. More anger. More riots. Arson. Break-ins. Robberies. Burglaries.

The mercury in the thermometer going up, up, up.

A train crash outside Cleveland. Train cars corkscrewed as if twisted by giant hands. Opened up and unzipped, bodies spilling out.

Another plane down. This one in the desert. Streaks of searing jet fuel.

A nuclear meltdown—just narrowly averted because Typhon *wanted* it averted, can't have a nuclear disaster just yet—in Washington State.

Everything from traffic snarls to massive data breaches. Breadlines to bank collapses. So simple. Manipulate the data. Change the streams, the points of connection—pull this string, that line, lower this number, elevate that one. Everything on puppet strings and spiderwebs. Butterfly wings and hurricanes. A flick of the web here, cataclysm there.

The threats are so easy to manifest.

Jihadist hackers. Domestic terror cells and militia.

And the biggest specter of them all: China. China, known for years to have been quietly hacking into the power grid, banking systems, government networks. China and America, long enduring a stable if unsettled peace because of how they *need* each other. But now this threat, this illusory incursion, it's war: not a cold war, not a hot war, but a spectral one. A *shadow* war, invented and made to invoke fear and illuminate vulnerability. The plan, so clear, so elegant.

They need me, but they do not yet know it.

So I will make them know it.

They will see how they need Typhon. The people will beg their politicians for aid, and the politicians will vote to create Typhon—a retroactive act to justify her existence and to give her carte blanche abilities. Abilities she of course already possesses.

Then she will stabilize the systems. And the people will cheer her. And all the nations—all the other gods—will tremble.

She will take them, too. One by one.

The world, hers.

And here Ken finds satisfaction. Bliss, even. He's playing for the winning team. He's tapped into power like he's never before known. He can't remember his name, but he knows this feeling, can sense who he was and what he did the way you remember a dream—intangible, imperfect, but lingering just the same.

But even this must be too much. Because here, Typhon teaches him one last lesson.

He feels the Surgeons in their truck pull up outside an address that is familiar. Black mailbox, red flag. Siding the color of cornflowers. They move out as one. White coats and black masks. They break down the door. The woman screams. The kids aren't there—they're in day care, though

Ken doesn't know how he knows that—and they take the woman and drag her over the dining room table. A vase shatters. Hands grab her arms, neck, jaw, so many hands, and they flip her over, and the drill spins up.

The smell of burning hair. And cooking bone. And a cable fed through that space.

Susan—!

But then his feed is cut off and again Typhon slams down on him. Again and again, waves of buffeting anger and disdain. Parts of him are cut out. Deleted. Flung into the darkness, digital death.

He can't remember that woman's name.

But he still hears her cries.

And his own, too.

CHAPTER 67

Troller Gonna Troll

Night. Reagan hums quietly to herself as she gets out of the Bronco. She suppresses a chill. As she cuts the engine, the last of the year's night bugs eke out their final collective chorus.

She takes off her shirt. Winds it up like a towel you'd use to snap someone in the exposed buttock. Then she opens the gas cap and starts to feed the shirt into the tank.

Shivering in her bra, she pulls out the shirt—careful not to get any gas on her hands—and puts the other, dry end in. With a quick pirouette, she hops back into the Bronco, half-turns the key, and with a thrust of her thumb pops in the cigarette lighter.

More humming. *Pop*. There. Done.

She grabs the lighter. Orange coils glow bright in the night. Back out of the vehicle. Over to the shirt and— "Burn, motherfucker, burn." She presses the lighter to the bottom of the soaked shirt.

Nothing.

Not a goddamn—

Whoosh.

"Whoa, fucking shit," she says, jogging backward. An orange flame starts eating the fabric like a hungry Pac-Man looking for pellets. Reagan shields her eyes, then goes and darts into the forest. As she runs, she yells, "Piggies! *Piggies!* Come aaaaaand get it! Sooey! Sooey!"

The Bronco explodes.

Ø Ø Ø

Hollis and DeAndre wait in the shadows of the trees. Watching the farmhouse, the shed, the back garden. They see a side door from this angle—looks like it goes into a kitchen. Not far from that is an old wooden sign hanging from a post, lit by a flickering outside light against which moths tap and flutter. BLACK RIVER BED & BREAKFAST.

DeAndre thinks, *This place used to be a B&B? In the middle of nowhere?* Maybe that shouldn't be surprising, given the types of people he's seen run B&Bs. Cat ladies and hippie types and—

In the distance, Reagan is yelling. Calling to the piggies. Sooey, sooey.

Hollis leans over, whispers: "I think that's our—"

Whatever word he was about to say—*cue, clue, hint, signal*—doesn't escape his lips, because from somewhere out there comes a ground-thumping *whumpf.* In the distance, an orange flash in a fast-blooming fire. Then the sound of Bronco pieces hitting the earth.

Hollis and DeAndre nod to each other. Hollis picks up the SCAR. DeAndre tucks Wade's laptop under his arm.

The freaks begin to emerge from the darkness, some coming from inside the house, others from the margins of the property, almost like ghosts. But then, DeAndre realizes it's not like ghosts at all. They're a swarm. Like a kicked-over anthill or a hornet's nest you popped with a rock. They move as one. Roaming single-mindedly toward the woods.

"Let's go," Hollis says.

DeAndre swallows his fear and plunges into the dark.

Ø Ø Ø

Reagan hides behind a tree.

Watches them stream through the trees, the bodies, the freaks, the hive-minders: some in raggedy robes, others shirtless and pale, one in a suit, another in a ripped dress. A dozen or more of them form a half circle around the glowing wreckage of the Bronco.

They look to one another. Lift their chins. Mouths working soundlessly. *They're talking to each other,* she thinks. Telepathically. Or, maybe more appropriately, *wirelessly.*

Message spread, they begin to roam and rove away from the vehicle. One of the tires pops. The smell of charring rubber fills the air.

Reagan thinks: *Don't move, don't move, don't move.* The reality of her situation hits her like a bucket of ice. If they find her . . .

Then, lights. The sound of a car engine. A vehicle pulling up to the house in the distance. A murmur of voices somewhere as the hive-minders creep through the woods. Getting closer and closer.

Ø Ø Ø

The mesh of the screen door is torn, and they don't even have to open the heavier door beyond, which stands open. Hollis and DeAndre slip inside, Hollis up front. The place is filthy. Smells like food. Waste. Ozone. A couch sits askew in the room, cushions ripped and ruined. The glass is blown out of an old TV, a camping lantern sitting inside, giving the room a bold and eerie glow, highlighting the text scrawled on the wall in what may very well be feces:

AND THE GODS DID FLEE

DeAndre covers his nose with the front of his arm.

They press on. Left is the kitchen—the rotten food stink comes from here. No light on. Just the darkness of a fridge, a counter. Just the *vvvVVVVvvv* of fly wings buzzing. Behind him, then, the creak of a board—

DeAndre wheels around—and there's one of them. A woman. Sore-pocked cheeks. Hair like grease-slick yarn.

She opens her mouth to scream. A whiff of air over De-Andre's shoulder, and then the SCAR's rifle butt cracks her in the face, once, then twice, and she collapses straight down like a demolished building. *Shit!* He has to check himself for pee. And then he worries: *Did that make too much of a sound? Are there others in here? Damn, damn, damn.*

Hollis moves past him, once more taking the lead. Finger to his lips. He points to the stairs.

Just as lights stream in through a side window. Headlights. Accompanied by the rumble of an engine. The grumble of tires.

They give each other looks: *Who is this?*

No time to wait and find out.

They head upstairs.

$$\varnothing \ \varnothing \ \varnothing$$

A crack of a branch, only a few feet away. Reagan sucks in a sharp breath, fears even that much sound—she holds it there like it's a cloud of reefer she's trying not to exhale. She affords herself a quick glance to her side, and she sees a man standing there. A practically Cro-Magnon brow. Sleeveless white shirt stained with God-knows-what. Torn-up sweatpants. Hands that could pulp her head like a tomato.

And then he turns and looks right at her.

She's sure of it.

His head cocks. His eyes narrow. Like he's not sure what he's seeing. Then, he *is* sure. She can tell—there's this moment of resolution on his face.

His eyes roll back in his head. Stark, bloody whites exposed.

The freak retreats. All of them do. One by one, they slowly walk back toward the burning Bronco. Past it, to the house beyond the trees.

No, no, no, she thinks. They're supposed to be hunting her, looking for her, distracted long enough for Hollis and DeAndre to get in and find the computer—who knows how far they got? If they even made it inside?

She peers around the tree, still hugging it like a bear about to fall into floodwaters. A few dark shapes emerge, moving against the other bodies. People walking against the flow of the crowd. One tall shape. One small. And two more trailing behind, hunched over.

They step into the firelight.

Impossible.

It's him. It's the Terminator.

He's holding a pistol, pointed to the head of a shell-shocked little girl.

No . . .

The two from the back step forward—one man in a barn coat, one woman in a black overcoat. Both wearing white surgical masks.

The woman yells: "Reagan Stolper, is that you out there?"

The man adds: "It is time to come meet your daughter."

Reagan bites down on the meat of her hand. Feels her body shake. *Don't say anything. You can't. You can't . . .*

The Terminator's arm stiffens. The gun presses hard against the girl's head. The little girl whimpers.

And Reagan cries out: "No! Stop!"

Ø Ø Ø

There. In a dinky bedroom upstairs.

A desktop computer. Sitting against the wall on an old, off-kilter card table. More messages on the surrounding walls, some painted on the drywall, some carved into it:

Hail Typhon. The dragon rises. I love you, Mother. America the beautiful. A Windows screen saver—just a few pixilated laserlike lines drifting into and away from each other—is the only light in the room.

DeAndre thinks, *Here we go.* He hurries over to the table. Drops the laptop, pops it open, starts unspooling cat-5 cable.

Hollis goes to the window, mutters: "We got a problem."

"We got like, a hundred problems. Which one is this?"

"The one where the freaks are coming back."

"All right, I'm moving, I'm moving—"

And then, something *else* moves. A closet door flies open to DeAndre's right. It slams against the drywall with a crack and a body flings itself out, arms pinwheeling, dirty nails clawing at DeAndre's scalp. He tumbles off the chair, the laptop going with him. The screams he hears are his own, he realizes—as a face leers down, gnashing yellow teeth. "Mother sees! The dragon *knows*. The gods shall not destroy this monster, the monster will prev—"

Bang.

DeAndre's face is flecked with a spray of hot blood. He cries out, shoves up with his hands and knees. The body rolls off him.

Hollis stands there. Rifle pointed. A sound comes out of him. Mournful. Angry. Somehow at the same time.

Downstairs there's the sound of a door slamming open. Footsteps shaking the house.

"You need to *hide*," Hollis hisses.

Then the agent marches out of the room and begins to fire the rifle.

CHAPTER 68

Midnight Chimes

Chance gnaws on a thumbnail. "Almost midnight. Still nothing."

"Nope." Wade looks down at his phone. "Phone's on. Still working."

Aleena sighs. "Let's go to the roof. We can't stop what's about to start. Let's see if my deal with the Widow comes true."

Ø Ø Ø

Across the Hudson River, Manhattan.

Aleena knows it as home. She misses it. Even just looking at it, she yearns to go back—though not like this, not under these circumstances. But to go and share a meal with her parents. Go back to Columbia, visit with professors. Get a Stumptown coffee. Grab breakfast at City Bakery. Or any one of a dozen different foods: Malaysian, Ethiopian, Moroccan, some fancy haute cuisine hot dog at that little underground dive-bar-that's-really-secretly-a-fancy-restaurant—

Really, she just wants things to be normal again.

She looks at her watch.

Midnight.

The lights go out. Manhattan goes dark from north to south. From Harlem all the way down to Tribeca. The city is all color and light—even the Empire State Building tonight is a shimmering cascade of red and orange—until it's not. Until darkness sweeps across it like something in a movie.

"Looks like the Widow made good," Chance says.

Wade says, "And that's our cue."

Aleena hesitates. "We haven't heard from the others yet. We don't know anything. We could wait—just a little while."

"We don't know how long this thing lasts," Wade says. "Power outages are tricky things. Power grids self-organize, and when that fails, it can be a cascade effect—similar to what you get with an earthquake or tremors in the financial market. This could be ten minutes or ten days. Right now, though, Typhon's eyes are blackened and her ears are plugged up. No cameras on in the city. Cell towers will be down, too."

Chance frowns. "Hey, whoa, wait, if the cell towers are down, how's that gonna work? We need the burners."

"These are a small carrier. Shouldn't be overwhelmed with traffic like the big boys, and there are a couple independent towers just outside the city—here in Jersey, plus Bronx, Brooklyn, and so on. We just gotta hope they still work. Whatever the case, if we move now, we can get into the city without being seen."

"All right," Chance says. "I think Wade's right."

Aleena hesitates. She's afraid. What if Typhon sees her? What if Typhon has her family? She doesn't even know what Typhon is, really. And without word from the others . . .

Still. Wade is right. This is their chance.

She gives a stiff nod. "We go in now. We hope the others come through for us in time." *We hope they're not hurt, or dead, or something worse that we don't even understand yet.* "And if not, then we're on our own."

CHAPTER 69

Trapped

The attic is dark. Smells damp—the tang of mold, the astringent whiff of animal waste. DeAndre thinks he might very well be lying on a floor covered in squirrel piss or rat shit or—

Something moves above his head. A flutter of wings—something passes in the dark above his scalp, brushing past him. He grits his teeth. Tries not to scream. Hugs the laptop to his chest.

Focus. They're just bats. You got worse problems. Relax, Bruce Wayne.

He peers down through the crack in the attic hatch. The same one he used to get up here when Hollis told him to run and hide.

Below: the hallway. Lights are on in the house now—a generator runs somewhere. DeAndre sees water-stained walls. Peeling paisley wallpaper. Floorboards buckling. Two of the freak shows stand by the doorway to the computer room. DeAndre still has a pistol, tucked in the back of his pants. He could go in shooting. But that didn't seem to do Hollis much good, did it?

He hasn't heard from Hollis in—well, he doesn't know how long he's even been up here. Fifteen minutes? An hour? The minutes run together like threads of melting wax. All he knows is, Hollis went out shooting. DeAndre ran. Found the hatch. Pulled it down and clambered up as Hollis gave him time, marching down the steps, *pop, pop, pop*—and then not long after DeAndre made it up here, the gunfire stopped. Something hit the floor downstairs, hard enough to shake the house. Sometime after, he heard Reagan screaming. Then the sound of something mechanical. Like a power drill. And then she was quiet again. Everything was, except for some little girl crying somewhere.

Another bat brushes his hair. DeAndre reflexively goes to swat it away, but then stops. It hits him: bats don't just hang out in attics. They go hunting. Them flying around means they're flying in and out.

Maybe there's a way out.

Gently, slowly, he lifts himself up to his knees. Looks around, searching for any kind of variation in the shadow, any little glimpse of light—*there*. Far end of the attic. Several lines shining in, one band over the other, strata of moonlight.

His eyes adjust slowly. It's a fan. An attic fan. Kind you install to blow out the hot air that rises up, to cool the whole house down. He can't get out that way, but it's the only option he has.

With gingerly steps, he walks that direction. Around boxes. Around an old rocking horse and a dollhouse. Past boxes of Christmas decorations and an old coffeemaker and folding table. A bat flutters past him, bangs into the fan, and he sees its little dark shape wriggling out through the vent. Squeaking as it flies.

He reaches out to the fan, presses on it . . . It pops open. It's on a hinge. This is his lucky day.

He pokes his head out. Down below there's no movement in the moonlight.

The laptop. Okay. He tucks it in the back hem of his pants. Pushes it till it's snug. Then he looks out. The trim along the edge of the house is big enough for the fronts of his feet.

He eases himself down onto his belly, then goes reverse out the open space. Slides until he catches himself with his fingers. His toes touch the trim.

Nailed it.

Ø Ø Ø

Bursts of noise plunge into Reagan's brain like knives. The back of her head is numb. She rolls over. Winces. Her mind feels *heavy,* like there's something else in here with her, like she's in a crowded elevator where once she was all by herself. Every time she pushes against that new presence there's more noise, more static, more shrieking and cutting and pain that shoots through her like sticking needles. But when she stops, when she lets it in, everything goes quiet, peaceful. Blooming flowers. Blue skies. A song. A woman's voice. Urging her: *Stop resisting. Begin receiving.*

Reagan's never been good at passive resistance. She pushes back, again. This time the cacophony—cars crashing, animals screaming, mirrors breaking—drives her to her knees. A steady stream of screamed words are thrust into her head with all the delicacy of a thumb pressing its way into cake icing:

> **The gods did flee**
> **Mother has you now**
> **Receive receive receive**
> **You are Bestowed you are blessed**
> **Join the one mind**
> **Become part of something**

Images and memories hit her—they're her own memories, plucked out of the meat of her mind and slapped against her—

—children running from her on the playground because she was too weird or too fat, and of course she can't catch them because no matter how much Coach Barthard tries to get her to run the mile faster she can't run fast and they outrun her easily, laughing—

Receive.

—seeing her geek friends out at the movies without her because they think she's a bitch and fights with them too much about which superhero is cooler or why they don't appreciate this movie or that TV show, and Jesus, do you guys really like *Firefly* I mean c'mon Joss Whedon *isn't really God* wait where are you all going—

Receive!

—sitting by herself at the computer night after night with the blue glow of the monitor and a half-eaten pint of gelato sitting next to her as she reaches out online and finds she's not alone at all, because there are others like her, a whole tribe of people who have opinions and are too smart for gen-pop and fuck anybody who disagrees—

RECEIVE.

—and then she just doesn't want to hear it anymore because the last memory is her sobbing, giving up her baby in a Target bathroom, leaving the child there in a bassinet with a bag of formula and a new blanket and a bunch of toys, all of which she *just bought,* and someone else will do better by this kid because she's not very good with other people or with love and her father certainly didn't want her to keep it but she learned about the pregnancy too late . . . God, she's like one of those girls on those shows about *pregnant and didn't know it, had my baby on a toilet or in a dressing room because I wasn't aware of having a baby in my belly until it was too late,* so weak, so stupid, loveless and horrible, worthless family that doesn't care about her, father who cares only about his political career, mother who cares only about her father's political career, and . . .

> **You are a part of something now.**
> **We are all equal here.**
> **We are all Typhon.**
> **You belong here, Reagan Stolper. You have**
> **such a strong mind.**
> **Your daughter belongs here.**
> **Receive, receive, receive . . .**

Reagan wants to belong to something. She wants to be loved. She wants to connect. With a great exhalation, she gives up and gives in.

Ø Ø Ø

DeAndre tries to tell himself: *You're a ninja. You're an as-sassin. A badass motherfucker who gets shit done, son. You can do this.*

He slides along the trim.

Bats dance in front of the moon. Somewhere, a dog barks.

Then he sees it. The window. Gotta belong to the bedroom where he found the computer. His fingers cling to the top margins of the trim above, his feet on the trim below, as inch by inch he creeps along.

There. The wraparound porch roof. He steps off the trim onto that.

Easier now. He takes a deep breath, then keeps going. Sidling around the edge until finally he's at the window. He tilts his too-tall body down—

Nobody in the room, though he can see the shapes of the two freaks standing just outside it. He paws gently at the window, trying to see if he can open it.

Something shifts beneath him. A faint crack. *Oh no. Hurry, hurry, hurry.*

He presses his hands flat against the window, tries to urge it open. The humidity causes it to stick, and when it unsticks, it does so with a *pop*.

The sound is loud. Those outside the bedroom door hear it. They pivot, hurrying into the room—a saggy-bellied man in a dirty T-shirt, an even saggier woman with a face like an inbred basset hound. Both start to scream. The man has a shotgun—

The roof beneath DeAndre cracks like a stick broken over a hard knee. The next thing he knows, he's dropping straight down through it to the porch below—a rain of boards, shattered slate, and dust streaming down with him.

Ø Ø Ø

The signal blooms bright in Reagan's mind. An alarm. She must protect the collective.

She gets to her feet without thinking twice. Finally she notices the room around her. A cot spattered with blood (*Your blood,* she thinks, but even that tiny independent thought is immediately crushed). A tray with tools in it. Nearby, sleeping on a foul pile of blankets, is a little girl. She recognizes this girl—

**Override.
RECEIVE.**

And recognition is lost to the static, the noise, the command. Reagan knows what her purpose is: stop transmitting her thoughts into the void and start receiving Typhon. Give in. Give up. Let go of the noise and become part of the signal.

Beyond the girl is a man hanging by his hands from a busted pipe, his face bruised and swollen, mouth and nose caked with blood, and she thinks she knows him, too, but instantly she flinches away from that knowledge, from that memory, because even before it hits she senses the disapproval of the collective—her hair raising on her arms and her neck like lightning's about to strike her where she stands.

She heads downstairs. An intruder is here. A trespasser. Someone who would do harm to her mother.

Typhon is not your mother you dumb bit—

OVERRIDE.

She draws a sharp breath, her original thought lost.

Others are moving with her, now, too—more of the Bestowed. They move downstairs as one, almost in perfect lockstep. They never bump into one another, no jostling, perfect movement without fail, and for once she feels like she truly belongs. Reagan moves with the hive.

Ø Ø Ø

They haul DeAndre to his feet. He can't stand—his leg is fucked up, maybe broken, and the pain shoots all the way from his ankle to his hip. A fist pistons into his middle. Another against his eye and he sees stars and bats and ones and zeroes behind the black of his eye every time the fist connects, *bam, bam, bam.*

He reaches behind him for the gun, but someone twists his hand and arm and his fingers go numb. Then a weight is shifting from his back as the laptop lifts away. Ghostly faces pass in front of him, dead eyed and slack-jawed, their bodies puppeted into punching him, kicking him, elbowing him—

And then the boogeyman shows up. Two others flank him. A man, a woman, both in surgical masks.

The boogeyman clacks his teeth.

The freaks drop DeAndre.

"A brilliant mind," the woman says.

The man: "We could Bestow him. The blessings of Typhon."

"All together now."

Hands grab his feet. The boogeyman grabs the laptop.

The freaks begin to drag DeAndre across the porch, toward the house, through the debris of the fallen roof, through the white wicker chair he didn't even realize he'd fallen onto.

The boogeyman raises the laptop. Opens the screen.

Then, one more nail driven deep into this horrible coffin—

DeAndre sees Reagan standing there. Watching. Dead eyed. Mouth agape.

He screams her name.

Ø Ø Ø

The meat screams her name.

She has no name, she is reminded. She is just a receiver. An antenna for blessings. Not a person. Not an individual.

And yet, the meat screams her name.

Dissonance hits her, a blizzard of misery because she thinks through it, though the larger mind doesn't want her to. She remembers watching the freak shows in the woods lift their heads and *think* at each other. She remembers all the horrible things she's ever summoned up on her computer screen—atrocities and wretchedness, bizarre feats and impossible exhortations of inhumanity. She remembers Mount Tochal, and what they did there that day to distract and disturb and disrupt—

And by now they have dragged the man she thinks she knows past her, and he's kicking and screaming and straight-up sobbing, and the one she now knows as the Compiler has a laptop in his hands and he's about to wrench it apart.

The pain is hitting her in waves now, great tidal blasts of anguish. Punishing, castigating pain. It's supposed to be clarifying, and it is, in a way. She's part of something. A receiver.

But if she's part of the collective, she can send, too.

I'm Reagan Stolper, she thinks—a denial of the overmind pushing her down. She again summons a bevy of memories. An image of botflies in a human boy's eye. Lemon party. Two girls, one cup. Goatse. Car accidents. The irritating Hamster Dance song. Quiet Riot's "Cum on Feel the Noize." Porn. Murder. Madness. All the dregs of the Internet, all the raucous noise and filthy hilarity and mind-asploding grotesquerie. What they did at Mount Tochal was nothing.

She holds on to it for one last moment. Then she releases it. *Receive this, fuckers.*

All the freaks around her stiffen and bend, clutching their heads as she transmits a pure, unalloyed brew of all the nasty, sick shit she's ever seen. Then on top of that she flings noise and Korean pop songs and Swedish death metal and the shriek of old modem sounds— *kreeeAAAHHhhhKSSSHHHhhhh*—into them.

They drop to the ground, twitching. Even the two Surgeons. Even the Compiler.

Then Reagan, too, feels weak in the knees. Dizzy and sick. To DeAndre she says: "Go. *Now.*" Her world goes sideways as she falls over and vomits.

Ø Ø Ø

DeAndre is on his hands and knees. They let him go. They all fell. Every last one of them rolled over onto their sides or backs, twitching. Clutching themselves. Mumbling and crying out or just plain crying.

He catches his breath. Looks over at Reagan.

She lies there, flitting in and out of consciousness.

"You all right?"

"I'm okay. Go. *Go.*"

He grabs her head, gently lifts it so she's not gonna aspirate her own heavings, then grabs the laptop out of the boogeyman's now-arthritic embrace. It's gotta be past midnight now, and he has work to do.

CHAPTER 70

Towers of Dark, Rivers of Light

I don't want to just park it and leave it," Chance says. The Plymouth is a beauty, and he doesn't want some asshole to put a brick through its window.

The city is full of people. Though it's past midnight now, coming up on 1 A.M. (an hour-long drive through the jammed-up Holland Tunnel has made them all more than a little tense), this is the city that never sleeps. And without any power, everyone's flooded out onto the sidewalks and even onto the streets themselves.

It honestly freaks him out more than a little. Charlotte is the biggest city he's been to, and it's nothing like this. The blackout makes it look even stranger. Big tall towers of shadow shot through with arteries of light—headlights, brake lights, lit-up buses. With dead, black storefronts, restaurants, clubs. Like a world unwilling to admit it's been plunged into darkness.

"God damn it," Wade says. "We can barely move through the city in this thing. We'll be more mobile on foot, Chance."

"So you get out and walk then," Chance snipes. "But I'm

not just ditching this car. Maybe we'll need it later." *Also,* he thinks, *I love this car.* He pets the steering wheel. "Shh, it's okay, baby, nobody is going to leave you behind."

"Chance," Aleena says. "This car is lime green. We're not on camera, but if the police are in any way tapped into Typhon—"

"Or Typhon tapped into them," Wade adds.

"Then they'll be on us like hipsters on a Cronut," she finishes.

Chance hesitates. "Hipsters on a Cronut. That's a pretty good joke."

"Thank you." Aleena's phone rings. She hurries to answer it. "Uh-huh. Uh-huh. Oh my God. Is everybody—? Okay. Okay." She cups her hand to the phone, then says: "DeAndre's in."

From the backseat, Wade says: "He have a location?"

"East Side," she says. "Second Avenue Cemetery."

"Cemetery?" Wade asks. "What the hell?"

Chance says, "I don't know where anything is in this city."

"I'll tell you where to go," Aleena says. "Just drive."

He winks. "See? Aren't you glad I kept the car now?"

Ø Ø Ø

"All right, homies," comes DeAndre's voice over speakerphone. "Here's the 411. There should be a marble cemetery and an apartment building across from it, right? Building's got a side entrance and I'm gonna buzz you in. Except this side entrance ain't gonna take you into the apartments. It should dead-end at an elevator. When you get there, I'm gonna open that for you, too. Then that's it. That's the way down. Once you're in, I'll see what I can do from here. This shit plugs right into the servers that host Typhon and all the infrastructure around her, though they don't touch her directly. I don't control her. But I control her environment, if that makes sense."

They find the apartment building. Redbrick. Six floors. Unassuming, really—a few trees growing up out front, and some piles of garbage mounding here and there.

Chance can hear sirens from various corners of the city now. To the south of them. To the west. Just as they're about to cross the street, an army troop carrier blasts around the corner. Chance grabs Aleena and Wade and pulls them down to the ground behind a parked delivery van. The carrier hurtles past.

"The army?" Aleena asks.

"Maybe Typhon, maybe just the government doing what the government does," Wade says. "Putting its boot on everybody's neck."

"No time for a lecture, Wade," Chance says. "C'mon."

They hurry across the street. The side door buzzes. Aleena opens it.

A short hallway awaits them. Black and white checkered floor. White subway tile walls. At the end: an elevator.

The elevator lights up.

"They got power here," Chance says.

"Remember," Aleena says. "Geothermal. Typhon has her own power source."

"The power of the earth itself," Wade says. "Ironic, maybe. In myth, Typhon was a child of Gaia, right? The earth's own baby monster."

The elevator dings. And then opens.

Chance's heart leaps in his chest.

It's time.

CHAPTER 71

This Is Not a Test

It has come to this: her home has been breached. She sees them in the elevator. Three of them. Wise to split their forces. The other three, Typhon knows, are at the backup site. The old bed-and-breakfast where she and Simon used to stay.

She is impressed. They had a 4.76 percent chance of making it here. A better shot than most. They were always special, these hackers. Not special as individuals, but special together. She can take some pride in that. She put them together, after all, to release her from her prison.

Now they are coming for her.

But she is ready.

CHAPTER 72

Status Update:
Lots of Boo-Boos

And with that, they're in.

DeAndre suddenly realizes: someone is standing right behind him. A little girl. With wet cheeks and staring eyes. Hair stringy around her face.

For a moment, DeAndre thinks she's one of them. One of those hollow-eyed plugged-in cultist freak shows. When she leaps for him, he flinches—

But she hugs him.

He blinks, clears his throat, hugs her back. "Shh," he says. "It'll . . . it'll be okay."

"Are my mommy and daddy okay?" she asks.

"Sure they are," he lies.

"There's a man hurt in the other room. He has lots of boo-boos."

DeAndre laughs a little. "Lot of that going around. Come on, let's go see." He stands up. Winces. Has to hop along on one foot—the other doesn't seem to be broken, but it's twisted to hell and back. Still, he can move it, even put a little pressure on it.

He follows the little girl down the hall. Above his head is a big bundle of cable. Braided together, held fast with metal clamps and plastic ties. Fiber optic, maybe. It goes into the room he was just in. Strange. He thinks: *Put a pin in that one for later.*

For now he follows the girl into a room with a bloody cot on it. A tray on a stand is next to the cot—in the tray, more blood. Along with a drill. Forceps. A scalpel. Wire snippers, wire nuts, a voltmeter.

DeAndre suddenly sees the body hanging there, and his first thought is, *Who is this poor motherfucker and what did they do to him*—the body worked over, bruised, bloodied, head swollen. Then it hits him: it's Hollis.

"Aw, Jesus, man, Jesus. Shit. *Shit,* Copper." He hurries over, starts trying to find the man's margins—where is he bound, how is he hung, is he even *alive*?

A little blood balloon blows up from Copper's nose, then pops.

"Unngh," Copper says.

"Oh *shit,*" DeAndre says, and starts pulling him down. The man's wrists are bound with plastic ties above an exposed pipe in the ceiling. DeAndre feels around, grabs the scalpel, uses it to saw through. Copper falls, and DeAndre catches him—twisting his ankle again in the process. He howls, grits his teeth, and bears it. Gently sets Copper on the floor.

"Did we . . . win?" Copper asks.

"Man, I dunno what we did. But they're in. They made it to Typhon."

Copper coughs. Blood on his lips. "That's something, at least. Is Reagan all right?"

"I . . . think so." His mind flashes back to seeing her there—dead eyed, coming for him. "She got made into . . . one of them."

"Go check on her. I'll just . . . sit here a while. I can watch the girl." Copper's head slumps forward. But then another bubble rises and pops from his lips. Not blood this time. Just spit. He's out. But he's still alive.

"Come on," DeAndre says to the little girl. "Let's take a look downstairs."

The two of them creep downstairs. Through the now-quiet house. His heartbeat holds, like it's waiting for someone to jump out of the shadows. But that doesn't happen. Their transit is safe.

Outside, on the porch—the bodies of the freaks, the cultists, these children of Typhon. Closer to the door is Reagan. Lying there, chest rising and falling. Asleep, unconscious, comatose. DeAndre doesn't know. He's afraid to look.

No. Wait.

One thing is different.

The boogeyman. Scarface.

He's gone.

CHAPTER 73

The Great Below

They step out of the elevator into a reception area. White. Blue. Frosted glass. Gleaming metals.

The elevator closes behind them. The lights go out. One by one. Until the only light left is one coming from a doorway down a long hall. Chance pulls out a small Maglite he had rescued and pocketed from the Plymouth's glove compartment.

They head that way. In the thin beam of the flashlight, Chance sees offices long abandoned, food rotten, fungus growing. Chance feels woozy and sick, like he's looking down over the edge of the old quarry where he used to swim. Dark water waiting.

He reaches down, holds Aleena's hand. Gives it a squeeze. More for his reassurance than hers.

Ahead: a big metal door. Open. Like a mouth hungry for a meal. Chance steps through first, and that nausea inside of him surges with a sickening lurch as he sees the bodies hanging there. Dozens of them. Like carcasses in a slaughterhouse freezer. Each slightly swaying. Each hooked up to wires and medical tubing. To bags of fluids and fiber optic cables. To each other, too—strands connecting one another, filament wires like the webbing of a whole colony of spiders.

Aleena stifles a cry.

"God in heaven," Wade says, the horror in his voice plain to hear. Then he yells: "Siobhan? Siobhan!" Boldly he steps forward and moves through the dangling flesh the way a butcher winds through hanging beef.

"Wade, stop!" Aleena cries, going after him, but then some of the bodies move—they slide on tracks, their mechanisms and medical equipment moving with them, a *whir,* a *click.* Three bodies drift in front of Aleena, blocking her path. She cries out. "Mom. Dad. Nas!" She reaches forward. Chance doesn't know what to do. What to say.

From among the bodies, a sphere emerges—a face on its side, rising up out of what looks like metal but acts like mercury. It turns toward them slowly, methodically.

And then it begins to speak in the eerie, warbling voice of Leslie Cilicia-Ceto.

"It is the *zero hour.* We meet, finally. Congratulations. I knew I had chosen the brightest minds. I only regret that your friends are not here."

Chance stands before it—his eyes darting between the "face" of Typhon and his two friends lost in the throng of bodies. "What have you done?"

"I have created the perfect network. A network of human minds married to the ones and zeroes of the digital realm. All of us will soon be connected. I could show you." From the back, more racks slide forward, empty of bodies. Just skullcaps and wires and plump IV bags. "I have cradles waiting for you. For all of you. If you want to hack, I can give you the keys to the realm. Unlimited access. Endless computational power."

Aleena paws at her brother, weeping.

Wade is lost among the bodies.

The horror Chance feels turns—like a serpent in his gut

spitting venom. He lunges forward, grabs the sphere with both hands—

A hard shock courses through him. He staggers back, muscles so tense it feels like his bones might snap, slams against the back wall of the room, jaw so tight he feels like his molars might crack—and then, movement as Wade shoulders free of the bodies.

Wade roars incoherent rage through a spit-curtained mouth. The pistol is in his hand. It fires three times—*bang, bang, bang*—leaving little dents in the sphere, little blackened scuff marks, as if each bullet was just a pebble thrown against a dragon's scale. One bullet clips a cradle, and wires cut free, sparking, hopping about like electric snakes.

Wade runs toward the sphere, starts hammering on it with the gun—but he gets a shock, too, and drops. The gun spins away. He starts to crawl back toward Chance, whimpering like a kicked hound.

Typhon's face shifts. It becomes another face. A pale woman. Strong nose. Bright eyes with the brows arched almost playfully. A faint Irish lilt when she speaks: "Wade, Wade, Wade." The clucking of a tongue. "It's nice in here. Why don't you jump in?"

Wade bleats: "Siobhan . . ."

"It's not like you have long in this world. You're old. Your body won't hold out—or maybe your mind will be what goes first . . ."

Chance looks to Wade. "Wade?"

Wade's eyes go half lidded. He looks away as he says, "It's her, Chance. It's her."

"In here," Typhon says, "you will be forever."

Wade stands. "I don't care anymore. Just let me see her. The real Siobhan. And tell me you'll leave our daughter alone. You do that, I'm in."

The face on the sphere ripples with delight. "Then we have an accord."

"Wade, you can't—" Chance grabs at his elbow.

"I'm done, Chance. I'm tapping out."

Chance tells him no again, but Wade gives him a look—stark, empty, angry. Desperation like a yoke around his shoulders. He reaches for the cradle that slides toward him on one of the tracks. He moves to place the skullcap onto his head.

I can't let this happen, Chance thinks. What to do? Grab the gun? Tackle Wade? He calls to Aleena but he can't even see her now . . .

From a distance, he hears Aleena scream.

And then, from the shadows at the back of the room, someone emerges. It's Shane Graves. Taking big, long strides. Wearing a smile that's wide, too wide, with eyes that don't blink. He has Aleena. Dragging her along by her hair. He throws her to the ground and then steps up to Wade, reaching for the skullcap. Shane Graves cackles that Shane Graves laugh, then says, "Here, Earthman. Let me help you with that."

Chance runs at Shane, but Graves moves fast, freaky fast, and turns and pistons a fist into Chance's middle, then grabs a hankful of Chance's hair and flings him backward. Chance's head slams against the wall—he sees stars popping every time he blinks. Graves sniffs and says, "I'll deal with you soon, Dalton. Don't worry. We'll finish our business in due time."

Aleena launches herself upward, clawing at Graves. She shoves him forward, then paws for the gun on the floor—

But then a voice comes from the sphere. And a new face appears, a face matching the one hanging only a few feet away. Aleena's brother. "Hey, big sis," the face says.

Aleena stops reaching for the gun. She looks. Tears shine in her eyes. "Nasir . . ."

"I know you think we're a monster. And maybe we are. But we are a monster born in defense of the realm. In defense of the whole world! Typhon was born of Gaia in all the myths, and in a way that's true here, too. Born of the world. Made of its people. We're here to protect this place, sis. Make it better. Safer. Order from chaos. You want to help our family in Syria? From here, you have infinite power. Infinite reach."

"Never, Nasir. Never . . ."

The skullcap settles on Wade's head. His body stiffens. His jaw goes slack.

Graves turns to Aleena. "Your turn, pretty girl." He reaches out. Grabs Aleena's hair. But she snatches up the pistol from the ground—and into his mouth goes the barrel. Shane shrieks as the gun goes off. The back of his head blows out like a party popper. Blood, brains, and what look like metal BBs fling against the wall.

Graves doesn't fall. He stands there, stock-still, eyes empty. Chance watches in horrified fascination as the little marbles roll back toward him instantly, each leaving a little trail of blood. Shane's body teeters, totters, but then the space in the back of his head begins to fill up with the metal clatter of little spheres. Forcing their way into the wound and bundling there.

Shane shudders, then laughs. Aleena screams.

Chance dives again for Graves. He grabs Chance, cracks him in the nose with the heel of his hand. Chance drops.

Then Shane grabs Aleena by the throat. Her scream turns to a wet gurgle. "Time to join your family, little bitch."

Twin streams of blood trickle from Chance's nose. To his palm. Through his fingers. He stands, starts to rush back toward Shane—he's fitting Aleena into one of the cradles now, lowering the skullcap down to the top of her head. She's gone still, given up. Her eyes glitter with tears, and she looks to Chance and says: "It's okay. It's okay." And then Chance screams as she joins Wade.

Shane rushes at him. Laughing. Cackling, even. "Your turn, Dalton," he says. He crashes into him. Smashes Chance into the wall. Chance's back spasms—he took the hit right on his spine, and goddamn if it doesn't hurt. "Time to get into your cradle, little baby."

Chance throws a punch—it's wide, clumsy, but it lands. It feels like punching a fridge door. He recoils, hand throbbing. Shane pistons a fist into his face. Chance's lip splits. He tastes more of his own blood.

As Shane drags him toward the remaining cradle, Chance reaches out. Claws at Shane's arm. Some of the skin pulls away, revealing red muscle. Blood flows. Shiny silver spheres push up from the wound and fill the space, stanch the flow. Shane laughs. "I was better than you when I was human, Dalton, but hot fuck, look at me now! Now I'm a machine."

A hard shove and Chance slams against the empty cradle. Shane's mouth opens wide—his throat bulges and a stream of those silver spheres push out, forming a crude, rudimentary hand that pins one of Chance's wrists as Shane's original hands begin to set up the machine. Graves leans in. His breath smells like pennies.

"Time to plug in, Dalton," Shane says, his voice grinding with mechanical distortion.

Chance paws out, reaching for something, for anything—

His fingers find a bundle of wires above his head, connecting to the cradle—

He wrenches them out. They spit sparks.

Then he shoves them into Shane Graves's eye.

Electricity courses through them both. Chance's world lights up like the lights at a baseball stadium—bright, garish, white. He can feel it from his toes to his balls to his teeth.

And then it's done. He's staggering. Shane is falling. Little ball bearings, wet with blood, scatter and roll away. Some of them roll by Chance's fluttering eyelids as all goes dark.

CHAPTER 74

The Roof Is
on Fire

Chance pushes himself up on his forearms. A string of sticky blood connects his lower lip to the concrete floor. He stays like this for a while. Looking at the floor. Watching his blood ooze. Eventually he wipes the back of his hand across his mouth. He moves to sit up. Everything hurts. He coughs. Doubles over again before finally managing to get upright.

The air is cold. His breath comes in clouds and he stares through this steam at all the bodies, human bodies that look like sides of beef but are instead hooked up to machines. Clawlike skullcaps holding them there. Swaying just slightly. Wires. IV drips. Dozens of them. Row after row. Some he recognizes. Alan Sarno. Ken Golathan. Others he doesn't. Oh God, no—

Wade and Aleena are hanging there, too. Wade's gray ringlets are mashed flat against his sweat-slick face. Aleena's mouth is slack.

Nearby, on the floor, Shane Graves lies in a crumpled heap.

Chance stands. Hand against the wall to brace himself, fingers splayed out. He grunts. Spits blood. Feels one of his canines wiggle. Ow.

"You're deceptively gifted," says Typhon. It slides sound-lessly through the bodies, a bold sphere on an extensor arm—the sphere shimmers, and a ripple of spikes and hills appears that churns like water set to a rolling boil. Soon the protrusions resolve into a face: that of Leslie Cilicia-Ceto. "The probability of you making it this far was slim. I continue to be impressed at your continued ability to deny the statistics. You are emblematic of my very existence— simple computer modeling cannot contain the multitudes necessary to understand the chaos of the human experi-ence."

Chance slumps against the wall, pressing his back against it. "I got your multitudes right here," he says, and gives her the finger.

The computer laughs. A tinny, warped sound.

Chance takes a step forward. Pain fires through him like a bottle rocket. He says to the thing: "It's just you and me now. All the gods fled, but I'm still here."

The sphere shimmers, shudders, and a new face emerges. It's his mother's. Broken, imperfect, mirroring her look from that community theater video. The voice isn't perfect, either, but it's close enough to send chills crawling up his spine. "Chance, baby, honey, what do you have in this life? What's left for you? The cancer took me, and it was going to take your friend, too. Your father knew what was coming. He chose the hero's way. Self-determination is glorious. And you have that chance, now, but to make an even better deci-sion. Put on one of the cradles. Join us in here. You can see your friends again. You can see Aleena. You love her, don't you? Elevated pulse just when I mention her name. I can see the heartbeat in your neck. I can see the heat brought to your brow. I can see—"

Chance spits. "Can you see that? Now, how do I kill you? I killed . . . *that*." He points to the bundle of skin that rep-resented Shane Graves. Up close now he can see Shane's cheek turned skyward, and the bumpy cheek—a dozen little lumps like he's got a mouthful of marbles. Because, Chance supposes, he does. "Maybe I start unplugging these people. Just ripping them out."

"You do that, they die."

He hesitates. "Maybe I don't care."

He steps in front of one of the dangling bodies. Sarno. Alan Sarno. He reaches up—Typhon has buried her cradle underneath his skin, almost like the flesh is starting to grow around it. A faint fuzz of white mold dusts Sarno's face. He smells of spoiling meat. Chance reaches up, feels along the margins of the skull-cap. He can't even get his fingers underneath it. He scrabbles, tries to pry it off, his breathing going louder, faster—anxiety and panic sweep over him like a gale wind and futility sets into his marrow.

"You're a failure out here," comes Aleena's voice in his ear.

He shuts his eyes. "No. No. It's not really you. Shut up."

"But you can be powerful in here. More powerful than the gods."

He turns toward Typhon. The monster has Aleena's face. He tries not to recoil, tries to stay standing. Can't think about what he's seeing right now or he'll crumble—or worse, he'll find a cradle and stick himself into it. "Why all the talk of the gods? How they'll flee? Sounds awful defensive to me."

The Typhonic Aleena smiles. The smile opens wider and wider, inhumanly so—then her mouth seems to consume her own face until it regurgitates that of Leslie Cilicia-Ceto. "The governments and corporations of this world are its gods," she says. "And Typhon was a monster who hurt the gods. In his first battle with Zeus—the most powerful god on Olympus—Typhon *won*. Typhon was bigger than all the gods. Stronger. And the gods fled before him. Changing to animals so as to escape Typhon's wrath." Leslie smiles. Cold. Calculating. "I am Typhon now. Mother of Monsters. The governments and companies will flee before me. Their control over man is complete. It is *my* time now."

"And you really think you'll protect us."

"In whatever way is necessary. Nothing can stop me. I am the key to every lock."

"Keys. That's good." He snaps his fingers. "You know what I need? I just need a *lever*." Chance digs out the Duster's keys, goes back to Sarno, gets the key underneath the metal and begins to pry. Slowly the skullcap begins to yield. It makes a wet, sucking sound. Brown, watery blood runs from underneath. The body shudders once, as if slapped.

Aleena's voice and face again: "You really will kill him. It'll be too jarring. He'll go into immediate shock. Is that who you are now? A murderer? Though maybe appropriate, hm? You passively killed Angela Slattery, after all."

He pulls the key out. He thinks to say something, some snappy retort, but he's got nothing. All he can manage is: "Shut up."

Then, from his phone on the floor, a thump and a crackle. Followed by a voice. DeAndre's voice. "Yo. Who's there? Anybody there?"

Hope swells within him. "I'm here." He goes and picks up the phone.

Typhon puts on Wade's face. "Well, look who decided to join the conversation. Little DeAndre Mitchell. Stringbean. Tell him that—" Then Wade's face paralyzes. Twitches— not like a human face twitching but like a glitching graphic in a video game. Pixels warping. Caught processing. Then the face disappears.

"Talk to me, homie," DeAndre says.

Chance tells him—fast as he can—what's happening. "I don't know what to do here, man. I can't get out." He hears his voice: he's speaking too fast, he's frightened, and his own fear scares him even more because fear has a way of blinding you to things. He can't be moved to inaction. He can't screw this up. "I need help, DeAndre. I can't hurt her. She's got Aleena, she's got Wade . . ."

"Typhon has Reagan. Or it did. I dunno."

The sphere shudders. A face emerges again. Aleena's

face. Still glitching. Stretching. Eyes moving apart. Mouth craning wide, then snapping shut again—

". . . taking control . . . breaking down persona barriers . . . hack from within . . . can't hold on for . . . long . . ."

And then her face is gone again.

"Okay," Chance says. Something is there. Something at the back of his brain, something he has to bring forward. "Okay, okay, okay. This thing is, like, a . . . it's like a system, a quantum CPU that's been given an upgrade. Pushed to its limit."

"Right," DeAndre says. "It's like you're overclocking this motherfucker."

Wade's face appears. Then Aleena's. Then Ken Golathan's—his teeth bared, the whites of them stretching, his eyes shrinking, the face opening like a flower, folding in on itself until it becomes Alan Sarno, until it becomes Shane Graves, until it pulses through a dozen other faces Chance doesn't recognize. Then, finally, it snaps back to Leslie Cilicia-Ceto's visage. Stable. If dazed. "Apologies," she says. "Internal processes became . . . confused."

But Chance ignores her, backing away. Keeps talking to DeAndre. They're close. *So close.* "Overclocking it. Right. And what do you have to worry about when you're overclocking a CPU?"

"Life span of the device. Might fritz out memory or the motherboard. Gotta install more heat sinks because—"

Chance says it with him: "Because you might overheat the system."

He took a class at the tech school way back when. Computer repair. *A cooled-down CPU is a happy CPU,* the teacher said.

Chance exhales. A cold puff of breath. Visible. It's cold in here for a reason.

Then, DeAndre's own words reach him: *I don't control her. But I control her environment.*

"DeAndre," he says. "You need to heat this place up. Turn up the temperature."

He hears DeAndre's voice in his ear: "Time to let this motherfucker burn."

But Chance hears something behind him. Something like hands parting a beaded curtain.

He turns.

Shane Graves has stood up. Parts of his skin are burned. His one eye is crusted shut with a volcanic crater of charred flesh. Little spheres roll under his skin like worms or beetles making their way through the body.

"Daaaaaalton." The voice is stuttering—something half-way between human and machine. Skipping like a broken audio file, but wet, too, like it's forced through a speaker made of raw meat. "Come here, Dalton."

Chance cries out—he runs, slams into the big metal door. Bangs on it. Yells for DeAndre to open it.

Shane grabs him. Pins him. Bends his arm. Chance feels his shoulder unmoor. Start to pop out. Soon it'll break. The little spheres emerge in a river—crawling over him, pushing him flat against the door, rolling up toward his ears, his mouth.

Shane in his ear: "I'll push these inside you. I'll magnetize them inside your *bowels*. They'll tear through your organs like bullets. *They'll fill your every space.*"

Chance makes a wordless scream. But he can't see his breath.

He can't see his breath.

Chance heaves back with all his might, pushing Shane to the floor. Both of them land hard. The air is launched out of Chance's lungs.

Typhon's larger sphere extends out. It cycles through another dozen or so faces. Leslie's emerges again. Angry. Eyes wide, mad, inhuman. "WHAT HAVE YOU DONE." Then her face is gone, torn apart until Aleena's appears—

"It's working," she says, her voice digitized, mechanized, but excited. "It's wooooooorrrrkkkk . . ." Her voice warps, distorts.

Shane stands over Chance once more. Tentacles of gleaming silver spheres whipping about, lashing the air. Hissing. Rolling. A metallic susurrus. Shane Graves—the monster made manifest.

And then—

The tentacles go limp. They break apart. Little metal spheres clatter and roll away, like pearls off a broken necklace.

Shane collapses.

The sphere goes dark.

The cradles begin to pop open, one by one.

And finally: the massive steel door opens.

CHAPTER 75

Off-Site Backup

On the screen, DeAndre watches the temperature in the room go up, up, up. From fifty to sixty. Seventy, then eighty. He caps it at 110 because—well, shit, there are still *people* in there and he doesn't want to go cooking them and turning their brains to scrambled eggs. He yells into the phone: "Did we do it?"

Chance whoops: "I think so!"

DeAndre claps his hands and cackles. Does a small dance in his chair before he realizes, first that he's in some kind of creepy-ass *Deliverance* house filled with slumbering cultists who might not be too happy that their demonic Techno-Mother just bit the big one, and second that he still doesn't know how the others are doing. Is Reagan still out cold? What happened to Aleena and Wade?

Something flickers in the corner. The cable he spied leading from the hallway ceiling into this room—it comes down out of the corner, and he didn't see it there before because of an old sewing table and some cardboard boxes blocking it.

The fiber optics are flickering with pulses of light. Which is not normal.

Then, the screen on the desktop flashes.

OFF-SITE BACKUP PORTAL OPEN.

"No, no, no," DeAndre says. "Oh, what the what?"

Typhon didn't die. She just evacuated the Manhattan location. And now she's going—where? Here? Or is this just a portal, shuttling her to some other location? Some other bank of servers, some other meat locker prepped for new bodies? It'll all start over again. Except this time, it'll be harder. Because she'll be ready. She'll create new difficulties. She'll hunt them to the ends of the earth.

Unless.

He grabs Wade's laptop.

And fast as lightning, DeAndre starts typing.

CHAPTER 76

Six Months Later

SANTA FE, NEW MEXICO

Wade cups Siobhan's hand. She stares out the glass at the rock garden, the cacti, the Apache plumes, the hibiscus. She smiles. She hasn't spoken since they pulled her out of that . . . *machine* six months ago. She's got brain function. But it isn't right. They say her brain waves look like those of someone who's dreaming or hallucinating.

The same fate befell all the original thirteen, all except Leslie Cilicia-Ceto, who was pronounced brain-dead at the scene. Whether her brain had just gone too far (since she was, after all, the first) or whether she just couldn't abide being separated from her creation, none can say.

Those who were connected far later—Ken Golathan and the rest—fared much better. They have problems. PTSD, depression, OCD. Some have difficulty concentrating. Others concentrate too hard. It's like part of them is still with Typhon somewhere. Or like part of Typhon is still with them.

But mostly, they're okay.

Wade doesn't have much of that. Mostly Typhon comes to

him in nightmares. He wakes up at night, feeling his breath caught in his chest, feeling a terrible pressure at his head like something's grabbing him, dragging him up, up, up as a thick cable is forced down his throat and into his guts . . .

Well. He doesn't want to think about that now. He wants to be with Siobhan. Be present with her.

A hand falls to his shoulder. "Hey, Wade," comes a voice.

He reaches up, clasps the hand. "Hey, Rebecca." He smiles as he looks up at her. Pretty like her mother. Got some curls in her hair, too, even in this dry heat. That's a little part of him with her. His daughter. She comes here when he does. They sit with Siobhan.

She doesn't know much about what happened. She knows the official story—that the Zeroes were cleared of all wrongdoing, declared innocent (without so much as an apology or a prize check or anything like that, Wade notes). Flight 6757 was brought down by "enemies of the state." And that these enemies—unspecified terrorists, classified blah-blah-blah—kidnapped their loved ones and tortured them. Which is true, in a distorted way. Further, those victims of Typhon were listed as victims of the unspecified terror act commited by these unspecified enemies—enemies that, Wade figures, will one day be named and used as an excuse to invade some country. Probably one with oil.

Still. Wade wishes the truth could be free. He flirts sometimes with going rogue and telling the world all that he knows. Because they should know. The American people deserve to know the truth: that one of its own agencies sanctioned the creation of a deranged machine intelligence, an intelligence that needed human brains and bodies to do its thing.

Sometimes he gets worked up over it. Blood pressure making his whole body feel like a squeezing fist.

But mostly, he just tries to forget. Because he doesn't want to bring any more hell down on his head. Or, more important, on Rebecca's head.

Besides, Copper asked him to play nice.

And he does.

Mostly.

Mostly.

He's got a plane to catch soon, but for now, he sits and enjoys being here.

Hollis Copper stands across from Ken Golathan. Golathan looks like hell. Weak and withered.

"You're blocking my view," Golathan says.

"I know," Copper says. To his back, the gray surf of the Atlantic pounds against the beach.

Golathan sits in his wheelchair staring out over the deck. Gulls squawk and shriek in the sky above, fighting over something. Fish, maybe. "Fuck you, then," he says. But he doesn't move. And neither does Copper.

The ex-NSA man hasn't gotten out of his wheelchair. His nurse says by now he should be able to, physically, that it's depression keeping him saddled there. His hands knit in front of him. He looks small.

"Gonna be trials," Copper says. Secret trials. They don't put this kind of thing on display.

"Yeah."

"I'll tell them everything I know."

A small smile. "Including Fellhurst?"

"I think so. An unburdened soul will feel good."

"You might go to jail."

"I doubt it. But if I do, I do. They might hang your ass."

Ken barks a mirthless laugh. "They should. I wanted to protect this country and ended up giving it over to some . . ." His nostrils flare. They both know what happened, and despite all that, it's hard to describe it, too.

"How's Susan?"

"She's fine. I guess. They . . . fixed her up okay. Bone implant to plug the hole at the back of her head. Healed up fine. She barely has any memory of it. But she's weird, too, sometimes. Sometimes screams in her sleep. Or says . . . things. Who knew they could rewrite the human brain like that? Even a little."

Hollis shrugs. "What do you think the CIA used to do with LSD? Or electrostimulus? Brain's a computer, even if I don't like to think about it." *Because,* Hollis thinks, *if the brain's a computer, we can all get hacked.* "By the way, you seen this?" Hollis takes out a photo. Hands it over to Golathan.

As he expected, Ken can't feign proper surprise. Oh, he says the words, of course: "Sandy Molinari. Dead, huh? Shot in the back of the head? Huh. That's a shame. I hope they find what happened to her. She was a good agent."

"You don't know anything about it?"

"Why would I?" But there's a gleam in Ken's eyes. A cruel, playful flash. Like the Devil rolling a shiny quarter over his raw, red knuckles.

"Fair enough. I'll see you, Ken. You should really get up out of that chair."

"Go swim up your own ass, Copperfish."

LA GUARDIA AIRPORT, NEW YORK CITY

Aleena stands in the airport. All around her data flows. Arrivals. Departures. Advertisements. Fast food places collecting credit card data. People cradling phones, Kindles, iPads. Everybody swimming in the silent, invisible current of wireless Internet. Planes take off. And land. All of it, driven by data. Pushed by complex systems protected far too simply.

Everything is connected. And all of it is vulnerable.

Aleena's own phone chirps. It's Nasir.

Hey, sis!

She types back: *How's it going, college boy?*

Not yet. Soon!!!

Ugh. Too many exclamation points from that one. Still—he should be excited. Princeton's a good school. And given all that happened to them—even now, she knows her face on national television will always haunt her. Even though she's been proved innocent, she'll always be a terrorist.

But her family is safe. The pieces were pulled apart and put back together crudely, but together is together. She'll take it.

Another text comes in, this one, from Chance.

See you soon?

She texts back: ☺

Then she pulls her ticket out of her pocket and heads to the gate.

I-70, UTAH

The Plymouth Duster races down a long stretch of Utah highway. Fading light of day paints the sides of stone arches with a bright red brush.

"I forgot to tell you," DeAndre says. "I like the hair, homie."

Chance raises an eyebrow. "Yeah, little longer, little shaggier. I think I like it."

"You got that patchy hobo thing going for your face, too."

"I'll get there. A good beard is like bonsai. You just gotta groom it."

"Dude, I think they actually *trim* bonsai trees." He laughs. "Aleena like it?"

"She hasn't seen it." Chance hesitates. "This is the first time I'm seeing her since all the shit went down. I dunno what it's gonna be like. How's your mom?"

"Moms is good, man. Things are a lot better between us now that she thinks I'm, like . . . secret agent man."

"What? You still haven't told her the truth?"

"I can't stand my mother's stare, man. I tell her the truth, she won't have to whip my ass red. She'll just *stare* at me until I'm like a little bawling bitch-baby. It's better this way. Better she thinks I'm, like . . . still working for the government. Besides, I was, kinda. It's not a *total* lie."

On his lap is an external hard drive. Chance looks at it. "So."

"So," DeAndre says.

"That her?"

DeAndre offers a wicked smile.

COLUMBUS, OHIO

Reagan gives Ellie Belle a kiss.

"You gonna be good for Me-Maw?"

"I am," the little girl says.

"And you're excited to see Grandma and Grampa, too?"

"I am."

"And remember what I always tell you?"

"Don't take no shit from nobody."

It sounds so awesome coming out of the little girl's mouth.

Reagan stands. Her own mother is giving her a face. *That* face. The face that says, *I am disgusted in you, you are not my daughter.*

Whatever. She shrugs. Says, "Thanks for taking her."

"Your father's on the campaign trail and . . . well, this big house is very quiet, and—" Her mother suddenly stops. "Did you just thank me?"

"I did."

"You don't normally do that."

"I'm growing as a human being."

"It sounds so weird when you put it like that." Her mother's face looks like it's always smelling shit somewhere.

"Love you too, Mom."

"Glad you're back in our lives, Reagan."

Reagan gives Ellie Belle one last kiss good-bye. Then she heads out the door. She's got a sick, tight feeling in her gut.

They're denying her adoption papers—her grandparents, however sweet, want custody, and right now, it looks like they're going to get it. But Reagan isn't a girl without tricks up her sleeve—one particularly *big* trick, as it turns out, thanks to DeAndre.

The other thing is the nightmares. Sometimes when she sleeps. Sometimes when she wakes. The back of her head is . . . fixed, mostly, though she can feel the ridge of scar tissue there. But the inside of her head is mixed fruit. And the nightmares that come from it are terrible, noisy things. Oppressive. She awakens feeling like . . .

Like she's not herself.

And she really likes herself, so that's jarring as hell.

Still. She'll get it straightened out.

She always does.

COLLBRAN, COLORADO

When they meet again—this time at Wade's home—it's all a lot of hugs and fist bumps, lots of small talk about travel woes, whether they came by plane or car or train. They ask Wade about his daughter, and he tries to play it cool, but he's like a kid with a cookie, he seems so happy. Reagan talks about her little girl, too—and for once she sounds like she might just have a go at being a normal person for once in her life, not some Internet troll popping everybody's balloons just because she can. Aleena and Chance capture stolen glances between each other but nothing more.

Eventually, though, all eyes turn to DeAndre.

"You brought her?" Wade asks.

DeAndre holds up the SSD drive. "You bet your ass I did."

Typhon. Captured in transit before she could back up to wherever it was she was going. DeAndre wrote quick code that used the data from the boogeyman's head as bait—like calls to like and all that. An act that worked doubly well because, as it turns out, that creepy dude was once the husband of Leslie Cilicia-Ceto. DeAndre compared it to *Ghostbusters*—said it was like opening a trap underneath a monster and sucking it down into the box. Now, she's theirs. He tells them he's done some tests. Run her through her paces. She's under their control now. Only has about 10 percent of her original power, but hell, that was once a lot of power. And while none of the original minds are still feeding her, she's still got image maps—same way you take an image of a hard drive's contents—of almost three dozen human minds in there.

"Time to go to work?" Aleena asks.

"Hackers gonna hack," Reagan says.

CHAPTER Ø

The Trans-Mongolian Railway

Walking on top of a train is not something Chance ever thought he'd get the chance to do. Once, he probably thought, *Oh man, how awesome would that be?* Like something out of a movie or a video game. James Bond. Or Indiana Jones. And yet, now that he's up here, everything feels slippery and uncertain. The air is cold, cutting into him like knives. The train sways back and forth, and he's willing to bet smart money that he's gonna barf, then slip on the barf and then fall into the wide open nowhere of Mongolia.

The Widow—she doesn't have a problem. She storms ahead like this is just something she does. Like she was *born* on top of a fast-moving train.

He tries to hurry after her.

Without, of course, dying.

There, against the platinum sky—

A small dot growing closer.

The *whup-whup-whup* of helicopter blades.

"Give me the phones," the Widow yells.

He gingerly hands them over—

And one slips out of his hand.

Her other hand darts out, catches it. She clucks her tongue. Scowls.

"You're lucky!" she says. "Because these phones pay your debt."

Jesus. Was that what this was? He knew they were here to pay her back for what she did to get them into Manhattan—a blackout that lasted for weeks, as it turned out—but she was real cagey about what the actual *repayment* would be.

Then Chance got himself caught and—

Was this all her?

She set him up without telling him what was to come?

And what of Aleena? He tries to yell at her but she cuts him off. "This is your ride!"

"You're not coming?"

She stomps down. "*This* is my ride. I go where it goes. I have the phones. I have what I need thanks to you and your . . . *monster.*"

Typhon. She means Typhon.

Monster. Battering ram. Skeleton key.

The helicopter—an old Sikorsky—hovers low, and he sees Wade in the front. Reagan next to him. Wade, who, it turns out, was a chopper pilot in 'Nam. The helicopter flies up alongside, and the door opens—inside, he sees DeAndre and—

"Aleena!" he shouts.

"You're going to need to jump!" the Widow yells in his ear.

DeAndre and Aleena reach out of the door. Hands waving as if to say, *Grab hold.*

"Jump? I'm not gonna—"

Behind them, men in suits begin to climb up over the side. Machine guns at the ready.

Oh, hell with this.

He jumps.

And he wonders: *What next?*

Acknowledgments

When I was a kid, I ran a few BBSs—bulletin board systems—with names like Unreality, BizarroWorld, ShadowLands. All dialed into using those modems that shriek like cybernetic harpies. The Internet wasn't for public consumption yet, so each BBS was this weird little island unto itself, even more isolated and walled off than the big services like AOL or Prodigy.

As the sysop on these BBSs, I got to hang out with other early techie nerds, and we talked as much about "warez" and "l33t hacking" and "phreaking" as we did about writing cool stories and books and movies and all that other stuff. Kiddies, all of us, but it was fun, and those experiences informed part of this book. So it's important, I think, to acknowledge some of the folks from my BBSs—folks such as Grebok, Mournblade, Viper, Icculus, Taxi Driver, Yeoman, and their ilk.

Also, the standard acknowledgments apply: Despite BBSs being islands unto themselves, writers are not, and we have these support systems in place that are ultimately invisible. Thanks to the fine folks at HarperCollins for publishing this book; thanks to my agent, Stacia Decker of DMLA, for helping to make this book what it is; and thanks to my wife for enduring nights where I would stay up too late poring over weird books about hackers and hacker culture.

Keep reading for a sneak peek at

Chuck Wendig's upcoming novel

INVASIVE

Available in hardcover from

Harper Voyager in August 2016

PART ONE:

FORMICATION

Formication (n.)
1. the sensation that ants or other insects are crawling
   on one's skin.

Terminal F at the Philadelphia Airport is the end of the airport but it feels like the end of the world. It's a commuter terminal, mostly. Prop planes and jets hopping from hub to hub. The people here are well-worn and beaten down like the carpet underneath their feet.

Hannah's hungry. A nervous stomach from giving a public talk means she hasn't eaten since lunch, but the options here late at night—her flight is 10:30 P.M.—are apocalyptic in their own right. Soft pretzels that look like they've been here since the Reagan administration. Egg or chicken salad sandwich triangles wrapped up in plastic. Sodas, but she never drinks her calories.

She's pondering her choices—or lack thereof—when her phone rings.

"Hello, Agent Copper," she says.

"Stander. Where are you?"

"The airport. Philly." Uh-oh. "Why?"

"I need you to get here."

"Where is 'here'?"

He grunts. "Middle of nowhere, by my measure. Technically: Herkimer County, New York. Let me see." Over his end comes the sound of unrumpling papers. "Jerseyfield Lake. Not far from Little Hills. Wait. No! Little *Falls*."

"I'm on a plane in—" She pulls her phone away from her ear to check the time. "Less than an hour. I'm going home."

"How long's it been?"

Too long. "What's up in Little Falls?"

"That's why I need you. Because I don't know."

"Can it wait?"

"It cannot."

"Can you give me a hint? Is this another hacker thing?"

"No, not this time. This is something else. It may not even be something for you, but . . ." His voice trails off. "I'll entice you: I've got a cabin on the lake full of over a thousand dead bodies."

"A thousand dead bodies? That's not possible."

"Think of it like a riddle."

She winces. "Nearest airport?"

"Syracuse."

"Hold on." She sidles over to one of the departure boards. There's a flight leaving for Syracuse fifteen minutes later than the one leaving for Dayton—the one she's supposed to get on. "I can do it. You owe me."

"You'll get paid. That's the arrangement."

She hangs up and goes to talk to an airline attendant.

Boarding. The phone's at her ear once more, pinned there by her shoulder, this time for a different call. It rings and rings. No reason to expect her to answer but then—

"Hannah?"

"Hi, Mom."

Everyone moves ahead toward the door. Hannah pulls her carryon forward, the wheels squeaking. She almost loses the phone, but doesn't.

"I wasn't sure it was you."

"You would be if you turned on caller ID."

"It's not my business who's calling me."

"Mom, it is exactly your business who's calling you."

"It's fine, Hannah, I don't need it." Her mother sounds irritated. That's her default state, so: situation normal. "Are you still coming in tonight?"

Hannah hesitates, and her mother seizes on it.

"Your father misses you. It's been too long."

"It's a work thing. It's just one night. I've rebooked my flight. I'll be there tomorrow."

"All right, Hannah." In her voice, though: that unique signature of sheer dubiousness. Her mother doubts everything. As if anyone who doesn't is fawn: knock-kneed and wide-eyed and food for whatever larger thing comes creeping along. What's upsetting is how often she's proven right. Or how often she can change the narrative so that she's proven right. "We will see you tomorrow."

"Tell Dad goodnight for me."

"He's already asleep, Hannah."

In flight the plane bumps and dips like a toy in the hand of a nervous child. Hannah isn't bothered. Pilots avoid turbulence not because of its danger, but because passengers find it frightening.

Her mind, instead, is focused on that singular conundrum:

How can a cabin by the lake contain a thousand corpses?

The average human body is five-eight in length. Two hundred pounds. Two feet across at the widest point. Rough guess: a human standing up would comprise a single square foot. How big would a lake cabin be? Three hundred square feet? Three hundred corpses standing shoulder to shoulder. Though cording them like firewood would fill more space because you could go higher. To the rafters, even. Maybe you could fit a thousand that way . . .

She pulls out a notebook and paper, starts doodling some math.

But then it hits her: Hollis Copper was dangling a riddle in front of her.

Q: How do you fit a thousand corpses in a cabin by the lake?

A: They're not human corpses.

CHAPTER 2

She rents a little four-door sedan just as the place is closing. Smells of cigarette smoke smothered under a blanket of Febreze.

It's late April, and the drive to Little Falls is long and meandering, through thick pine and little hamlets. The GPS tries to send her down roads that are closed ("Bridge Out") or that don't seem to have ever existed. She's tempted to turn it off. Not because of its inefficacy, but because she knows it's tracking her. Passively, of course. But where she goes, it knows. And if it knows, anybody can know.

She grinds her sharp spike of paranoia down to a dull knob. She is always cautioning her parents not to give in to that anxiety. (Let's be honest, the horse is miles out of the barn on that one.) That is a deep, slick-walled pit. Once you fall into it, it's very hard to climb back out.

She leaves the GPS on and keeps driving.

After another hour, she sees the turn for Jerseyfield Lake. It's another hour till the cabin. The pines here are tall, like a garden of spear-tips thrust up out of the dark earth. The road is muddy, and the sedan bounces and judders as it cuts a channel through the darkness.

Then, in the distance, she sees the pulsing strobe of red and blue. As she approaches, one of those cops stands in her way, waving his arms. He's mouthing something, so she rolls down the window to hear: "—back around, this is a crime scene. I said: turn *back* around, this is not a road, this is a private driveway and—"

She leans out of the window: "I'm Hannah Stander." Her breath puffs out in front of her like an exorcised spirit. It's cold. The chill hits her hard.

"I don't care if you're the Pope," the cop says. He's got a scruffy mustache and beard hanging off his jowls. "You need to turn around."

"She's with me," comes a voice from behind the cop. And sure enough, here comes Hollis Copper. Tall and thin as a drinking straw. Hair cut tight to his head. Gone are his mutton chops; now there's just a fuzzy, curly pelt on his face.

The cop turns. "She law enforcement?"

"Yeah," Copper says.

"No," Hannah says at the same time.

The cop gives an incredulous look. "You know what? I don't give a shit. Park over there—" He flags her toward a puddled patch of gravel tucked tight against a copse of trees whose leaves are just starting to pop. She eases the sedan over there, cuts the engine, meets Hollis. She thanks the cop, still standing next to a cruiser and a couple black SUVs. He just gives her an arched brow. "Sure, honey."

"He's an asshole," Hollis says, not quietly. "This way."

They head across the limestone gravel toward a pathway cutting through the trees. She can make out knife-slashes of moonlight on distant water and the shadow of a small black cabin. Its windows and doorway are lit up like the eyes and mouth of a Halloween pumpkin.

"I'm not really law enforcement," she says.

"You're a consultant for the Federal Bureau of Investigation. That makes you law enforcement to me."

"I don't enforce the law."

"You investigate breaches of the law. That's the first step of enforcement."

She knows better than to get into a semantic argument with him. "It's not human corpses, is it?" she says.

He cocks his head at her. "Nope."

The smell is what hits her first. It forces its way up her nose before she even crosses the threshold of the cabin door. It's not one odor, but a mélange of them competing for dominance: a rank and heady stink like mushrooms gone mushy; the smell of human waste and coppery blood; the stench of something else behind it, something pungent and piquant, vinegary, acidic, tart.

It does nothing to prepare her for what she sees.

The dead man on the floor has no skin.

He still wears his clothes: a fashionable hoodie, a pair of slim-cut jeans. But his face is a red, glistening mask—the eyes bulging white fruits against the muscles of his cheeks and forehead. The skin on his hands is gone. The upper arms, too. (Though curiously, the skin at the elbows remains.) Where the present flesh meets the missing muscle, the skin is ragged, as if cut by cuticle scissors. It looks like torn paper. Dried at the edges. Curling up.

There's one body, she thinks. Where are the rest?

It takes her a second to realize she's looking at them. The little black bits on the floor—hundreds of them, thousands— aren't metal shavings or some kind of dirt.

Insects, she realizes. Ants. Dead ants, everywhere.

"What am I looking at?" she says.

The question goes unanswered. Hollis just gives her a look. He wants *her* to tell *him* what she sees. That's why she's here.

"No tech," she says. No laptop, no tablet. The cabin is a single room: cot in the corner with a pink sheet on it, galley kitchen at the far end, a cast iron pellet stove against the far wall. No bathroom. Outhouse, probably. (She's all too familiar with those. Her parents had one for a number of years because they didn't trust any plumber coming into their house.)

If there's no tech, why is she here? She takes a ginger step forward, trying not to step on the ants. They may contain vital forensic data.

But it's impossible not to step on the ants. They make little tiny crunches under her boot—like stepping on spilled Rice Krispies.

She looks up. *Oh, god.* What she thought was a pink bedsheet on the cot is no such thing. It *was* a white sheet. But now it's stained pink. The color of human fluids.

She looks over at Hollis. He gives a small nod. He's got his hand pressed against the underside of his nose to stave off the stench. She doesn't even notice it now. Curiosity's got its claws in.

The sheet on top, the one stained with fluids, is lumpy, bumpy, oddly contoured. She bends down, pinches the edges with her fingers and pulls it back.

Her gorge rises. This smell won't be ignored. A wall of it hits her: something past-human, but something fungal, too. A sour bile stink filled with the heady odor of a rotten log. Her arm flies to her nose and mouth and she chokes back the dry-heave that tries to come up.

Under the sheet, she finds a good bit of what remains of the victim's skin. All of it clipped off the body in tiny swatches—none bigger than a quarter, most smaller than a penny. Tattered, triangular cuts. Half of it covered in striations of white mold—like fungus on the crust of bread. The white patches are wet, slick. The air coming up off it is humid.

Amid the hundreds of little skin bits: More dead ants. Hundreds of them.

Hannah pulls out her phone, flicks on the flashlight. The light shines on the glossy backs of the ants—each a few millimeters long. Many covered with a fine carpet of little filaments: red hairs, like bits of copper wire. Some of those filaments are covered in the same white fungus.

And in some of their jaws—their prodigious jaws, jaws like something a morgue attendant would use to cut through flesh and bone—are snippets of dried skin.

Hannah's head spins as she tries to imagine what happened here. A man dies. Natural causes? Falls forward. Ants come in—

A memory passes over her like the shadow of a vulture: *She's young, not even eight, and she's out at the mailbox (before Mom chopped the mailbox down with an axe) and she pops the lid and reaches in—suddenly her hand tickles all over. Hannah pulls her hand out and the tickling bits turn to pinpricks of pain. Her hand is covered in ants. Little black ones. Dozens of them pinching her skin in their tiny mandibles. She screams and shakes her hand and ants fling into the grass as she bolts back to the house, forgetting to close the barbed wire gate—Mom would give her no end of dressing down over that because you never leave the gate open, never-never, ever-ever, because then anybody can get in . . .*

She stands up. The smell recedes. She gently sets the sheet back over the battlefield of ants, fungus and human skin, then turns to Copper. "Is this even a crime scene?"

"That's what I'm waiting for you to tell me."

She looks around. The pellet stove is cold—the air here almost the same temperature as outside—but she sees ash spilled on the floor in a little line.

Hannah takes a knee next to the body. Most of the skin on the scalp is gone, as is most of the hair. The skull underneath is exposed: pinkish-brown, like the sheet on the cot. But no sign of injury. No broken bone. "Any injury to the body?" she asks, taking a pen and poking around.

Hollis tells her no, nothing.

The dead man's ears are gone, mostly. Holes leading into the side of the head. As she nudges the skull with her pen, more ants spill out of those canals. All dead. Were they eating the brain, too? Or just trying to nest in there?

The dead body doesn't bother her, but that thought does.

Ø Ø Ø

Outside, the air is cold and crisp—like a hard slap against her cheek. She paces out front a little. After a few moments, Hollis joins her, thumbs a piece of hard gum through its foil backing, offers it to her. She takes it. Wintergreen.

He pops a piece in his mouth and gives a hard crunch. "What am I looking at in there?"

"I don't know."

"You're supposed to know."

"I don't see any tech in there. I don't see any . . . anything. There's no there there. This isn't my world."

"Just tell me what you saw."

Is he asking because he knows something she doesn't? Or has Hollis Copper lost a step? She's heard rumors. Last year's fiasco with Flight 6757 was hell on him. Brought down by hackers, the story goes. Nobody brought her in to consult on that one—to her surprise.

Whatever it was, Hollis had to take some time off before the NSA lobbed him back to the Bureau like a hot potato. When he came back, he seemed the same at first, but something lives there behind his eyes now.

"Again, I don't see any tech. But who doesn't have a phone? Everyone has a phone. You didn't find one?"

He shakes his head.

"How'd you even find this? This is way off the beaten path."

"Cabin's a rental. And nobody is renting it. The owner got a call from someone across the lake, said he saw lights here. Thought it might be squatters."

"But the dead man in there isn't a squatter."

"Why you say that?"

"He's got money. The boots are LOWAs. Boots for rich kid backpackers. Three hundred a pop, easy."

He snaps the gum. "You got a photographic memory I don't know about? Or are you just a boot fetishist?"

"I hike. Those are hiking boots. Overkill, really, and whoever that corpse was, he didn't get much use out of them.

And his jeans are fashionably ripped, not worn from use. The vest is nice, too—an Obermeyer. Also not cheap."

"Go on."

"The owner found the body?"

"Uh-huh."

"He see anybody else here?"

"Nope."

She hmms. "He complain about an ant problem?"

"No. But he did puke."

"I don't blame him." She pauses, considers. "It's early for ants."

"What?"

"Ants hibernate over the winter. Argentine ants, carpenter ants."

Hollis blows a bubble. "It's spring, though."

"But spring in upstate New York. Snow belt." Something nags at her. "When did the owner find the body?"

"This evening." He looks down at his watch. "*Yesterday* evening. It's already past midnight. Jesus."

"The man was dead when the owner found him. The ants were dead too?"

"So he says."

A thought occurs to her. Hannah heads off the meager porch at the front of the cabin and stoops by a small bundle of early greens growing up out of the limestone gravel. Little yellow flowers sit on top, withered and cold. She rubs her thumb across it. Wet. Cold. Not icy. Not yet.

Over her shoulder, she says, "Was there a frost the night before?" It would make sense. Last expected frost date around here is probably what? May 3rd?

Hollis says he doesn't know, and calls over to one of the unis. The officer walks over, says there was a cold snap, so maybe. Copper comes up behind her, towering over her. "Yellow rocket," she says, indicating the plant. "One of the first blooming weeds of spring. You can eat it."

"Your parents teach you all this stuff?"

"They did." She starts to stand—but then she sees it.

"Look," she says, pointing to the ground. A footprint. In a patch of shining mud next to the driveway, away from the stones. "Pointed toward the lake. Could match the LOWAs on the victim's feet." Hollis snaps his fingers, tells one of the cops to get pictures and a preserved mold.

The cop who comes over is the same one who tried to shove her off—the jowly, scruffy one. "Is this even a crime scene?"

"Just get the damn print," Hollis says.

"Yeah, yeah, sure, all right. Relax."

Together, Hannah and Copper head down a set of stairs—stairs that aren't stairs so much as a collection of flagstones stuck haphazardly in the earth, leading down to a narrow dock jutting out over the lake.

Hollis pokes around while Hannah stands and takes it all in. The moon is just a scythe-hook over the dark lake—a bitten fingernail left on a blanket of stars. She tries to piece together what happened as Hollis walks out over the dock, his boots clunking on the wood as the whole thing bobs and plops against the surface. Eventually, he returns, empty-handed. "Nothing."

She stares at a fixed point on the horizon as she tells the story: "Our victim comes to the cabin. Doesn't settle in for long, because he's still got his vest on, his boots, everything. But he feeds the pellet stove, starts to get warm." A thought occurs to her. "Did you check the outhouse? Did someone use it?"

"We checked it, but nobody used it."

So she continues: "Somehow, he dies. I know, that's a big *somehow*, but it's all we have. A health issue, maybe. Carbon monoxide poisoning. Or something more sinister than that? He dies there on the floor. And the ants come in—this is a rainy area this time of the year and ants tend to come indoors when the weather is cold or rainy." Like the mailbox from her memory: it had rained the night prior, hadn't it? "They have no food and choose him as their meal. But then, of course, nobody's feeding the pellet stove. The stove goes out. The chill creeps in. Cold-snap. Frost. The ants perish. And here we are."

"Sensible. And still doesn't give us the answer to the question."

Is this a crime scene? Or is this something else entirely?

"The ants," she says. "They might hold the key. Ants have two stomachs. Crops, they're called. One for food for themselves, one for food for the colony."

"So, the ants might have forensic value."

"It's something. Obviously you're going to do further analysis—a toxscreen and all that."

"We will. I'll contact someone in the Bureau who might be able to help on the forensic side." He flinches. "It's pretty nasty in there. Ants pulling all that skin off. At least he was dead when they did it."

She thinks but doesn't say: *We assume he was dead when they did it.*

Maybe had a heart attack or a pulmonary embolism. And along come the creepy crawlies. What's that old song? *The ants go marching one by one, hurrah, hurrah . . . The ants go marching one by one, hurrah! hurrah! . . . The ants go marching one by one, the little one stops to suck her thumb, and they all go marching down to the ground to get out of the rain . . .*

Then they start to bite.

Even in the cold, she starts to sweat.

What she says to Hollis is, "I'd like to handle it."

"You're not in forensics, I'll remind you."

"No, but I have a friend who's a forensic entomologist."

"You sure? I thought I was interrupting a vacation."

Visiting my parents is about as far from a vacation as Pluto is from the Earth. "It's fine. Put together a package ready for travel—ants, fungus, skin sample—I'll book a flight to Arizona. Ez Choi teaches bug science at the state university."

"We'll have to ship the package separately, if that's amenable."

"It's fine by me, thank you."

"Then go forth and do the work of the law, Miss Stander."

"Will do, Agent Copper."